"I am so amazed by this bo ,
Biblical references, charac
ing, but what really enthralls and overwhelms me is her imagination. I want more!"

DONNA DELORENZO
Exec. Director, College Relations, Flagler College, St. Augustine, FL

"A gripping tale! I had a hard time putting this down, and can hardly wait for the next book in the trilogy! Groux has shown herself to be a masterful weaver of fantasy."

CELIA KING, EdD
Educator and lover of great books, Fairbanks, AK

"This is a delightful story, delightfully told. All in all, a fine piece of work, reminiscent of C.S. Lewis."

MAJOR GENERAL J.R. CURRY, U.S. ARMY (RET.)
Author and Recording Artist, Haymarket, VA

"A great read... very well written and very creative in the way the author weaves the King Arthur story with the present day. Definitely piqued my interest in King Arthur! Enjoyed it thoroughly."

DIANE TURRELL
Graphic Designer, Tunkhannock, PA

"*Finding Truth* is a beautifully written book with the perfect blend of mystery, fantasy and faith. I can't wait to see what Rosemary has in store for Cassie and her friends in the books to come!"

VIRGINIA CARPENTER
Reader, age 13, Purcellville, VA

Brenwyd
Legacy
Book 1

Book 1

Finding Truth

Rosemary Groux

Illustrations by Margaret Syverud

Believe Books
Stories That Inspire
Washington, DC

Believe Books is a registered trade name
of Believe Books, LLC of Washington, DC.
www.BelieveBooks.com

Print ISBN: 978-0-9817061-2-2
E-book ISBN: 978-0-9817061-3-9

Cover design: *Jack Kotowicz, Washington, DC, VelocityDesignGroup.com*
Layout design: *Annie Kotowicz, AnnieKotowicz.com*
Illustrations: *Margaret Syverud*

First Edition

Printed in the United States of America

Publisher's Cataloging-In-Publication Data
(Prepared by The Donohue Group, Inc.)

Groux, Rosemary.
Brenwyd legacy. Book 1, Finding truth / Rosemary Groux.

p. : ill. ; cm.

Issued also as an ebook.
ISBN: 978-0-9817061-2-2

1. Gifted persons—Fiction. 2. Kidnapping—Fiction. 3. Quests (Expeditions)—Fiction. 4. Animal communicators—Fiction. 5. Good and evil—Fiction. 6. Christian fiction, American. I. Title. II. Title: Finding truth

PS3607.R689 B741 2013
813/.6

This book is dedicated to God, who is
the Master Storyteller and the only one
who knows how all stories play out.

And also, to all the readers of this book,
I pray that you will find the truth for yourselves
and hold to it tightly in this world full of deception.

"SEE, I HAVE PLACED BEFORE YOU
AN OPEN DOOR THAT NO ONE CAN SHUT.
I KNOW THAT YOU HAVE LITTLE STRENGTH,
YET YOU HAVE KEPT MY WORD
AND HAVE NOT DENIED MY NAME."

Revelation 3:8

Contents

Acknowledgments

First, I would like to thank God for putting the idea for this story into my head, and setting up all the events that eventually resulted in my typing this story out on my little six-year-old laptop. When I look back and consider everything that eventually led to this book being created, I feel amazed that it all tied together, and fully understand the truth of Jeremiah 29:11.

Next, of course, comes my family. Mom and Dad, thank you for encouraging me through this process and really getting it started, because if it had just been left to me this story would still only exist in my head and in my computer (and the various flash drives I've been through). Margaret, even though I know reading is not your favorite activity, you played an important part in getting me to type the first word of this story. If I hadn't started pouring out my rather jumbled thoughts to you in the car on that trip, it probably would have taken me a much longer time to start writing them down (hopefully now my storyline is a lot more coherent).

Annie, thanks so much for going through the manuscript with me so many times to make sure everything's crystal clear. I cringe to think of what the story would have been if my very first original draft had been published.

Mrs. Haskett, thanks for helping my family through the publishing process and letting us be so involved. It's helped a lot. Thanks also for thinking the story is good enough to get published, because without your offer to publish it I don't know where we'd be.

Mr. Kotowicz, thanks so much for doing the cover art. It's really beautiful, and I've honestly never seen anything like it on the cover of a book before.

Thank you to Celia King, the copy editor, for going through the manuscript and catching all the little errors that hadn't been caught previously, despite multiple read-throughs, whether they were grammar errors, spelling errors, or places where the all-important words "to" or "and" were somehow forgotten.

Thanks also to Meg Syverud for her excellent work on the illustrations, and for dealing with our comments and suggestions with grace.

To everyone who has pre-read copies of *Finding Truth*, thank you for doing so and for encouraging me with your words of praise that the story's good. I won't name names, as I'm sure I would forget someone, but you all know who you are. I really appreciate your comments, and they help give me confidence that this whole publishing thing will work.

Foreword

I am very honored to be writing this foreword. Not only do I love a good adventure, but it is an honor to see such creativity and expertise come out of a youth group where my wife and I once served.

From the first evening when Rosemary came to join the group, she brought a sense of calm to an energetic and sometimes crazy environment. To the unsuspecting, she is a quiet and reserved bookworm, but to those who get to know her, there is so much more – she is a very caring and thoughtful young woman who has an incredible touch of creativity and poise.

In any discussion about life, Rosemary adds insight and wisdom far beyond her years, and I have been privileged to spend some amazing moments of growth and development with her. Most of all, I am impressed with her desire for the truth, and her depth in understanding people, life, and of course, anything equestrian.

Through the *Brenwyd Legacy*, Rosemary has created characters that connect with teens in every way. Having interacted with parents of teens for over twelve years, I have been asked many times for suggestions of good books, and this is by far one of the best adventures that I have read. Chapter after chapter, Rosemary adds new situations that young people will relate to and learn from. The settings are so tangible, yet also push the boundaries of any reader's imagination. *The Secret Garden* and *Narnia* had settings that took you from one world to another, but Rosemary brings a mysterious and fantastic world right to your living room. As a youth worker, I appreciate how Cassie (the main character) lets us in to see her thoughts as she deals with the huge obstacles that she faces, taking responsibility at an early age to protect herself and others.

The book touches on many themes, but really the biggest for me is to trust God and not ourselves. This theme is woven into a story that, like many that stand out through the ages, is a tale of rescue. As I stand here rescued by a Savior, I personally felt that I could recognize the great rescue of the Gospel reflected all the way through this book – and not to spoil it for you, but even more so as I read ahead into the second and third part of this incredible trilogy.

Rosemary has the uncanny ability to take an intense moment that would seem impossible, and make it come alive in a way that will have you stopping to take a breath and check your heart rate! You will be wanting to dive back in for more, over and over. Although this is an intense adventure filled with great drama and action, Rosemary has left just the right amount of room for pondering deeper meanings, helping young people discover their identity in Christ.

Bryce Taylor
Young Adults Pastor and Youth Speaker
Lancaster, PA

Prologue

England, Early October, 516 A.D.

Long ago in Dark Age England, a woman slipped out of her house late at night, about to play a crucial role in a drama that would not end for many centuries. Behind the woman walked a large dog, and in her hands she carried a small bundle. She went to the stable beside the house and quickly saddled her dark bay mare. The mare sent an inquiring thought toward her rider, wondering at her determination to go despite the danger of this mission, but she received no reply and so did not inquire further. The woman led the mare out of the stable, latching the door behind her. She mounted, looked around to verify that no one had heard her leave, then urged the mare into a canter heading northeast toward a hill beyond her sight on which a city-fort lay. *It will be safe there*, she thought as they moved away from the house. Although she could be there and back in twenty minutes if she wished, she knew that for this night to unfold as it should, she must travel in the usual way and not take advantage of her mare's special ability. She repeatedly looked at the bundle hanging from her saddle, as if to reassure herself it was safe. A good while later she was on her way home, but without the bundle. She was starting to think that she might get home after all, that they had all been mistaken and he was not aware of her midnight trip. Suddenly, the mare halted at the same moment the woman heard a twig snap, and she knew then her hope had been in vain. Her dog bared his teeth in a silent snarl and told her, *They have come.*

The woman didn't have to ask who, as she listened to the intruders moving while quietly drawing the knife belted at her waist. The mare shifted in the direction of the noise, moving her head back and forth as she looked around them.

The dog sniffed the wind, wrinkling his nose in distaste at the unpleasant odor he knew all too well. *He has come for it,* he said.

He is too late, the woman replied calmly. No sooner had she thought this than seven men appeared out of the trees, completely surrounding the woman, horse, and dog. The dog growled menacingly at the men while the mare pawed the ground, wanting to attack these men who had the audacity to threaten her mistress.

The woman looked around and said, "Very well, Mordred, you have the advantage of me. Now what do you want?" even though she knew why he had come. One of the men stepped forward with a grin, but it was not friendly. His hair was a light brown and his face was square and open, giving off an aura of warmth. His eyes, however, were icy gray and glittered with a maniacal gleam.

"I believe you know, Caelwyn. If you give it to me without any fuss, I'll let you go back to your family and you can try to stop us at the battle. If not, I'll kill you. The choice is yours. You wouldn't want to leave your children all alone, with Siarl in the north... would you?"

Caelwyn met his eyes squarely without a hint of fear. "I wouldn't give it to you if Arthur himself commanded me, even if I could. It is no longer in my possession, Mordred. You'll never find it. Killing me won't help you any. Leave now, while you still can."

The man glared at her, hand on his sword hilt. "Then you now have the choice to tell me where it is freely, or I will make you. I have some things at my hall that are for just that purpose."

"Do you really expect me to tell you?" Caelwyn asked. "You know the disaster wreaked upon this kingdom the last time it fell into evil hands. I will never tell you. Go."

Mordred stared at her for some time. "Very well," he said at last. "You have made your choice." He signaled to his men and they began to close in around Caelwyn, the dog and the mare, drawing their swords. When they were within kicking distance, Caelwyn vaulted off, giving her mare free rein as she lunged at a man to her right, moving with astonishing speed. She and the mare disabled several men each, the dog taking care of the rest. Finally, only Mordred was left standing. Caelwyn looked at him with pity in her eyes. "Mordred, stop following this path you've chosen. It won't work and many innocents will be killed because of it. Please, turn and go before God to beg forgiveness, and then go to Arthur."

Mordred laughed. "A valiant attempt, Caelwyn, and I expected no less from you, but I think I shall decline your noble offer." He drew his sword. In the faint starlight, flames seemed to reflect off it. Caelwyn paled as she saw it and backed away. Mordred chuckled, "Ah, yes, you have heard of my blade. Made of devil's iron, you know, very rare, perfect for my work in keeping the human race pure and untainted by Brenwyd blood. Which you, unfortunately, have in abundance." He considered her for a moment. "I had planned on taking you back to my castle, to join the others you have been looking for. But surely you are not the only one who knows where the *item* is. Your children would, perhaps, or Siarl. Maybe even your wards. It would serve my purposes admirably to kill you now. But I will give you one last chance. You tell me where it is, and I will let you go free... for now. Whether or not you agree, I will still have taken Seren." He gestured to the knife in her hand, which also appeared to give off flames, but brighter than those given off by Mordred's sword. "Arthur will fail, and he has no sons to avenge him for me to worry about. And as for his queen, I have already sent my men to deal with her. Arthur will be much more cooperative if I have his lovely wife and daughters with me to help move negotiations along. Merlin has already fallen, and if you choose to die, so much the better for me. But if you choose to live, you will have the pleasure of seeing all you have striven for fail."

The dog growled at Mordred threateningly, ready to spring for his throat, but Caelwyn checked him. She looked at Mordred, her sea-colored eyes flashing defiantly. "You will never find nor have what you seek. You underestimate the people. They will not submit willingly to the rule of a tyrant," she said, at the same time sending a message to her horse to go get the girl and tell her it was time. The mare hesitated for a moment, and then sprang away through the trees at a full gallop. "And you are overconfident. You have been beaten already, Mordred. This is pointless. God will have the final victory. His plan has already been set in motion."

Mordred's eyes blazed with anger, any vestige of warmth gone from his face. "That was the wrong answer!" he snarled as he leaped at Caelwyn. But the dog got in his way, sinking his teeth into Mordred's thigh. Mordred howled in pain and slashed his sword at the dog, but he was too slow.

Dragon, get back! Caelwyn shouted at him mentally. *This is my fight*. The dog paid her no heed and was leaping through the air again, this time going for Mordred's throat when, thwack! The dog yelped as something smashed into him, knocking him to the ground. One of the men who hadn't been killed outright had grabbed a nearby tree branch when he saw his master in danger, and had hit the dog as hard as he could, then keeled over and died.

"No!" Caelwyn cried as she saw her dog hit the ground. She knew from the sound that the blow had broken bones. She lunged at Mordred, quicker than any normal human could, stabbing toward his heart. Under any other circumstances, the man would have stood no chance. But tonight, as Caelwyn's blade closed in, her foot suddenly slipped on a stone, and she lost her balance, distracting her for a precious moment. That moment was enough for Mordred to avoid her blade, raise his sword, and drive it into her side. Caelwyn screamed in pain as the sword cut through her and burned as only devil's iron could. As she fell to the ground she looked up at Mordred, who stood leering over her. She gasped for breath, summoning just enough strength to utter a few final words that she knew would plague Mordred for the rest of his life, words that she knew would come true. Mordred bent over in an effort to hear her clearly. Her dog lay where he had fallen, wishing to aid his mistress but unable to move because of the pain. His keen dog ears picked up her message, and he felt hope lift his sagging spirits.

Mordred stood with a strange look on his face, a look he tried to hide from the dying woman by issuing one last threat. "She might try, but she cannot bring me down if she is never born!" he hissed. Caelwyn gave him one last look, filled with surprising pity, compassion, sadness, and also a certain knowing. Her eyes turned heavenward and a smile grew on her face as she saw her Savior waiting for her. Then she went still.

Mordred looked at her body, but did not feel the satisfaction he would normally enjoy after killing one of his worst enemies. Instead, he felt something that he had rarely felt: fear. Caelwyn's prophecies were never wrong; but this one had an added level of certainty to it that Mordred knew nothing about, a certainty that doomed him to failure before he even started trying to avoid it. He stooped down and picked up Caelwyn's knife, then hurried away from the clearing, forgetting that her dog was still breathing, anxious to find out how the mission to capture the queen was progressing. He had planned to attack Caelwyn's house and eliminate the possible threats that lurked there, but he hadn't expected his force to be so decimated and couldn't risk an attack now. *Besides,* he thought to himself as he left the clearing and headed toward where he had left his horse, *they are only children. How much of a problem could they be?*

After Mordred left, the dog got up stiffly and walked with great pain to where his friend and companion of many years lay growing cold on the grass, a peaceful expression on her face. Then he sat on his haunches, lifted his nose to the sky and began to howl. He howled with loss, making an eerie, mournful sound that people miles away heard and shut their doors tight against. He howled so the sound woke Caelwyn's children several miles away, who followed it to where she lay. The dog was joined in howling by two other dogs staying with the family, and animals of the forest also came and mourned. After a while they fell silent. The only noise that remained in the clearing was the sound of the children sobbing, because Caelwyn – leader of the Brenwyds, speaker to animals, healer of the sick and wounded, wielder of the legendary knife Seren, student of Merlin, counselor to the great High King Arthur Pendragon of Britain, and dearly loved wife and mother – was dead.

A Strange Reflection

Soft, golden rays of morning sunshine passed through a window and fell across a child sleeping in a bed. The child rolled away from the piercing sunlight, but her mind had been awakened from slumber and it refused to go back to sleep. *Should have remembered to close the blinds*, the girl thought sleepily. So she opened her eyes, blinking, and looked out the window, slowly adjusting to the brightness as she gazed on the familiar panoramic view. There was the barn, with the horses in the paddock next to it. There was the grass-filled meadow, which served as a playground for herself and her friends. The woods beyond the meadow contained many wild animals and covered most of the valley in which the girl lived, as well as the mountains surrounding it – the same mountains that framed this view better than any picture frame could. The girl loved the mountains. They made her feel secure, like they were ancient sentinels guarding her from any and all harm. She yawned and stretched lazily. It looked like a lovely summer day out there, and though the girl enjoyed the slow sensation of her body waking from a night of peaceful sleep, she disliked wasting time once she was awake.

Looking back out the window, she could see the top of her friends' house. She smiled as she recalled that they had gotten back from their Florida vacation late the night before and would be over today. That thought provided a good reason for getting out of bed. The girl heard her mother in the kitchen and sniffed the air. *Pancakes*, she thought. *Yum*. Her father was likely in the kitchen, too, eating breakfast before going to his job at the University of Virginia. The chance of saying goodbye to him was another good reason to get up. She stretched and yawned again before making up her mind. *Well, Cassie, you might as well get up so David and Sarah don't come over and find you still in pajamas*, she told herself.

Resolute, she rolled from bed and went to the bathroom, brushed her teeth quickly, and threw on some clothes, humming to herself, not even bothering to brush her hair or glance into her bathroom mirror. Her dad stuck to a strict morning schedule, and she didn't want to miss him. It was just before she left her room that Cassie's day took a decidedly unexpected turn.

Now feeling completely awake, Cassie was headed for the door when she threw a passing glance toward the mirror above her dresser... and froze in mid-step. She turned more fully toward the mirror; she was sure she had seen something strange in it. She looked carefully in the reflection's background and, finding nothing wrong, turned her attention to herself. She scrutinized her face, seeing at first just her usual features: strawberry-blond hair, vivid gray-blue eyes, delicate-looking facial features, and small, pinkish lips. Then Cassie's gaze turned to her ears.

Her mouth dropped open and her heart skipped a couple of beats. *Check again*, she told herself. So she did, leaning closer for a better look, almost pressing her nose against the mirror. She stared at her reflection for several minutes, trying to understand what she was seeing. The tips of her ears, which she knew had been rounded yesterday, now had slight points, which most people would not have noticed from the corner of their eye. Cassie, however, was not most people. She put a hand up and felt what her eyes were telling her, then sat down hard on the bed, trying to digest the information.

Cassie stared at her reflection. The tips of her ears, which she knew had been rounded yesterday, now had slight points.

Cassie knew she was a little different from other people. She had far better sight and hearing than everyone else she knew, and people noticed, commenting on it. It didn't bother her that much, but her keen hearing did become problematic in crowds. As such, she had learned to avoid large crowds, or to take earplugs to crowded places, which diluted her hearing enough that the noise was bearable. Sometimes, too, she overheard things she knew she shouldn't, which put her in a very awkward position. She generally resolved it by going to the person concerned in private and confessing what she had overheard. The people were grateful when she told them, but remained a little wary around her ever after, which made her feel sad. Even grown-ups sometimes acted warily around Cassie, though she was of the opinion that they should behave differently from the kids at school.

School, in particular, was a bit of a struggle, as she knew she was exceptionally bright for someone her age, so bright that her parents and teachers had decided it would be best for her to skip a whole grade. So she had been placed in third grade after first, instead of going to second with the rest of her classmates. The older kids had been surprised, but on the whole they didn't mind, and Cassie loved the more advanced things she was learning. Her friends in the grade below were happy for her, as they knew that what they were studying had been boring for her. But not everyone felt the same. Some of the kids in her old class who weren't her friends resented her for her intellect and bullied her a bit, though she tried to downplay her intelligence and offered to help them with their schoolwork. Eventually she gave it up and avoided places where she would be teased, because she had overheard her parents debating one day whether or not to homeschool her because of the days she occasionally came home from school in tears. She liked school, and she had a few close friends who didn't mind her differences. She didn't want to stop school, and if that meant having to take the long way to the water fountain or playground, that was okay with her.

But what really marked her as unique went beyond just having keen sight, acute hearing, and a sharp intellect. For some reason she didn't know, Cassie had the talent of being able to talk to animals. She had been able to do it for as long as she could remember. Until her parents told her otherwise, she had assumed all people could do it. This ability was top secret. Only six people in the world, besides herself and the animals, knew about it: her parents; David and Sarah, whom she told pretty much everything and who were sworn to secrecy; and their parents.

But none of those differences were physically obvious. Cassie had never heard of anyone with pointed ears, except for elves. That thought gave her pause, as she remembered that Dad had told her on many occasions that elves only existed in books or movies, yet here she stood with the identifying elven mark.

She was still thinking about her problem when the big family dog Kaiser, or Kai as everyone called him, came into the room. He was a dark brown wolfhound mix who had been with the family since before Cassie was born. He showed no signs of aging, however, something that regularly amazed their veterinarian, as dogs of his size and breeding did not generally live past ten years or so. *Your mother says you need to come downstairs if you want to see your dad before he leaves, and if you would like hot pancakes,* he told her. *Why are you standing there staring at the mirror? Having trouble with your hair this morning?* he asked in a teasing tone.

"I have a problem," Cassie replied, perplexed. She positioned her head near Kai's so he could see the problem. "Look."

Kai was silent for a minute, then shoved her from behind and said, *Go, you need to show your parents before your father leaves.* All teasing was gone from his voice. Cassie tried to protest, but there was no arguing with the over-a-hundred-pound dog when he decided she needed to go somewhere. He then took hold of her sleeve and pulled her down the stairs to the kitchen, where her parents were talking about plans for the day. They stopped when they saw Cassie and Kai in the doorway, the former with an annoyed look on her face.

"What is it?" Cassie's mother Leah asked. Kai rarely dragged the delicate-looking ten-year-old anywhere, and whenever he did, it was generally important. Kai released Cassie's sleeve with a final directive to tell her parents, and sat down with his head nudging her toward them. Cassie looked at her parents, trying to figure out how to explain. Both looked at her with curiosity. Neither was quite sure what to expect from their daughter at any given time.

Any onlooker observing them would see how like the parents the child was. Her mother, Leah, had dark red hair and gray eyes; was slender, around five inches over five feet; and although she might not be considered classically pretty, her face was friendly and open. Tyler Pennington, or Ty as his friends and associates called him, was a respected history professor and archaeologist, specializing in the early Middle Ages, and was considered quite handsome, with fair hair, brilliant green eyes, and a six-foot frame.

Cassie heaved a breath. "Ummm... this will sound weird, but... my ears are pointed."

"What?" both parents asked, sounding alarmed.

"My ears are pointed," Cassie repeated, saying the words in an almost detached manner. "Look." She pointed and turned her head slightly so her parents could see, pulling her hair back to reveal the strange shape.

They looked. Her dad knelt next to her and lightly ran a finger along the edge of her ear. Strangely enough (in Cassie's opinion), there was no confusion on either parent's face, only worry, shock, and a resigned look, like something each had feared was confirmed and they could do nothing about it. Ty put a hand on each of Cassie's arms and looked her in the eye. "When did you first discover this?" he asked in a tone that was deadly serious.

Cassie gulped, having rarely heard her father speak in such a way. "J-Just this morning," she replied, stuttering slightly.

"Are you sure? Absolutely sure, Cassie?"

"Yeah." She wondered why Dad was asking her like it was a life-or-death question. "Why did my ears get pointed? This is definitely *not* normal, and they weren't like this yesterday." She looked from one parent to the other. Both seemed tense, and they looked at each other as if holding a silent conference.

Finally Ty sighed. "I have to go to work. To answer your question, Cassie, in another person, you're right, it wouldn't be normal, but for you..." His voice trailed off and he turned to grab his coat and briefcase. He bent down to look straight into Cassie's eyes. "Don't show or tell anyone about your ears, Cassie. It could attract... unwanted attention."

She gazed fixedly back at him, wondering what "unwanted attention" meant, but knowing by the veiled look in his green eyes that she would get no answer to that particular question right then. She went with a safer one. "Not even Sarah and David?" It was almost unimaginable to her not to tell her best friends something.

"Even them. I promise I'll explain everything tonight. Just don't worry about it too much, okay?" He tried to smile, but his effort was overshadowed by the worry in his eyes.

"Do you have to go today, Ty?" Leah asked.

Ty sighed and grimaced. "Unfortunately, yes. I told Evan I'd do the college tours scheduled for today while he's on vacation. Otherwise, I would definitely stay." So saying, he went out the door to the car after giving Cassie a quick hug and kissing Leah on the cheek. Leah and Cassie listened until the car couldn't be heard any longer.

"What did Dad mean when he said that... this... was normal for me?" Cassie asked her mother.

Leah sighed. "He meant that only certain, special people have pointed ears and such people are in your family tree," she explained. Cassie frowned as she considered this.

Kai looked over at Cassie and said, *Do not worry about it, girl. It means you are strong, and we need a strong one. There has not been a strong one for a long time.*

Cassie looked at him, her confusion growing by the minute. *What do you mean?* she asked him silently.

Just what I said, the dog replied mysteriously.

"Cassie, eat some pancakes. They have chocolate chips," Leah said as she placed a plate on the counter, unaware of the silent exchange. Cassie decided to do what Dad had said and not worry. For the rest of breakfast anyway.

During the drive to UVA, Ty mused over what he had learned that morning. *Yes, I suspected the Blood was strong in her,* he thought, *but not that strong! She's only just turned ten!* None with the Blood had had pointed ears for several centuries, and the fact that Cassie showed such signs of her unique ancestry heightened the risk with which the family already lived. *It will be that much easier for the Brotherhood to find us,* he worried. *All someone has to do is look at Cassie closely enough to find the secret. At least we don't live in a town, where such things are more likely to be noticed.* Ty's thoughts turned from his daughter's ears to figuring out what explanation to give her. The real trick would be telling her just enough to satisfy her curiosity without letting her know how much potential danger she was in from the Brotherhood. As he parked his car in the university lot, he decided to give the matter more thought in his free time, and began to focus on what he would be talking about with prospective students that day.

After breakfast was finished and the kitchen cleaned up, Cassie followed her mother to the master bedroom. Cassie sat on her parents' bed while Leah rummaged around in a drawer, pulled out a headband, and walked over to where Cassie was seated. "Now, Cassie, this is important. From now on you need to wear this headband when you are in public or with anyone other than myself or your father. Understood?" Leah looked intently into her daughter's eyes for understanding. Cassie nodded.

"I have to wear it even when I'm with David and Sarah?" she asked, just to be sure. Wearing something over her ears all the time was going to be annoying.

"Yes, even with them." Leah positioned the headband on Cassie's head, making sure that it covered the tips of her ears, but wasn't so tight that the shape of the ears showed through the fabric.

"But what will I tell them it's for? I don't want to lie." Cassie raised troubled eyes to her mother.

Leah thought about this for a minute. "Tell them it's for protecting the tips of your ears from the sun," she finally said. "It *will* help protect them, and it should satisfy their curiosity. They know you burn easily. If they keep asking, tell them that I'm making you wear it. Which I am." Leah smiled, but it was fragile. "Don't worry, honey, you may be able to tell them someday, but for now you need to keep quiet. Okay?"

"Okay," Cassie agreed, feeling more confused than ever. She put a hand up to the material. "Wait, did you know my ears would become pointed? How come you knew what to do?" she asked suspiciously.

Leah sighed. "No, Cassie, we didn't know. But I am ready because your father and I talked about what we could do to hide pointed ears if it happened, unlikely as it seemed, because your father, as you know, believes in preparing for every sort of eventuality." Cassie nodded. She did know that. Her dad was the most prepared person she knew. She had decided a long time ago that his life's philosophy could be summed up in two words: *Semper Paratus*. It was Latin for "always prepared." She wanted to ask more questions – such as, how had her father known to prepare for this situation? – but she knew she would get no hard, concrete answers until Dad returned that night. So all the questions that were going around in her head stayed there, until her thoughts were interrupted by a message from Penny, Leah's horse, that David and Sarah's car was pulling into the driveway.

Cassie jumped up and raced for the door. Leah looked up, a little startled by her daughter's sudden departure, but she had a good idea as to the cause. *You'd think she hadn't seen her friends in two months instead of two weeks*, she mused.

In the meantime Cassie had reached the door, and she opened it as the Thompson family hopped out of the car. She ran to the twins who had been her best friends since age five, when Cassie's family had moved to the valley. She hugged them enthusiastically.

"You're back! I've missed you so much. It gets boring when you're the only kid around, even with all the animals."

David laughed. "I'll bet."

Sarah grinned widely. "Well, the trip was pretty fun. It's too bad your family couldn't come. We went to SeaWorld, saw Shamu, and swam with dolphins."

Her brother laughed. "No, Sarah, *you* took an unplanned swim with the dolphins." Sarah rolled her eyes.

"It was still fun," she retorted.

"Unplanned swim?" Cassie asked, looking them over. The resemblance between the Thompson twins was easy enough to see, but they weren't identical. They both shared the same dark brown hair, but Sarah had hazel eyes and her hair was curly, while David's eyes were as dark as his hair, which was as straight as a board. The children were interrupted by Leah coming out and greeting Hannah, the twins' mother.

"Why don't you kids go and play in the meadow? I'm sure you three have a lot to catch up on," Leah suggested. The idea was greeted with enthusiasm by the youngsters and they raced each other to the barn, with Kai following to keep them out of trouble. Leah and Hannah went inside to the living room, where they could talk and observe the children at the same time through the window. Leah asked Hannah about her trip and received a lively account of the wonderful time the family had had.

Throughout the conversation, however, Hannah noticed a tension and worry on her friend's face that hadn't been there two weeks ago. "So what's been going on here?" she asked during a lull.

"Not much of note," Leah replied, avoiding the double meaning in the question. "Cassie and Kai found a bald eagle's nest in that big tree by the pond."

"Really? That's wonderful. Benjamin will be excited," Hannah said, referring to her husband. "But you said not much *of note*. What else has happened?" Her blue eyes probed Leah's gray.

Leah sighed, knowing she couldn't keep her friend in the dark long, one of the few people outside the family who knew the secret. "Cassie came down to the kitchen this morning and showed us the tips of her ears. Actually, it's more accurate to say Kai dragged her. Her ears were – are – slightly pointed."

Hannah took in a quick breath. "What? But how? I thought that she's too far removed from a full-blood to have pointed ears."

"That's what we thought. But apparently we were wrong. I don't know how it's possible."

"Have you told her anything?"

"Not yet," Leah said, "Ty had to go to work, so we're going to explain things tonight."

"What have you told her for now? If I know Cassie, she won't be content to wait for tonight."

"I told her not to worry and that it was normal for people like her. I also warned her not to say anything to David or Sarah about it. But she'll likely try to quiz Kai and figure it out for herself."

Hannah nodded, with a little smile on her face. "That would be Cassie for you. But I'm glad you told her to keep it hidden from the twins for the time being. It wouldn't do them any good to have a secret of that magnitude to conceal. They have enough with hiding her animal speech right now. Don't worry..." Hannah assured Leah as her friend's face took on a look of alarm. "Nothing's slipped, although it was close a couple of times. But they remind each other not to tell, so the secret's safe enough."

Leah sighed again. "Sometimes I wonder just how safe things really are."

Outside, Cassie was also receiving an account of the Thompson family vacation. The trio was lying in the horse pasture getting caught up on all the things that had happened in the last two weeks that mattered to ten-year-olds. They had just finished this and were quietly watching the horses when Sarah, glancing over at Cassie, asked, "Are you upset about something, Cassie?"

Cassie looked at her friend, surprised. "Why do you ask?"

"You seem upset," Sarah replied, sitting up. "You've got that look on your face that you get when you're upset about something."

Cassie thought for a minute about how best to answer that. "I'm much better now that y'all are back. I'm fine. Really."

David piped up with an idea. "Why don't we play blind man's bluff?" The girls readily agreed.

"But what can we use as a blindfold?" Cassie asked.

"What about the headband you're wearing?" Sarah asked.

"Um... no," Cassie said, feeling uncomfortable.

"Why not?"

"Because... because I have to wear it to prevent sunburn. My parents are enforcing it and Kai will tell if I take it off and I'll get in trouble. There's a bandana in the barn we can use." The words tumbled out of her with such speed that the twins barely understood her. She sprang up quickly and ran to get the bandana, leaving David and Sarah feeling very confused.

"What kind of explanation was that?" David asked, looking at his sister.

"I don't know, but it was weird," Sarah said, gazing thoughtfully after Cassie. Wearing a headband to prevent sunburn? She'd never heard of such a thing. *Still*, she reasoned, *Cassie does get burned easily. But why couldn't she take it off for a quick game?* Both twins got the feeling there was another explanation for their friend's uncharacteristic behavior. However, Cassie soon returned with the bandana and the incident was pushed to the back of their minds as they became engrossed in their game, with the horses and dog looking on.

At the university, Ty was in his office packing up his things for the day. He was reaching for a small, leather-bound journal when he was startled by a sound in the hallway. "Is anyone there?" he called. There was no answer. Frowning, Ty opened the door and looked up and down the hallway. No one was to be seen. *Odd*, he thought as he closed the door again, *I could have sworn I heard someone.*

After thinking it over for a few seconds, he dismissed the sound and went back to his work. Picking up the journal, he paused in his packing to flip carefully through the pages, occasionally scanning one here and there. He was about to put it away in his briefcase when he felt something not quite right. He opened the book again and turned to the very last page, where he had felt the anomaly. Carefully comparing that page to the others, he realized that it was slightly thicker than the other pages, something he hadn't noticed before and doubted anyone else would. As he looked at the edge, he thought he saw a very faint seam. He realized that two pages had been pasted together somehow, concealing what lay between. Curious, he put a fingernail to it and pulled gently. The seam widened and a piece of paper fell out. Wondering why he hadn't discovered it before, Ty unfolded the paper and read it. His expression quickly changed to one of shock, which was almost immediately replaced by one of anxiety. *Good grief*, he thought, *if this is true, then Cassie may be in more danger than I thought.* Hearing noises outside the door indicating classes had been let out, he tucked the journal and the mysterious piece of paper into a pocket of his briefcase and hurriedly finished packing his things. One thing was clear in his mind: before he told Cassie anything, he would show Leah the piece of paper, get her take on it, and decide where to go from there.

Ty picked up his briefcase, opened the door, turned off the lights, and headed to his car, unaware of eyes watching his progress.

Two stories above where Ty walked toward his car, two men stood at a window, watching him as he got in and drove away. "Are you sure?" asked the taller of the men. He spoke in a British accent.

"Well, no," the other replied in an American accent with the slight southern drawl customary to the central Virginia region. "But I'm suspicious. He's rather handsome, but that doesn't have to mean anything. However, I've looked around his office when I've cleaned it, and I've discovered certain documents that make me most curious as to how he got them. He bears watching. I've been trying to trace his family ancestry but I'm having an unusually difficult time."

"Very well, I'll convey your suspicions to the Master. *He* thinks that the time the ancient witch spoke of is drawing close, and he would very much like to go on living and have her line completely destroyed."

"I understand," replied the second man, who leaned against a janitor's cart and carried a broom. "Oh, by the way, you may want to tell the Master that Pennington has a daughter. A very pretty one too, I must say, and I've heard she's somewhat... unusual."

"Really?" the first man responded. "The Master will certainly be interested in that. How old and what sort of unusual?"

"Ten. I remember because he brought her in on her birthday a couple of weeks ago. She had a very developed mind for ten, with endless memorized facts floating around in her head – some knowledge way beyond her years – though some of it may just be from having grown up in a history professor's household. Her name's Cassie. Additionally, I've heard that she got pushed ahead a grade in school when she was younger."

The first man's black eyes glinted with interest, and it wasn't the good kind. "Fascinating. I will be sure to let the Master know." He strode from the office, leaving the other man at the window. The man stayed there for a time, then went about attending to his work.

A Shocking Revelation

Cassie watched the driveway like a hawk as the time drew near for her dad to come home. She had been wondering all day about the strange comments that had been made that morning, and felt the tips of her ears repeatedly to make sure she wasn't imagining the points. After David and Sarah left, she went to the family library and read all she could find on humans and elves, making notes about the differences, and did an Internet search as well. The most obvious difference she could find was that elves had pointed ears and humans did not. Elves' faces were sometimes angled, and all the different fantasy books agreed that elves were much prettier than humans, and were immortal. The books also said that elves were generally much keener of sight, smell, and hearing than humans; they were wiser; and in several books they were stronger than regular people. The more Cassie thought about these differences and took her own characteristics into consideration, the more uncomfortable and confused she felt. She wasn't quite sure how her appearance compared to elves (though she was frequently told what a pretty child she was), and there was certainly nothing special about her strength or sense of smell. But the other characteristics lined up with her personal traits alarmingly. *Could I be part elf?* she wondered, despite the fact that her father had told her elves didn't exist. But she also recalled that he had told her several times that most myths were based on at least one small grain of truth. Was there more truth to elves than she thought? But neither of her parents had pointed ears. So why did she?

Suddenly she recalled the Brenwyds, a people who inhabited her father's fantastical stories. He had told her of them often, mixing them with stories of King Arthur and early Britain. He taught European history at the University, but his special love was the Celts who once inhabited much of Western Europe, particularly those who had lived in Britain. Even more specific was his fascination with King Arthur, and he had passed that fascination to his daughter. Tales of King Arthur that Cassie's father told her, which were quite different from the traditional legends, held a special appeal for her, and included a race of people called the Brenwyds. They also had pointed ears and elf-like characteristics. Were they once actually real? Was she one? No, she couldn't be, she decided. Dad had said that they were his version of elves combined with elements of Celtic faerie folk. Brenwyds simply brought her back to the elf idea.

At that point Kai walked in. *What are you doing?* he asked.

"I'm trying to figure out why my ears got pointed. I know they weren't this way yesterday."

And books are supposed to help you with that? Your father told you he would explain everything this evening.

"I suppose you already know what he's going to tell me. You've been acting strange all day," Cassie groused with a frown on her face.

Of course I know.

Yes, yes, a second animal voice added. *We all know that Kai knows everything there is to know about this family, a fact that we have heard him proclaim many times,* Smokey said sarcastically as he padded into the room in search of a patch of sun to sleep in. Smokey was a soot gray cat that Leah had rescued, along with his female litter-mate, from being put down two years before at the local animal shelter. His sister, Calico, had grown to prefer the barn while Smokey took the house as his domain. He hadn't been present in the kitchen that morning, but had been filled in by Cassie and Kai as to what had happened. Now he leaped onto the table Cassie was working on and stretched out in a patch of afternoon sun. He lifted his head to look at the other two. *If you ask me, you are dramatizing the affair. Her parents should have let her grow up with the knowledge instead of waiting until she showed signs, or they should have told her when they realized she could talk to us.*

They had their reasons. And she is just reaching the age when she can fully grasp the concept and be able to keep the secret, Kai answered the cat, sounding slightly annoyed. The pair got along well enough, but they had a habit of goading and mocking each other.

Cassie felt irritated with both, because they obviously knew what was going on and each refused to tell her. It also bothered her that they spoke as if she were not in the room. "Hey, I'm right here, you know. If you're going to talk about me, you shouldn't do it right in front of me," she said. Both animals regarded her as if she were a puppy or kitten that didn't know how to respect its elders.

Books will not help you find the answers you are looking for, Kai said. He put his forepaws on the table and looked at the piece of paper on which Cassie had written her observations. *Why are you researching elves?*

"Because they're the only beings I know of that have pointed ears! And all my research makes me wonder if I am one."

Well, if it is any comfort, you are not. In fact, you are what elves were based on, Smokey answered her, sounding amused.

"What's that supposed to mean? The Bible never says that God created anything like elves – just man," Cassie cried in vexation. She was getting heartily tired of mysterious answers.

It means exactly what I said. The One did indeed just make man on the sixth day, but the One can decide to bless faithful followers with unique characteristics if He wishes, can He not? Smokey replied smugly in a typically evasive cat answer as he leaped down from the table and moved toward the door, deciding to go elsewhere for a nap.

Cassie looked after the cat with frustration. "Oh, yes, *that* was helpful," she muttered, turning to Kai. "Do you have anything to add or are you going to keep on being stranger than any dog has a right to be?" she asked. Kai stared back at her.

You will find out everything later and then you will understand, he finally replied, and left the room, leaving Cassie to stare after *him* in frustration.

At present, she was sitting on Chance's back, taking comfort from him and Penny. Horses were generally not given to deep thoughts, although it wasn't unusual for them to share one occasionally. For the most part, however, horses thought about things like food, when they would next be ridden, and the peculiarities of their human owners. Neither of the Penningtons' horses concerned themselves much with human problems or spoke mysteriously. They would simply state things the way they were or should be, and sympathize with human heartbreaks and issues, providing comfort and necks to cry into. Cassie loved horses for their relative simplicity, and often went to them after Kai or Smokey gave her evasive answers to important questions (at least ones *she* deemed important), such as what had happened in the library. The paddock also offered a clear view of the road and driveway entrance, perfect for watching for incoming cars. She had just finished pouring out her woes to the horses and was waiting for a reply. Oddly, both horses were silent. Finally Cassie couldn't take it any longer and blurted out, "Well?"

Kai and Smokey have their reasons for being mysterious, Penny replied in a slow, deliberate tone. *Your parents should be the ones to tell you... what it is they need to tell you.*

"You two know what the secret is already, don't you?" Cassie asked, feeling the horses' reluctance to discuss the subject.

Chance swished his tail at a fly. *Well, yes. We have often heard your parents talk of it when they have been alone. It takes a very special kind of person to hear us, and such a person has not been born with the strength for many years. We have all known for years, girl. We just did not think you would show physical characteristics. This pointing of your ears... it means you are strong, and that is a good thing, nothing to be ashamed of.*

"What kind of special person? What strength?" Cassie asked. "I've heard things like that all day. I'm tired of half-answers. I want whole ones!" She knew she sounded whiny but she didn't care at this point. Her patience was wearing very, very thin.

Penny snorted, bobbing her head up and down. *I know you do, but we cannot give them to you. I can tell you that your parents always act with your best interests in mind, and they were not expecting your ears to form points,* she said.

Cassie sighed. "Alright, but what did Smokey mean when he said, 'Can't God grant unique characteristics to His followers?'"

You will find out. We will not tell you before your father does, Penny said. The three lapsed into silence. Cassie was still mulling over Smokey's comment when she spotted her father's car turning into the driveway. She dismounted from Chance so quickly that the gelding brought his head up in surprise.

Ty was barely out of the car when Cassie skidded to a stop in front of him, looking up with demanding eyes. He put on a weary smile, knowing what she wanted and knowing she would not be pleased with waiting until after dinner, which he could smell cooking on the stove. "Well, Cassie, how was your day?"

Cassie wanted her dad to tell her right then and there what he had promised to tell her that morning, but knew that if she pestered him he would just put it off longer. “Fine. David and Sarah came over. We played in the meadow and I showed them the eagle’s nest. The mama eagle says the eggs will hatch soon.”

“Really? That will be exciting.” By this time they were in the foyer and Leah was coming toward them, smiling at her husband.

“How was work?” she asked as Ty pecked her on the cheek.

“Fine. Dinner smells good. Roast chicken?” Leah nodded. Ty turned to where Cassie was standing, Kai behind her. “Cassie, why don’t you go tend the horses? I’m sure they’d appreciate it.”

“But...” Cassie stopped herself. Her dad obviously wanted time alone with her mom, most likely to talk about how best to tell their daughter their big secret. Besides, he was giving her the “if you don’t do what I tell you, you’ll be in trouble” look. So she meekly went outside, pausing at the doorway to ask Kai if he wanted to come. He declined, so she continued out into the yard to wait until her parents were done talking.

After Cassie left, Leah closed the door and she and Ty went into the living room with Kai following them. Smokey looked up from where he was sprawled on the window seat and debated whether or not to leave, as it was clear his humans were going to be in here awhile. He decided against leaving, as he had a feeling the following discussion was going to be important and he prided himself, like many cats did, on knowing everything of importance that went on in his house. The whole day had been extremely interesting to him, and Smokey wanted to see what would happen now that Ty was home.

Leah knew it was serious when Ty closed the door behind them. He sat down on the couch and Leah sat next to him. “What is it?” she asked. She rarely saw such a serious expression on her husband’s face.

“Has Cassie been asking questions today?” he asked.

"Not of me, which I found surprising, but I found notes in the library about the differences between humans and elves. She's definitely been trying to figure it out, but I don't think she's made the connection to... your stories. Not yet, anyway."

She has been asking me, Kai said, *I have not told her anything definite, but it has made her frustrated. Smokey has not helped*, he added, coming as close to glaring at the cat as a dog could.

Smokey propped himself up nonchalantly, flicking his tail idly. *I have not told her anything more than you have, dog. I merely alleviated her of her notion of being part elf.*

Kai made a little half-cough, half-growl in his throat that was the dog equivalent of a "humph," and turned from the cat. Ty and Leah watched the animals, only able to hear part of the conversation. Kai was a unique breed of dog that could talk to any person he wished, even if they didn't have the gift of animal speech that Cassie had. *I think she may have figured out she is only part normal human. She has no idea what the other part would be, though*, Kai told Ty and Leah.

Ty sighed. "I expected her to suspect as much. She's smarter than other kids her age. Sometimes I think she's smarter than some of my students." He smiled a little, but it faded quickly. "But I found something today that, if true, places her in even more danger."

"What?" Leah asked, alarmed. Ty took the piece of paper from his coat pocket and showed it to her, also giving her a slip of paper on which he had written the translation. Leah read the contents and gasped. Her face grew pale. "Is this true?"

"I wouldn't doubt it. My family has said for years that we're descended from her, but I'm going to double-check. They may have been wrong."

"But what if it is true? Cassie's only ten!"

"I know, I know. But if it *is* true, it may be Cassie's best protection."

Leah looked at her husband as if he'd just said that pigs fly. "Her best protection?! How?" Kai nuzzled her clenched fist comfortingly. Smokey got up from his napping position and leaped to the sofa where he examined the piece of paper in Leah's lap.

Ty grabbed his wife's hands reassuringly. "Leah, listen. If that prophecy *is* talking about Cassie, which it may or may not be, then she'll have to be able to get older to fulfill it. It could be that she'll be safe until the time comes for her to do it. Do you understand?"

Leah nodded slowly as his words sank in. "I suppose. I don't like the thought that she'd have to oppose... *him*... someday."

"Neither do I. But someone has to do it, and Cassie stands a good chance of succeeding with the proper training. The fact that her ears have become pointed means she's strong. Very strong. I'll show her how to fight with the sword and bow, like the Brotherhood do, teach her how to hear songs and use them to heal. We also must encourage her in the faith, because to defeat someone as strong in the dark arts as he is, she must be strong and unshakable in her faith."

"Don't you think she's a tad young to be waving a sword around?" Leah asked, her motherly instincts objecting to that particular part of Ty's idea.

"She's young, but she's responsible. And I wouldn't start her with a real blade anyhow, even if she were older. She needs to know how to defend herself properly first. My father taught me after he told me. If my family's been right about our ancestry, then Cassie may very well be God's tool to do the deed, and if so, she'll need to know how to defend herself with a sword. It's never too early to start. If I'd known about this sooner, I would have started her years ago."

Leah desperately wished for some time to think through all this herself, but if Ty was right... She steered her thoughts away from that scenario and took a calming breath. "I'll just trust God to take care of her and show her the path she must take. If it leads to a duel with *him*, then so be it."

Ty smiled charmingly and reassuringly at her. "I hoped you'd say that. Now, how about some dinner and then we shall tell our daughter the answers to her questions."

Despite all her doubts, fears, and worries, Leah laughed. "You're always thinking of your stomach. Go call Cassie in; I need her to set the table."

The couple left the room, leaving the dog and cat with the all-important piece of paper. Smokey sniffed it and looked at Kai, a strange light in his eyes that Cassie would have identified as excitement. *It is from* her *book*, the cat said, his tail twitching.

Kai bared his teeth in a dog grin, which really looked quite ferocious. *Then she* is *the one. I suspected so. The downfall is close.*

Yes, the cat agreed.

We must tell the others. We all must double our watch on the girl. She must be protected.

She will be, Smokey said. *I will go tell Calico.* He jumped down from the table and left the room, eager to tell his litter-mate what he had learned.

Kai turned his gaze toward the window, where he saw the girl grooming Penny. He'd always known this girl was special, and now he'd been proven right. Her face at this moment was relaxed, having no idea of the plans the One had in store for her. *It is better that way*, Kai decided; *it should wait until she is older. I will tell Ty to keep it hidden for now.* He left the room, but not before he took the piece of paper gingerly in his mouth to give back to Ty.

All through dinner Cassie stayed quiet, saying nothing unless she needed a different dish. She could feel her parents eyeing her, probably expecting questions, but she ignored their looks. Finally, after all the dishes were cleaned, she went to Ty and said, "Tell me now, please," looking at him beseechingly with big, pleading eyes.

He nodded slowly. "Very well, come to the living room with me and I'll tell you." Cassie followed him to the living room with Leah behind. Her parents sat on the couch and gestured for her to join them. She shook her head and sat on a chair nearby, hugging her knees to her chest. Kai also came into the room, followed by Smokey. Kai lay on the floor near Cassie's chair, looking alert. Smokey jumped on the couch and crawled into Leah's lap. Cassie felt a little uncomfortable about what her dad was about to tell her, but had no idea that the news would turn her world almost upside-down. Ty cleared his throat, feeling apprehensive about what his daughter's reaction might be.

He thought for a minute about how to start, then began to speak. "Cassie, remember all the King Arthur stories I've told you?" he asked. She nodded, puzzled by the question. Of course she remembered the stories. He'd been telling them to her since she was a baby and she never tired of them. Why would he ask her that? What did King Arthur have to do with her ears becoming pointed? Her thoughts turned again to Brenwyds. Was this some sort of prelude to saying elves were real? "Well, all the stories I've told you... they're all true. All of them, to the last detail."

Cassie blinked. "Really? But I thought you said that they were just stories your father told you."

Ty got up and started pacing. "And so they are. He learned them from his father, and his father from his mother. Those stories have been passed down since the time of King Arthur's reign, by those who witnessed the events as they happened. You remember Caelwyn, the king's advisor and close friend?"

"Of course, Dad, she's my favorite character."

"And do you remember what was special about her?"

Cassie thought for a minute. "She was part Brenwyd, and..." She stopped short as the implications of his previous words hit her. "So Brenwyds were really real? If that's so, then..." She stared at her father as full comprehension of what he was trying to say dawned on her. "Are you saying that... ?" She didn't need to finish the question.

"That's exactly what I'm saying," Ty answered. "You are part Brenwyd. That's why your ears became pointed." A half-smile appeared on his face. "Where else did you think the stories of elves came from?" Cassie continued to stare in astonishment at her father. What he was telling her seemed almost too fantastical to believe, but then again, so was the fact that her ears had become pointed, and that was definitely true. She felt slightly disgusted with herself that she had discounted the idea of Brenwyds so readily in the library. Brenwyds, she recalled from her father's stories, were a people blessed by God for their faithfulness. He had given them special abilities, as well as pointed ears to physically set them apart. They could heal people by singing, communicate with animals, and sometimes talk mind-to-mind. Cassie felt even more disgusted with herself after remembering what she saw now as Smokey's blatant hint in the library. Her thoughts turned to Caelwyn. Caelwyn had been a Brenwyd leader during Arthur's reign in the sixth century A.D., despite being a woman living in a male-dominated society. And to think that she had really been real... but how could she, herself, Cassie, have pointed ears? Neither of her parents had pointed ears. It didn't make sense.

Ty saw she was struggling a bit to accept the information he was telling her, and decided more detail was in order. After all, no matter how bright she was, she was still only ten. "Cassie, listen to me. After Caelwyn died, the Brenwyd race had no... representative, I guess you'd say, to normal humans. As Caelwyn's death coincided with Arthur's, the Brenwyds eventually withdrew into their forests and islands, slowly living more and more apart from the rest of the world. Remember, the king served as a... patron, you might say, of the Brenwyd race. It was because of his open mind and friendship, and that of his father, that Brenwyds were able to come out and become a real part of Celtic society, instead of just being on the fringes. But as the Brenwyds came to the towns and villages of England less and less, they came under suspicion that eventually gave way to fear, especially given their special abilities. The normal humans thought the Brenwyds were witches and wizards who used dark magic to accomplish what they did, the healings and such, though it was just through natural abilities that God had given the original Brenwyds in return for their faithfulness. The people did not understand this, or chose not to, and eventually their fear led them to inflict a devastating war of persecution on the Brenwyds. Many were killed. But some learned of the impending persecution and, after warning their communities and gathering what belongings they could, they fled Britain to places where they were still respected and welcomed and would be relatively safe. The Brenwyds melded into normal human culture and communities, and over time they started keeping their true identities secret, hiding their ears to escape persecution and witch hunts. Many Brenwyds married regular men and women, passing their abilities to their children and preserving their legacy. Descendants of Brenwyds still exist today, though most are unaware they have Brenwyd blood. It's not as strong as it once was." Ty stopped speaking and looked at Cassie.

Cassie felt as if she were a bystander watching all this happening. *This sort of thing happens in books,* she thought, *not in real life.* She saw her father looking at her expectantly. Taking a deep breath, she said, "Sooo, I'm guessing I get it from you, since you're the one explaining all this?"

Ty nodded. "Yes."

"Then why aren't your ears pointed? And how can people be unaware that they're part Brenwyd? Wouldn't that part of family history be remembered?"

"Well, my ears aren't pointed because the Blood isn't very strong in me. Brenwyd blood needs to be pretty strong in a person for them to have pointed ears. So, it's much stronger in you than it is in me. The only way it really affects me is by having keen senses. As to how people don't know, the secret was jealously guarded by families and often lost throughout the centuries. In the later Middle Ages, being Brenwyd could get you killed for supposed witchcraft. Often it was safer for the secret to be lost than to be preserved for the next generation. As far as I know, you're the first person with Brenwyd blood to develop pointed ears in a very long time."

Well that's just great, Cassie thought, turning toward the window. *But why me?* Kai stuck his head in her lap and she rubbed it absently. "Why am I the only person with Brenwyd blood to have pointed ears in so long? That doesn't make sense. And why did they become pointed just now?"

Ty sighed. Cassie always tried to get as much information out of a conversation as she could, delving deep to find the how and why of everything, a fact that sometimes stumped her teachers and frustrated her parents. "Honestly, Cassie, I don't really know. I never thought that you would develop pointed ears. As to why they've just now become pointed, it's likely because Brenwyd blood has become so diluted that it takes time for that kind of change to develop. And why they have at all... well, quite frankly I think it was an act of God."

"An act of God? He specifically wants me to have pointed ears?" Cassie sounded doubtful.

"No, not exactly. Having pointed ears means that you are likely as strong as a real half-blood Brenwyd. They could do... amazing things. I've told you the stories. Pointed ears are just... part of the bargain, you might say."

Cassie felt overwhelmed. "This... this isn't a joke, is it?" she asked, just to make sure, hoping against hope it was, even though she knew very well that it wasn't. "Because if it is, it's *so* not funny!"

"Of course not," Ty replied, frowning. "Why would I joke about something like this?"

Cassie jerked her head up, the blue almost completely gone from her eyes as she felt a wave of anger rise up inside her. "Then why didn't you tell me sooner? Like when you found out I can talk to animals? When I came home crying because of bullies? And if I hadn't come down this morning with pointed ears, you probably wouldn't have told me until years from now! Am I even human?" She felt tears pricking the backs of her eyes and forced them away. She saw her dad's eyes become filled with sadness and hurt.

This time, it was Leah who answered. "Of course you're human, Cassie. Don't ever think otherwise. You just have blood in you that enhances certain characteristics and causes you to have a slightly different appearance. It was how God marked the original Brenwyds as a faithful people. I don't know why He did it in that particular way, He just did. We haven't told you before now because we wanted to be sure you were ready. With the animal speech... well, we just figured it was best to wait."

Cassie reflected on that. "Why can't I tell David and Sarah? They can keep secrets. They've kept the one about my animal speech."

"I know, but the fewer people who know about it, the less chance it will slip out. That would not be a good thing. Also, if they knew, it could place them in danger," Ty said.

"How?"

Ty knew he would have had to tell her sooner or later, but he had been hoping for later. He scolded himself for his last sentence. Still, considering it was Cassie, he wasn't surprised she wanted to know more. "Well, because of the people who forced the Brenwyds to go into hiding in the first place. It was mainly a group who named themselves the Reficul Brotherhood. They swore to hunt down Brenwyds until not a drop of Brenwyd blood was left on Earth. They're still around today and they want to finish what the original members started. And... they don't always leave normal people who know part-Brenwyds alone."

Cassie really felt like her brain was drowning now. First, she was part Brenwyd, a people she had thought were only figments of her dad's imagination, the "faerie folk" of Celtic lore. Second, she was the first person to have pointed ears as a result of Brenwyd blood in several hundred years, because God wanted her to for some reason. And now – "You mean, there are people out there who want to kill me? And just by knowing me, David and Sarah are in danger too?" The idea was mind-boggling. She was only ten, for heaven's sake, and so were her friends! What kind of people went around wanting to kill ten-year-olds just because of their heritage or their friend's heritage? *Not anyone* I *want to meet,* she decided.

They do not care how old you are, girl, Kai said, interrupting her thoughts. *All they care is that you have Brenwyd blood and therefore, by their twisted thinking, you must die.*

"But why? I haven't done anything to them," Cassie said aloud, then looked at her parents. "Kai said..." she began.

Ty held up a hand to stop her. "I know what he said, and he's absolutely right. They don't care. That's why I wanted to delay telling you. I didn't want you living out your childhood with the knowledge that there are people out there who want to kill you."

"You know what he said? How?" Cassie asked.

"Because Kai is descended from the dogs the Brenwyds had. They have the ability to speak to anyone they choose, not just those with animal speech," Leah answered.

"Really?" Cassie asked, looking at Kai.

Really, he replied, looking amused. A thought struck Cassie.

"That's why you don't age like a normal dog, isn't it? I remember that Brenwyd animals generally lived a long time."

Yes. It was part of the Blessing. Their animals often lived as long as their owners. Cassie wondered what blessing he was talking about, then remembered that he was referring to the original giving of the Brenwyds' special abilities by God, thousands of years ago. She wondered what the original Brenwyds had thought of suddenly finding themselves with pointed ears.

Her father interrupted her thoughts. "So Cassie, you cannot, I repeat you *cannot* tell *anyone* about your Brenwyd blood. If word gets around to the wrong ears..." his voice trailed off, but everyone knew what he meant.

"Would they really kill me?" Cassie asked, still finding it all hard to believe.

"Yes, they would. You must be careful, and choose your friends carefully, too. It could be the difference between life and death. Do you understand me, Cassandra?" Ty asked, looking into her eyes. Cassie knew it was serious because he almost never called her Cassandra.

She stood abruptly. "Yes, Dad, I understand. I understand everything. I'm going to the pasture. I need to think." With that, she ran out of the room. Ty and Leah listened as the front door opened and closed, and watched as Cassie ran out to the horses. They were silent for a few minutes.

"Well, that could have been worse, I suppose," Leah said at last.

Ty put his arms around her. "She'll be alright. I remember how I reacted when my dad finally told me. I had many of the same thoughts. She just needs time to adjust herself to the whole idea."

Outside, Cassie buried her face in Chance's neck and cried as she told the horses what she had learned just a few minutes before. She could hardly believe what Dad had said, but deep down, she felt the truth of it. Penny nuzzled her hair. *I understand that what he told you is hard for you to believe, but why are you crying?*

"Because I don't want to be different," she sniffed into Chance's mane. "I want to be normal. I've heard kids say how cool it would be to talk to animals and I'm glad that I can, I really am, but if it comes with this much danger, I say it's so *not* cool. I don't want to get killed." It seemed like a reasonable concern to her.

You are not going to be killed, Chance said firmly. *Not while I am around.*

Penny snorted and pawed the ground. *They will find it hard to get past two horses.*

Not to mention us, a new voice said from behind them. Cassie turned to see the barn cat, Calico, approaching, along with Kai and Smokey.

Kai growled agreement with Calico. *We will all fight to protect you, girl, do not forget it. As for your animal speech, it has already proven useful and will continue to do so. Do not wish you did not have it.*

Cassie looked around at them. She felt their resolve, and her fear began to melt away. It would take determined men indeed to get through all of them. What she didn't know was that they knew about the mysterious paper – a paper she knew nothing about, but the contents of which had been in animal lore for countless generations. "You would fight for me?" she asked, very much touched. Affirmation rose from all around her.

Kai approached Cassie and looked her in the eye. *Of course we would fight for you,* he said. *You are our friend. For you, we would do anything.*

A Planned Trail Ride

Four years later...

Several deer grazed on a mountaintop on a quiet and peaceful summer afternoon. A slight breeze rustled through the woods behind them so that the leaves murmured to each other. The sun shone down, not yet with the relentless heat of high summer, but with rays that bathed the land in an intense warmth a few degrees above a completely comfortable temperature. Shining through the trees, the light created leafy shadows on the ground that moved in response to the breeze, as if dancing for joy that it was summer. The mountain was mostly tree-covered, like the other mountains surrounding it, but about a third of its top was taken up by a roughly circular clearing. It was in this clearing that the deer grazed on the patches of grass poking up toward the sun from the brown earth. The clearing extended to the edge of the mountaintop, at which point the earth ended abruptly in light gray rock that jutted out from the mountainside into the air. A peek over the side revealed a long way down.

One of the deer lifted her head, ears alert. She had caught the sound of something like distant thunder, but there were no clouds in the clear blue summer sky. As the sound got closer, the others also picked up on it and became poised to run, but they hesitated, wondering if it could be the girl. Then, as the sound got closer, the doe who had first heard it caught familiar smells. The whole group of deer relaxed as they proceeded to the far end of the ridge, to get out of the way of the horses moving toward them. Before long, three horses and three dogs came out of the tree cover into the clearing, with two girls and a boy on the horses' backs. The deer looked on as the riders slowed their horses to a walk, and then one headed toward a girl of about fourteen on a pretty, delicate-looking black mare with a slightly dished Arabian face. The girl saw the deer coming and smiled, halting her horse. *Hey, Faline*, she thought toward the approaching doe, *How are you?*

I am well. You have not been here for a while, Faline replied, sticking her head under the girl's hand for an ear scratch.

Sorry. It was unavoidable. End of school exams, you know.

No I do not know, but I do not wish to know, the deer declared as she went back to the herd, happy the girl was there but dismissing her as she concentrated on grazing. The girl stood there for a moment sending the rest of the deer greetings, as two of the dogs wandered up to her, waiting for her to move. The mare nudged the girl with her muzzle as a not-so-gentle reminder that she wanted to graze with her two fellow equines.

The girl chuckled as she retrieved a halter from her pack. "A person might think you never got grass," she remarked as the mare tore into the grass with enthusiasm. The mare tossed her mane in reply, not bothering to speak. Her horse seen to, the girl went to join her companions already standing near the edge of the rock cliff with the other dog, taking off her riding helmet as she did so. "Well, what do you think?" she asked them.

The boy, the tallest of the group by an inch or so, was the first to respond, his dark brown eyes never leaving the vista. "You're right. It's definitely one of the best views in the Blue Ridge. I can't believe we didn't remember it earlier." The vista in question was an impressive one, stretching as far as the eye could see. What immediately grabbed the eye were two neighboring, tree-covered mountains, which rose up and nearly obscured the view beyond them, but not quite, as their descending slopes created a gap between them. Through it, more mountains could be seen with the same cover of trees along their sides, forming the Blue Ridge range, which in the distance did, indeed, look blue and hazy. Several gaps between mountains representing valleys were also distinguishable, though what they contained was a mystery to the viewers. Best of all, there were no real signs of civilization save for the occasional, isolated house built onto a mountainside, and a highway in the distance, too far away for the sound of traffic to disturb the quiet of the mountaintop.

The girl shrugged. "Well, you were the one who insisted on checking out all possible sites at the creek down in the valley first." With a slight smile, she added, "Besides, who was I to go against your judgment about camping sites, especially since I remember that when we first saw this place a year ago you were the one who declared it as perfect for a campsite?"

Now the boy shifted his gaze to the girl, the corners of his mouth twitching upward somewhat ruefully. "Hey, it's not my fault I didn't remember it right off. We haven't been here since then, and anyway, you're the one with the perfect memory. Who needs to remember stuff with you around?"

The girl laughed. "So you just keep me around for my memory? Oh dear, I suppose that means you'd be absolutely crippled without me," she teased, rubbing the head of the black and white Border collie at her left side. Some people, observing the girl more closely, might have noticed that, although her strawberry-blond hair was secured in two tight braids, she also wore a headband that partially covered her ears. This, taken into account with the other two humans and the animals around them, identified the trio as Cassie Pennington and the Thompson twins, David and Sarah. The three were very close, and adults and peers alike often called them the Three Musketeers. The reason for their closeness, in their own words, was that they were the only kids their age in their valley, and had known each other since the age of five. On this particular day, the threesome was looking for a place where they could camp out on an overnight trail ride. Cassie's fourteenth birthday was in a few days, and their parents had finally consented to an overnight in the mountains by themselves. This might have seemed irresponsible to some people, but Cassie, David, and Sarah had been riding alone in the Blue Ridge for several years and knew the area surrounding their valley like the backs of their hands. Cassie's ability to talk to animals ensured that none would attack them – no sane ones anyway – and the fact that they had several dogs with them also helped ease their parents' minds. They had been looking for a suitable place since they had gotten permission, but so far they had just not found one.

Sarah laughed at Cassie and David's banter, her hazel eyes dancing with amusement as they often did. "It's a good thing you two don't live in the same house; otherwise no one would get anything done because they would be laughing so hard 'cause of your teasing."

"Nonsense," Cassie said. "I can be very serious when I want to and am good at ignoring people. So I take it this is the place?"

"Definitely," David said, glancing around. "There's plenty of room for a couple of tents, and grass for the horses, and the view faces west so we can watch the sun set."

Cassie nodded. "Yeah, that's part of why I like it so much. This place okay with you guys?" she asked, turning toward the animals. The horses stopped their grazing and ambled over to their humans.

I like it. The grass is sweet, and water is not far off, Twi, Cassie's horse, replied. The mare's full name was Twilight's First Star because of the star on her forehead, but everyone called her Twi.

The other two horses agreed with her. David's bay gelding, Wildfire, commonly known as Fire, added, *And there are no fences, so we do not have to worry about running out of grass.*

The vista in question was an impressive one, stretching as far as the eye could see... a place where they could camp out on an overnight trail ride.

Cassie chuckled at his response. "When have you run out of grass?" The bay just looked at her, and Cassie remembered the dirt lot covered in weeds where they had found the three horses and some others, all of them terribly skinny. Her smile faded as she remembered the fight it took to get the horses and dogs away from the man to whom they had belonged, and the weeks and months it then took to gain the horses' complete trust, even with her animal-speaking ability.

Dassah, the Border collie, nuzzled her hand and said, *Do not worry about it, girl. We are not there now, and have plenty of food. In fact,* she said looking at Fire critically, *he is looking a bit chubby. Perhaps you should bring a grazing muzzle.*

Fire snorted indignantly. *I am* not *chubby. I am merely... well filled out.* The other animals made their various noises of amusement, and Cassie started giggling. They all tried to conceal it, but realized they had failed miserably when Fire glared at them, pinning his ears back in annoyance, and pointedly turned away, swishing his tail as he did so. David and Sarah looked on and waited for Cassie to explain the source of her amusement. They were used to such outbursts, knowing they were caused by the animals they were unable to hear. Getting in control of herself, Cassie told them what had been said.

Sarah started giggling as well, while David assumed a look of injured dignity. "I take very good care of him. He is just the right weight," he declared, which just sent the girls into more giggles. David finally allowed a grin, for he knew as well as they did that his horse *was* a little chubby, in spite of the teens' habit of riding frequently.

Suddenly Kai whirled to face the forest, all amusement forgotten, every muscle tense, nose twitching. The horses and other dogs looked in the direction he was staring and tensed as well, forming a line in front of the kids. Even the deer stopped grazing and raised their heads, looking toward the forest with full attention, bodies poised to run, their big ears at full alert. Cassie felt apprehension and worry from all of them and stopped laughing, as did Sarah. They knew that Kai did not act like this without cause. Cassie slipped a hand behind her back to grasp the hilt of a knife she had concealed in the emergency bag that she always wore on rides, strapped diagonally across her back.

What is it? She asked Kai silently.

The dog waited a few moments before replying, putting his nose in the air. He relaxed slightly and turned toward Cassie. *I do not know. Whatever it was, it is gone now. We should go.*

Can we use this place for our overnight?

Maybe. You may want to find other places just in case. His tone was cautious and guarded.

Sarah had grabbed her mare Dreamer's halter and was now looking curiously at Cassie. "What alarmed them?" she asked as the blue roan tugged against her hold.

"Kai says that whatever it was, it's gone now. He doesn't know what it was, but we should go," Cassie said as she took off Twi's halter and put the bridle on. She continued, "He also says that it's probably okay to camp here, but we may need a backup spot."

David frowned as he took Fire's bridle out of his saddle pack, where he had put it when they'd arrived at the site. "What could set him off like that? Couldn't it have just been an animal, or maybe someone hiking? What's the big deal?" He looked at Cassie with probing eyes, trying to figure out why the animals had gone tense.

Cassie waited until she had Twi's girth tightened and was in the saddle before she answered, not looking at them. "It... it *could* be nothing," she allowed as Sarah and David mounted, waiting for her friends to get settled before pressing Twi into a walk. "But then again it *could* be something, and I don't want to stick around long enough to find out. I'm sorry," she said, lifting her head to look at them, "but I can't tell you what it could be and I can't tell you why it's a big deal. You just have to trust me."

David and Sarah looked at each other, similar confused expressions on their faces. They knew Cassie was different. Anyone who could talk to animals was different. They were also puzzled by the fact that ever since they had gotten back from that trip four years ago, she always wore a headband. When they had asked her about it, she'd said something about her parents making her, and beyond that she wouldn't say. They had also noticed that Cassie was physically quicker than other people, and everyone knew she was very smart. Technically, she should be in the grade below the twins, but she had been bumped up. This occasional jumpiness about things was another one of her quirks, but as with the other characteristics, David and Sarah had gotten used to it, though it was certainly the oddest and most mysterious of her traits. "Cassie, we may not understand all that's going on, but we do trust you. Although that could mean we need our heads examined," David said. He grinned at her, trying to lift her spirits with memories of various little adventures they'd had – mostly after Cassie had decided to investigate something further.

Cassie smiled and chuckled a little, but her expression was strained. "Thanks." There was silence for a long time as each contemplated their own thoughts. As Cassie mulled over their answer, she knew that she would have to tell them her secret soon. She had kept it from them for four years, and she wasn't sure how much longer she could keep it. It made her feel like there was a barrier between herself and her friends, and she would like nothing better than to tear it down. *I'll talk to Dad about it,* she decided. Later, as they were approaching the houses, she halted Twi and turned toward Sarah and David. "I'd appreciate it if you didn't tell your parents about this right away, okay?"

Sarah frowned. She hadn't necessarily been planning to, but she wondered why Cassie was asking them specifically not to, and why she looked so uncomfortable. What wasn't she telling them? "Okay, but are you going to tell yours?"

Cassie hesitated a little. "Maybe," she said. "I don't want them worried over nothing. I've been thinking about it, and I realized that the wind was blowing from the trees to us, so it may have carried a scent that was a ways away."

David nodded. "That's possible, but what scent would cause the animals to tense up like that?"

"I don't know. A bear, maybe? I'd better get home now. See y'all tomorrow?" Cassie asked.

"Yep. See ya," Sarah said. Cassie turned Twi toward her house and startled the twins by squeezing her into a fast canter. They stayed where they were until Twi's hoofbeats faded. At length Sarah voiced what was going through both their minds: "Well, that was weird."

David nodded. "It's unlike her to take off like that so close to home."

"That too, but I was thinking more about the other stuff. There's got to be way more to this than meets the eye."

"Yeah, definitely. Cassie's always been... different, but she's never been so vague about stuff. Except for the headband."

"Oh? I know she's a little touchy about it, but she did explain why she wears it," Sarah said.

"But it was a pretty lousy explanation for Cassie, in my opinion. Think about how she reacts whenever someone suggests she take it off. And that time Bob Mallory almost got it off. If she wears it just to prevent sunburn, she wouldn't be so touchy about it." The incident to which David was referring had happened several years earlier, a few months after Cassie had first started wearing the headband. Bob Mallory had been the school's worst bully, and Cassie had often been the recipient of his cruel remarks, even though he was a couple of years older than her. One day during recess, she had been sitting a little away from everyone else studying for a test, and he had gone over to her and tried to forcibly remove the headband, having noticed she was sensitive about it. They had been out of sight of the teacher and most of the other kids. Cassie had retaliated by kneeing him in the groin and whacking him on the head with her schoolbook, giving the right side of his face a big bruise. Not long after that, Bob had been expelled for cheating on tests and provoking fights. People had long wondered who had managed to nail him, but Cassie never said a word. David and Sarah, who had been the only others to see the altercation, also kept quiet, per Cassie's request.

"Yeah, I remember that. You're right; it's a little weird, as you pointed out. But I fail to see how the whole headband thing is connected to what happened on the ridge," Sarah said, berating herself for giving David an opening about the headband. David wondered about the headband frequently. He'd tried asking Cassie about it many times, but she completely clammed up whenever he mentioned it blatantly, and changed the subject if he tried to bring it up subtly. Sometimes Sarah wished he would just quit wondering about it and simply accept it as another of Cassie's quirks.

The twins turned their horses the opposite way Cassie had gone, and started walking. A suspicion began to form in David's mind. He tried to dismiss it as crazy, but couldn't help thinking about it. "Sarah?" he asked.

"Yeah?"

"Do you think that the answer to why Cassie's different could be what she's hiding under that headband?"

Sarah thought about it for a moment, frowning slightly. "I don't know. How do you know she's hiding anything? She was different even before she started wearing it, you know. And what could she hide under it? She said it's needed to help prevent sunburn, and she does burn easily. Remember that time she went to the beach and came back with her ears completely burned, and had to stay inside until they healed? That wasn't too long before she started wearing the headband all the time," she reminded her twin.

"But she acted funny when she told us that, remember? She was looking off to the side and avoiding eye contact. Besides, she keeps it on even when we're inside, or it's cloudy out, or it's winter. I know she's hiding something about it. What, I have no idea. Could it be some sort of girl thing, d'ya think?"

Sarah rolled her eyes and stifled a sigh. He'd asked her that before, and she always gave him the same answer. "No, it's not a girl thing. It's most definitely a Cassie thing. But you think she was lying to us? Come on, David. Cassie's the most honest person I know. She wouldn't lie to us." David had not raised that possibility with her before, and the idea made Sarah uncomfortable. Why would Cassie lie to them about something as simple as a headband? It made no sense, and it didn't go with Cassie's personality.

"Normally, she wouldn't," David said, "but I think she did about the headband and I think she did today. Why, I don't know, but I get the feeling she has an idea why the animals got tense and didn't tell us because of the reason she wears the headband." He frowned as he finished speaking, staring off into the distance. The idea that Cassie would lie to conceal something from them rankled his mind. *She had better have a really good reason for having hidden whatever she's hiding*, he thought heatedly.

Sarah shot a look at her brother, eyebrows raised. He'd never been so fixated on Cassie's headband before. She shook her head. He was overthinking the incident, big time. "David, seriously, what could she hide under there? Pointed ears? You think she's part elf?" Sarah asked, amusement in her voice.

"Maybe, Sarah. You never know. Whatever it is, I want to find out," David answered, hard determination and resolve in his voice.

Sarah stared at her brother. He had answered her flippant remark seriously. Much too seriously, in her opinion. "You've been watching too much *Lord of the Rings*. Elves don't exist."

David sighed, deciding not to pursue the subject any further at the moment since Sarah was clearly more than ready to drop it. It would be rather pointless to continue thinking about it anyway, as Cassie wasn't available to question. "I can see I'm not going to win this argument. Wanna have a trotting race?"

"You're on." David tried to quiet his suspicions by absorbing himself in the race, but he couldn't get Sarah's comment about pointed ears out of his head. He resolved to look up anything and everything he could find on elves and their characteristics and behavior. *Who knows,* he thought, *the legends have to have come from somewhere, right? What if there really were elves once?* Then he realized what exactly he was thinking. *I really have been watching too many movies*, he thought, unaware that Sarah, for all her teasing comments, was wondering along similar lines.

Neither had any idea just how close they were to the truth.

As the trees passed by in a blur on account of Twi's speed, Cassie thought about what had happened up on the ridge and tried to discount it. *It was probably just a bear or wayward hiker,* she reasoned. But still her doubts grew. Her mind envisioned terrifying possibilities of what it could have been, anything from a passing bear to the worst thought of all, a member of the shadowy Brotherhood come to kill her, having discovered her secret at last. Twi's speed increased as the mare caught her rider's apprehension, but Cassie paid almost no notice. Suddenly Kai jumped in front of the horse, growling and snapping. Twi reared up, startled, and Cassie grabbed a chunk of mane just in time to keep from falling off. "What was that for?" she demanded, glaring at the dog.

He met her gaze steadily. *You were going too fast*, he replied calmly. *You wish to keep what happened a secret, but if you come charging into the yard your parents will realize something happened and will press you for details. If they get them, they will likely not allow you to continue with your plans for this trail ride, and you do not want that, do you?*

Cassie accepted the logic of Kai's reasoning. "But that's still no excuse for nearly making me fall off! You could have just asked me to slow down."

We tried, Dassah said, breathing hard as she caught up to them. *You were not listening.* She stared reproachfully at Cassie. Chastened, Cassie nudged Twi, still blowing hard, into a slow walk.

"But Kai, why did you tense up like that? You guys, too, Twi and Dassah." The animals remained silent. "Well? I'd like to know what happened."

Twi answered. *There was a passing smell of... wrongness in the air, like the scent before a bad storm. A... disturbance that causes an unnatural silence, or an absence of animals where there should be many.* The mare sounded cautious and uncertain, very different from her usually confident tone.

"So in other words, you don't know what it was, it just smelled wrong and dangerous?"

Yes, Kai said. *It seemed important that we get out of the area quickly.* Cassie breathed a small sigh of relief and started to relax. If it hadn't been Kai who'd raised the alarm, she would have dismissed it right then as the animals sensing a predator on the prowl and wanting to get away. The deer had seemed to confirm that thought when they got skittish. But Kai did not get tense like that for no good reason. The last time was when they had gone on a dig with her dad in England, and Kai had sensed thieves sneaking into the camp to steal the artifacts the archaeologists had found. *There's something he's not telling me,* Cassie decided. *But it can't be too serious or he would have said outright that we shouldn't use that place as a campsite.* Kai was very protective of her.

The trees started to thin out, and soon Cassie was able to see her house. But before she left the shelter of the trees, she posed the animals a question: "If we go back to the clearing and stay there an hour or so without any alarms, would it be okay to camp there?"

She heard the three conferring for a moment, and then Dassah replied, *Yes.* Cassie smiled. That was what she had wanted to hear.

As she rode into the stable yard and heard Penny and Chance give their greetings, she said, “Remember, don’t tell Mom and Dad. I don’t want them to be worried about nothing.”

This was directed primarily at Kai, as the others could communicate only with Cassie. *And if we go back and sense a similar feeling?* the dog asked.

“Then I’ll tell them, but not before.”

Very well, Kai said, *as you wish.*

As Cassie entered the barn with Twi to untack, Kai and Dassah stayed outside, the smaller dog coming as close to a glare as a dog could. *You should have told her,* Dassah accused. *She should know.*

We do not know for sure, and she has wanted to do this since her tenth birthday. It could have been nothing.

And it could have been something, the female argued. *We cannot let her do something that could put her in danger. Remember the prophecy.*

Kai growled a little, showing his teeth. *If anything or anyone wants to harm her, they will have to get through me first. And I do remember, Dassah. There is no need to remind me.* He left abruptly, not wanting to prolong the conversation. Deep down, he had a feeling that Dassah was right. They had not told Cassie everything. They had told her about a general feeling of wrongness, but not about the specific scent of a sinister evil that Kai had caught. It had been there, and then was gone so quickly that Kai was not sure he had smelled it. So he decided not to tell Cassie or Ty or Leah. It was sometimes better that they did not know everything. In a few days, however, Kai would regret that he had ever hidden the smell.

The animals had been right to get their humans away so quickly. A scant fifteen minutes after they left, another horse and rider came onto the mountaintop out of the woods. The rider was clothed all in black and his horse was the same hue. Normally he wouldn't have attracted much attention – many people rode in the area – but he had a long sword hanging by his left side, something not at all normal in the area. He dismounted and examined the ground with dark eyes, finding the tracks he was looking for quickly and without difficulty. The rider grinned as he remounted, and it was the grin of a hunter closing in on his helpless prey after a long chase. *At last,* he thought. *After years of searching and dead ends, we are close to eliminating the last of the witch's line.* He rode down the mountain to the valley, and then to within view of the Pennington's house. He watched as Cassie led Twi out to the pasture, then as she headed up to the house with the two dogs in tow. Before she reached it, she looked around, as if sensing she was being watched. After a few seconds she apparently satisfied herself that everything was alright, and went into the house. The rider watched for a while after she disappeared from view, studying the house and making note of any and all entrances. He then went back up the trail to report back to his master that they could move on with their mission to exterminate *her* line, along with anyone else who shared Brenwyd blood.

Cassie went looking for her father after changing out of her riding clothes. She didn't have to look far, as she knew exactly where he would be: at his desk in the library. He had been working on something in there for the past few weeks whenever he was home, but had proved cagey when asked about what it was. Cassie decided to practice her stalking skills and figure out what he was up to. The library door was slightly open, and her keen ears picked up the sound of her father's muttering. He often muttered when working on things, but Cassie knew from past experience that listening to that wouldn't necessarily tell her what he was working on. He didn't speak clearly when he muttered, anyway.

Slowly and silently, she pushed the door open. Her father's desk faced the big bay window at the back of the library, so a person sitting at the desk had his back to the door. Cassie slid through the door opening and tiptoed up behind her father. It had been a kind of game since she was small to see if she could sneak up on her father. Although his ears were not pointed, he did have extremely keen hearing and Cassie had never been able to sneak up on him, despite her best attempts.

As she got closer to the desk with no greeting from her father, she started thinking that maybe this would be the time she surprised him. Just as she was about to announce her presence, he said, without looking up, "If you want to successfully sneak up on someone, Cassie, you must breathe more quietly."

"I was breathing quietly," Cassie protested. "I could barely hear myself."

"Ah, but you admit you could still hear yourself," her dad answered, turning his head to look at her. His green eyes twinkled in jest. "Although, to be fair, a normal person would never have heard you."

She grinned. "Thanks." She looked over his shoulder at the mess of papers on his desk. "Whatcha working on?" She frowned at the paper currently in his hand. "Why are you writing in Latin?"

Ty gathered the papers and placed them inside a binder, closing it in one fluid motion. "I hope to tell you soon. And... so people who shouldn't be looking at it can't understand it."

Cassie smiled smugly. "But I know Latin. Come on, Dad, tell me. Please?"

"No. I'm not quite ready yet."

Cassie spied what looked like an old leather-bound book, and snatched it up before Ty could put it away. "What's this? It looks old."

"It is. Fifteen hundred years old, to be precise. May I have that, please?"

Cassie gave her father a searching look. "Fifteen hundred years? Is this something from King Arthur's time?" She opened it and noted the style of writing. "A diary?"

"Mmm, yes. Now please give it back." Cassie complied and Ty put it under another pile of papers.

"Whose was it?" Cassie asked.

"I'll tell you..." Ty paused, thinking. "How about this: I'll tell you everything on your birthday."

Cassie brightened. "Okay. So I can wake you up at midnight and you'll have to tell me."

Ty laughed. "Try that, m'girl, and I'll make you wait until dinner. Not to mention you'll be up in the mountains with the twins. And speaking of that, how'd the ride go?"

"It was fine," Cassie said. She hesitated a moment, debating whether or not to mention the animals' odd behavior after all, but decided against it. Animals often acted in strange ways that even she didn't understand, and if Kai had really been concerned, he would have firmly advised against using the spot as a campsite. "I think we found a place. It's not too far from here and actually has a great view westward across the mountains that isn't obscured by trees."

"That's good." Ty narrowed his eyes at his daughter. "Is there something else?"

"Well..." Cassie started, uncertain of how to approach the subject. "I think... I think I should tell David and Sarah. I'm tired of hiding it from them."

"Hmm." Ty didn't have to ask what she meant. "Did something happen today to prompt this?"

"Um... not really. The animals were a little jumpy for some reason, and that made me jumpy, and the twins asked me why but I couldn't say."

Ty frowned. "Jumpy? Why?"

"It was nothing. I think it was just the far-off scent of bear or something. The wind was blowing in our direction." Cassie paused. "But beyond that… I just think it's time. It's been four years. They don't question the headband directly, not anymore, but I can see the question in their eyes whenever they hear me try to explain it to someone else. They want to know, and I think they deserve to know the truth about why you teach us swordplay, why we're always so careful around new people, why I get jumpy when odd things happen. We're not ten anymore, Dad."

He sighed. "I know, Cassie, I know. I've been expecting this." He paused. "You can tell them. I've taught you all enough defense skills that you can take care of yourselves. We can trust them. Their father is an old friend of mine, you know."

"I know. He knows, right?"

Ty nodded. "Yes. My father told me before I went to college. Ben and I ended up picking the same college, and I told him in the course of those four years. It's important to have some people who know, people you can relax around."

Cassie hugged him. "Thanks, Dad."

He hugged her back. "Will you tell them tomorrow?"

Cassie pulled back. "I don't know… maybe. I'll tell them when it feels right." Now that she had permission to reveal her biggest secret, she felt a little scared. How would her friends react? Especially knowing that she had kept quiet for four years?

Ty took one of her hands. He knew what was going through her head. "Cassie, they'll understand. Real friends do. And Sarah and David have proven themselves that over and over."

"I know." Cassie ran a hand along her ear. Some part of her had never gotten used to the shape, especially since it had happened literally overnight. She sat down on the floor. "Dad?"

"Yes?"

"If we were found out by the Brotherhood... what would happen?" Cassie wasn't sure what made her ask the question now, never having really wanted to ask it before. Whenever the subject of the Brotherhood came up around the house, it was in the context of hiding from them, and Cassie understood quite well that if the Brotherhood actually found them, they would be killed. Other than that, all the Penningtons took pains to never really discuss the Brotherhood, as active discussion would make them seem much more real. "I mean, I know... I know that they want to... kill us, torture us, but what if we had time to do something? What if we had some sort of warning? What would we do?"

Ty didn't answer for several minutes. "Well Cassie, there aren't many people with Brenwyd blood, but there are some, and there are means of... communication. We have ways to hide and warn each other. There are also ways to track the Brotherhood's movements as best as we can. If there were signs that the Brotherhood was getting close... we'd have to move."

"But couldn't they track us? All they'd have to do is ask for the forwarding address from the post office."

"As I said, there are ways to hide. I'll tell you, eventually, but not today. Don't worry; I've hidden our family records well. It would take a matter of years and an extremely determined person to uncover the fact that we're Brenwyd."

"Unless one of them happened to be in the area and took an educated guess as to why I wear a headband all the time," Cassie countered.

Ty shook his head. "Even then, I would doubt it. Since there hasn't been a part-Brenwyd with pointed ears in so long, they've probably stopped using that as a means of identification." He looked her over keenly. "Why are you being so negative today? Is there more to the animals acting jumpy?"

Cassie shook her head. "No. And I was just... wondering, I

guess." She looked up at him. "So you do know other people with Brenwyd blood? Can I meet them?"

"I don't know them well. It's just a sort of communication connection, a warning system that's been in practice since Brenwyds went underground. You might meet them someday, but as a rule it's safer to stay apart. Helps keep Brotherhood suspicions quiet."

"Okay." Cassie looked at the messy desk. "Can you even give me a hint of what you're working on?" she asked in a wheedling tone.

Ty laughed. "Alright, but I won't give you anything else until your birthday. It has to do with King Arthur."

Cassie blinked at her father. "That's all? I guessed that weeks ago! That's not fair."

"Oh yes it is," Ty said, grinning. "Now if you would kindly let me go back to work, I would appreciate it. I think your mother will be getting home from the store about now." At that moment Cassie received a message from Smokey that confirmed her dad's words.

She sighed dramatically. "Alright. See you later, Dad." She turned to leave.

"Cassie." Cassie looked back at her dad. His expression had morphed into one of seriousness. "Even though I don't think we're in any danger at the moment, if anything *does* happen, you just concern yourself with you. If something happens to me, or your mother and me, there is a plan in place. If something happens to just me, your mother knows what to do. But if something happens to us both, you'll need to go to your aunt's. I have everything in place to cover your tracks, and Mr. Thompson knows how to put that into action. You go to them first. Understand? You just worry about yourself."

Cassie frowned. "How would I explain to Aunt Janelle why I suddenly need to hide at her house? She doesn't know."

"No, but your mother told her that I occasionally take dangerous, undercover, classified jobs for the government and so you might need a safe place someday."

Cassie blinked. "Oh. That explains a lot." Whenever they visited her aunt, she seemed to enjoy asking coded questions and never directly asked about how Ty's work was going. "Why didn't you tell me that sooner?"

"You didn't need to know." At Cassie's skeptical look, Ty added, "Cassie, I know you like knowing everything, but please trust me to tell you what you need to know when you need to know it. Alright?"

Cassie sighed and nodded. "Alright." She smiled briefly. "It's all just making sure we're *Semper Paratus*, right?

Ty smiled back. "Right. But like I said, don't worry about it right now. I've received no indications that the Brotherhood knows where we are. You just worry about controlling that wild horse of yours."

"She's not wild anymore, Dad!" Cassie exclaimed indignantly.

Ty chuckled. "Just saying, Cassie. We'll be alright."

When Cassie left the room, Ty looked after her for a few minutes, reviewing the conversation. He suspected there was more to the animals being jumpy than she said, but he knew if he pushed before she was ready, she would clam up. She was like him in that respect. If it were serious, Kai would tell him. He was also glad that she now knew what to do in an emergency. He'd been planning to have that talk with her anyway. He realized he should have told her long ago, but he'd wanted her to have as normal a childhood as possible. He walked across the room to fully close the door, and then spread out his papers and set about his work.

A Heartbreaking Birthday Surprise

Cassie felt thrills of excitement running through her as she packed her duffel and saddlebags. *At last*, she thought, *we're really going*. Her excitement made her want to sing, so she did. She chose a song with lyrics about saddling horses to blaze a trail, which seemed appropriate. Smokey wandered into her room and sat right in the middle of her duffel. "Hey, I'm packing things into that, you know. Could ya get off?" she scolded the cat good-naturedly.

The cat stared at her with unblinking yellow eyes. *You be careful, girl. You never know what could happen.*

"It's okay, Smokey. There'll be Kai, Dassah, Twi, Fire, Dreamer, Gracie, David, and Sarah to keep me outta trouble. And I've got my knives, too. You know I'm good with them."

I also know that people with the best protection have been killed because they failed to pay attention to details. Do not get cocky.

"Cocky? I'm not cocky. I'm just stating facts. Why are you so concerned all of a sudden? You haven't worried about me in the mountains before." Cassie was puzzled and amused at the same time. Smokey was displaying decidedly un-catlike behavior, something he generally took great pains to avoid. The gray cat flicked his tail nervously. The smile slowly fell from Cassie's face as she considered the cat's unusual behavior and remembered how all the animals had been acting odd lately... ever since that visit to the mountaintop clearing. She, Kai, Dassah, and Twi had gone back to the site a few days later and had stayed there several hours. Nothing had happened nor had the animals smelled anything strange, so Kai had given his okay, but they had still acted jumpy and tense. Cassie didn't like it, but decided that the incident had just unsettled them and they would calm down soon. This, however, was the first time she had detected wariness in Smokey. "We'll be fine, Smokey. We'll all have our phones and there is reception at the campsite. I checked. And we all know how to fight."

I know girl, just pay close attention to what is around you, okay? He leaped down from the bed and left the room. Cassie looked after him for a while, then decided to not worry about it and went back to packing.

Her mother came into the room a few minutes later. "I thought you might go looking for this," Leah said, handing Cassie her cell phone.

"Thanks, Mom," Cassie said.

Leah looked over her packing. "Do you have everything?"

"Yep. I made a list this time."

Leah smiled. "That's good. Before you go, I would appreciate you dropping off your dirty laundry by the washer and picking up your clean clothes."

"Okay." Cassie went about finding a few odds and ends, but her mother didn't leave the room. "What is it?" Cassie asked.

Leah sighed. "Oh, nothing. Just remember to be careful, that's all."

"Mom, it's just an overnight in mountains that we all know well. What could happen?"

"I'm just saying, Cassie." She paused. "Your father told me that you asked him the other day about our plans for if the Brotherhood attacked."

"Oh. I was just wondering about it, that's all."

"I know, and it's a good thing to know. But don't you worry about it too much, okay? That's your dad's and my job."

Cassie nodded. "Alright."

"Have you told David and Sarah yet?"

Cassie shook her head. "No. I was planning to do that tonight."

Leah nodded. "It'll be good for them to know." She turned to leave.

"Mom?" Cassie's voice stopped her. Leah looked back with an inquiring look on her face. "How did you react when Dad told you?"

Leah raised her eyebrows slightly. "You know that, Cassie. I've told you many times."

"Tell it again. Please?"

Leah appraised her daughter with a thoughtful look. "Alright." She sat down on Cassie's bed. Cassie sat beside her. "Well, I wasn't sure if he was serious or not at first. He does love to joke, you know." Cassie nodded. "When I realized he was serious... I didn't know what to say. I was shocked, of course, but the shock wore off. I had noticed there was something different about your dad. Now I had my answer. It made sense. He had told me his Brenwyd stories beforehand." Leah smiled at the memory. "When he eventually told me everything, he did it to see if I would be turned off by it, or by the knowledge that there was an organization that could come after him. I wasn't. I thought it was rather exciting at the time, like something from a story."

"And now?" Cassie asked.

Leah put an arm around Cassie's shoulders. "I'm waiting to see how this story plays out. You, my dear, are destined for great things. Never, ever, doubt it."

"How do you know that?"

Leah chuckled and ran a finger lightly over Cassie's ear. "It's as clear as the shape of your ears, honey. Only God could make the

Brenwyd blood in you strong enough to give you pointed ears, and He always does things for a purpose. Never forget that."

Cassie nodded thoughtfully. "Thanks, Mom."

"Anytime." Leah squeezed her shoulders. "Don't worry about what Sarah's and David's initial reactions might be. They'll get over it."

Cassie smiled sheepishly. "I guess it's a little silly to be nervous about it. I never thought I would be."

"It's perfectly alright." Through Cassie's window, Leah spied two riders approaching the house. "And speaking of which, there they are. You go on down and get Twi ready. But remember what I said about the laundry."

A little while later, the three teens were ready to start. All the parents had come to the barn to see them off. "Have a good time," said Benjamin, Sarah and David's dad. "Steer clear of poachers, thieves, and animal oppressors, okay?" he added with a twinkle in his brown eyes. The kids grinned at the reminder of the adventures they had already had in the mountains and elsewhere.

"The artifact thieves were in England, Dad. I doubt they'd show up here," David said, laughing and glancing over at Cassie. She blushed at the memory. After Kai had discovered the thieves, the twosome had tried to recover the artifacts without the thieves noticing, but had been unsuccessful. A fight had resulted during which Cassie had almost been overcome by virtue of the thieves' superior numbers, but had been saved by the timely appearance of David and Sarah. With the assistance of Ty and Ben, all the thieves had been rendered unconscious. The group had then gone back to the camp to inform the archaeologist in charge of the dig that there were several thieves who needed to be put in jail. The incident had attracted media attention, but fortunately the identities of those who had caught the thieves had miraculously been kept secret, much to everyone's relief.

"Well, hopefully this won't be quite as exciting," Hannah said, chuckling.

Cassie's eyes gleamed with mischief as she said, "Well, if it is, David's handling it. It's his job as the only male member." Everyone laughed at this as David rolled his eyes.

Kai and Fire grew indignant. *We are males as well, you know*, they said. Kai nudged Cassie's foot out of the stirrup.

"I know that, I meant the only male human." The others looked at her inquiringly, so she told them what had been said.

"Have fun, but call if you run into trouble, got it?" Ty reminded the teens after the laughter died down. He looked at Cassie.

"Got it," she said.

"Be careful," Leah cautioned. "You never know what could happen."

"We'll be fine, Mom," Cassie assured her. "We'll be back tomorrow by around nine or ten."

Her mother smiled. "Try not to sleep in too late. It won't seem like your birthday without you here."

"We'll try to get her up, Mrs. Pennington. I think we're gonna get up early for sunrise," Sarah said.

"That early?" Ty asked, smiling. "I'd like to see that."

"I get up early just fine," Cassie said indignantly. "It's David that's going to be the problem."

David sighed as he swung into the saddle. "There are just too many girls around here for me to win. Let's get going before I think better of this excursion."

"Be patient, David, it's a virtue," his sister told him impishly.

"Pay attention to your mother's advice and watch the animals closely. They'll be aware of any danger before you will," Ty said, looking at Cassie. She nodded. "And you do have everything, right?"

"Everything," Cassie confirmed, putting a hand on her emergency bag strapped to her back. She knew he was really asking if she had her knives.

The parents said final farewells and watched until Sarah, the last rider, disappeared through the trees with the Thompsons' dog, Gracie, following. Ben and Hannah left and Ty and Leah went back into the now quiet house. As they walked into the kitchen, Leah noticed a tense, worried look on her husband's face. "What's the matter?" she asked as she began to gather the ingredients for a cake from the cabinets. "You look worried. The kids will be fine. They can take care of themselves, and they've got the animals with them."

Ty sighed. "I know. I just have this strange feeling that something bad is going to happen."

Leah stopped her preparations and looked at him. "You haven't heard anything, have you?" she asked, her gray eyes dark with worry.

"No, not exactly, but ever since that conversation with Cassie I've felt edgy for some reason. And I got a cryptic message from my brother this morning. He thinks they're moving."

Now Leah's eyes reflected alarm. "Are we in immediate danger?"

"I don't think so, but we should be extra careful for a while."

"Do you think Cassie telling Sarah and David is a bad idea?"

"No, not at all. It's time they knew. I just want you to be aware. I'll tell Cassie when she gets back. She should know as well. Now, are you going to bake that cake, or do I need to do it?" His face held a teasing expression.

Leah laughed, for they both knew the only things Ty could cook were microwaveable meals with directions. "I'll bake it, I'll bake it. I know Cassie would like her cake edible. But you can help me stir the batter."

The ride up to the campsite was pleasant and the teens arrived in good time. David and the dads had gone up earlier that morning to set up the tents, so the teens didn't have to worry about that.

They untacked and set the horses loose to graze. Cassie's talent ensured that they would not wander off too far. Next, they went into their tents and set down their bags. Cassie and Sarah occupied one tent and David the other. Since there was still a good bit of the afternoon left, they took bathing suits out of their bags and rode bareback to their swimming lake. After they finished swimming and changed back into riding clothes, they rode around the mountain, visiting all their favorite haunts and doing some sparring practice with sticks they found. As the sun began to set, they returned to camp. David built a fire and the girls took food out of a bag the moms had packed while the sun set in the distance, painting the sky with streaks of orange, yellow, pink, and violet. As darkness fell, they sat around eating and enjoying each other's company, discussing summer plans and past vacations. Sarah had just finished recollecting a memory from their trip to SeaWorld four years earlier, when she had accidentally fallen into the dolphin pool and gotten completely soaked, when David asked, "Hey Cassie, did you bring your guitar?"

She nodded. "Dad brought it up when you guys set up the tents. I asked him to because I knew Twi couldn't carry it up here with all the other stuff." She went into her tent and came back carrying the instrument. She had been playing since the age of eight, and was often asked to play at church and at school talent shows. After tuning it, she began to strum the opening chords of a worship song they all knew. Soon the ridge rang with the sound of three voices praising the Creator. They sang for a good half-hour, mixing worship songs with campfire songs. At last, Cassie laid aside her guitar and all fell into companionable silence, gazing into the fire as each became absorbed in their thoughts.

Cassie considered how to tell her friends her secret. Although she had known David and Sarah almost her whole life, she wasn't sure how they would react to what she was about to tell them. Her mother's words had reassured her, but she was still feeling a little nervous. This was the one thing she had never shared with them, and she was afraid they would be angry, or think she was legitimately crazy.

How can they think that? Dassah commented from where she lay near the fire. *You have the ears. They'll be able to see it with their own eyes.*

I know, Cassie said, sounding morose even in her thoughts. *I just don't know how they'll take it. Especially David. Sarah is very trusting and understands there's generally always a good reason for concealing information, but David isn't like that. He always wants to know everything and gets upset when people won't or don't tell him something. I don't want him mad at me.*

Do not worry about it, Gracie told her. *He gets upset, yes, but he calms down and accepts why he was not told something.*

If he thinks the reason given for not being told is solid and valid and not just an excuse, Cassie countered.

You have a solid and valid reason, said Kai. *Your parents would not let you. Besides, you did not want them exposed to danger. Do not let your fear of David's reaction cloud your resolve to tell them. They will understand. They are your friends. Why are you so worried about how David will respond? Do you fancy him?* The dog's tone had become mischievous.

Cassie stared at the dog. "Of course not!" she exclaimed, feeling grateful that neither of the twins could hear him.

"What?" Sarah asked, startled, jerking her gaze to Cassie at the sudden exclamation.

Cassie shook her head. "Nothing. But... I do need to tell you guys something." Her serious tone tipped off the other two that she was about to say something important, and they both looked at her attentively. As the firelight flickered over Cassie's face, Sarah thought she looked as ancient as the mountain on which they sat, and slightly ethereal. Slowly, Cassie began to speak. "It's... it's something really important, so before I tell you, I need you to promise you will never, ever, speak of this to anyone. If you do, it could be the death of me."

The twins were extremely puzzled. Cassie had never spoken to them like this before. It seemed a little spooky, as it was now around ten o'clock and fully dark. The sound of nighttime insects could clearly be heard. The air was still and humid, but starting to cool off a bit. The waxing moon would have completed the sense of a peaceful summer night if not for Cassie's odd remarks.

"What do you mean, the death of you? Why is it so important? And what is it?" David asked.

Cassie trained her eyes on him. "Like I said, before I tell you anything more, I need you to promise that you will not tell anyone, *anyone*, what I tell you. It's incredibly important."

The gray in her eyes became dominant as she gazed at them, no emotion evident in her face except a deadly seriousness. The twins felt like her eyes were boring into them, looking at their souls. Cassie's gaze could be intense, but it had never been like this before. They knew she was not joking.

Sarah nodded slowly, a little concerned by Cassie's solemnity and intensity. "I give you my promise I won't tell anyone whatever it is you're going to tell us, Cassie. Ever. Unless you say so."

"I give my promise too, Cass," David said. "So, what is it?" He was becoming more and more curious. What on earth could she be about to tell them?

She looked at them for a moment longer, then took a deep breath. "Okay. It's easier to show you first and then answer your questions, so hold on a moment." She started to raise a hand to her head. David narrowed his eyes, realizing that Cassie was about to take off her headband. Were her peculiarities connected to the headband after all? He shot a glance at Sarah, and could tell that she had also realized the possible implications. He returned his gaze to Cassie, his mouth pressed into a thin line, and crossed his arms, waiting for her explanation. Before Cassie's hand reached the headband, however, she heard faint hoofbeats rapidly coming toward them. She cocked her head slightly and turned in the direction of the trail, a perplexed look on her face. Everyone, people and animals, turned toward the forest. The dogs jumped up and growled deep in their throats. The horses moved closer to the campfire, heads facing toward the forest. Cassie now felt the approaching horse's panic and fear. Stunned, she realized who was coming to the campsite. "It's Penny! But she has no rider. She's completely panicked. I can't figure out why; her thoughts are all jumbled."

"What could panic her so badly she'd run up here without a rider?" Sarah asked, now able to hear the frantic staccato of hoofbeats for herself.

"I have no idea! Kai?"

Before the dog could answer, Penny galloped into view and slid to a stop in front of Cassie. *Quick! You must come. They came. They took them. They hurt him. You must heal him!* Her thoughts were edged with a tinge of hysteria, something Cassie had never heard in an animal's voice before. The other animals started talking to and over each other, trying to figure out the reason for the older mare's distress. They got so loud Cassie couldn't think.

She placed her hands on her ears (even though she knew it had no effect whatsoever) and shouted, "Quiet!" The silence that followed in her head was so sudden it was slightly unnerving. "Alright. Now, tell me what's going on. Slowly, so I can understand it."

Penny lowered her head until her eyes were looking into Cassie's. *Watch,* she commanded, and a series of images began streaming into Cassie's mind. Quickly becoming horrified, she watched Penny's memories of a van pulling into the driveway and men in dark clothing jumping out, drawing swords as they forced the front door open and rushed into the house. Several more men rode up on dark horses. Penny and Chance had begun whinnying a warning as soon as they saw the men exiting the van. Chance fiddled with the gate chain until it finally opened, and the horses ran out of the pasture and began attacking the enemy horses and two men left to guard the door. Sounds of swords could be heard clanging from inside, followed by Leah's scream of terror. One man fell to the horses' deadly hooves, but the other slashed at Chance. Cassie gasped as she saw blood stream from a long gash along Chance's stomach, and his high-pitched cry of pain sent chills down her spine. The enemy horses were shying and pulling back at their restraints. She felt Penny's anger and heard her challenging whinny as well as the cats yowling from the house. Suddenly the other men came out, their number diminished, but dragging her mom and dad with them.

Mom was crying, tears streaming down her face, along with blood from a shallow cut near her cheekbone. Dad was unconscious, and Cassie gasped again as his head rolled and she saw that he had been hit. Blood covered one side of his head. She saw a streak of gray as Smokey jumped for the throat of one of the men. A moment later Calico joined him. Together they downed the man, and Penny injured another. The rest of the men fought free of the animals and threw both parents in the van. They quickly drove away, followed by the men on horses, leaving Penny in the dust as she tried to run after them. Cassie saw a couple of empty saddles among them, and some part of her wondered why on earth they had used horses in a kidnapping. It didn't make much sense to her.

By the time Penny finished, Cassie had already called Twi to her and was halfway onto her back. Her mind was all in a whirl, her thoughts unclear save for one: somehow, the Brotherhood had found them. Part of her brain felt stupefied with shock, while the other part simply reacted instinctively. "Penny, stay here. Sarah, David, look after her. I've got to get home. I'm sorry." She closed her legs around Twi's sides and the mare sprang forward, Kai and Dassah following as fast as they could.

David and Sarah stood there dumbfounded, staring after her with open mouths, until the sound of Twi's hoofbeats completely faded. David was the first to speak. "Well, *that* was seriously weird."

"Yeah, I'll say!" Sarah exclaimed, completely bewildered and feeling no small amount of worry. "She was getting ready to tell us something really important, Penny shows up right before she reveals whatever-it-was, and then she goes charging off bareback with her dogs following as if the devil were after them! What on earth could Penny have said?"

"Whatever it was, it must have been really important for her to run all this way to say it, and then for Cassie to rush off like that. I wonder if it has anything to do with what she was going to tell us." He looked at his horse. Fire was gazing down the trail, ears pricked forward in alertness, his muscles taut beneath his skin. "I'll bet you know what's up," David said to the horse. Fire glanced at his rider with intelligent eyes, as if affirming the statement, then returned his attention to the trail. "Man, I'm really wishing I had Cassie's talent right now." He stared down the trail, hating the fact that he didn't know what was going on. He decided that the next time he talked to Cassie, he would somehow wrest the truth from her, along with her reasons for hiding it. For there was no doubt in his mind now that Cassie had a secret, a big one, and he wanted to know what it was.

"Me too," Sarah agreed, her voice pulling him from his ruminations. "But for the time being, Penny needs to be seen to."

As the twins began to cool down the exhausted horse, each thought up their own scenarios for Penny's sudden arrival and Cassie's sudden departure. None of their guesses were anywhere close to the truth.

Cassie urged Twi down the mountain trail as quickly as she dared, which was a good deal slower than she would have liked. Cassie knew she wouldn't catch the kidnappers, but what worried her most at the moment was Chance. She had seen through Penny's memories that his wound was bad. She hoped she would be in time to save him. She became aware of a wetness on her cheeks and realized that tears were trickling from her eyes. They hit a place where the downhill slope became level ground for several hundred yards and Twi opened up, accelerating to a gallop, stretching her legs to their fullest extent. Cassie thanked God for the speed and stamina that came to Twi naturally from being an Anglo-Arab, half-Arabian and half-Thoroughbred, though she worried about the speed they were gaining. In just a few seconds Twi would have to severely decelerate to safely navigate the trail. At that moment their surroundings seemed to blur from Twi's speed, and suddenly the house and barn appeared in front of them. Cassie gasped, astonished. The ride from the ridge campsite to her house was normally between thirty and forty minutes, but they had made it in well under half the time, and she didn't even remember traversing more than a third of it. How had Twi, speedy as she was, managed to get to the house so quickly? Cassie decided to ask later.

As they approached the paddock she began to slow the horse down. By the time they were almost to the front door, Twi had slowed enough for Cassie to vault off and run to a large form lying prone on the ground. It was Chance. The sight of the big chestnut's side covered in blood, both black dried blood and crimson fresh, sickened Cassie to the point she thought she might throw up – not because of the blood itself, but because it made her fear she was too late. There was blood on the ground as well. Then she looked closer and realized Chance was still breathing, but barely. His eyes were tightly closed, and he was in too much pain to hear her. She knew that if she didn't do something quickly, the horse would die. It was a miracle he'd survived this long already with so much blood loss, and though she noticed that the blood was slowly clotting and congealing into a scab, it wasn't happening fast enough. She wiped her tears away hastily with the back of her hand. She couldn't break down right now. Chance needed her.

She knelt, not caring about the blood getting onto her clothes. As she ran her hand over the wound she discovered that, although the laceration was long, it had not penetrated too deeply into his body. The main reason for Chance's unresponsive state was that he had lost so much blood. Despite the wound's relatively shallow depth, it had been bleeding freely for a while now, and if it had been any deeper, Chance would have been dead before Cassie got there.

She was so focused on the horse that she jumped when Smokey bumped his head against her leg. *You came.* He leaned heavily on her leg, confirming the tiredness she heard in his voice.

"Of course I came." She pulled her emergency bag from her back, brought out all the gauze from the first aid kit, and began pressing it on Chance's stomach. The white gauze quickly became red. She also poured some disinfectant on the wound.

I am sorry, the cat said sadly from where he stood at her side.

"For what? You did all you could, Smokey. I don't blame you." Cassie took out her cell phone, but before she dialed the vet, she realized several things. It would take the veterinarian at least half an hour to get here, and by that time Chance would be dead. He was at death's door as it was. She would also have to think up a convincing explanation as to how he'd gotten the wound and where her parents were. Chance's fate was up to her. But what could she do? She'd seen the local vet stitch up wounds. He'd even explained to her how to do it. But she had never done it herself, and if Chance was to have a chance at survival he needed sutures. They had sutures and a needle in the barn for emergencies. She would have to try. She ran as quickly as she could to the barn, which was very fast indeed. She quickly found the sutures and needle and returned to Chance's side. By this time Kai and Dassah had arrived and were standing by Chance. She assumed they had found some sort of shortcut. She knelt by his side and threaded the needle. *God, please help me save Chance*, she prayed.

As she was about to insert the needle, Kai stopped her. *Sing his song, girl. You do not need this needle and thread.*

"Whose song? What do you mean I don't need the needle and sutures?" she asked, confused.

Chance's. Remember what your father taught you? If you heal him in the Brenwyd way, you have no need of stitches.

Of course, Cassie realized, *the Brenwyd way of healing. Why didn't I think of that?*

Her dad had taught her how to do it, explaining that everything that was alive had a song ingrained in them that made up who they were. People with strong Brenwyd blood could sense that song when they wanted to, and when a person or animal was injured, their song became disjointed and confused where the wound was. A Brenwyd could heal them by listening for the discordance and singing the correct tune, which in turn caused the wound to seal up and the person or animal to become whole once more. This ability was particularly useful with internal wounds and bleeding, and was why Brenwyds had been such good healers, though it was also why they had eventually become the objects of superstition and fear. Cassie hoped she would be able to use the ability effectively.

She closed her eyes in concentration and placed her hands on Chance's wound, opening her hearing on a deeper level the way her dad had taught her, listening for Chance. Fortunately, her dad had made her learn the songs of all the animals in the vicinity, and she didn't have much trouble finding Chance's. She homed in on his melody, hearing it interrupted by discordant sounds that represented the large wound. She started singing softly, trying to coax the discordant melody back into its normal tune. The song had no words, only notes, but the melody she sang created a slight vibration in the air. It was uncomplicated but powerful and gentle, as befitted Chance's personality. She had healed animal hurts before using this ability, but never something this large in an animal already so far gone. She kept singing until she sensed awareness

Cassie placed her hands on Chance's wound and started singing softly, trying to coax the discordant melody back into its normal tune.

and awakening from Chance's mind and his song returning back to normal.

She rocked back on her heels and watched Chance anxiously. She had done everything she could, but was still uncertain whether Chance would pull through or not after losing so much blood. Where the wound had been, Cassie now saw a well-formed scar and, if she hadn't known better, she would have guessed the injury was months old. The sight gave her a slightly eerie feeling. No wonder people had gotten scared of Brenwyds. If she didn't know better she would have assumed it was some sort of magic. Twi walked to the chestnut and nuzzled his mane. Chance stirred and lifted his head, shaking it as if trying to throw off a bad dream.

Cassie breathed a sigh of relief as he lurched unsteadily to his feet. "How do you feel?" she asked. He started slightly, not having registered that she was there. Cassie backed up in case he went down. She had no wish to be crushed under a thousand pounds of horseflesh.

Chance considered the question for a moment. *I think I need a drink of water and a rest. My side twinges,* he replied. Cassie put her fingers under his jawbone to feel his pulse. It was weak, but it was beating regularly. She had a feeling he would be alright.

"Come on, I'll put you in the barn and give you some pain meds and water. Don't scratch at your scar, it's counterproductive."

He turned a large, gentle brown eye to her. *They are gone, are they not? Those men took them.* Cassie was unable to answer as the full force of what had occurred that night finally started to sink in.

Yes, Calico answered, tail lashing. *But only because they had larger numbers and caught us by surprise. We will win next time.*

Cassie heard her words, but barely heeded them. Her parents were gone, kidnapped by an organization that had existed for centuries to kill Brenwyds. *They don't always leave people who know part-Brenwyds alone,* her father's words from four years ago echoed in her ears. It didn't matter that her parents had been captured instead of killed. They would be killed eventually. She would be an orphan. She would have to follow her dad's plan, go to her aunt's, try to act as if everything was normal. But wouldn't the Brotherhood just track her there? All they would have to do is look at her mother's family records. Dad had said he had a plan to cover her tracks, but could that really stop the Brotherhood? Cassie remembered him saying that throughout the Brotherhood's history, they had proven that nothing, not even police intervention, could thwart their plans once a target was discovered.

She sank to her knees. How had this happened? It had only been a few days ago that Dad had assured her they were safe. Could things really have changed so quickly? Kai and Dassah pressed against her, and she wrapped her arms around them. Her dad had warned her many times about the dangers of falling into Brotherhood hands. They were the ones who had thought up many of the medieval torture devices that had been used throughout Europe. They wouldn't just kill her, wouldn't just kill her parents. No. The tears started and she let them flow, sobbing her heart out into Kai's fur. It wasn't fair. It just wasn't fair. *God, why?*

What Now?

Cassie stared at the wreckage strewn about the living room. *This is hands down the* worst *birthday surprise in history,* she thought as she bent to pick up the shards of a lamp from the floor. After finally regaining control of her emotions, though tears still ran down her cheeks now and then, she tended to the animals. She put Chance into the barn instead of turning him out into the paddock, not wanting him to risk reopening his wound, and put Twi beside him for company. She also checked over Smokey and Calico to make sure they had no wounds. Finding none, she turned her attention to the house.

The kitchen, hallway, and den all seemed untouched, but the acrid, stomach-churning stench of death and blood permeated the house, emanating from two dead men she found in the hall. Smokey informed her that her father had killed them while trying to fend them off. When Cassie looked into the living room she stopped, aghast. All the lamps were knocked over, as were most of the pictures. The chair into which she liked to climb and read was overturned, and the cushion was ripped to shreds. The couch pillows were all over the floor as well. *It'll take a week to get this room looking like normal,* she fretted as she picked up the pillows. Suddenly a thought struck her, and she rushed to the library. When she reached it, she stared in absolute horror. Most of the books were on the floor, loose pages scattered everywhere. Furniture had been overturned, and two movable bookcases were knocked askew as well. Her eyes went to the case where her dad had kept swords that he collected from various places, the ones they practiced with. All the weapons were gone.

Kai, Dassah and Smokey entered the room and went to Cassie's side. They were silent, taking in the destruction. Tyler Pennington had one of the best personal libraries on the East Coast. Few outside friends and family knew about it, but many ancient books and manuscripts were kept there, as well as more modern ones. The books in that room ranged from history to fantasy, biographies to epics, and everything in between. Cassie loved that room. She had spent many hours curled up on the window seat between two of the built-in bookshelves, learning as much as she could about the Middle Ages, the Crusades, legends like Robin Hood, and all the different versions of the King Arthur story. She had met many characters that had fed her lust for adventure. And adventure, she realized with a sickening lurch as she picked up a book, had just arrived on her doorstep. *Things like this happen in books, not in real life,* she thought. *Maybe I'm dreaming.*

At that thought Kai came over and gently head-butted her side. *This is no dream, girl,* he said. *They found us and took your parents. Chances are, they will come back for you.*

"They won't catch me unprepared," she muttered. She collapsed on the window seat, feeling completely drained of energy. It had all gone into her grief. She felt hollow, fragile, like she might break apart at any moment. The animals gathered around her, pressing against her, trying to comfort her as best they could. Smokey leaped into her lap and she held him close, taking comfort from his warm, furry body, feeling herself relaxing and her mind calming. Still clutching the cat to herself, she asked, "Smokey, can you show me what happened in the house? Penny could only show me what was going on outside."

Of course I can show you, Smokey replied. As the images flowed, Cassie felt as if she were watching a movie. Tears began running down her cheeks anew as she saw her parents and Smokey sitting in the living room, her dad working in his binder, her mother reading a book.

Smokey had just curled up against her mom when they heard the horses whinnying madly. They all jumped up and raced to the window. They saw men drawing swords and running to the door. Her dad ran out of the room, binder in hand, and down the hallway to his study. He had no sooner reached it than the first of the intruders burst into the house. Smokey ran to meet them and, even through the memory, Cassie felt his determination to stop these men and protect his people. He jumped on the first man, scratching and yowling, and knocked him down, causing the next few men in line to fall, which gave her dad enough time to grab a sword and dash up the hallway. Through Smokey's memories, Cassie heard her dad shout something at the men, but she didn't hear what it was. It seemed to have no effect, however, as the men proceeded to attack him. He killed one man, then was overwhelmed by several others setting on him at once. The rest divided into the living room or went through the door to the study, squeezing carefully by the combatants in the hallway. Two went up the stairs. Smokey helped as best he could, biting, scratching, and yowling to deter the men. Calico jumped into the fray as well, having been wakened from her bed in the barn by all the commotion. Ty downed a second man right before a third smashed a sword hilt down on his head. He slumped to the ground, unconscious. Cassie shuddered as Smokey remembered the scream her mother emitted when she saw her husband fall. She had been bashing men with a baseball bat they kept in the living room, for which Cassie just now realized the purpose. One of the men shouted a command, and the men who had entered the study reappeared, carrying all of the weapons along with lots of old books and manuscripts. As Cassie saw what the men were taking, she felt a burning sensation in her chest as if a spark had landed on it. Penny had not shown her that. She made a mental note to check what was missing. Two of the men now grabbed her mom, who fought them all the way, and they tied her hands behind her back. Cassie's anger grew as she saw how the men handled her mother. Another grabbed her dad, and the men who had gone up the stairs also reappeared. The cats had been thrown against the wall and were dazed. By now Cassie felt like strangling something, and the burning sensation grew to a white-hot flame of anger that started overtaking her grief.

The man who had spoken earlier spoke again. "Well, where is she?" His voice was gruff and authoritative, and the sound of it made Cassie shudder. He had a British accent. His facial features were craggy, and not at all attractive.

"She's nowhere to be found! We searched all through the house." That voice also had a British accent, but sounded young, which intrigued Cassie. She thought it came from the shorter of the two men. She couldn't tell anything about him because his hood completely shadowed his face.

"She's the main one the Master wants! Go check the barn." The two men left through the back door, which explained why Cassie had not seen them in Penny's memories. She felt her blood go cold as she got the affirmation from Smokey that the men had been looking for her, and her anger was dampened slightly by a shadow of fear. Why would they want her in particular? The gruff-voiced man put the tip of his sword under her mom's chin and forced her to look up at him. "Where is your daughter? The Master expressed a strong desire to meet her." The words were spoken with mock politeness. Leah didn't answer. The man's tone grew harsh. "Well? Where is she?" When the only response he received was a silent glare, he hit her across the face with the flat of his sword, cutting it and causing her to fall over with a small cry. The two men returned from the barn with the report that Cassie was not there. The leader snarled something at them that Smokey didn't catch, and they hurried from the house. The rest of the story Cassie already knew.

She sat back, trying to take it all in. *Why would I be the main one their master wants?* she wondered to the animals. *I feel like there must be some reason besides my pointed ears. How would they even know about that, anyway?* She felt a current of unease run through the animals' minds, and she looked at them sharply. "Do you know why?" she asked. No one answered. "Well?"

Kai finally answered. *Yes, but I will not tell you yet. I will tell you when I think you can handle it.*

"What? Why shouldn't you tell me now? I deserve to know!" Cassie demanded, the ember of anger growing again.

Yes, you do, Kai said calmly. *But not now. Not when you are this distressed. It may overwhelm you in this state.*

"Overwhelm me..." Cassie repeated dumbly. She felt her temper rise. Smokey, sensing her change of mood, wriggled out of her grip. Cassie barely noticed. "Overwhelm me! Kai, my parents just got kidnapped by an organization that wants them dead – my dad, anyway – we learn that I'm the main one they want, you know why, but you won't tell me because you think it will overwhelm me?!" Her voice rose louder with each word.

Your ranting just proves his point, Calico said. *You are not in a state to know at the moment.*

Cassie rounded on the cat, giving her anger free rein. "Oh, the rest of you know, too? Of course. Why should I be surprised? I should know by now that my animals find it a great amusement to know everything there is to know about me – even things I don't know myself – and laud their knowledge over me when they feel like it," she said. "I suppose I should be used to it by now. I bet my parents know, too, don't they? Another thing they haven't told me. Why should I know anything? Why shouldn't I go through my life in blissful ignorance?" She glared at the animals. They wisely stayed silent. "I'll tell you why: because I like knowing things that put my life in danger, such as the fact that I exist at all. Knowledge – truth – is important, because you'll die without it. You think truth will overwhelm me? Try me!" she challenged. The animals gazed back at her sorrowfully.

Abruptly, she felt ashamed of herself. She knew they only wanted what was best for her, as did her parents. She sank to the floor, sobs bursting forth, hot tears cascading over her face yet again, the burning sensation of anger transforming to the dull ache of grief in the blink of an eye. "Oh, I'm sorry, I'm sorry! I don't mean it. I know you only do it for my own good. You're right, learning that tonight would probably overwhelm me. I just... I just feel so... so... so helpless and out of control!" She wept as the animals pressed in around her.

Dassah licked her nose. *It is alright, girl, we forgive you. And remember, the One is always in control and is always ready to help you when you feel this way.*

Cassie nodded, taking deep breaths, trying to regain control of her emotions. "I know, I know. It's just... oh, why did this have to happen? Why now? Dad said that he had a communication system in place. He said that he would know if the Brotherhood was getting close!"

I do not know about all that, Dassah said. *But I know that the One always works for good.*

Cassie heaved in several more deep breaths and the sobs stopped. The sensation in her chest settled, but her voice was still shaky. "Alright. I'm better now. I think I'll go see if my room is still intact." Calico found a packet of tissues on Ty's desk, picked it up in her mouth, and offered it to Cassie. She took it gratefully.

You do that, Smokey said. *We will go investigate more outside.*

Cassie wondered what they wanted to investigate, but didn't feel like questioning him at the moment. "Okay." She stood and climbed the stairs to her room, then stopped as she beheld it. It was most certainly *not* intact.

Clothes were everywhere, as were all her pictures. Her dresser drawers were open, and her bookshelves stuck out from their usual places at odd angles. It looked like the men had messed up the room just for fun. Despite all she'd already discovered, she now just felt extremely annoyed. "Seriously?" she said to the air. "They have to turn over all my stuff just to make sure I'm not hiding under the rug. And I'd just cleaned all this. Ugh." She changed out of her blood-spattered clothes and rummaged around a little, straightening the room, but stopped when she found her Bible. She needed some divine guidance right now. She opened it randomly and found herself looking at Jeremiah 29:11. Oddly enough, it lined up with what Dassah had said: "'For I know the plans I have for you,' declares the Lord, 'Plans to prosper you and not to harm you, plans to give you a hope and a future.'"

Letting tears flow once more, she collapsed onto her bed and hugged her pillow, feeling angry yet again. She felt as if her emotions were working on some sort of yo-yo system between anger and grief. She was becoming tired of the pattern, but she didn't feel she had the strength to fight it. "God, how is this Your plan? How is this supposed to give me a hope and a future? How is this not supposed to harm me? I don't understand," she railed, utterly despondent, repeating her words from downstairs. "Mom said you have something special in mind for me. Is this it? If so, I would very much like it if you picked someone else, someone stronger. I can't take this, God. I'm not even fourteen until tomorrow!"

As she lay there, the story of Job came to her mind. God had blessed him because he was faithful, but Satan wondered if Job was only faithful because God protected him from bad things, and thought Job would turn away if persecuted. God allowed Satan to test him, only warning him not to take Job's life. So Satan had destroyed all of Job's herds, took his wealth, and caused his children to be killed. He made Job get really sick. But through it all, Job remained faithful to God. He didn't understand why it was happening, but he never renounced God, even when his friends pressured him. As a reward for his faithfulness, God gave him double of everything he'd had before.

Cassie heaved in several deep breaths, then a few more, trying to get her emotions back under control for what she hoped would be the final time that night. She didn't like going to pieces every other minute. Not to mention, going to pieces every other minute would definitely not help improve matters. "Okay, God. I don't get what's going on, but I'm going to trust You're gonna get me through it," she whispered into her pillow. "Like Mom said, this is like a story. And in stories things always get worse before they get better." As she lay there, she felt peace seep into her soul, pushing out the anger, and she felt stronger, steadier, better able to cope, although the sadness was still very much present. She took several more deep breaths for good measure.

Feeling calmer, Cassie remembered the mental note she'd made. "First things first," she told herself. "I'm going to see what they took." She stood up and, for a reason she couldn't explain, stuffed her Bible in her bag, along with a change of clothes. She had a strange feeling that she wouldn't be seeing her room for a while. The bag had been a gift from her father when she was eight, the first time she had ever gone on an archaeological dig with him, before she'd had any idea of her Brenwyd blood.

"Put only the necessities of what you would need for several days in here," he'd told her. "And keep it close. That way, if anything happens, you can just grab it and know you have stuff to see you through until help comes." It was a small duffel that she had refitted to strap diagonally across her back so her hands were free. It wasn't especially large or bulky, which was a good thing, but was still big enough to hold a change of clothes, a couple of books, a water bottle, a box of granola bars, and a small survival kit with things she'd gathered herself, like duct tape and matches. Last but definitely not least, the bag always held a first aid kit, which Cassie had put together based on her dad's suggestions over the years. And after her dad had declared her skilled enough to carry a weapon, she'd added her knives and knife belt, making a little opening near the bottom of the bag that allowed her to reach behind her hip and grab a knife in an instant, if needed. She had put in a loop that attached the knife hilt to the bag so it couldn't slip out, and had practiced pulling the knife out until there was no hindrance to her ability to whip it out in emergencies. It was a very useful bag. More than that, knowing she had things on hand for emergencies settled her nerves and made her feel prepared and in control. It was a feeling she enjoyed.

When she reached the bottom of the stairs, Kai and Dassah approached her excitedly. *We found it, we found it*, Dassah chanted, sounding pleased.

"Found what?" Cassie asked. Neither answered, but they started pulling her toward the front door. Once she got outside, she could hear the excited thoughts of the cats. They were crouching over a certain spot on the driveway. Smokey was bent down like he was smelling something on the pavement. Which was, Cassie realized, exactly what he was doing. "What's going on?" she asked.

This time Kai did answer her question. *We have found the trail of the riders. It goes toward the Eagle's Trail. We can follow it.* Eagle's Trail was a trail going northwest out of the valley, and Cassie had named it as such because an eagle's nest was at the start of the trail.

Cassie gasped. This meant she could go after the men. Then she frowned. "But those riders have over an hour's start. How could we catch them?"

We may not be able to catch them, but maybe they have already set up a camp that we could investigate, Dassah said logically. *They may even have stopped, in which case we can rescue your parents.* Cassie thought for a few minutes, trying to make sense out of the confused tornado of thoughts spinning around and around inside her head. Everything in her told her to go after the men and her parents, but what would come of it? Would they just be captured again, this time with herself included? Dad had told her that if anything happened to him and Mom she needed to be concerned with getting herself to safety. But surely he had just meant if he and Mom had been killed. She couldn't abandon her parents while they were still alive. Then again, if she did manage to rescue her parents, where would they go? They couldn't go back home and stay there, and they couldn't place the Thompsons in danger. David and Sarah! They were still on the ridge with Penny. What would she tell them? Should she go get them before she started on the trail of the kidnappers? No, she couldn't place them in such danger. If she went to the ridge personally, she knew they'd follow her, no matter how hard she pleaded with them to stay behind. Should she call Mr. and Mrs. Thompson? Dad had said she was to go to the Thompsons first if something happened. Mr. Thompson knew Dad's plan.

She considered it for a few moments. *No,* she decided. *I'll go after them by myself. I'll call David to tell him and Sarah to come down. I'll call the Thompsons to ask them to look in on Chance. I'll leave a note explaining a little. Yes,* she thought, *that is what I'll do. The rest is up to God. Jeremiah 29:11.*

Having decided on a plan, she started to put it into action. She wrote a note explaining that the house had been attacked and her parents abducted, that she had gone after them, and that she did not want them to follow her. She also asked them to pray.

Next, she checked on the horses. Chance said that he felt okay, but the scar ached a little. His appearance was much improved, and his gum color was almost back to normal. She gave him a little bit of painkiller and told him the Thompsons would come by and check on him. She also tacked a brief note to Chance's door with the time he could have more pain medicine. She asked Twi if she felt up to another ride. Twi answered that she was more than ready. Cassie then dragged all the dead men to the back of the house so they weren't so easily seen. She figured she'd deal with cleaning up the house when she got back. If she got back. *Don't think that way, Cassie,* she scolded herself. *Of course you'll be back. You'll find Mom and Dad, and Mom will have a fit about her house being ruined, then set me and Dad working like bees to get it right again.* The idea cheered her. She tacked Twi up with an extra set of tack kept in the barn, as she'd left her main set on the mountain.

She got her knife belt out of her bag and buckled it around her waist. Keeping her knives in the bag gave her quick access to one of them, but tonight she wanted both readily available. It made her feel a little more confident about going after the Brotherhood. Her dad had given her the belt for her twelfth birthday, signaling he was satisfied enough with her knife skills to trust her on her own with them. The belt was special because it was made for two knives, which was how Cassie preferred to fight as it gave her more options, though she could use a sword or bow just as well. When her father had first started teaching her how to use medieval weapons, he had tried to get her more interested in using swords, but she had wanted to learn how to fight with knives. That was how Caelwyn had fought, and once Cassie had discovered her dad had a replica of one of Caelwyn's knives, there was no convincing her to fight otherwise. One knife rested on her left hip and the other on her right. Most people wouldn't go around giving their children knives, but Ty had been teaching Cassie how to use swords and daggers since she was ten. He told her that, being part Brenwyd, she had to know how to defend herself against the Brotherhood, who fought with swords as the original members of the group had done. David and Sarah had also learned, because once they'd found out what Cassie was learning, they wanted in on it, even if they didn't know the exact reason behind the lessons. Their parents had given them permission, thinking that if the Penningtons were ever found by the Brotherhood, the art of weaponry would be a good skill for their children to have.

Cassie's knives were delicate-looking, but they were strong. Each knife was designed in the Celtic way, with a leaf-shaped blade that thickened slightly in the middle before tapering to a point. Each hilt was made of dark wood, with the cross-guard curving down toward the blade, and two additional points curving in the opposite direction, mirroring the cross-guard in the unique Celtic style. Each knife had a ridged hand grip, making its total length about sixteen inches, with each blade being twelve inches long. The knife that hung on Cassie's right hip was plain, but the one on her left had a Celtic-designed star engraved on the blade just below the hilt, with a vine-and-leaf design stretching down toward the point. The same engraving was on both sides of the knife. This was the replica of the dagger Caelwyn had used, which had been called *Seren*, a word that meant *star*.

Going back into the house to grab some more granola bars and a water bottle, she opened a cabinet and discovered a wrapped package with her name on it. It was small, about the size of boxes that necklaces come in. Cassie hesitated to open it. It was obviously a birthday present and she preferred opening those with her parents. If they had been home, that's exactly what she would have done. But they weren't, and who knew if she would be successful on her mission? Her curiosity and circumstances won out, and she tore off the wrapping paper. A small box was revealed, and on it she recognized the name of the jewelry store in town. She opened the box slowly. A gold locket was inside, one she had pointed out to her mom at the jewelry store a month ago, commenting that she liked it. It was a simple oval locket with a small, delicate, flower pattern engraved along the circumference, surrounding an intricate

"C" in the middle. She swallowed down the lump in her throat. Mom had gotten it monogrammed with her initial. There was a card, too. She opened it. It had a standard birthday card sentence inside, but she recognized her mother's handwriting below. It read:

My dear daughter, has it already been fourteen years? How the time has flown. I am proud of who you are, and who I know you'll become. I thank God for you each and every day. I know life hasn't been easy the last four years, and I fear it will get no easier, but I know you will be able to handle whatever happens in the future. You are a strong, beautiful young lady. Never let anyone convince you otherwise. Always trust in God's plan for you, for He will never lead you wrong. I hope you will treasure this locket as a reminder of how much I love you.

Love, Mom

Cassie couldn't help but cry again. It was almost as if Mom had known what would happen, and it was yet another reminder from God that He was still in control of this situation.

She raised her tear-stained face to look up. "Thank you, God, for letting me find this." She closed her eyes and willed herself to stop crying. She didn't have all night. She took the locket out of the box and threw the wrapping paper in the trash can. She hurried back up to her room and grabbed a photo album from the shelf. She found her favorite picture of her parents, and after a brief moment of hesitation, cut out their faces and placed them in the locket, then fastened it around her neck. Before leaving the house, she opened it and smiled. Her parents' faces smiled back at her, strengthening her resolve.

Before Cassie mounted, she took out her cell phone and called David. He picked up immediately. "Where are you? What's going on?"

"I'm at my house. Listen, you guys should come down. There's been some stuff that's come up and I have to see to it."

"What stuff? Is everything okay?"

"Well, no, but I can't tell you what. I need you to come down with Penny as soon as she's able. How is she?"

"She's fine. We'll start down right away. So what was it you were going to tell us?"

"I'm sorry David, but I can't tell you now. Not after..." Her voice trailed off as her throat closed up.

"Not after what? Cassie, tell me what's going on. You can tell me." His tone sounded worried and a little hurt.

"David, I'm sorry, but it's too dangerous. I see that now. I've got to go now. I have something to do."

"What?"

"Something that I have to do by myself. I don't want to risk you or Sarah getting hurt."

"Getting hurt? What are you talking about? Cassie, we're your *friends*. You can trust us with anything. Tell me what's going on. We can help you."

Tears began flowing down Cassie's cheeks yet again as she choked out a reply. "I know I can trust you, but it's because you're my friends that I won't tell you yet. It's for your own safety. I'm really sorry, but I've got to go now."

"Cassie–"

"Soon you'll know why I'm doing what I'm doing. But not now. Watch Penny and Chance for me, okay?"

"Sure, Cass, but–"

"Goodbye, David." She hung up.

David stared in bewilderment at his phone. She had actually hung up on him! Never had Cassie done something so rude before. And the call itself! Cassie had sounded scared. Very scared, and grief-stricken, almost. David hadn't heard her sound quite like that before, and it unnerved him. What on earth was going on? Cassie always seemed so sure of herself, not scared of anything. *Well, except spiders and cockroaches,* he amended to himself. Sarah broke in on his thoughts. “What on earth did she say? You look like someone just told you the president died or something.”

David shook his head. “I don’t know what to make of it, Sarah. This night keeps getting stranger and stranger.” He told her what had occurred during the phone conversation.

Sarah frowned. “That makes no sense. Why wouldn’t she tell you anything?”

“I don’t know. But it worries me, Sarah. That goodbye sounded very final. Let’s get going.”

“I’m with you there, but you said she sounded like she was crying? What would she be crying about? Tomorrow’s her birthday, for heaven’s sake.”

“I have no idea. Hurry up, I want to get to the bottom of this mystery.”

Cassie stopped as she reached a ridge that looked out over the whole valley. She could see the Thompsons’ house and barn, as well as her own. She’d decided she would call Mr. and Mrs. Thompson when she was a little way up the trail so they would get to her house around the same time as David and Sarah. Looking at the valley, she wondered if she would see it again. *Don’t think like that,* she scolded herself, *of course I’ll see it again.*

Yes, you will, Twi said, sensing her rider’s anxiety. *We will all see it again. Your parents, too.* Kai and Dassah stood by her. Smokey had decided to come as well, feeling somewhat responsible for Ty and Leah’s predicament. Calico had decided to stay behind, to keep an eye on Chance, and to help the Thompsons understand what was going on (or so she’d said).

Kai nudged Cassie’s stirrup gently. *Come, girl,* he said, *we need to get going.* He walked into the forest, Dassah and Smokey following.

Cassie looked out across the valley one more time, committing every feature to memory. Then she, too, entered the forest, the deep shadows under the trees swallowing her until there was no sign the group had ever stood on the ridge.

Questions & Answers

Hannah hung up the phone, all sleep gone from her eyes. When the phone had rung, she'd assumed the kids had a question, something they deemed important enough to call about in the middle of the night. She had been surprised to hear Cassie on the other end, asking if she or her husband could check on Chance. Hannah had pressed for details, but Cassie had been unusually cagey. She had said that David and Sarah were fine, but that she had to go somewhere and likely wouldn't be back for a while. Hannah had a gut feeling that the Penningtons had been discovered, although Cassie hadn't said so. Her tone seemed to confirm it, as she had sounded weepy, which was definitely unusual for the girl. Hannah ran back to the bedroom, calling for Ben.

She flicked on a light and saw him sitting up, rubbing sleep from his eyes. "What is it, hon? The kids hear a bear?"

Hannah shook her head. "It was Cassie. She wants us to check on Chance and call the vet in the morning. She didn't say, Ben, but I think it's the Brotherhood. They've found them."

Ben jumped out of bed and headed for the closet, instantly wide-awake. "What about David and Sarah? Did she say anything about them?"

"She said they're fine, and that they're coming down from the campsite. She wouldn't say where she was, but the connection wasn't great, so she might be in the mountains. I think the Brotherhood may have come already and taken Ty and Leah. One of the animals probably went to get Cassie, and now she's going after her parents."

Ben stopped what he was doing and looked at Hannah. "Surely she knows how dangerous that is! For her, of all people, as well."

"She was very vague." Hannah changed from her nightgown to jeans and a short-sleeve t-shirt. "I'm going to call David, to make sure they're coming down and find out if they know anything we don't."

"You can call him from the car. Let's go." Hannah grabbed her phone and started dialing as they hurried down the hallway.

David picked up as they were getting into the car. "Hey, Mom. What's–"

"You and your sister had better be on your way down from the mountain right now."

"We are, Mom. Relax, we're almost to the Pennington's. Cassie called and–"

"What did she say?"

"Not much. Something about checking on Chance, and she was going somewhere."

"Was that all?" Hannah heard her son hesitate before answering.

"She kept talking about something that had happened, something she couldn't tell us about because it was so dangerous."

"Did she give you any hint as to what it was or why it was so dangerous? What happened? She called us, too, asking me and your dad to check on Chance, but she didn't say much more than that, except that you two were coming down."

"That's basically what she told us, but she started acting a little strange while she was still up here, around ten or so. She was getting ready to tell us something when Penny came galloping toward us. She must have told Cassie that something was really wrong, because Cassie galloped out on Twi, like, two minutes later. We cooled Penny down, and then Cassie called me. She sounded like she'd been crying. I've tried calling her back, but I think she's turned her phone off. "

"I wouldn't be surprised."

There was a short pause. "Why would Cassie want us to check in on Chance? Is he sick or something?" David asked.

"I don't know. We'll find out when we get there."

"Well, I guess it makes some sense if Penny came up here to tell Cassie Chance was sick, but why wouldn't her parents call her or call the vet? They're not the kind of people who do nothing if an animal is hurt or sick. And besides, if that's all it was, Cassie would have said so."

Hannah paused before answering. She knew from what David told her that Cassie had not revealed her secret, and she felt Cassie should be the one to tell them. "I'm not sure, honey, but I'm sure it'll make more sense when we see what's going on at the house."

"Okay, Mom. I gotta go now. We're about to hit a dead spot."

"Alright, but you two be careful now, hear?"

"We will, Mom. See ya soon." Hannah closed her phone.

Ben glanced over from the driver's seat. His dark eyes were filled with concern. "What did he say?"

"They're on their way down. Cassie didn't tell them much, either."

"Did he say anything else?"

"He said that Penny came galloping into the clearing and Cassie left a few minutes later. He also said Cassie was on the verge of telling them something when Penny appeared."

"So Penny interrupted before Cassie told them anything?"

"I think so. I'm really worried, Ben. If it *was* the Brotherhood..."

"I know, Hannah. I'm praying we can catch Cassie before she leaves, or that we're just completely wrong."

By now they had reached the Pennington's driveway. They drove up to the house and parked. The house and yard were dark, but it looked like there was a light on in the barn. Ben grabbed a flashlight from the car and flicked it on. He handed it to his wife as he reached into the back of the car for another flashlight. He had just found it when Hannah gasped and grabbed his arm. "Ben, look! There's blood on the driveway."

He pointed the light toward the ground and saw that Hannah was right. Dried blood coated a spot on the driveway near the front door. Looking more closely, he saw red footprints all around the spot. "Hannah, look at these." As he flashed the light around, he saw human footprints mixed with paw prints and hoof prints. "I'm guessing these prints are from Cassie and the animals. The larger paw prints are likely from the dogs, and the smaller ones from the cats. It looks like Cassie went to the barn and came back, and then went into the house with the dogs and cats, or vice versa."

Hannah nodded. It made sense, but all the blood worried her. "Whose blood is it?" she worried aloud. She shined her light on a spot near the doorstep. "Ben, look at this. It looks like something was dragged from here."

"It does. Let's go investigate." They followed the trail and found where Cassie had deposited the dead men in the backyard.

Hannah gasped and backed away in horror. "Well, this confirms our suspicions, doesn't it?" she asked.

Ben was silent for a minute as he examined one of the men, kneeling down to get a closer look. "Yes. Take a look at this." He pulled something off the man and held out his hand. Hannah leaned down and her breath caught in her throat. In his hand was a metal object that seemed to reflect flames in the starlight – a broken cross with dagger-like points all around it, resembling a swastika, but with the points going the opposite way. It was the symbol of the Brotherhood. Hannah knew that the Reficul Brotherhood had existed since the early sixth century, for the sole purpose of extinguishing the Brenwyd race. She recalled Ty saying once that they also wanted to stamp out Christianity. Brenwyds were considered their main opponents in achieving that goal, because their God-given abilities could help prove His existence to the world.

Hannah's throat tightened. Leah and Ty had told them their secret long ago, but she had never really thought about the danger. Now, the point was driven into her heart so that she would never forget it.

"We should see if Cassie's in the barn. There's a light on in there, and we told her we'd check on Chance," she said to Ben, who nodded in silent agreement. They headed for the barn, but before they entered, they heard a bark from the woods. They turned and saw the twins riding into the meadow. Gracie bounded ahead of them. David was leading Penny. The palomino looked more tired than Hannah had ever seen her. She also looked about as worried as a horse could look. Sarah urged Dreamer into a trot as soon as she spotted her parents. She rode up to them and started dismounting before the mare had even halted completely. Confusion and worry were written all over her face.

"Do you have any idea what's going on?" she asked, searching her parents' faces. "First there was that time a few days ago when the animals acted up, then–"

"Wait, what do you mean the animals acted up last week?" her father asked. Sarah blushed guiltily and looked down at the ground.

David rode up and dismounted. "When we went to the clearing last week, all the animals got really tense all of a sudden, kinda like something was wrong. It wasn't just normal shying, either. Kai tensed up first, then the others did and they all got in front of us, like they were trying to protect us. Cassie got worried, too, but the animals weren't sure what was wrong. We left, and Cassie asked us not to tell anyone. She acted really strange, like she had an idea of what caused them to tense up, but she didn't say anything to us about it. She didn't want you to know because she was afraid you might not let us go," he explained.

"But you camped out at this clearing anyway?" Hannah exclaimed. She disliked it when her kids kept things from her.

"Cassie said she went back another day and everything was fine, so Kai said it was okay. Plus, it was the best spot we investigated to camp. I'm sorry. We didn't think it was that big of a deal at the time."

Sarah jumped back in. "Yeah, like maybe the animals were catching the scent of a bear or something, but it was a little odd, and now this... whatever this is... has happened. David and I talked on the way down, and we think that whatever is going on is connected to what Cassie was going to tell us tonight, and may even be connected to what the animals sensed last week. The problem is, we have no idea what that might be."

Hannah was about to make a reply, but was interrupted by an impatient whinny from the stable. "Let's check on Chance," David said. "It's the one thing Cassie stated clearly in her call." So the family entered the stable, with horses and dog in tow. Chance had his head over his stall door, and whickered eagerly when he saw them. Calico was lying on the stall door ledge, which was the perfect width for her to do so. Hannah went up to Chance, scratching him behind the ears.

"Hey, big guy," she said softly. "What have you done to yourself?" He made a whiffling sound and pulled his head from Hannah's hand, pointing his nose toward his right side. Hannah looked at it and gasped, attracting the attention of her husband. She went into the stall to examine Chance's side as Ben came to the door. He saw the large scar and whistled softly. Blood still dirtied the chestnut's coat.

"I guess we know where the blood by the front door came from now," he said softly to Hannah. She nodded as she eyed the length of the wound.

"But how is it so healed?" she asked quietly.

"Cassie must have done it," Ben answered in the same low tone. "Brenwyds have their own ways of healing." Hannah nodded again. The twins put Penny in the stall on Chance's left and their own horses across the aisle.

Sarah's voice broke the quietness of the stable. "Hey, there's a note here in Cassie's writing!" she called from the tack room entrance.

Ben went to her side. "May I see it, please?" he asked his daughter. She handed it to him, her hazel eyes wide in confusion and concern. Ben scanned the contents. "Oh, dear God," he muttered, "Please say it isn't true!"

"What's not true, Dad?" David asked, coming down from the hayloft. Instead of answering, Ben walked quickly to Chance's stall with the twins in tow. David looked at his sister. "What'd it say?" he asked. She shook her head, and David felt that the note had upset her greatly. He began to feel even more uneasy. What could Cassie have said? He looked into Chance's stall and his mouth fell open. A huge scar covered Chance's right side and it looked like there was blood in his coat. Where had that come from? David knew Chance hadn't had a scar earlier that day. How had he been hurt? Was this why Penny had been so panicked? A wound that size certainly bled a lot, but if Chance had just gotten it, why did the scar look so old? And what could cause a wound like that? If they had been living a thousand years ago, David would have said it was a sword wound, but this wasn't a thousand years ago. Something was bothering him about this situation. Suddenly it hit him. "Hey, where are Mr. and Mrs. Pennington? They should be here."

His dad swiveled his gaze to face his son. "This will answer your question, David." He handed him the note, and confusion and incredulity filled David as he read it.

Dear Thompsons,

I'm sorry I can't be there, but I had to leave. My parents have been abducted by a group known as the Reficul Brotherhood, and I have gone after them, because some of them were on horseback for whatever reason. David and Sarah, I know you have no idea what I'm talking about, but your parents do. They can tell you. I was going to anyway. I can't explain it all right here, but I promise I'll explain everything when I get back if you still don't know by then. I know that following people who want to capture/kill you isn't generally the best idea, but I have to do this. DO NOT*, I repeat,* DO NOT FOLLOW ME*, no matter how long I am gone. And don't bother calling the police, either. They can't help in this kind of situation. I would appreciate it if you looked after Chance, Penny, and Calico. The others are with me. Also, if you could do something about the dead men in the backyard before they really start smelling, and maybe clean the stink out of the house, I would really appreciate that too, as would my mother, I'm sure. I hope and pray I'll see you again soon. I have one last request: Would you please pray for me? And my parents?*

Love,
Cassie

P.S. There's a note by Chance's stall door with the time he can have more painkillers if he needs them.

David read it again, making sure he'd read it right the first time. *It can't be,* he thought. *It just can't be.* But the words were the same. "Who are these people who abducted Cassie's parents? And why on earth would they do such a thing?"

Ben and Hannah looked at each other, communicating silently. Each understood that they needed to tell the twins, and Ben nodded slightly toward Hannah, indicating that she was to handle it.

She put her arm around her son's shoulders and looked at Sarah. Calico sat up on top of the stall door, looking interested in what was happening. Across the aisle Fire and Dreamer stuck their heads over the doors, and Penny shifted so she had a clear view of the humans in Chance's stall.

It was quiet enough to hear a pin drop as Hannah began to speak. "Did Cassie tell you anything on the mountain? Anything at all?"

David and Sarah looked at each other. "Well... she was about to tell us something," Sarah answered. "Something important. She made us promise that we wouldn't tell anyone what she was gonna tell us, that it could be the death of her." She shuddered slightly, then went on. "It was really kinda spooky. I've never heard her sound so serious. Then she said something about it being easier to show us and answer questions, and she started lifting her hand to her head, like she was gonna take off her headband. Then Penny interrupted and Cassie left. She said she was sorry, but she had to get home." Sarah stopped talking and David picked up.

"When we had gotten Penny cooled off and taken care of, and were talking about what to do next, Cassie called and told us to come down. She said she had to go somewhere, and she couldn't risk taking us because we're her friends. She sounded really upset, like she'd been crying, and it sounded like she started crying again as I was talking to her. I tried to ask her what was happening, but she wouldn't tell me anything and hung up." Hannah could feel David's muscles tensing as he related the phone call, clearly frustrated with the fact that Cassie had told him practically nothing. He turned abruptly toward his mother, his face dark with emotion, though she wasn't sure which one. "What is this secret? What's going on? Cassie said you know. She said you could tell us."

Hannah nodded. "That's true. Now, I don't know everything, but I know most of it. For starters, Cassie's family isn't exactly normal."

"I figured that. I know she herself isn't, and her parents wouldn't have been abducted by the... um... Reficul Brotherhood, was it, if they were normal, right? Who on earth are they? And why wouldn't she want us to call the police?"

"And there was something in the note about... dead people... in the... backyard?" Sarah asked, looking slightly queasy. Anything and everything having to do with blood made her feel sick.

Ben patted his daughter on the back reassuringly. "Don't worry about it. We won't make you help dispose of them."

"Then there really *are* dead people in the backyard?" Now Sarah *really* started feeling queasy.

"Don't worry about it," her mother advised. "She probably doesn't want the police to get involved because there's more going on than just a kidnapping. It's a hatred that goes back over a thousand years. Not to mention that the presence of two dead people in the backyard would be hard to explain without getting into... details the Penningtons prefer to keep hidden from the rest of the world. The Reficul Brotherhood is an ancient organization sworn to eliminate... a certain, and very rare these days, race of people called Brenwyds. The Brotherhood is brutal and merciless, and they spare no one with so much as a drop of Brenwyd blood." She looked at David and Sarah, waiting for them to get it.

David responded first. "Sooo, would I be right in assuming Cassie's family is... Brenwyd?" The name sounded familiar to him. Where had he heard it before?

Sarah answered his unspoken question. "What?" she asked, sounding skeptical. "Brenwyds? I thought Brenwyds were a people Cassie's dad made up in his King Arthur stories. You know, his name for the faerie folk."

"Partially right, Sarah," Ben said. "It is a name for the 'faerie folk' or whatever you wish to call them, and they are in Cassie's father's stories, but they are very real. Cassie is part Brenwyd, as is her father... that's why he knows those stories." Ben smiled. "Don't you two remember the Brenwyds' identifying mark?"

David thought for a moment. "Oh yeah, wasn't it pointed..."

His voice trailed off as he stared at his father. "You're kidding," he said in disbelief.

"Not at all, David. Cassie happens to be a very strong part-Brenwyd, and as such she does have–"

"Pointed ears," Sarah finished, eyes wide, her tone a little breathless. "That's why she wears the headband. She has pointed ears."

"Exactly," Hannah said. The twins looked at each other, shocked.

"Why weren't we told sooner?" David asked heatedly after a few heartbeats, frowning. Did Cassie really not trust them? "You knew."

"Ty told me about the whole Brenwyd thing in college," Ben said. "We've been friends since we were your age, you know. I told your mother after they moved here, with Ty's permission. Cassie found out when she was ten, because that's when her ears became pointed. You weren't told because we wanted to protect you. Also, you were a little young."

"Protect us from what?" Sarah asked, using a calmer tone than her brother. "This Brotherhood?"

"Yes," Ben said, his expression serious. "Because you two are so close to Cassie, you were – are – at risk. The Brotherhood has been known to get to Brenwyds by targeting their friends. The less you knew, the less chance the secret would slip. Even if a Brotherhood operative caught you, your lack of knowledge might be able to get them off her track, and you would stand less chance of getting hurt yourself. Does that make sense?" Sarah nodded. David didn't respond.

"And Cassie didn't want you to treat her any differently," Hannah said, watching her son's expression. "She was afraid that if you found out, you'd treat her more warily and would become standoffish toward her. She gets enough of that anyway, you know that, and she didn't want it to happen with you. She still doesn't, but she felt she couldn't keep the secret from you any longer."

"That's ridiculous!" David said, turning to his mother. "Whether she has pointed ears or not, she's still Cassie."

Hannah smiled. "Then why don't you tell her that the next time you see her?"

"I will."

Sarah looked thoughtful. "But why do Brenwyds have pointed ears? And don't they have some special abilities to do with healing? Is that why Chance just has a scar and not a stitched-up wound?"

Her father was about to answer, but he was cut off by a loud meow from Calico. They all jumped, having forgotten the cat was there. She thought the humans were taking too long in explaining things, and decided to help them out so they didn't stand there all night and prevent her from sleeping. She knew the girl wouldn't mind. She jumped down from the stall door and started for the barn door, pausing halfway to look back at the humans, flicking her tail in an unmistakable gesture for them to follow. Gracie walked to the cat and barked at her family, also indicating for them to follow. The Thompsons left Chance's stall, latched the door behind them, and followed the cat. Calico bounded ahead of them, leading them into the house. The family paused after coming in the door, wrinkling their noses as the metallic scent of blood hit them. Ben turned on the hall light, and they gasped as they saw the blood spattered on the walls and floor. Sarah turned green and closed her eyes. Calico walked on calmly toward the back of the house. She turned around and meowed again, sounding impatient, encouraging them to move forward.

David was the first to follow, beckoning to the others. "Come on! She obviously wants to show us something. We can clean up the house later." Sarah wasn't particularly eager to go on, but Gracie put her head under Sarah's hand and gently tugged on her shirt. The animals led everyone to the library and headed toward the desk where Ty kept his computer. It was a desktop, not a laptop, so the men had left it. Calico jumped up on the table and pressed the "on" button with her nose.

Sarah blinked, not quite believing what she was seeing. "Hey, look! Calico wants to show us something on the computer." The others had been surveying the damage and hadn't paid attention to what the animals were doing. They turned to look. By this time the home screen was up and the cat was maneuvering the mouse.

"Cassie taught the cat how to use the computer? Cool!" David exclaimed, watching her.

"But why would a barn cat, or any animal for that matter, need to know how to use a computer?" Hannah wondered aloud. If the family was surprised that Calico could work the computer, they were shocked speechless by what she did next. While they were talking, Calico and Gracie had been having a debate as to which icon to press. Calico did not see computers in use as much as Gracie, so the dog won the argument. Calico clicked on Microsoft Word and opened a blank document. It was what came next that truly shocked the Thompsons. She began pressing the keys to form words, and the words made sense. Or, mostly. They all stared as the cat typed. Sarah was the only one who didn't act surprised, and she bent down to see what Calico was typing.

David looked at his sister. "You don't seem surprised. Did you know about this?"

Sarah flashed him a grin. "Yep. Cassie told me she was teaching her animals to read and type. Something about them being able to communicate with other people in an emergency. She didn't really want anyone to know, though, even her parents. I found out because I snuck up on her while she was first teaching them the alphabet, but I never saw any of them use the computer until today."

"That girl thinks of everything," David said. It was one of the things he liked about Cassie. She always seemed prepared for every eventuality, no matter how far-fetched. And now that he thought about it, teaching animals to type was a Cassie-like thing to do. "So, what does Calico say?"

They were shocked speechless by what Calico did next. She began pressing the keys to form words, and the words made sense.

Sarah waited several minutes before answering, and not just because of the bad spelling. What Calico was typing seemed so fantastic it was hard to believe, but it was because it was so fantastic that she believed it. She doubted Calico could be making it up. "Umm... I think it's like a history of Brenwyds. Apparently they came about after the Flood, when pretty much everyone else turned away from God. They stayed faithful, so God blessed them with special abilities, like..." She frowned as she re-read the next part.

"Like?" David prompted.

"Hang on a minute. You try reading this in a hurry. There's no punctuation and the spelling is awful." Calico meowed loudly in protest. "No offense," Sarah said to her. "It's extremely good spelling for a cat."

"Their abilities consisted of things like talking to animals, speaking with their minds, and healing people by singing," Ben said. "The pointed ears were to clearly set them apart as faithful."

David frowned at his father. "Healing people with songs? What, you mean magic?"

At that suggestion, Calico hissed loudly, the fur on her back standing up, and Gracie barked sharply, startling the humans. "Nope, not magic," Sarah said, still bent over the computer. "That's stated pretty strongly. Calico says here that some humans called it magic, but it wasn't because, quote, 'magic is bad.'" She paused. "There's something about living things emitting songs that Brenwyds can hear, and if a song, um, sounds wrong they can fix it."

"How?" David asked.

"By singing," his father said. "Ty explained the concept to me once, but it was awhile ago. Brenwyds do not practice magic, but they do have certain God-given abilities that would seem like magic to an unknowing observer – and healing by singing is one of them."

"So anyway," Sarah said, "the Brenwyds went to England, and lived peacefully with regular humans... Mr. Pennington mentioned some of this stuff in his stories... okay. So it looks like things started going downhill for the Brenwyds after Caelwyn died." Sarah glanced at her father. "Caelwyn existed?" He nodded. She went back to summarizing. "So anyway, humans started getting scared of the Brenwyds for some reason, which eventually led them to attack the Brenwyds. So they went into hiding and married regular people, passing some of their Brenwyd blood to their children. For some reason Cassie has stronger Brenwyd blood than her father, which is why she has the pointed ears. Her parents have been kidnapped by this Reficul Brotherhood group, who apparently were founded by Mordred to persecute Brenwyds. The group still exists, and Cassie has gone after them." She reached the end and looked at her father again. "Mordred? As in the knight from the King Arthur legend?"

"The same," Ben answered. "He had a personal vendetta against Brenwyds. I have no idea why."

Glancing at the computer's clock, Sarah saw it was almost midnight. "That's all," she said.

"So Cassie just went after a group of people who want her dead, with no one but a cat, two dogs, and a horse to help her?" David said, his jaw set. "We have to go after her!"

"No!" Ben said sternly, looking at him. "This is Cassie's situation, not ours. Not to mention, it's extremely late. I think now we should go home, get some sleep, and deal with everything else tomorrow."

"But Dad, Cassie's just one person! Yeah, she's a good fighter and her animals would die before letting anyone harm her, but she might need help! We can't just stay here while she goes off into the unknown. What if she gets caught? Who will help her then? Animals aren't exactly great with ropes and locks, you know."

David's mother rubbed his back sympathetically. "Hon, I know you're worried. We all are. I wish Cassie had waited before leaving, but we can't fix that. She's smart and she knows how to take care of herself. She's also part Brenwyd, and that will help her. The most we can do right now is pray for her, like she asked."

Sarah nodded. "Why don't we all pray right now?" she suggested.

"That's a good idea, Sarah." Ben said. They all got on their knees and prayed silently, each one asking God to keep Cassie safe and to help her find her parents. They got up after several minutes and headed out, Ben doing a last-minute check on the horses. They decided to leave Dreamer and Fire there for the night, so they all piled into the car and went home.

An hour later, when he was sure everyone was asleep, David crept cautiously down the stairs to the door, holding the sword Mr. Pennington had given him in his hand. He softly called Gracie from her place in the kitchen. "Quiet, Gracie," he whispered. "We don't want to wake anybody up." He opened the door and the dog followed him, sensing what he was up to. He hurried to the Pennington's barn, startling the horses from their rest positions. David walked to Fire's stall and stroked the horse's cheek. "I need ya to wake up, boy. We're going after Cassie." The horse bobbed his brown head, and David smiled to himself. *It's nice knowing your horse can understand you,* he reflected as he grabbed his tack. *Too bad I can't hear what he's thinking.*

He heard Gracie yip softly and froze as he saw someone come into the stable. "Just what do you think you're doing?" a voice asked. David relaxed as he recognized it.

"Sarah, what are you doing here? There's a reason I didn't wake you up." The twins did most things together, but this was something he wanted to do by himself, and he was slightly irritated that his sister had shown up. He knew how she felt around blood, and didn't want her to get sick or possibly hurt. He noticed she had her bow and arrow set in her hand, and a long dagger strapped to her waist.

"Well, too bad. I figured you'd do something like this, and I also figured that two would be better wandering around the forest than one. I know you'd like to play the noble knight rescuing the damsel in distress, but Cassie's my friend, too, you know. Besides, she's not exactly a damsel who automatically goes to pieces when in distress... and neither am I." Her hazel eyes looked hurt as she passed David to get her own tack.

He turned and followed her. "You can't come, Sarah."

"Why not? I can defend myself."

"Sarah! Did you not hear what we were told tonight? Cassie: part-Brenwyd. Reficul Brotherhood: bad, wants to kill all Brenwyds. It's too dangerous!"

"For a girl? Or me specifically? I heard, David, and I'm wondering if you did. You'd be in just as much danger as Cassie is, and in no less danger than I would be. I can fight just as well as you can, even if it's not my favorite activity. If you don't let me go, I'll just follow you, or I'll go back home and tell our parents what you're doing. You're not getting rid of me so easily." She was glaring at him, but he thought he saw a hint of mirth behind her expression.

He released a gusty sigh of exasperation. "Alright, but if we get into a fight and there's blood and you get sick, don't blame me!"

"Of course not." The twins hurriedly saddled their horses and went to the driveway, pausing to let Gracie pick up the scent. She found it in a matter of seconds, and they headed out to find Cassie.

Searching for the Lost

Cassie paced up and down part of the wooded trail. Kai and Dassah had gone ahead to scout, giving her time to puzzle over what they had found so far. It was late in the afternoon on the day after the abduction; in other words, it was late afternoon on her birthday. The previous night, they had found that the men had abandoned the van not too far from the valley, mounting horses and meeting those who had ridden there. While this made it easier to track them and helped Cassie and her animals make up for lost time, Cassie could think of no reason to dump the vehicle in favor of horses and head deeper into the Blue Ridge. She and the animals had pushed on nonstop, not wanting the Brotherhood men to gain any more of a lead. All were tired, but they were determined to keep on. This was the first real stop they'd had.

She addressed Twi, who grazed nearby. "You would think they would dump the horses for a car, not the other way around. Very medieval thinkers, this bunch."

The mare didn't bother to stop grazing as she made her reply. She was making the most of the sparse grass along the trail, sometimes stripping leaves from low-lying vegetation to supplement her meal. *They could not have driven a car up these mountain trails,* Twi said. *Horses are logical methods of transportation. We do not need gas every few hours. We can eat as we go.* Cassie had had this conversation with her animals several times before, and she smiled slightly at her horse's disdainful tone. Twi did not fully understand why horses were no longer the main method of transportation for humans, and was scornful of all things with four wheels. Privately, Cassie was of the opinion that if gas prices got any higher, people would start using horses for regular transportation – and if that happened, Twi would soon long for the days when horses were only used for showing and pleasure. Right then, however, she did not feel like debating the point. Horses, although relatively simple in their concerns and thoughts, could carry on a debate longer than any politician.

"Well, yes, but if I were those men, I wouldn't have used horses at all" – at this, Twi did raise her head to look at her rider in disgust – "and would have instead driven to, say, a small airport, and gotten away in a plane piloted by a buddy or something like that. What would be the purpose of heading into a mountain wilderness? Do they have some kind of outpost here full of torture devices? And why wouldn't they have made a road to get to it?"

You have asked these questions several times. Have you gotten any closer to the answers by repeating them? Smokey commented, coming up behind her. He had gone hunting and had been absent from the group since they had stopped about thirty minutes ago.

Cassie paused in her pacing. "No."

Then do not repeat them. Find the answers. The cat sat on a fallen tree trunk and started licking himself. Cassie sighed in exasperation, but could think of no reply. Smokey's logic was, as usual, correct. But Cassie resumed her pacing and continued asking herself the questions anyway, hoping the answers would come eventually.

After about another fifteen minutes, Dassah appeared out of the forest. "Did you find anything? And where's Kai?" Cassie asked her.

He is waiting for us. We followed the scent for many paces and then the trail split, as did the riders. Kai is investigating further and I came to get you. Cassie frowned. She didn't like the sound of that. *Come. We need to keep moving.* Dassah started tugging on Cassie's pant leg.

"Alright, alright, I'm coming." She got up and picked Twi's tack up from where she had put it. Twi ambled over and Cassie began the process of tacking up. She had just gotten the saddle cinched up and was about to put the bridle on when Twi jerked her head out of reach and turned toward the way from which they had come. Smokey and Dassah also stared in that direction. Cassie heard faint hoofbeats coming up the trail, likely at a trot. Her hand dropped to the knife on her left hip. "What is it?" she asked. No one answered, but Twi gave a loud whinny that sounded like a welcome, making Cassie wince at the high-pitched sound right next to her sensitive ears. She grabbed Twi's head and hurriedly started to put the bridle on. "What on earth was that for?" she whispered to the horse, irritated. Twi broke out of Cassie's hold and fully turned toward the trail, whinnying again. This time there was an answering whinny and a dog's bark.

Cassie gasped, then frowned. She knew those sounds. She knew them very well. *How on earth did they manage to track me?* she wondered. She now felt in her mind the two horses and dog coming up the trail. She suspected they'd been blocking her from sensing their thoughts, which would explain why she hadn't felt them before. She grabbed her headband out of her bag and quickly placed it on her head. Though she was fairly sure they would know by now, it never hurt to be too careful. Smokey jumped onto Twi's saddle and Dassah ran back down the trail. Cassie sighed in frustration and annoyance, arms crossed and face glaring as David and Sarah came into view. They were trotting quickly, following Gracie and Dassah. Sarah caught sight of Cassie and waved, a relieved expression coming over her face at the sight of her friend, unharmed. The two urged Fire and Dreamer into a canter for the rest of the way.

"What are you guys doing here?" Cassie asked as they halted, even though she already knew the answer. "I believe I mentioned specifically in my note *not* to follow me. In fact, I distinctly remember writing that in capital letters and repeating the 'do not' part twice." She tried to sound stern and disapproving. Neither of the twins paid any attention to her expression or tone of voice.

David walked up to her with his usual easygoing smile, though Cassie saw tension in his face. "We thought you might need some help. Generally, if one goes after blood-thirsty villains, they take a friend or two to watch their back." He stared right back at her, his brown eyes even darker than usual with concern.

She softened her gaze slightly, looking from him to Sarah. "Look, it's not that I don't appreciate you coming after me. I do. I really do. But it's just way too dangerous. You see, as I was about to tell you a couple of nights ago, I'm–"

"Part Brenwyd? We know, Cass. Our parents and your cat told us."

Cassie released a pent-up breath, feeling relieved. No more need for hiding. She looked to her right. "And you don't mind that I hid it from you for four years?" she asked somewhat timidly.

"Well, we mind a little," Sarah said. "But we understand why you did. It's alright." Sarah discreetly elbowed her brother as Cassie returned her eyes to the twins.

"Right. It's okay, Cassie. We know now, and that's what matters," David said hastily.

Cassie eyed David a moment longer. She'd glimpsed Sarah elbowing him. David noticed her gaze and correctly interpreted it. He sighed. "Cassie, as much as I might not like the fact that you hid that you're part Brenwyd from us for four years, you did have some pretty darn good reasons. It's alright." David did admit to himself that he was a little hurt by Cassie's silence, but he wanted her to know he didn't hold it against her.

After gazing at him for several more seconds, Cassie nodded. "Thanks for understanding. So I guess this isn't really necessary now." She slipped her headband off, revealing the slight points at the tips of her ears. Sarah blinked and her eyes widened slightly, and Cassie heard David take in a sharp breath. She felt some amusement at her friends' reactions, knowing full well that it was not just her pointed ears causing the response. She had observed in her mirror that when she had her headband on, her face looked more rounded and normal. When it was off, her features looked slightly more angled and, well, her looks more startling. The Britons of the Middle Ages had had good reason for calling the Brenwyds "the Fair Folk" and Cassie was no exception, though it wasn't the ethereal beauty that elves are often described as having. It was more human, but still enough to draw people's attention to Cassie when her headband was on, and even more so now that it was off.

Anxious to get their attention off her looks and back to the issue at hand, she said, "But even though you know now, you guys have to go back home. I don't want to put you in danger. That's part of why I didn't tell you. The Brotherhood is dangerous. I didn't want you guys to be at risk of being killed just because of me."

Sarah's gaze met Cassie's. "You didn't put us in danger. We did. We're not going to let you face a bunch of bad guys by yourself. I know," she continued as Cassie began to protest, "that you have your animals, but it can't hurt to have two humans who can use weapons guarding your back as well." Cassie glanced in the direction of David's and Sarah's saddles, and saw the weapons fastened to their packs.

"You can't make us go back, Cass. We'd just keep following you," David added, with as serious an expression as Cassie had ever seen on his face. "You're our friend, and friends stick by each other. We do not care about what shape your ears are. That doesn't change who you are." Cassie looked from one determined face to the other and sighed, rolling her eyes upward toward the sky. The twins both grinned, knowing they had won.

Cassie called Twi over and mounted, and the twins followed suit. Just as they were about to leave the small clearing, Cassie turned in her saddle to look back at them, gray dominating her eye color. "Remember, you guys volunteered for this. If you get caught with me, you'll be treated as if you were part Brenwyd even though you're both regular humans. These people don't always just kill you, though. They can torture you first, take you close to death's door, but not kill you just yet. They can drive you insane, break your will, get you to admit to anything to stop the pain. This is real stuff, guys, not something I or someone else has made up. Are you sure you still want to come with me? I won't blame you if you want to turn back."

David and Sarah stayed silent for several minutes, taking in what they had heard. Then David said earnestly, "It doesn't matter, Cassie. We stand a better chance together than you do alone. Besides, we've got God on our side. That does count for something, you know." Sarah nodded affirmation with what her brother had said. Cassie studied them for a moment longer, then turned and squeezed Twi into a trot. Inside, she felt a huge sense of relief blooming and spreading like a warm current throughout her whole body from her heart to her toes, stemming from the fact that her friends would stand by her and she would have human companions with whom to confront the Brotherhood. "Hey, Cass," David said as they left the clearing.

"Yeah?"

"Happy birthday. For what it's worth."

Cassie turned slightly to look at him. A smile appeared on her face for the first time that day. "Thanks."

About twenty minutes later, the group came to where the trail split. The humans dismounted and looked at the ground. There was obvious evidence of hoof prints, but they diverged, and Cassie thought that about the same number of riders had gone on each trail. "Now what?" Sarah asked of no one in particular. Cassie's eyebrows slanted downward as she examined the area. She looked for Kai but didn't see him. That worried her, but then she caught a wisp of his consciousness approaching from their left and turned in that direction. Several minutes later he walked into view, pausing as he saw David and Sarah, but Cassie sensed that he was not too surprised by their presence.

In truth, she wasn't all that surprised they had followed her either, at least, not that David had. Sarah was more timid, the kind of person who preferred to stay at home and pray for people in dangerous situations rather than get involved in them herself. However, she invariably found herself in such situations because of following Cassie, and actually handled herself pretty well. David was bolder than his sister and liked doing more dangerous things. He was still cautious and generally didn't take unnecessary risks, but had highly protective instincts. Nothing ever really seemed to visibly bother him, which Cassie was grateful for, as his steadiness had helped her stay in control of herself in previous situations they had encountered. Cassie was the kind of person who acted instinctively and impulsively if she saw people doing wrong, often causing the threesome to get into trouble, but generally finding ways to get them out of it, too. She admitted that she had a temper, though she kept it under a very tight rein. All together, the trio balanced each other out.

Kai continued on toward Cassie, who asked him, "Which way?"

I am not entirely sure, he replied. *All the paths go on for some distance and I did not have time to investigate them very far. I cannot tell which group has your parents with them.* As he spoke, David and Sarah both gasped.

"I heard him!" Sarah exclaimed.

"So did I. How does that work? I've never heard him before," David added.

Cassie was slightly startled, as she had not realized Kai had extended his words to her companions. *Why did you do that?* she asked him silently.

He tilted his head up at her to reply. *Because they are with us now, they know the secret, and it is quicker than you translating everything.*

How did you know they know?

You are not wearing your headband. He sounded slightly amused, as if it should have been obvious.

Oh. She looked at her friends' shocked expressions and had to laugh a little. "You can hear him because he allowed you to hear him. Among other things, Brenwyds were renowned for their animals. One of the things that set their animals apart was that they could talk to anyone, Brenwyd or human, that they chose. Kai has Brenwyd dog blood in him, so he can do it as well. You haven't heard him before now because if he had let you, I would have had to tell you the secret sooner."

"Cool!" said David, grinning. "Now you don't have to tell us what he says all the time."

Sarah agreed, then asked, "So what do we do now? Pick a trail and hope we're right?"

"We might have to, but if we pick wrong, we lose a lot of valuable time," Cassie answered, frowning. "We can't afford that."

"We could split up," David suggested. "We have our cell phones. When one group finds your parents, they can call the other and wait for them to catch up, then we can rescue them together. Since the kidnappers have split, we should be able to take them on."

Cassie thought about it. "We'd still lose time waiting for the other group to catch up. And what if one or both groups get caught? The other would have no way of knowing. Not to mention cell reception is pretty spotty up here. And even if we succeeded, we might have the other Brotherhood group on our tail all the way home, and just go through this whole thing all over again." They fell silent, trying to find a way out of their predicament.

Sarah looked between the two trails, and saw the dogs and cat having what looked like a silent conference. She smiled at the thought that Kai could really speak to her. Often she had wished she could communicate with animals like Cassie – her eyes widened as an idea struck her. It was quite simple, and she wondered why no one had mentioned it yet. "Cassie, are there any wild animals around?"

Cassie's eyes met hers, surprised by the question. "Well, yeah, but why?" she asked.

"Well, I was thinking that maybe some of the wildlife that live around here could tell us which way the group with your parents went." Cassie stared at her. "What?" Sarah asked. "You don't think so?"

"No, I do," her friend said with a rueful grin. "I just should have thought of that sooner. I knew there must have been a reason I let you guys come."

David snorted at that. "*Let* us come? We decided to come on our own, thank you very much. And you couldn't have forced us to turn around anyway."

"Who says I couldn't have?" Cassie retorted. Then her eyes focused into the distance as she reached her mind out to the wildlife in the area. She sensed the presence of several deer, squirrels, and various birds, and sent out a silent query to them. She felt them shudder in fear as they remembered the riders passing through the area. Through their memories, she saw the riders approach the fork and halt. Several of them conversed, one gesturing toward the different paths. Her heart lurched as she saw her parents riding double with two of the riders, hands bound. Apparently the riders reached an agreement and split, the group carrying Ty and Leah heading to the right. The animals said that the trail to the left circled back to the trail Cassie and the twins had been following. That made Cassie nervous. Had the Brotherhood guessed that she would come after her parents? Or had they just gone back to get her, assuming she would return to the house? If so, why hadn't they just backtracked on the original trail? In any case, the teens needed to get going. There was no telling how close the group who had circled back was, and Cassie didn't fancy getting captured or being the cause of her friends' capture. A vulture, who had been listening in on the conversation, said that he had seen a valley not far down the trail where a camp of men and horses was set up. He was fairly sure that's where Cassie would find her parents.

Cassie thanked the animals profusely. Despite the worry that the other Brotherhood group could be closing in, she felt a spark of excitement. This endeavor might just succeed. A smile broke through her serious expression and the twins knew she had been successful.

"So which way?" Sarah asked.

"Right," Cassie answered, turning Twi toward the trail. "Let's get going. We're burning daylight, and the animals said that the left trail circles back and eventually joins this one again."

"Then that other group is following us? How could they know we're here?" David asked.

"I don't think they know we're here *per se*, but they may be trying to get back to the valley to get me. My concern is that there are some muddy patches left over from the rain the other day, and if they find one of those and make out our tracks heading this way, they could get the idea to come up behind us."

Then come on, Kai said, already partway down the right-hand trail. *We cannot risk them catching up*. He started to run, as did Dassah and Smokey, and the teens set off at a canter. There was no time to waste.

Found! ... and Lost Again

David scanned the trail in both directions as he rode. Kai and Smokey acted as scouts to warn Cassie of any difficulties in front, but David still kept a sharp eye out, glancing back often to see if the other Brotherhood group was, in fact, following them. Cassie rode behind him, with Sarah bringing up the rear. All three teens refrained from speaking, not wanting to give away any hint of their presence. The trail they were following was clearly angling downward and occasionally zig-zagging back and forth through the trees. David guessed they were close to the valley Cassie had mentioned. He looked down the mountain through the trees, but couldn't make out any valley floor. The thick foliage and underbrush made it difficult to see clearly, and they were still a ways from the mountain's base. Focusing on the trail before him, David spied an area where the trees thinned out into a small clearing. He halted Fire and turned to face the girls. They halted as well and looked at him expectantly. "There's a clearing of some kind up ahead. I think we should check it out on foot first, just to be safe," he said in a low voice.

Cassie nodded. "I see it, too. Let me call Kai and Smokey back first. They must have gone by it."

"Okay."

Cassie looked beyond him and focused on calling the animals. Suddenly her eyes went wide. "They've found them! They're not that far ahead. Kai says to go around the clearing because the camp is right below that ridge in the valley at the bottom. There's a break in the trees we can see through."

"Then let's go! We shouldn't waste time," Sarah said, her eyes showing excitement. She started to urge Dreamer off the trail.

"Hold your horses there, Sis. We have to go carefully," her brother told her sternly. "We can't risk getting caught."

Sarah turned Dreamer back to the group, a little surprised by her own eagerness. "I know, I know, I just can't stand the thought of Mr. and Mrs. Pennington in the hands of those men," she said, blushing a little in embarrassment.

"I understand you perfectly, Sarah, but David's right. We can't do anything if we're caught." Cassie dismounted and continued, "Kai says that there aren't any sentries this far up the mountain, but there are some when we get closer, so we have to be quiet. And that goes for you guys, too," she added, turning to Dassah, Gracie, and the horses. They all bobbed their heads in understanding.

Let us go. We are not accomplishing anything by standing here talking, Twi said, pawing the ground.

We're going, Cassie assured the mare. The twins dismounted and the group turned off the trail and into the woods, stepping carefully over fallen branches to decrease the noise they were making, and keeping a sharp eye out for poison ivy. Despite their care, the snapping of small twigs and the crunching of leaves from last fall made Cassie cringe. It sounded so loud. She took the lead and concentrated on Kai and Smokey, following their directions to their location. Dassah and Gracie helped by smelling the path the two had taken. After a few minutes, Cassie spotted Kai's head by a fallen log and Smokey in the tree above. The animals turned their heads toward them when they heard them. *So what did you find?* Cassie asked, her thoughts growing excited. The idea that her parents could be free by nightfall made her want to charge into battle right then. Hope burned brightly in her chest, sending a warm, comforting feeling through her body, though she sternly told herself not to let her expectations rise too high.

Come and see, Kai said. *The horses must stay here.*

And why should we? Twi asked tartly.

You are too big to hide where we need to go, Smokey said. *You would give us away. There is a watch-human not far below the place.* Cassie looked back toward the trail, mentally retracing the route they had taken. There was little sign of their passing, but someone going by who looked in their direction would be able to see the horses, albeit with a bit of difficulty.

"It's not just sentries I'm worried about," she said. "If that Brotherhood group comes up behind us, they'll be able to see you if they look this way. You're going to have to lie down."

With our tack on? Dreamer asked.

"Your saddles can come off." Cassie quickly unsaddled Twi, David and Sarah doing the same for their horses. The horses folded their legs and went to their bellies, keeping their heads down. Cassie gathered some brush from around the area and arranged it in front of the horses to completely conceal their position. She didn't worry too much about anyone deciding the arrangement looked unnatural, because the Brotherhood men, if they passed, would most likely not be expecting to see built-up brush hiding horses. Her dad had often told her that if someone didn't expect to see something, most of the time they didn't. Then the group crept through the trees and undergrowth to the vantage point Kai and Smokey had found, where a log was conveniently positioned; beyond it was a bit of a break in the forest. The three teens crouched behind the log, peering over the top to look below them.

Cassie had often thought that the expansive, dense forests of the Blue Ridge, with their tall trees, creeping vines, and ground strewn with dead leaves and small plant growth, would fit right in on the set of a fantasy movie. Often she imagined knights or Civil War soldiers moving through the woods. Now the reality that she saw seemed to reflect scenes from her imagination. The valley itself seemed normal enough. It was not too large or too small and was mainly tree-covered, like most valleys in the area. The camp in the middle of the valley, on the other hand, was a different story. Some of it was obscured by trees, but the teens could make out most of it well enough. Tents were set up around a central area, and a picket line of horses was tied between a couple of trees. Men were walking around casually with swords hanging from their waists. Cassie, with her keen vision, noticed a pole at the center of the camp with a couple of things tied to it. She narrowed her gaze and let out a small gasp. The things were her parents. Three men were nearby, apparently guarding the prisoners. Scanning the entire valley, she noticed that beyond the camp was a clear area running the length of the valley which she suspected might serve as an airplane runway.

"Do you see your parents?" Sarah whispered to Cassie.

"Yeah. They're tied to a pole near the middle of the camp. Several men are guarding them."

"This place looks like something from the Middle Ages or a fantasy movie. These guys do know it's the twenty-first century, right?" David asked from her other side.

Cassie shrugged. "Obviously their thinking is stuck somewhere in the past, but don't underestimate their appearance, no matter how strange it seems. They're all killers. You guys could still go back, you know," she said.

"Of course we won't go back," Sarah protested. "You can't take on all those men by yourself. And I don't fancy running into that other Brotherhood group. It's probably safer for us at the mo-

The valley itself seemed normal enough. The camp in the middle of the valley, on the other hand, was a different story.

ment to be with you." At this, Kai, Dassah, and Smokey gave her dark looks.

What are we, invisible? Smokey grumbled. The cat sounded so offended, Cassie had to grin.

Of course you're not invisible. She meant any other human help, Cassie reassured him. She returned her attention to the camp, noting there were about seven men around it. Everything she observed made her believe the Brotherhood had been planning the attack for weeks.

But why take her parents prisoner instead of just killing them? There was always the torture machine idea, but something told Cassie there was more to this than simply sadistic pleasure. Why so much planning ahead? Why the big set-up? That didn't go with what her father had told her of the group. According to him, they would find their targets and kill them. Occasionally they would capture Brenwyds for torture first, and Cassie had given David and Sarah some extreme examples of Brotherhood behavior to discourage her friends from following her. But most of the time it was simple murder. But why so many men for just two people? Well, three, since they'd been planning to take Cassie too.

David interrupted her thoughts. "Any ideas on how we're going to do this?" he asked, frowning as he studied the camp. "As it stands, we might - might - be able to take them on, but those sentries Kai mentioned bring their number up several men, not to mention that other group that went left at the fork. It's not like we can just sneak in there in broad daylight."

"Whatever we decide to do, we've got to do it quickly. The fact that they kidnapped my parents instead of outright killing them confuses me. There's something else going on here that we don't know about. I think that clear strip running the valley's length is a runway. That could be their getaway. The smart thing to do in their position would be–" Cassie stopped short as she heard a slight noise in the forest near them, a little way down the path behind them, a noise just loud enough she knew no wild animal had made it. "Don't move!" she hissed, turning around quietly to get a better view. Several horsemen came into her view, making no attempt to move silently, riding along the same path the teens had left. The teens crouched down into the brush, praying they wouldn't be seen. Cassie pressed herself against a tree and peeked around it so she could see the men's faces. They looked frustrated, upset, and also, she thought, a little fearful. *Why on earth would they be scared?*she wondered to herself. The riders continued following the zigzagging trail. When they had come around the trail about ten yards in front of the log the teens had hidden behind, and were getting just far enough away that Cassie started to relax, a loud voice suddenly hailed them, making Cassie jump.

"Well, so you're back. That was quick. Where's the girl?" The group behind the log exchanged glances. They knew who the sentry was talking about.

One of the men – Cassie assumed he was the leader – responded. "We didn't go all the way back. I think she's tracking us. When we rejoined the main trail, we kept finding tracks of unshod horses leading in this direction, along with some dog prints. I thought we would run into her. You mean she hasn't shown up yet?"

"No. You seem to have miscalculated. The Commander won't be pleased with you about this, Raymond." The sentry sounded a little nervous. Cassie wondered who this "Commander" was. She berated herself for not thinking to cover their trail.

"I know. I was sure we would find her... well, at any rate, I would tighten your watch. She might be hiding around here somewhere, biding her time and waiting for a chance. Tricky folk, Brenwyds. And there's no telling what this girl might be able to do. She's strong by all accounts."

"Yes, good idea. But don't worry. The little witch won't get through on my watch."

The "witch" epithet made Cassie feel disgruntled. Her father had explained to her that Brenwyds were not like witches in any way, shape, or form, since their special abilities came from God and not from an evil source. Besides, they used their ability to hear songs for healing only. Well, Dad had mentioned something about being able to use the songs they sensed in battle against actual witches or wizards, but she didn't quite understand that. At any rate, she greatly disliked being referred to as a person who practiced magic.

"We're leaving soon, anyway," the sentry continued. "If she comes around here looking for us, she'll be sorely disappointed. And once we do find her, it surely won't be that hard to capture her. Who knows? Maybe she'll bumble right into me. That would be convenient." The sentry laughed. *Not at all a nice laugh,* Cassie thought. She noted that both men spoke with British accents, though the sentry's sounded weaker than Raymond's. Cassie guessed he must be some other nationality by birth, likely American. So the Brotherhood was still based out of England, as her father had said. That must be where they were taking her parents, which added another level of urgency to the rescue mission.

"It would at that," said the other man, Raymond. "We'd best be going on."

"Good luck, you'll need it," the sentry said in parting. The horsemen rode toward the camp and the sentry watched them, then disappeared into the trees. Cassie made a note of where he was and what features she could see under his hood. An idea was forming in her mind. It was very dangerous, but they didn't have much time. She motioned for David and Sarah to follow her, and they quietly retreated back to the horses.

Sarah's face was full of worry as she looked at her friend. "Cassie, you heard them. They know they missed you. Now they're watching for you, and the sentry said they're leaving soon. Do you think you should keep going?" she said with no small concern.

Cassie nodded. "Absolutely. I could never forgive myself if I don't give it my best try. And I have an idea." The twins examined her face for signs of what she was thinking. The gray in her eyes almost completely washed out the blue. Her face was set in a determined, almost fierce expression.

"What is it?" David asked. "Wait for dark, then sneak into camp and free your parents?" She looked at him in a way that made him feel uncomfortable.

She was recalling a comment he had made earlier about possible ways to get into camp. "Nope. We'll need all of the night to cover as much ground as possible. I was thinking of hiding in plain sight."

"And that means?" he probed. Her face took on a sly look, with a hint of amusement. David had a feeling he would not like this plan, and it was confirmed by her next words.

"How do you feel about playing the enemy?"

The leader of the group that the teens had seen waited anxiously for the Commander to reply. After hearing his subordinate's report, the Commander had been ominously silent for many minutes. When he did speak, his voice was dangerously quiet and his black eyes hard as iron. "Do you know what your failure means, Raymond?"

Raymond swallowed nervously. "Surely a thirteen-year-old girl isn't that much of a threat, Commander. And like I said, I'm sure she's hanging around here somewhere. The tracks I saw confirmed it."

"Fool!" the Commander bellowed, making Raymond flinch. "She may be young, but Brenwyds are clever. You should have found her on the trail, or not come back until you combed every inch of the woods around here! She more than likely heard you conversing with Karl and is now on guard. Because she has Brenwyd blood in her, she can continue the race – and she is in the line of that thrice-accursed witch! Do you have the slightest idea what that could mean for our mission, dimwit?!"

"N-no, Commander," Raymond replied, stuttering. Never had he seen the Commander so angry. He started to sweat.

"No, of course not," the Commander mocked. "Very well, then, you and your group shall stay here *until* you find the girl. Remember, don't kill her. If you do manage to find her, don't be fooled by her youth or any innocent looks. She is dangerous and tainted with blood of the devil. And to make sure you do the job right..." He turned to the back of the tent where a figure stood watching and listening with interest. He beckoned to the figure and it stepped forward. "William will accompany you and report back to me. Is that understood?"

"Yes, Commander," Raymond said, gritting his teeth. Did the Commander really think him that incapable?

"Very well. As a reward for failing, your group will relieve those currently guarding the prisoners. Once we take them away, you are to scour every inch of this place, turn over every rock, until you find her." The Commander paused, looking at Raymond with a dangerous light in his eyes. "And if you don't find her... don't come back. Now go!" Raymond left the tent hurriedly, and the Commander turned to William. "What do you think about this, William?"

William scowled. "I think you are right. If she is around here somewhere and has been alerted that Raymond was following her, she'll be very hard to catch. But Raymond fears you, as he should. He won't dare fail a second time. I'll make sure he doesn't."

The Commander nodded. "Make sure you report their every move. Because of your youth, they will likely let more slip than if I sent one of the older men. In fact, perhaps you will be able to get the girl to trust you and then lead her into our arms."

William smiled at the thought. "Perhaps, Father. I am honored you think so highly of me. I will prove myself worthy of your trust."

The Commander gazed at his fifteen-year-old son fondly. As fondly as he ever did, that is, which meant a slight softening of the harsh lines on his face and a relaxed look in his eye. William had already shown himself to have the true spirit of the Brotherhood. "You have proven yourself trustworthy already, my boy. Now prove yourself capable. Go and get ready for your assignment." He put a hand on William's shoulder and squeezed it briefly.

"Yes, Father." William left the tent. The Commander sat down and mused over what had occurred. If William did run into the girl, he was confident that his son would be able to pull the wool over her eyes. *Girls have a weakness for handsome boys,* he thought, *and so the Pennington witch will be caught.*

"I still don't like this, Cassie," David grumbled. "Something's bound to go wrong."

"Oh, be more trusting, David. Cassie hasn't made a bad plan yet," Sarah told her brother, though there was a hint of nervousness in her voice.

"Thanks for your trust, Sarah, but we still need to be careful. No plan is completely foolproof, and this is probably the riskiest one I've thought of to date." Cassie had her eyes fixed on the sentry's hidden position, every bone in her body determined to succeed. "Ready?"

"I suppose," David muttered. Cassie slowly and silently started to move toward the sentry, first backtracking up the trail so she could cross to the other side without him seeing her. She smiled briefly at the thought that her dad would be proud of her. Not even she could hear herself breathing – although maybe that was because, for the moment at least, she was holding her breath entirely. The plan was for her to knock out the sentry, and for David to take his place. Then David would drag Cassie down to the camp with the story that he had found her lingering in the woods, planning to attack the camp. The sentry was roughly David's height and had his coloring, so with the cloak he was wearing David should be able to pull it off. Cassie wondered why anyone would want to wear a cloak in Virginia's hot, humid summer climate, but it gave them an opportunity they could use. Another thing working in their favor was the fact the man did not have a particularly strong accent, so David would be able to imitate it well enough. The animals would spread out around the camp, with Sarah waiting for David's signal to come down. Cassie would then play up the "witch" role the Brotherhood had assigned her and cause a distraction. She had heard the nervousness in their voices when they mentioned the strength of her Brenwyd blood. Hopefully she would be able to bluff them long enough to get her parents free. Her dad could help from there, and Sarah would shoot arrows into the camp. It was a risky plan – extremely so, as David had pointed out several times – but it was the best they had. Cassie also planned to enlist the support of the Brotherhood horses, which would help greatly.

Cassie was still some yards away from the sentry when a buzzing noise made her look up – and she realized in an instant that they were too late. She spied an airplane through the canopy of leaves overhead, and saw that it was descending. She estimated the distance between the plane and the runway, and concluded that its descent rate would put it right smack-dab in the middle of the valley right next to the camp. The sentry had spotted the plane by now, and began walking unhurriedly down toward the camp. He'd been expecting this. Cassie wondered if the men who had doubled back on the trail would have been left behind if they hadn't arrived in time, or if the others had just been waiting for them to come back and the airplane had been on call. She decided to follow the sentry into the camp and see what would happen next, even though she knew it would be a futile effort. She just couldn't stand watching helplessly as her parents were snatched from her again.

She was about to move when she saw a flicker of movement behind her and felt Kai pull her back. She tried to break free of the dog's grip, but David grabbed her as well. "Don't you dare, Cassie. You'd be caught in a minute," he breathed into her ear as he started pulling her back toward the log.

She glared at him, trying to struggle out of his grip. "Don't you see? That airplane's their way out of here! I have to try..."

"You'd just get caught, Cass. Listen to me. You are your parents' best chance of escaping. If you're caught, there's no way you – or they – will ever get out of there." David's eyes were dark with concern, as was his tone of voice, and his passion surprised Cassie. It made Sarah examine her brother more carefully, suspicious of why he was being so insistent.

Kai tilted his head up at Cassie until he looked her in the eye. *He is right, girl. We will free them, but now is not the time.*

Sarah interrupted the three. "Um, guys? You should be watching this." She had binoculars trained on the camp.

"Let me see those," David said to his sister. She handed them to him. He raised them to his eyes and watched the camp. The plane was now within a minute or two of landing, and a group of people had gathered by the runway. Others were untying the horses, and taking down tents with astonishing speed, though they left a few up for some reason. David focused on the plane, searching for any markings that might give away who owned it. He found none. His attention was diverted when Cassie emitted a choking sound and Kai growled deep in his throat. "What is it?" he asked.

Cassie pointed to the group by the runway. "Look." David couldn't remember ever hearing her sound so upset. He looked again where she was pointing, and stiffened. The group had grown, and he saw two very familiar forms in their midst. Mr. and Mrs. Pennington had their hands tied behind their backs. They weren't gagged, which struck David as odd, but then he reasoned that it was unlikely any sane person would venture out here in the middle of nowhere. *Does that mean I'm insane?* he wondered briefly. He brushed the thought aside and focused in on Cassie's parents. Mrs.

Pennington looked okay, just scared, for which he didn't blame her. Mr. Pennington, on the other hand, had blood encrusted on one side of his head. David felt his temper flare when he saw that.

Sarah tugged on his arm. "Can I see?" she asked. David gave her the binoculars and looked to see how Cassie was doing. She was pale, but he saw sparks of anger in her eyes. He also saw something he had not seen before: despair. It shocked him. Never had he thought Cassie could give up anything as a lost cause. He moved over to her and put a hand on her shoulder, giving it a gentle squeeze. The trio watched as the plane was loaded with passengers and then took off, quickly disappearing into the sky. Cassie abruptly burst into silent sobs, burying her head against David's shoulder, which made him feel slightly awkward. But after a moment of hesitation, he put his arms around her comfortingly as the others gathered around, wondering what on earth they were to do now.

Friend or Foe?

William watched the plane disappear into the clouds, still hardly believing that his father had entrusted him with such an important mission. He was determined to succeed and prove himself worthy of the Brotherhood. It had been his dream since he was small, and it had spurred him to master the weapons of the Brotherhood while still young. Now here was the ultimate chance to prove he was not too young, as so many of the men seemed to think. If he succeeded, he might be able to take the rite of initiation that would make him a full-fledged member of the Brotherhood. He was also curious to see a young Brenwyd up close. He had seen several adults, but none had been below twenty-five or so, and all had had blood so diluted it didn't really show. This girl, however, was reputed to be close to, if not exactly, half-and-half, and as a result to have pointed ears. At least, there were rumors that she had pointed ears; according to the Brotherhood's source, she always wore a headband to cover the proof of them. He turned to his right, where Raymond stood with a scowl on his face. He obviously didn't like being left behind with a teenager supervising him. He snarled at William, "You just do as you're told and stay out of the way. The girl's clever and likely knows she's being hunted. We'll have to surprise her."

William nodded. "Very well." He was accustomed to being treated as a nuisance and unimportant, despite who his father was, though he was treated with more respect than other initiates his age in the Brotherhood. It was part of why he knew so much about the mission and their target. People forgot he was there, allowing him to pick up all sorts of conversations. He even knew why capturing this girl and her parents alive was so important, which Raymond did not. The men and boy went back to the tents to gather supplies. All the horses had been taken on the plane, so they would have to hike across the country. They were gathering up their belongings when William looked up toward the forest from the half-open tent window and caught the barest flicker of movement among the trees up the mountain slope. He stopped what he was doing and looked more carefully. Yes, there was definitely someone there. He went over to Raymond. "Have your men stop what they're doing. Someone's coming down toward the camp."

"Are you sure?" the man asked.

William nodded. "Look for yourself." They gazed out the window and saw three dogs emerge into a bare area along the trail, sniffing cautiously. Then one turned toward the trees, and three teenagers became visible, horses following. The distance was too great to make out details, but one was obviously lighter haired than the others and female. They quickly crossed the open space and disappeared into the forest shadow on the other side. A smile slowly spread across Raymond's face.

"Well, well, well, looks like the witch is coming to us. How convenient. Looks like she's not being so cautious with the others gone. We'll wait until they reach the center of camp and surround them. This will be easier than I expected." He went to the men to tell them to hide themselves. The sun was setting behind the mountains, its rays shining into the eyes of the party in the trees. *That's good,* William thought. *They won't be able to see clearly.* Twilight began to spread across the landscape as the group proceeded slowly, keeping inside the tree line as they crept toward the camp. They were hard to see, at times disappearing completely behind the trees. But having already spotted them, William was able to keep an eye on them, especially as they got closer to the camp. He could tell all were on high alert, as they kept looking around and moved quickly.

When they had reached a place where more details could be seen, William frowned thoughtfully. They were all armed. He had half-expected the Brenwyd girl to be armed, but he hadn't thought she'd bring anyone with her, or that they would be armed, too. He wondered if her companions were also part Brenwyd, or if they were merely friends of hers. Either way, by accompanying her, they had sealed their fate.

The light-haired girl had a knife scabbard buckled around her waist. The knives were still sheathed, one on each hip, but her left hand rested on the knife on her left. The figure to her right, a dark-haired boy, had a hand on the hilt of a sword, and he looked like he knew how to use it. The figure to the far left, which was also a girl, appeared to have a bow with an arrow on the string, though it wasn't drawn. *But,* he reasoned, *they can't have ever fought in a real fight and spilled blood before, and they can't be all that skilled. They'll likely be squeamish, especially the girls.* Still, he wasn't sure he liked the look of one of the dogs.

At last the party got to a distance where the undergrowth no longer impeded William's vision through the binoculars. The boy, the tallest of the group, looked around warily. William could tell he was ready to spring into action at the slightest provocation. A blood-red bay followed him, William was surprised to note, without being led. The horse looked from side to side, as if it knew that this was a place in which to be wary. William knew that was ridiculous, but the other two horses, a black mare and a blue roan, also looked as if they knew exactly what was happening. A gray cat followed in their wake, as if guarding the rear. The dogs were in front of the humans, the two smaller ones on the edges and a big brown one right in front of the light-haired girl. William examined the girl next to the light-haired one. She, like the boy, was dark-haired. In fact, she and the boy looked enough alike to be related. She looked worried, furrows dug in her brow as she looked this way and that. She had an innocent look that made William feel a little sorry she had to be captured and then likely killed, but he coldly pushed the feeling aside. She was consciously consorting with a Brenwyd, which made her tainted. He scrutinized the boy, guessing him to be the most challenging. He appeared to have an air of fierce protectiveness around him.

Lastly, he turned his gaze to the girl in the middle. She was obviously the Brenwyd. Her hair, which looked red from a distance, he now saw was more of a titian color, highlighted by the setting sun. Her facial features were delicate and perfectly suited to her. All in all, she was very pretty, in a fairy-tale princess sort of way. But he saw a hard, determined look on her face, and knew she was no helpless fairy-tale princess. She would be challenging by virtue of her Brenwyd blood. The best way to capture her would probably be to threaten to kill her friends. Focusing on her head, he saw that her ears were, indeed, covered by a headband of some sort.

Returning to a full view of all three of them, his frown deepened and his brow furrowed in puzzlement. Something seemed incredibly familiar about the trio, though that made no sense. He'd never seen them before, he knew that for sure. But he couldn't shake the feeling that these were people he should know. He glanced around the camp and saw that the men had hidden themselves well. Now all they had to do was wait.

Cassie, David, and Sarah halted before entering the seemingly abandoned camp, unaware that they were being observed. Cassie scanned the camp, looking for any sign of movement. She saw none. "It looks safe enough," she decided.

"That doesn't mean it *is* safe," David said, scowling darkly at the tents. "If they were all leaving, why did they leave some tents?"

"But they took all the horses," Cassie countered. "Why would they do that if some were staying behind?"

"I don't know, but I don't like it. What if I go ahead to scout it out? No sense in us all getting captured if there are still people there."

I will go with him. It would not take long to check the camp, Kai said, agreeing with David.

Cassie frowned. "I don't think that's a good idea. We should all go as a group. We're stronger that way," she argued.

"I agree with Cassie, David. I'd rather us all go together than wait out here with my nerves on edge," Sarah said. "Besides, if anyone's there, they have to have spotted us by now, and we've seen and heard nothing from the camp."

"Then they've probably set up some sort of trap, so if just one person goes and doesn't come back in, say, ten minutes, the others will know it's a trap and can go get help," David said.

"From where?" Sarah asked her brother. "We're in the middle of the Blue Ridge wilderness. There isn't exactly anyone we can run to for help, and cell reception's spotty at best. Cassie's right, we stand a better chance as a group."

"Exactly," Cassie chimed in. "Besides, we can handle ourselves, David. You don't have to be our protector just because we're girls, ya know."

David rolled his eyes. "I know that. I was just volunteering to go ahead. You definitely should not go ahead, Cassie."

You know, Gracie commented to Dassah, *if they keep bickering, I am just going to check around myself, no matter what anyone says, and be done in five minutes. We could have finished by now.*

Definitely, Dassah agreed. *Humans can be so dense sometimes. They think too much, even if they are part Brenwyd. Used to be, humans would just go ahead and do things. At least, I think they did. Then they learned about all the possible dangers of things, and got so safety-conscious that they do not do anything for fear of getting hurt.* The dogs gazed quizzically at their humans. Cassie had picked up on their conversation and now glared at them, but they assumed an innocent air. She opened her mouth to give a scathing reply, but shut it as she realized they were absolutely right.

Twi pushed her from behind. *If you do not start moving soon, I am going to whinny so loudly that people in the next state will be able to hear me*, the mare said.

Cassie sighed. *It's very hard to argue with animals,* she reflected. "Guys, if we don't get going, the animals are going to stage a coup. We're going together and that's the end of it." She moved off with Sarah right behind her and David a second later. He made a mental note not to be the only guy on the next trip.

They moved into the camp, each looking around and on the alert for any suspicious sound or movement. They reached the center of the camp without incident, and Sarah felt her nerves begin to calm as it appeared no one was left. Cassie, however, was not too sure. Something just felt wrong. She had understood the sense of David's argument, but she just couldn't bear to stay up on the trail anymore. She had to do something, anything, that might help her get her parents back, or she felt she might go mad. She hated feeling helpless, and it was a feeling she'd felt too often in the last twenty-four hours. She heard a very slight noise, metal scraping against something, as if someone had just drawn a sword.

She glanced in the direction of the sound, as Kai growled low in his throat. *Someone is there*, he said.

Several someones, Gracie supplemented as she sniffed the air. *All men, all around us.*

David sent Cassie an inquiring look. She mouthed, *There are people here. Get ready.* He nodded.

Cassie took a deep breath, thinking what she was about to do was crazy, and started talking, taking her companions by surprise. "You may as well come out. We know you're here. We don't want to hurt you. Just come forward peacefully and lay down your weapons. We have some questions we need answered." She hoped she sounded more confident than she felt. Her throat felt like a dry cotton ball and her palms were slightly sweaty. There was a floaty, nervous feeling in her stomach, like it was doing somersaults and back flips. She recognized the sensation from when she competed in horse shows, but now it was magnified a hundred times. She hoped it wouldn't come to killing, but knew that was unlikely.

A sardonic chuckle answered her words, followed by a raspy voice. "So, the Brenwyd witch shows herself and demands we lay down our weapons. How considerate. Why don't I ask you to do the same? I'm sure we'll get along a lot better that way. Besides, it would be a pity to kill children so young." The speaker stepped into view, followed by several others, completely surrounding the kids. Each had a naked sword in hand. Cassie gulped. Sarah went slightly pale. David didn't appear to change, but his eyes flickered from man to man, fully taking in the threat facing them. His heart started pounding hard as he noticed how easily the men held their weapons. The dogs growled, and the horses pawed the ground and snorted.

The man continued speaking, and Cassie recognized him as the man who'd talked to the sentry. "Unfortunately, the game ends here for you. It was not a good move to show yourself. Now put down your weapons, prevent your animals from attacking, and allow us to take you with us. If you come peaceably, we'll let your friends go. Understand?" Cassie swallowed, looking at David and Sarah. What could she do? This is what she had feared would happen.

Kai moved in front of her and addressed the speaker. *Look, human. You cannot take her without getting through me. And we outnumber you. Put down your weapons and we will spare you. Attack, and you will die*. The other animals made various noises of affirmation.

The speaker's eyes widened. The other men murmured in astonishment. One said, "Hey, Raymond, maybe we should take the dog, too. He probably has Brenwyd dog blood in him. The Master might like to see him."

Raymond was silent for a few moments. Then he simply stepped forward and said, "If it's a fight you want, it's a fight you'll get." He struck at Kai, but the dog leaped nimbly out of the way. He lunged for Raymond's forearm, but the man was too quick. The other animals started attacking the men threatening their humans. The teens stood watching in awe for several minutes, seeing their normally gentle pets turn into savage fighters. Then Gracie let out a yelp of pain as a sword scratched her leg, and the sound galvanized the teens into action. David charged toward the man assailing Gracie, while Sarah aimed her bow and Cassie went for a man coming up behind Twi. Before she struck, Cassie hesitated, not wanting to be responsible for taking a life. But as she saw an overhead swing coming toward her horse, she forgot her inhibition and drove her blade home. The man went down, never knowing what hit him.

From that moment, Sarah, David, and Cassie fought for their lives as well as those of their pets. The battle seemed to last an eternity, but in reality was only about ten minutes. The men of the Brotherhood had vastly underestimated the training Tyler Pennington had poured into his pupils, and it proved to be the men's downfall. They also had not counted on dealing with animals so intent on protecting their humans. The fight ended when Cassie, involved in an exchange of blows with Raymond, was able to get through his guard and disarm him. She stood with her knife to his throat, breathing hard. The fight had become a blur to her, a series of blocks, parries, cuts, and slashes with her knives. She was mildly surprised to be finished. Raymond snarled at her, "Well, girl, are you going to finish the job, or are you too squeamish? That's the problem with you Brenwyds, you're all cowards."

Cassie glared at him coldly, her eyes stormy. "I'm not a coward. I have morals."

"Oh, really? A Brenwyd with morals? Ha, that's a fine joke. Well, since you lack the guts to kill me, I'll do it myself." And before Cassie could do anything, he grabbed her knife hand and drove it through his heart, pulling her toward him, a slightly crazed expression on his face. She jerked back, but it was too late. Raymond slid to the ground, dead.

It had become patently clear to William within the first few moments of the battle that he would have to think of a way to capture the Brenwyd girl without use of arms. Fortunately, he'd already thought of a plan to cover that possibility, which was quickly becoming a reality outside the tent. He threw off his sword belt, then found a length of rope and rubbed it back and forth across his wrists. Next, he took a bandana out of his pocket and tied it around his neck, making it appear that he had been gagged. He then tied his hands expertly behind his back, a skill taught to him by his father, and sat in a chair in the tent. His plan was to make himself appear to have been a prisoner himself, left by the others to die of starvation. His hope was that the trio would take him in, and he would be able to guide them into the Brotherhood's hands. He would be, he thought with a smile, the Brenwyd girl's Judas Iscariot.

Through a crack in the tent flap, William saw Raymond disarmed by the girl. She held the tip of her knife to his throat and appeared to speak to him, but William could not hear her. Raymond snarled at the girl and grabbed her knife wrist, stabbing the knife into his chest as the girl jumped back. William could clearly see she was distraught. He puzzled over this behavior. He had been taught that, while Brenwyds abhorred fighting and were cowardly, they would kill ruthlessly and not think twice about it. Yet the expression on the girl's face told him that she felt horrified about Raymond's death, even though it had been by his own hand. He saw the dark-haired girl get sick, and the Brenwyd went up to her, comforting her. The sight moved him strangely. His training had taught him that any kill he made was for the glory of the Brotherhood and he should not feel guilt or sickness. But these teenagers appeared to be very upset that they had taken life, even though it had been in self-defense. It intrigued him. He saw them conversing and pushed such thoughts from his head. His masquerade was about to begin, and perhaps he could learn the reasoning behind their actions.

Cassie turned away from the man who'd just killed himself on her knife, trembling slightly, feeling absolutely horrified. How could someone just do that when she was prepared to offer mercy? It didn't make sense. She looked around at the other men, all dead, and felt sick to her stomach, but it had nothing to do with the blood. It was the guilt she felt from ending a fellow human being's life, even if he had been about to capture and likely kill her. It was the thought that these men were surely condemned to an eternity in hell, and the fear that she may have sent them there, even if it was in self-defense.

She wrapped her arms around herself and looked up at the mountains, recalling something her father had told her once. "*Never grow accustomed to killing, Cassie. Always try to offer mercy before you have to kill someone, no matter how evil they may be. Jesus died for them just as He did for us, and we were no better before He found us. The men of the Brotherhood have been deceived into thinking they are serving a good cause when in fact they are working for evil. They need to be rescued from the hell they've fallen into. They have been trained to kill with no second thought. That is what makes them such villains. You must remember this: Avoid killing like they do, or you will become like them. But do not hold yourself accountable for their choices. Even if they make a choice that forces you to kill them, it is their choice. Sometimes, no matter what you do, you cannot save someone, but always give them a chance if the situa-*

tion allows." She had given the man a chance, and he had refused it. She wondered just what it was that made people feel obligated to kill children. She heard retching sounds behind her and turned to see Sarah emptying her stomach onto the ground. Cassie sympathized with her. David looked very disturbed, clearly averting his eyes from the battle scene. The animals were looking around, apparently unaffected.

Kai came over to her, his coat flecked with blood. *I do not smell others, but we must be cautious. There could be others I cannot sense because of all the blood.* Cassie nodded acknowledgment.

She walked over to Sarah and put a hand on her back. "Are you okay?" she asked gently.

Sarah looked at her with glassy eyes. "I don't know. This," she gestured to the bodies on the ground, "this is just wrong."

"They chose it," David said. "Don't blame yourself for their choices, sister. It'll just tear you apart." He had a look of infinite sadness on his face, as if this was the thousandth time he'd seen battle.

Cassie smiled faintly at him. "You sound like Dad," she said quietly.

He met her eyes. "We should bury them. It would be disgraceful to just leave them here. Not to mention they'd give the next hikers to come across them a heart attack."

Cassie nodded. "Yeah, but I'm not sure–" Her words were cut short by a faint cry from one of the tents. Her knives were out in an instant, as was David's sword. The dogs gathered in front of them, growling. Cassie and David advanced toward the tent. Sarah stayed where she was. She'd had enough blood and gore to last her for years. Maybe even her whole life.

As David and Cassie got close, Kai turned his head to them slightly. *Stay there, I will investigate*, he ordered tersely. He went into the tent, Dassah and Gracie staying outside. Cassie watched through Kai's eyes as he discovered that the tent's inhabitant was a boy, who looked a little older than her, sitting bound on a chair with what had likely been a gag around his neck. She relaxed and David looked at her inquiringly.

"Looks like my parents weren't the only prisoners," she told him in a low voice. "There's a boy in there with his hands tied behind his back."

David raised his eyebrows. "Wonder what he did to get himself captured," he mused, sheathing his sword.

"Maybe he's another Brenwyd," Cassie said, excitement flaring in her eyes. "Dad told me there are others." The two entered the tent with the other dogs and Smokey in tow.

The boy looked up as they entered, relief obvious on his face. "Oh, thank God you've come," he croaked hoarsely. "Those awful men were just going to leave me here to starve." He did look as if he'd had a rough time. His lips were chafed, likely from the gag, and he sounded as if he hadn't had water in a while. His black hair was tousled and he spoke with a British accent. It was hard to tell much more about him because of the tent's poor lighting, but Cassie could see he did not have pointed ears. Still, that didn't mean he wasn't part Brenwyd. Kai stood before him, his teeth half-bared.

What do you think? Cassie asked the dog silently.

I think he is not a threat at the moment, but something about him bothers me, the dog replied. *I do not know what.* He stared so intently at the boy that he started to squirm a little. *He is not part Brenwyd,* Kai decided. *He is all human.*

Cassie felt a little disappointed, but she shrugged it off. *Is it alright to help him?*

Of course. Just be mindful of what you say and do around him. Kai backed away and sat down.

The boy gave the dog a wary glance before raising his eyes to meet Cassie's. "I tried to wriggle out of the bindings on my wrists, but they're too tight. I had just managed to get my gag off when I heard a huge commotion and decided to stay quiet. Then I heard voices outside that sounded friendly, so I called out. Then that dog came in. Is he yours?"

Cassie nodded and moved around to the back of the chair. She saw that he had very nearly succeeded in getting his bonds off, but his wrists were badly chafed by the rope. She used her knife to cut him free. He brought his arms in front of him slowly, flexing them to get his circulation moving again. "Thank you," he said, smiling at her.

"You're welcome," she replied.

David moved to stand in front of the boy. "How were you captured?" he inquired.

The boy's smile vanished. "Oh, I wasn't captured," he replied. "I came with the men to help them. But when I learned what they were about, I tried to escape and warn their targets. Unfortunately, I was found out and placed under guard." Cassie and David exchanged glances.

"Did you? That's... thoughtful of you," Cassie said. "Let's go outside. Sarah's waiting."

"Sarah?" the boy asked, standing.

"My sister," David answered. The boy nodded and they walked outside. Cassie studied him. He walked with a natural grace and confidence, apparently perfectly at ease. He seemed to be what he had told them (at least, he hadn't pulled out a hidden dagger and stabbed her – yet). But something told her he was hiding something – something that could prove disastrous for her and the twins. Sarah had gone to the edge of the camp, likely to escape the sight of blood and dead men.

The boy stopped for a minute to take it in. "You did this?" he asked, sounding surprised. David nodded. "You must have been taught well," the boy observed, turning a little to look at Cassie. "Brotherhood men are very well-trained. It takes an above-average swordsman – or swordswoman – to take them down."

"I guess we got lucky then," Cassie said.

"You do not just 'get lucky' with the Brotherhood," the boy said. "You must be extremely skilled." He sounded admiring. Cassie shrugged, closely examining his face now that it was in better light. He was definitely good-looking, with strong, Romanesque facial features and eyes a deep shade of blue. She especially searched his eyes for hints of guile, but could find none, leaving her to conclude he was either an exceptional actor or telling the truth. The boy also, inexplicably, had a strange air of familiarity about him. Cassie didn't see how that could be, as she was positive she'd never seen him before. He certainly didn't act as if he knew her. She realized she was staring at him rather openly and quickly looked toward Sarah instead.

Sarah turned around as she heard them come up behind her, and she looked curiously at the stranger. "Who's this?" she asked, glancing at her brother.

"We found him tied up in one of the tents. Says the Brotherhood tied him up to prevent him from getting a warning out to their targets," David explained.

Sarah examined the boy more closely. "Really?" she asked him. He nodded. "What's your name?" she asked.

He smiled winningly at her. "My name is William Douglas, and yours is Sarah, if I'm not mistaken."

"You're not, but how did you know that?" Sarah asked a little warily.

"Your brother told me, but he did not give me his name, nor did your friend give me hers."

Sarah looked at them reproachfully. "You'll tell a complete stranger who I am but don't give him your own names? Shameful."

"It hadn't come up yet," Cassie answered her, then faced William. "My name is Cassie and that's David." She extended her hand to shake William's. He took it.

"Pleased to make your acquaintance. Uh, this is a little unrelated, but do you have a place to spend the night? Or were you planning to spend it here?"

"We hadn't thought about it, actually," Cassie replied. "We've just been getting our wits about us again... after..." Her voice trailed off.

William nodded understandingly, but looked at her intensely. "You've never killed before, have you?"

"No. It's not something I want to be in the habit of doing," Cassie said flatly and stared off into the trees. David looked at William keenly. It seemed odd to him that the Brotherhood would leave a prisoner behind, especially if – as William had hinted – he really had tried to get a warning to the Penningtons. He was a smooth talker and looked honest enough, but David wasn't ready to trust him yet, not until he was proven a friend beyond a shadow of a doubt. He also didn't like how the guy was looking so intently at Cassie.

"If we're gonna bury those... bodies, we should do it quick. Otherwise we'll have to do it in the dark or wait till morning, and I don't want to do either," Sarah declared. "Anybody got a shovel?"

William looked at her with surprise. "You're going to bury them?"

She nodded. "Of course. They may have been rotten to the core, but they are people and deserve to be buried. Also, one of the number one rules in the wilderness is to clean up after yourself. Though I don't think the people who made that rule were thinking of... bodies."

"Sarah's right," Cassie said. "Let's get a move on." The teens found a shovel in one of the tents. The boys and dogs started digging while Cassie and the horses moved the men toward them. Sarah had excused herself on account of a queasy stomach, and was exploring the rest of the camp with Smokey. They managed to get the men in the ground by last light, then decided to stay the night in the camp, since it was obvious by that point that no one else was there. Besides, they didn't want to risk getting lost in the mountains at night. They built a fire in the middle of the camp, and Cassie lit it with matches she had in her bag. Everyone watched silently as the flames spread hungrily from log to log, making a fire reminiscent of the one Cassie and the twins had made just yesterday, though it seemed like years ago in another life. David studied William in the firelight. He'd helped willingly enough with the shovel, but his gaze had kept straying to Cassie throughout. Once, David had thought he'd caught a look of eagerness on William's face that he hadn't liked, but it was gone so quickly that he wondered if he'd seen it at all. He hadn't liked all the other looks William had given her, either. It gave him a strange feeling inside, one he couldn't identify, but he decided William had no right to be giving Cassie that much attention, no matter how pretty she was.

Sarah broke his train of thought by speaking to William. "So, William, why were you left after everyone else went off in the plane? I would think that the Brotherhood would take all their prisoners with them." She gazed at him intently, eyes serious. Cassie shifted her gaze from the fire to William, and the animals also moved their heads so they could see the strange boy.

He leaned forward slightly in preparation to speak. When he did, he directed his speech at Cassie. "You can take your headband off. I know of Brenwyds and their attributes, and what the Brotherhood intended to do here." Cassie narrowed her eyes slightly, but kept her thoughts to herself as she slipped the headband off her ears, figuring there was no point in pretending now. William stared at her pointed ears, wonder on his face.

Cassie fidgeted under his gaze. She'd developed a self-consciousness about her looks, not liking the attention they attracted, and disliked such open scrutiny. "Your story?" she requested.

He cleared his throat and stared into the fire, the flames reflecting in his blue eyes. "Right. Well, you see, I have no family because my parents died when I was quite small. I was put into the foster system, but no family wanted me for long, and all the foster homes I was put in were horrible, so I kept running away. The last time, a few years ago, I stumbled upon a Brotherhood outpost. I overheard several of them talking, and they mentioned King Arthur. I've always been interested in the King Arthur legend, so I listened. I didn't understand much of what they were saying, but they caught me and took me to their commander. He questioned me, and I told him all he asked. Something I said must have pleased him, because he didn't have me killed or sent back to my foster home. They kept me there, and he told me what he called the 'real story' of King Arthur.

"After a few weeks of telling me their group's philosophies, he asked me if I would like to join. I had been completely taken in by him and agreed eagerly, to my regret. He then told me of their goal: to eliminate an evil race who served as servants of Satan on earth and practiced all kinds of magic. His words, not mine." At this, Cassie stifled a noise of objection. She noticed David glowering at the description of Brenwyds as seen by the Brotherhood. Sarah looked indignant. "I was, of course, shocked at hearing of the existence of Brenwyds. He then gave me a history of the Brenwyds, though now I very much doubt the version he gave me is true. Nevertheless, I believed him and entered training to become a full member of the Brotherhood. I felt like I had finally found a home.

"About a month ago, the Commander who had taken me in asked me if I'd like to go with him on a mission of the highest importance. I immediately agreed, wanting to prove my worth. I didn't know at the time what the mission entailed. The Commander gave the impression that it was taking down a particularly powerful," he paused, glancing at Cassie, "Brenwyd, one who was a severe threat to Christianity." Cassie suspected he'd been about to say "witch," and was grateful he had changed the reference, but then she focused on the last part of his sentence.

"Wait, what?" she said, her brow wrinkling in bafflement. "The Brotherhood thinks I'm a severe threat to Christianity? Why on earth?"

"Because you're such a strong Brenwyd," William answered. "The Brotherhood thinks that all Brenwyds are a threat to Christianity."

Cassie raised her eyebrows in astonished disbelief. She had always wondered how the Brotherhood had justified their actions, but this... "So the Brotherhood claims to be Christian, then?" William nodded. "I find that rather hard to believe, since they just kidnapped my parents and happily kill innocent people."

William paused for a moment before continuing, apparently gathering his thoughts. No emotion was evident on his face. "Well, I agree with you there. Anyway, we arrived in the States two weeks ago, and it was after we got here that I learned we were really after a family with a thirteen-year-old girl who had committed no crimes, and her father who had no Brenwyd powers to speak of. Well, despite what I had been told about Brenwyds, my conscience was horrified by the idea of killing someone so young – I don't know what came over me, really, but I just felt deep down that what they were proposing to do was wrong. So I went to the Commander to tell him of my concerns. He listened to me politely, and then explained that capturing the Pennington family was necessary because they had the potential to become major obstacles to the Brotherhood and must be removed. I pretended to completely understand and go along with this reasoning. But inside I decided to go find the Penningtons and warn them of their impending danger, because my instincts told me this was wrong, and one of the first things I learned in the Brotherhood was to trust my instincts. Unfortunately, the Commander anticipated me and had some of the other men catch me when I tried to leave. They brought me before him, and this time he was not at all polite. He shouted at me. I have never seen a man so enraged. He then had me tied to that chair and placed under guard. He made a point of showing Mr. and Mrs. Pennington to me, and sneered that I had been able to do nothing. He then told me that I could regain my position if I helped track down the girl – that is, you, Cassie. I refused, and so he condemned me to stay behind anyway. He left me to Raymond, the leader of those left behind, and told him to do whatever he liked with me."

William's gaze shifted from the fire to Cassie, a convincingly grateful expression on his face. "Your appearance saved me a beating at his hands, and then you killed him and his men, saving my life. I'm eternally grateful to you, and I'll help you in any way possible. I can tell you where they're taking your parents and I can help you recover them. But if you decide not to trust me, I'll understand. I wouldn't trust me, either, were I in your shoes." William felt pleased with himself. His story was believable, and was mixed with enough truth to give it an authentic ring. The last bit about giving them the choice to trust him or not made him appear all the more genuine, and he'd also reminded the girl what he could do for her. She seemed to be deep in thought. That big brown dog, apparently called Kai, had come up beside her and the two appeared to be having a silent conference. William had read in the old records that some Brenwyds held power over animals, and it appeared that this girl had that particular power. The boy, David, studied him carefully. William had a feeling he'd have to careful around him, as David suspected that William was not who he said he was and William had noticed he seemed highly protective of Cassie. That left Sarah. She appeared to be the most trusting of the trio. The way her big, soft, hazel eyes gazed trustingly yet warily at him made him feel slightly guilty about lying to her, but he paid no attention to the feeling. His father had told him time and time again that emotions were fickle things, and that listening to them only got you in trouble.

David moved to sit next to Cassie. He wanted to hear her take on William's story. It seemed true, but the way William had looked at Cassie at the end made him nervous. It was almost as if he were challenging her to believe his story at her own risk. Cassie glanced at David as he settled himself next to her. "What do you think?" she asked quietly so William couldn't hear.

"I think his story could be true," David replied in the same low tone, "but there's something wrong I can't put a finger on, like he's hiding something. However, he could be a big help. If I were you, I would bring him along, but watch him carefully. Your call."

"I agree with you, and so does Kai. I think we might be able to help him with whatever he's hiding. Not to mention that saying about keeping your friends close, but your enemies closer. If he is dangerous, I'd rather have him where I can watch him than have no idea where he is."

"Agreed," David said. "Besides, whether he's telling the truth or not, he probably wouldn't survive out here on his own for long, so it'd be cruel to leave him." Cassie nodded.

Sarah came over. "So what are we going to do?" she asked.

"Bring him with us, but watch him," her brother answered.

"You think he's lying?"

"Maybe. What do you think?"

"Well, the fact that he was found in the enemy camp and was a member counts against him, but his story sounds true. Besides, what are the odds those men actually thought we could beat them and so came up with a back-up plan?" David and Cassie absorbed this view and found it feasible, but their suspicions remained.

Cassie looked across the fire and met William's eyes. "If you're still wondering, I'm most definitely *not* a witch. No Brenwyd is. We're hunted by the Brotherhood because *they* are the ones who want Christianity removed from the earth... and exterminating Brenwyds is a part of that, for a reason that I honestly don't know."

William looked genuinely surprised. "You don't say? That's certainly opposite from what I was told."

"I'm not surprised. The Brotherhood probably says that to attract followers. I happen to be a Christian; so are my parents, and so are those two." She indicated David and Sarah. "Destroying Christianity is something I would never do under any circumstances."

William gave her a look, and a corner of his mouth twitched up in a half-smile. "I get the feeling that you're telling me this to reassure me about yourself."

Cassie smiled a little and nodded. "I don't imagine that all the Brotherhood doctrine just disappeared out of your head as if it had never been there. You've given us reassurances as to your character. It's only right I give you some as to mine. And having said that, we are not going to drive you away, but..." She paused and fixed him with her gaze. "You have to help me rescue my parents."

He nodded. "Of course. And thank you. It's nice to know that my instincts were correct. But then, how do *I* know *you're* telling the truth?" he challenged.

"You don't," Cassie replied simply. "We both have to trust each other on that score."

William smiled fully. "With that answer, I think you are being truthful." He shifted. "If you want to rescue your parents, I would suggest going back to where you live first. We're going to need at least one adult to get where we need to go. Would one of your parents be willing to help us?" he asked, directing the inquiry at the twins. They looked at each other and groaned.

"You didn't tell them you were coming after me, did you?" Cassie asked, sounding amused. "I had wondered how you convinced them to let you follow me."

"Not exactly," David said, grimacing at the thought of what his father would say when they got home.

"He means not at all. In fact, he tried to leave me behind," Sarah supplied. "I left a note, but they will *not* be pleased."

Cassie chuckled at the dismay in their voices. "Well, it can't be helped. Let's get some sleep. Oh," she said as she thought of something and turned to William. "I don't suppose there's an extra horse hidden away around here, is there?" she asked.

He shook his head. "No. They all went on the plane. I can walk. I enjoy running. You just can't go at top speed."

"Okay. We'll take turns riding and walking." She thought for a moment. "So if it took us roughly a full day and night to get here

"We are not going to drive you away, but..."
Cassie paused and fixed William with her gaze.
"You have to help me rescue my parents."

with everyone mounted... it should take us two to three days to get back."

At that, everyone made themselves comfortable on the ground by the fire. No one felt like sleeping in the tents. Cassie stared up at the sky and listened to her companions breathing. She felt like she was wandering through a pitch-dark forest with only one way out, but kept going in circles because she couldn't see the path that otherwise would have been clear. Tears started coursing down her cheeks as she thought about what might have happened that day and what she had lost. Kai and Dassah nestled against her sides and Smokey curled up by her head. Twi stood over her. *We are here for you, girl. And He is here, too, and He will never leave you.* Cassie felt peace come and smiled, then quickly fell asleep.

Looking for Secrets

"So we went to sleep that night, and started heading back here the next morning. We had to go slower because we had three horses and four people, plus the rain, but it was uneventful. Unlike last week." Cassie finished telling Ben and Hannah the story of their journey and silence descended upon the Thompsons' living room. The adults were thinking about what Cassie (with interjections from the others) had just told them. David and Sarah were watching their parents' faces closely, hoping they wouldn't be in too much trouble. Cassie shifted her gaze to look out the window, where she saw the horses grazing in the field. William was considering all that had happened since he'd joined Cassie and the twins, feeling extremely puzzled over much of their behavior.

When they'd ridden into the yard, all of them, animals included, had been dead tired. Hannah had come running out to meet them, demanding to know if they were alright. Once they had reassured her that they were, they had taken care of the horses and staggered into the house. Hannah had accepted William's presence without much question, and had made them all go take showers and put on clean clothes, orders they had gratefully obeyed. She hadn't asked any of the obvious questions or scolded them, saying it could wait until Ben got home from UVA, where he was clearing things up with the university regarding Ty's sudden disappearance, and told them all to take naps. Hannah had told Cassie that, so far, everyone was buying the story that her family had been called away suddenly for personal reasons and weren't sure when they would return. Even though there were no classes, Ty often gave tours of the college to prospective students and helped run summer programs the school offered. Cassie had nodded, looking relieved. William had guessed that she had started worrying about that on top of everything else going on.

Cassie completely and utterly baffled him. He had been taught that Brenwyds were masters of black magic and filled with evil. They weren't even considered human by the Brotherhood, being, instead, descendants of fallen angels working for the devil on earth, assisting him to take over all mankind. That's why the Brotherhood had been formed, to counteract that evil and purge it from the earth. At least, that was what William had always been told. But the way Cassie acted seemed to dismiss all those ideas, not to mention her casual reversal of Brotherhood and Brenwyd roles around the campfire. He could tell she had told the truth, or at least she believed she had been telling him the truth. The way she had so readily admitted that he had no proof he could really trust her had surprised him as well. He had thought she would provide all kinds of explanations as to why he should trust her. Never once had he heard her complain on the trip home, even though it had rained and none of them had had rain gear. She'd interacted playfully with her friends and had been friendly to him, though with some reserve, for which he didn't blame her. It's how he would have behaved in her position. Actually, he would have acted with extreme coldness toward anyone he wasn't sure could be trusted. She apparently believed what he'd told them about breaking from the Brotherhood, although William had caught her looking thoughtfully at him several times, as if evaluating his honesty and sincerity. Her eyes had never completely lost some vestige of grief, even when she smiled.

David had remained aloof, talking with him in a friendly enough manner but answering almost zero questions about his life, and William knew he was very suspicious of him. He needed to be careful around him.

Sarah had been the most forthcoming, appearing to genuinely like and trust William. She was curious about where he came from, and asked him many questions. She, in turn, had answered some questions he asked of her as he tried to form a more complete picture of Cassie. The information he had garnered from her deepened his puzzlement about the Brenwyd girl. Apparently, Cassie was well liked by their community and enjoyed helping people and animals alike. She did extremely well in school, and the only thing people thought really peculiar about her was the headband she wore all the time, though none realized it was to conceal her ears. Sarah had hinted that Cassie had suffered from bullying, but hadn't elaborated on the subject.

In short, the more William had learned about Cassie, the more she seemed completely contrary to what he'd always been taught, and the more she mystified him. He decided he needed to learn more about her, preferably from someone not as close to her. He knew that there was a Brotherhood informant in the area. He would have to ask his father who it was so he could contact the person and ask about the Pennington family.

Ben broke the silence. "So did it ever occur to you three that some adult help would be a benefit?"

His tone was stern, and Cassie thought it also sounded hurt. He was looking right at her, so she answered. "Mr. Thompson, believe me when I say I just didn't want to put anyone else in danger. Also, the time it would have taken to explain to you fully what had happened and then convince you to let me go would've been time lost in getting on the trail. The faster I went after them, the better chance I had of catching them. Although in hindsight, it wouldn't have really mattered. I still missed them." She stopped talking as a lump rose in her throat. She still couldn't believe how close she had come to rescuing her parents, only to lose them again. Dassah put her head in Cassie's lap to give comfort. Ben looked at her compassionately. He knew the logic behind her reasoning, and also knew he likely would have done the same thing at her age and in her situation, but he turned a disapproving frown in the direction of his two children.

"That explanation does not get you two out of trouble. Especially when I specifically told you not to go after Cassie right then. Did it occur to you that I may have been thinking of going after her in the morning?" Sarah's look told David he was taking this one. He supposed he had it coming, but his look to her said, *I'll get you later*. Sarah shrugged slightly. She was used to such things.

David met his father's glowering expression squarely, if not too confidently. "Well, no sir, I didn't think that. I thought you would say we had to wait until further contact to do anything, and not doing anything would drive me crazy. And I figured any kind of help is always welcome when pursuing dangerous people–"

"Funny, no one told me that," Cassie interrupted from her chair.

David glared at her. "Welcome by most people, I mean. I also knew that Cassie would have traveled pretty far already, and I needed all the time I could get to catch up to her. And I didn't ask Sarah to come with me. She followed me." He ended with his glare transferred to his sister.

"I went so you wouldn't get lost. Which you would have done if we'd followed your sense of direction. Besides, it would've been boring around here without you or Cassie around," Sarah said in defense.

"And I still don't remember asking you two to come after me!" Cassie interjected. "Although I do admit that your help was appreciated–" David smiled triumphantly at this "–I could've taken care of myself. You guys didn't have to put yourselves in danger. I don't know what I would've done if you had been captured or..." Cassie stopped, unable to utter the last word, though everyone knew what she'd been about to say.

Sarah got up and stood over her friend, looking down at her almost fiercely. "Cassie, the point is that you didn't make or ask us to go with you, so you couldn't've blamed yourself if either of those scenarios had happened. But neither did, so quit worrying about it. And you had to know we would come after you. You're our friend, Cass, and David and I don't care if you're a regular human or a part-Brenwyd or part-whatever. So stop saying that we should have stayed at home. If we had, we'd be pretty lousy friends. And Dad," she said, turning to her father, "please understand... that's why we went. We had to. I was already going to head out when I heard David pass my door. If you hadn't taken the initiative, David, I would've gone to your room and dragged you from bed." She finished her declaration and returned to her seat. Cassie felt stunned. She had thought that the revelation of her Brenwyd blood would cause her friends to drift away from her, at least for a little while. Who wanted to be friends with someone who put them in danger just by being in the same room? But it seemed that it had only bound them tighter to her. Cassie silently thanked God for giving her such loyal friends.

Ben and Hannah looked at each other. They reached a tacit agreement and Hannah spoke to the twins. "We understand how you felt and so we won't punish you. This time. But please don't do anything like this again without telling us first, and trust us to make good calls, alright?"

"Yes, ma'am," David and Sarah chorused, relieved to escape punishment.

Hannah turned to William, smiling. "Now, William," she said. "Do you have anyone in England you want us to contact? You must have someone outside the Brotherhood."

"Thank you for offering, Mrs. Thompson; however, I can contact the people I need to myself. But aren't you all going to go to England anyway in a few days? You did mention something about my guiding you to the Brotherhood headquarters, Cassie," William said, looking at her, knowing his ability to get Cassie to the Brotherhood depended on what she was about to say.

"I plan to go as soon as I can," Cassie said, looking at Mr. and Mrs. Thompson. "Please don't try to stop me. Dad told me about plans he has for this scenario, but I can't just leave them when there's a chance of getting them back." She pleaded with her eyes.

Mr. Thompson's brow creased in concern. "If you're firm on going, Cassie, I'll go with you, since your dad wants to make sure you'll be taken care of and safe. But I really don't think you should go. It would be very dangerous. And your dad is clever, you know – he, himself, may figure out a way for him and your mother to escape."

"That's highly unlikely, Mr. Thompson," William put in. "No one has ever escaped from Brotherhood headquarters. If they're going to get out, they'll have to have outside help." Inwardly, William was starting to feel anxious. If Mr. Thompson forbade Cassie from going to England, it would be much harder to get her into Brotherhood hands.

"See?" Cassie said. "I have to help them. I couldn't live with myself if I didn't try."

Ben sighed. "I know, Cassie, but I promised your dad I'd look after you if anything happened to him. I'll have to think about it, alright?" Cassie just looked at him. "And besides, even if we did go, it would take a few days for me to tie some things up here and get plane tickets."

Cassie nodded reluctantly. "Okay. I can live with that, for a few days, anyway." Inwardly, however, she wondered if she could. But there was something else on her mind that could occupy her while Mr. Thompson thought about the proposed venture. She turned her gaze to William, staring at him with her penetrating, twain-colored eyes. William felt as if she were staring into his mind, pulling information from it, trying to read his soul and discover his secrets. *It's Brenwyd witchcraft,* he thought. *That's why everyone else sees nothing wrong with her. She's bewitched them.* This assessment eased his mind and he stared back at her, undaunted. "I do have a couple of questions for you," she said. "Where are the Brotherhood taking my parents, and why did they capture them instead of kill them?"

William appeared to have been expecting the first question, though Cassie saw some surprise in his eyes at the bluntness of the second part. "Well, the first question is simple enough to answer, but the second requires more explanation, and I'm afraid I'm not able to answer it fully. Your parents will be taken to the Brotherhood headquarters outside Carlisle, in the county of Cumbria in northern England. As for the reason... well, as I told you already, supposedly your family is a big potential threat to the Brotherhood. Would you know anything that might explain that idea?"

"Um... I don't think so. Like I told you, we have no desire to end Christianity or whatever it is the Brotherhood thinks we want to do. We've just been trying to live normally and not attract Brotherhood attention," Cassie said after a moment's thought. She looked at her animals, frowning. "I don't suppose you lot have any idea as to what might give the Brotherhood that idea beyond the fact that we're Brenwyd?" she asked. *Like maybe what you didn't want to tell me the other night?* she added silently.

Yes, Kai said, making sure only Cassie could hear him. *But we will not tell you now with everyone here. Later, I promise.*

"Was there anything else, William? If the Brotherhood thinks my family's a potential threat, they wouldn't have wasted time capturing my parents when they could have just killed them. There has to be another reason," Cassie said aloud. She was starting to have a suspicion of what it might be, but she wanted to hear William's answer.

Cassie sounded so desperate that William couldn't help but feel a little sorry for her, though he quickly distanced himself from the feeling. He thought about how to answer her. There was something else he'd overheard his father and the Master discussing, and he didn't think it would do any harm to tell the girl. She might even be able to help him understand it. And if she could unwittingly lead him to what it was the Master wanted, all the better. "Well... there was something I overheard in a conversation between two higher-ups. Apparently, another thing some Brenwyds do is guard ancient, holy artifacts. The conversation I overheard seemed to suggest that your family knows the location of one that the Brotherhood wants, but doesn't know where to find."

"And Dad, being an archaeologist, might," Cassie said. It sounded like her theory was right. "That makes sense."

"What kind of artifacts?" David asked.

"Legendary ones," Cassie said. "Dad told me about this. Okay, so can you think of some supposedly powerful holy artifacts?"

"The Holy Grail?" Sarah offered.

Cassie nodded. "Alright, so I'll use the Holy Grail as an example. Lots of people know about it, how it supposedly is the cup Jesus drank from at the Last Supper, or perhaps it caught his blood on the cross, and as such became imbued with miraculous powers. I don't know if that's true or not, but the legend itself has gained strength over the centuries and still resonates with people today. If something like that were found by a nefarious person or persons like, say, the Brotherhood, they would try to use that power – or at least, the reputation of power that it gave them – to do bad things. Brenwyds guard such esteemed objects to make sure that doesn't happen. Make sense?" David and Sarah looked slightly confused.

"Your father explained this to me once, Cassie," Ben said, seeing the confused faces of his children. "The main thing is that since people have believed it's powerful, its cultural associations have given it power in society. So, it would be bad if said nefarious people got a hold of it."

"So the Grail has no power even though Jesus touched it and used it?" Sarah asked.

Cassie shrugged. "I don't know. It might. There is that story about the woman who was healed just by touching Jesus' robes, but he was wearing them at the time. My personal opinion? It's a cup. If it exists, it may have some sort of power, but I don't think any cup could pick up the amount of power attributed to the Grail, even if Jesus was the one who used it. I just used it as an example. And the cup itself might not even exist, or have existed at all, but something must have existed to prompt the legends about it. The Ark of the Covenant would probably make more sense, seeing as there are several Bible stories about its power, but do you get the basic point?"

David nodded. "So does your family guard an artifact?"

"Not that I know of," Cassie said slowly. "But I think I know what the Brotherhood's after. Dad has been working on something for the past few weeks that he's been suspiciously cagey about. It's entirely possible that he was working on finding the location of some artifact the Brotherhood wants, and they decided it would be easier to kidnap him to get the location than wait for him to actually find it himself. Although I have no clue how they would have found out about the project's existence, much less what it specifically contained. I couldn't find out what it was about, and I live in the same house. Not to mention he was writing his notes in Latin."

"Latin?" William asked.

"Insurance against snoops. Most people can't read a dead language fluently."

"Can you?"

Cassie chuckled. "Oh, yes. Dad made sure I learned Latin as soon as I had a good grasp of English. The consequences of having a historian specializing in the Middle Ages for a father."

"Oh." William wondered if she knew any other old languages. "So you have no idea what he was working on? Not one clue?"

Cassie shrugged. "The only clue he would give me was that it has to do with King Arthur. But that doesn't help much, in my opinion. About half of what he does has to do with King Arthur. He's determined to prove his existence to historians and the world at large. It was probably something along those lines, but I'm not sure exactly what." She became aware of the animals discussing something amongst themselves. She looked at them suspiciously. "I don't suppose any of you would happen to know what he was working on?"

Kai rose from his position lying at Cassie's feet, and sat upright. When he spoke, he addressed Cassie but made sure his words could be heard by all in the room so she wouldn't have to repeat. William's eyes widened as he finally heard the dog for himself, having only seen the animals converse silently with Cassie until now. *You are close, I think,* Kai said. *Your father was onto something. A big thing. I am not sure what, but it was something that could change the modern perception of King Arthur among the historical humans. It is possible the Brotherhood got wind of this and captured your parents to prevent it. The Brotherhood hates King Arthur for some reason, though he was a regular human.*

David looked puzzled. "Hang on, wouldn't Mr. Pennington need to prove Arthur's existence to begin with? No one knows for sure if he really existed or not. It's just as likely that he didn't exist as it is that he did."

"Uh, David?" Cassie said. "Remember all my dad's stories about King Arthur?"

"Yeah, but they're still just stories."

"No, they're not. They're what actually happened. King Arthur existed, reigned from about 495 to 516 A.D., and it was toward the end of his reign that the Brotherhood was formed and Brenwyds began to be persecuted."

"Really? But he liked the Brenwyds, didn't he?" Sarah asked.

Surprisingly, William answered the question. "He did, which is why the Brotherhood doesn't like him. He protected the Brenwyds while he was alive, so the Brotherhood couldn't really start moving until after his death."

"I thought you said that you joined the Brotherhood because of overhearing two members talking about King Arthur," Cassie commented.

"I didn't say they were talking charitably about him, did I?" he asked, meeting her eyes coolly. She shook her head.

"Okay," Ben said, getting the conversation back to what the dog had revealed, "but what Kai said still doesn't explain why they were captured instead of... killed. People who are captured can escape, and it could still get out."

At this, William laughed humorlessly. "Escape the Brotherhood? Mr. Thompson, as I said before, such a thing has never been done. They keep their headquarters locked tighter than a drum, and not even a fly goes in or out without notice."

David frowned at William. "Thank you for that estimate of the Pennington's chances, Captain Sunshine. We really needed to hear that. Now does it make sense that Mr. and Mrs. P. would be captured for something Mr. Pennington had been workin' on?"

"Is it hot in the Sahara?" William snapped back. "Many have been taken for doing less or nothing. It's one of the flaws of the organization."

Cassie sensed the tension rising. "Alright," she interjected before David could make a reply. "But there's another level to this. Capturing them for a project Dad's been working on doesn't really explain why–" she stopped abruptly.

"Doesn't explain why what?" Sarah asked.

Cassie sent an inquiring thought toward the animals. *Is it okay to tell them?* she asked, recalling something Smokey had overheard the night her parents had been taken.

Yes, Smokey replied with assent from the others. *It is important. And it might jar that boy into dropping something he should not.* Cassie cocked her head questioningly at the cat. *He is hiding something from you, girl. Watch your step around him. And his voice sounds familiar to me. He may have been there when your parents were captured.* Cassie stored the comment in her mind for later pondering. Smokey confirmed her own thoughts about William, but she couldn't think about that at the moment. Besides, Cassie reasoned that she could only be telling William what he pretty much already knew.

"It doesn't explain something Smokey overheard... that night." She paused as her mind tried to combine all the information she had gathered into a likely scenario.

"What did Smokey overhear?" Hannah asked, feeling concerned. It was unlike Cassie to not say something outright. She was generally blunt, and sometimes painfully so.

Cassie looked at the floor and stroked Dassah's head as she answered. "Smokey heard a man say that *I* was the main one their master wanted. And they clearly wanted to capture me, not kill me." Heavy silence descended upon the living room at that pronouncement. William looked at her sharply, wondering if she knew why the Brotherhood wanted her so badly. Sarah and David exchanged alarmed glances. Now they understood a little better why Cassie had been so concerned on the trail. Cassie continued to stare at the floor, trying to work out why she had been wanted in particular. The obvious answer was because of the strength of her Brenwyd blood, but something told her that there was another reason. Based on what she knew of the Brotherhood, they would have killed her straight out if that were the only reason.

"Well, William? Do you have any idea why Cassie would be especially wanted by your boss?" David asked. Cassie jumped a little at the suddenness of the question. She looked up.

"My *former* boss, David. And as to why she would be wanted especially..." William paused, a little unsure. He did know why Cassie was wanted, but he couldn't blurt that out. And he couldn't feign complete ignorance either. "It's likely because she... that is, you, Cassie... are such a strong part-Brenwyd. As far as I know, it's been a while since a part-Brenwyd who actually has pointed ears has existed."

Cassie frowned. "I know that. But something tells me there's some other reason." She stood abruptly, disturbing Dassah, who grumbled. Cassie ignored her and headed to the door, leaving the others staring in bewilderment.

"Um... Cassie? Where are you going?" David asked, already getting up to follow her.

She answered without turning. "My house. If I know Dad, he'll have left some trace of what he was working on in his office. Maybe we can find it and figure out what the Brotherhood was after." She amended herself after a reminder from Smokey. "That is, if they didn't take it."

The sound of approaching footsteps shook Ty out of his thoughts. He looked toward the door of the room in which he and Leah had been imprisoned, praying the footsteps would pass them by. Unfortunately, they stopped and Ty heard someone outside fumbling with keys. He put his hand on his wife's shoulder and shook her gently to wake her up. He still had trouble believing what had happened. He and Leah should be back in Virginia with Cassie, celebrating her birthday and doing the things they'd planned. Instead, they were prisoners of the Brotherhood, and Ty feared they would never get free. His only scrap of comfort was that Cassie had evaded capture, though for how long, he didn't know. As long as she stayed free, there was a chance of freedom for all of them... if that prophecy in the diary was true. Ever since he'd first read it four years ago, Ty had feared it might be true. Now it was his only hope. He smiled slightly at the irony. As he watched Leah sit up yawning, he felt an immense sense of failure that he hadn't been able to protect her from the Brotherhood. *She doesn't deserve this*, he thought.

Leah caught him looking at her and smiled, knowing what he was thinking. "Don't blame yourself," she said softly. "I'm the one who said yes, after all. I knew what I was getting into when I married you. And I don't regret any of it."

The door opened before Ty could respond. Ty recognized the man as the one in charge of the abduction. He didn't know the man's name, having only heard him referred to as "Commander." Now he was smiling as he looked at the captives, his black eyes cold. "You're in for a treat today," he said with the tone of a man who knows suffering is ahead and is glad for it. "The Master himself will be seeing you. Perhaps you'll be more talkative for him. Hurry up. He dislikes being kept waiting." The man shoved them out the door. Ty and Leah both experienced pangs of alarm as they shot glances at each other. *He* was here? What did he want? Yet in their hearts, they knew the answer. They walked down a long hallway, stopping before a room with a closed door. The Commander knocked, and a voice answered, "Come in. It's unlocked."

The Commander opened the door and shoved Ty and Leah inside. Leah nearly fell, but Ty caught her. As she steadied herself, she looked around the room curiously. Her first impression was that it was big and airy. There were large windows that let in plenty of sunlight, and through them Leah saw a forest and peaceful English countryside in the distance. Turning her attention to the rest of the room, she saw it was set up like a study, with built-in bookshelves along the walls as well as, she noted, suits of armor. One wall did not have bookcases and was covered by a huge tapestry, depicting a black boar standing over a red dragon as if in victory. There were also display cases holding almost every medieval weapon she could think of. Some looked like they had rust stains on them. Leah felt a chill go down her spine as she realized that what looked like rust was actually blood.

The Commander startled her by clearing his throat behind her. "Here are the prisoners, Master." A man Leah had not noticed before stood up from behind the desk and walked around it. Her first impression was that he was better-looking than she had thought he would be. He looked to be in his late forties, with streaks of gray showing in his light brown hair. His jaw was square, firm, and well-set. His eyes were light gray and betrayed no emotion as he stood surveying his prisoners. Ty noted he moved with no signs of stiffness and was built like a swordsman, with broad shoulders and a narrow waist.

The man walked in a circle around the couple. When he reached his starting point again, he was smiling satisfactorily. "Well, well, well, Professor Tyler Pennington. I have followed your exploits, although until recently I was not aware of your... shall we say... unique ancestry. It does explain much, though. And Mrs. Pennington," he said, meeting Leah's eyes, "what an honor to have you here with us as well. I apologize for the forcefulness of the invitation, but I couldn't have you refusing me now, could I?"

His voice was smooth and pleasant, but Ty heard the gloating concealed beneath it. He glared at the man. "What do you want with us?"

The man ignored the query. "But where are my manners? I know who you are, but you don't know my name. That is, I doubt you know my current one. My... traditional one, shall we say, you know quite well, but you can call me Morton." He paused. "And as for what I want, Professor... I believe you know that as well." He was still smiling, but it did not reach his eyes. They were as cold as the ice they resembled. "But I was extremely *disappointed*," he said, looking beyond Ty and Leah to glare at the Commander, "to hear that your lovely daughter has not come with you. The invitation was for your whole family."

The Commander accepted his superior's rebuke calmly. "As was I," he said. "However, she was absent from the house when we went to... ah, extend your invitation, and my *incompetent* subordinate was unable to locate her in time for our departure. I left him to capture and bring the girl. I'm sure she'll be here soon."

Morton raised his eyebrows. "Did you? Well, your 'incompetent' subordinate had better succeed," he said in a warning tone mixed with doubt.

"I'm quite sure he will, my lord. I left William with him to keep an eye on him." At that, Morton started to chuckle as if amused. Ty and Leah looked at each other, puzzled. Who was William?

"You left William to keep an eye on things? Excellent move, Commander. William is focused on our goal. He has a devious mind, that one. And the blow to the man's pride, being watched by a teenager! Yes, I'm sure he won't fail you now." Reminded of his prisoners, he regained himself. "Well done, Commander. This will be a true test for the boy."

"Thank you, sir," the Commander said, sounding pleased.

Morton returned his attention to Ty and Leah. "Your daughter is proving hard to catch, like the Brenwyds of old, but she'll be here soon enough. Once she's here, then things will really start happening. But in the meantime, Professor, I would like to talk to you about your project. It's an interesting one, to say the least. And I believe you are heading in the right direction. You understand that I could not have those artifacts come to light, and there is one in which I'm particularly interested. Yet I, myself, am not completely sure where they–"

"No." Ty said.

Morton met his gaze. "What was that?" he asked softly.

"No, I won't work for you. I know what you're after. And do not touch Cassie. You cannot have her." Ty's green eyes were hard, as was every line in his face.

His expression failed to intimidate Morton. "Really? Says who? The man who is my prisoner? Ha! You can't do anything to protect her. And as to your refusal to work with me... there are ways around that. I'm sure you would do anything to prevent harm from befalling your wife, wouldn't you?" Ty's expression turned harder and he put an arm around Leah's waist, holding her in a tight grip. She glared daggers at Morton as he looked her up and down suggestively. "But perhaps it won't come to that. I'll let you think about it. Commander, take them back to their room."

"Anything else?"

"Contact your son. I want a report on the girl."

"It will be done."

Ty and Leah were taken back to their room. They stood silently until footsteps could no longer be heard.

"What can we do, Ty?" Leah asked softly. Ty took her in his arms and hugged her hard.

"We can pray. It's all in God's hands. We'll get out of this. And if I know our daughter, she's not just going to let herself be captured. Not to mention any Brotherhood members would have to get past the animals first."

"Well, the place looks a whole lot better than it did, but we still haven't found a clue as to what your dad was workin' on, Cassie," Sarah said as she gazed around the library. The four teens had just finished reorganizing the whole thing with help from the twins' dad. It had taken about two hours, but the end product was very satisfying. All the books and papers had been picked up, sorted, and put away in such an organized fashion that Cassie remarked it looked even better than before the Brotherhood sacked it.

Sarah's comment brought a frustrated sigh from Cassie. "I know. The only other place I can think of that he'd leave research for something like that would be his office at the university. But if it's as important as we think it is, that's pretty unlikely. I guess the Brotherhood took it." She surveyed the room, trying to find the binder they had hoped the men had somehow missed.

William was examining the bookshelves, astonished by the number and variety of books in the room. "Your family is extremely well read," he said, taking a book off a shelf and leafing through it. "I don't think I've ever seen such a collection in a private home." He sounded slightly envious.

"You like to read?" David asked. William nodded.

Cassie looked at the book he'd picked up. "My dad wrote that," she said quietly.

He looked up, slightly startled. "Really?" he looked at the cover, and his eyes got big. "Professor Tyler Pennington. I didn't realize. I remember hearing about the big discovery of those tunnels in the hills of western England two years ago."

Cassie rolled her eyes. "Yeah, that was exciting," she muttered, remembering the events leading to that discovery.

William looked at her curiously, about to ask for more information, but Ben's entry into the room stalled any further conversation on the subject. "Did you find anything?" he asked.

"Nope," Cassie said. "I tried to see if I could find any references, but came up with zilch." She stared blankly at a gap between some books, wondering what to do next. "You don't think he'd have left a clue in his university office, do you?" she asked Mr. Thompson, knowing it was highly unlikely, but asking anyway.

Ben winced. "Actually, I got a call from the university the day after the abduction. Someone went through your father's office and ransacked it. They found it because one of the janitors heard noises coming from the office and went to investigate. Whoever did it must have had to leave in a hurry. The university wanted an inventory to see if anything had been taken, but the only person who knows exactly what all was in there is–"

"Dad," Cassie finished for him. She sighed in frustration. "I wish he wasn't so secretive. But who could have gotten into his office? He locks it whenever he goes home."

Ben sighed. "I didn't want to tell you, but... the initial investigation suggests that whoever did it had a key. There's no evidence that the lock was tampered with."

Cassie stared at him. "You mean someone at the university is working for the Brotherhood?"

"I don't know that, but it's possible. It's also possible that a Brotherhood agent stole a key from someone."

Cassie stared at the shelf in front of her. Was it really possible that someone they knew had betrayed them? And if so, who? "Do you know anything about it, William?" David asked.

William shook his head. "No. I wasn't of a rank to know such things." That was partially true. He knew that there was a Brotherhood mole somehow connected to the Penningtons, but he didn't know exactly who it was. His father had told him a name, but he couldn't remember it, only that the last name sounded like some sort of tree. But he wasn't about to reveal that little tidbit of information.

"Cassie, what *are* you doing?" Sarah asked. The two boys turned their attention to Cassie. She had taken several more books off the shelf and dropped them to the floor, and was now feeling the back of the shelf as if she was looking for something. "You do remember that we just organized that." Sarah sounded slightly reproachful, and Cassie smiled at her friend.

"I thought I saw something... here it is." Her searching fingers had found a slight protrusion in the wood. She pressed it – and got whacked in the head by a section of the shelf above that dropped. "Ow!" she exclaimed, rubbing her forehead. The others stared in astonishment at the small, boxlike compartment that had swung down. It was now lying at an angle to the shelf above, connected by two well-hidden hinges. Cassie realized just then the reason why the shelves were so thick.

"Now that's pretty cool," David said, walking to the shelf. "Did you know about this?"

Cassie sighed. "Yes, David, I deliberately let myself get hit in the head by a dropping shelf." She paused. "Of course I didn't!"

David smiled a little at her droll tone. "Okay, dumb question. Sorry."

She grinned at him. "It's okay. I'm more interested in seeing what's in this mysterious shelf than worrying about dumb questions."

David made an exaggerated bow. "Then be my guest," he said in a grand tone. Cassie rolled her eyes with a smile and saw Sarah doing the same, though her expression looked a bit more like she was embarrassed to be related to David. The others gathered around the spot as Cassie lifted a binder stuffed with paper out of the compartment. Her heart rose. It was the binder she'd been looking for. Dad must have had just enough time to put it back in the secret shelf compartment before the first of the attackers burst into the house. She held her breath in excitement as she opened it. Now they were getting somewhere.

"Well?" a chorus of voices asked. David, Sarah, and William looked at each other in surprise, having all spoken at the same time. Cassie and Ben chuckled.

"Give me a moment," Cassie answered. "Like I said, it's written in Latin. Give me some time to translate. It is the binder he's been working in." She examined it more carefully. "Actually, he uses this binder for any and all research he's doing related to digs. That's why it's so big." She scanned the opening lines and frowned.

"What?" Ben asked.

Cassie sighed. "His current project is in here, but it's not the only thing. Like I said, this is basically a complete record of all his digs, discoveries, and projects. It'll take me a bit to find the right section and translate it. Maybe it's just as well we can't leave right away. Before we go over there, I'd like to know what it is the Brotherhood wants so badly that they kidnapped my parents for it."

"And then what?" William asked.

Cassie raised her eyebrows. "What do you mean?"

"Well, when you find out what your father was working on, what will you do about it?" He gazed deep into her eyes. "If you want to free your parents, we'll have to move fast. There won't be time for a lengthy archaeological dig."

Cassie nodded. "I know. My first priority is to get my parents out. That trumps everything else. As to what to do with this," she hefted the binder, "I'll figure that out after I find out what my dad was working on. Knowing that will probably help us."

William glanced fleetingly at Mr. Thompson. "Sounds like we're definitely going, then."

"I'm still thinking about it," Mr. Thompson said, looking at Cassie. "I would have an awfully hard time explaining things to your father if anything went wrong."

"But if they went right, you wouldn't have to explain at all," Cassie said in her most persuasive tone.

Mr. Thompson sighed. "Cassie, I need you to give me at least a day, alright?"

Cassie nodded. "Very well." She looked at William. "Are you sure you're okay with guiding us if we get permission? It'll be dangerous for you to go back there."

William was surprised by the concern in her voice. "Not as much as it would be for you if you went without a guide. I know all the ins and outs of the place. One of the first things I learned. And helping you out *was* part of the deal for letting me come with you." He tried to sound as genuine and convincing as he could. Kai looked at the boy suspiciously, sensing that there was more to this offer than met the eye.

Dassah, who had come in from outside at the beginning of the conversation, sensed it as well. She tugged gently on Cassie's shirt to get her attention. *Careful, girl*, she warned.

"Hey, I'd go on this expedition, too," David said. "Don't even try to leave me behind, Cass." Sarah also declared her desire to go.

The four teens looked back at Mr. Thompson. He looked upward. "It's hard to say no to you all, but I'm going to reserve judgment until Cassie gets those notes translated, and nothing will change my mind about that," he said firmly in a tone that brooked no discussion. The teens nodded acceptance.

"So now that we've got all that straightened out," Sarah said, "let's go back home. Mom's probably got dinner ready by now."

"Good. Doing all this cleaning makes a person hungry," David said, rubbing his stomach.

"Great. I'm famished," William said at the exact same time. The two boys stared at each other as Cassie and Sarah burst out laughing.

"Well, since we've established that," Ben said, chuckling, "let's go eat before dinner gets cold."

A Sermon on Grace

David watched Cassie with the horses. She was sitting on Twi's back, leaning forward onto the mare's neck and likely having a conversation with the small herd. What really caught his attention was the peaceful expression on her face. A bystander observing her would never have guessed that her life had just been turned upside down by an ancient organization. The thought reminded him of the reason he'd come outside. William was inside, talking with Sarah. David had already confided his concerns about the British boy to her, and she'd promised to be on the lookout for anything suspicious from him. However, David wanted to talk to Cassie about William. If he'd met him under different circumstances, he would have really liked the guy. But the mystery surrounding him prevented David from trusting him, and he wanted to know what Cassie thought now, after spending several days with him. She looked up just then and saw David at the fence. Twi headed in David's direction, no doubt responding to a mental command from her rider. The way the setting sun caught Cassie's hair made it seem to be on fire, and the fading daylight clearly outlined the slight points on her ears as well. David was still having a hard time adjusting to that. Sure, Cassie had always been unusual. It was part of what made her Cassie. But now David felt as if he barely knew his friend. He knew in his head that it wasn't true, but it still made him feel a little uncomfortable in her presence.

"What's up?" Cassie's voice interrupted his thoughts. "You look like you've got a lot on your mind."

"Yeah, I do. It's about William."

"What about him?"

"What do you think of him? He's been with us several days now."

She considered his question. "I think he's feeling a little lost. And I still think he's hiding something. But he's very pleasant, and has a sense of humor, even if it is a little stiff. If I'd met him anywhere else under any other circumstances, I'd like him. He seems to be who he says he is."

David nodded at her answer. "Those are pretty much my thoughts. But what do you mean by him feeling a little lost? He seems pretty confident to me."

"You haven't noticed? Several times I've seen him with a confused expression on his face, mostly when he's been looking at me. I think it's because the Brotherhood paints Brenwyds as being devil spawn, and now he's learning that isn't the case. At least," she said with a wry smile, "I hope he is."

David chuckled. "I'm sure he is. But seriously," the smile slipped from his face, "what do you think he's hiding? If we let him be our guide, he could lead us into a trap."

"I've thought of that. In fact, one of my theories about him is that he may have been left behind on purpose to do just that."

"Then why are you considering going to England with the guy? He's already told us where they're centered. We could go there ourselves."

"No, we can't. We have no idea where in Carlisle this headquarters is. And who knows? It's completely possible he's telling the truth. But even if he is a plant, what are we gonna do with him? Imprison him in your basement for eternity?" David harrumphed at that statement. "The point is, we kinda need him. And I think he needs us."

"Why would he need us?"

"To show him the truth. This is a great opportunity, David. We can learn some of how the Brotherhood operates, and at the same time show William that the Brotherhood has Brenwyds all wrong. If he is a fake, maybe we can help him become who he says he is."

David thought about it. He hadn't thought about it that way before. It was possible, he supposed. After all, Cassie could be very convincing. "The way you can see the best in people and put up with them amazes me," he said.

She shrugged. "I learned early that people don't always behave well. I was different even before my ears became pointed. But if I didn't go around believing the best about people, I don't think I'd be a very nice person." She paused. "I know why people feel wary around me. They're jealous, don't understand, or just aren't sure how to act around me. That's why I got bullied when I was younger and still do a bit. I know that all people have at least some good characteristics, so I try to remember the Golden Rule."

"All people? Even Bob Mallory?"

Cassie chuckled, but blushed a little. "Even him. He had his reasons, David. Did you know that his father would beat him when he got bad grades? That's why he cheated, and why I became his personal target. The way I apparently just made good grades without effort infuriated him."

David blinked. "Really? I didn't know that. How did you find that out?"

"The day I decked him, I noticed welts peeking out from under the back of his shirt. I investigated the cause. I hope he's alright now, wherever he is." David thought about her words. They were very typical of Cassie. "But anyway, I'd rather be positive and try to see the best in people than be negative and only see the worst. And that goes for William," she finished.

"I'm not trying to be negative. I'm being cautious. You can't trust him completely, not yet."

"I never said I did. I know better than that." She cast a look over him. "Do you have a personal grudge against him or something?"

David frowned up at her. Her voice betrayed some amusement, though it didn't show on her face. He climbed to the top rail so he was on her level. "Why would I have a grudge against him? I just met the guy. But if he's lying, I definitely have a grudge against him."

"I thought it might be because he seems intent on seeking out your sister." Cassie nodded toward the house.

David blinked at that suggestion. It was one thing that hadn't crossed his mind when he thought about the British boy. "Sarah's fine. He probably just thinks she's the best one to pump for information. It's you I'm most worried about." Cassie raised her eyebrows in inquiry. "You've lost your parents, there's a guy in my house we're not sure can be trusted, and you can't really do anything about either at the moment. I know how you hate feeling helpless."

Her expression grew distant. "Believe me, I know. I've really been trying to distract myself out here. This is not exactly a promising start to my fifteenth year of life." She gave him a pained smile.

David smiled back at her half-hearted attempt at humor. The mention of her recent birthday reminded him of something he'd forgotten to do. He jumped down from the fence rail. "Come with me, Cass. I need to show you something."

She dismounted, curious. "What?"

"You'll see." He led her into the house, past the living room, up the stairs, and to his room.

She stopped at the entrance and looked around. "Do you ever clean this place?" she asked. It was the same question she asked whenever she had the occasion to go to David's room.

"When forced. There is a method to my madness, you know," David said in his typical answer. It certainly seemed like madness to

Cassie, who examined the room more closely and shook her head. How anyone found something in here was beyond her. The fact that the room was on the small side didn't help matters. Clothes were congregated in haphazard piles near the closet, the desk had papers scattered all over it, and the bedcovers, while pulled up, were rumpled and added to the general aura of untidiness. However, the mess seemed to be no problem for David. It could be neater, he admitted to himself as he crossed the room to his closet, but he could find his way around, and right now he knew exactly where to find the item he wanted.

"Okay, Cass. Close your eyes for a minute." She complied, keeping the obvious questions to herself. She heard him take something down from a shelf and come back to the door. "You can open your eyes now." She did and gasped. David was standing next to a guitar case – a very nice one, way more durable than the one she had. David smiled at her reaction. "Happy belated birthday, Cassie. Sorry it's not wrapped. We couldn't figure out how."

"That's alright. How did you get it?" she asked, taking it.

"I helped," Sarah's voice said from the hall. "We each contributed from our allowances, and your dad knew which one you'd like. We knew you needed a new case. Your old one's not so great." Cassie nodded, examining it from every angle.

"So you like it?" David asked.

"I love it! Thanks, guys." She hugged each in turn.

"It was David's idea. He noticed your old case was falling apart." Sarah smiled to see Cassie so upbeat.

"Well, I'm going to go switch out the cases. Then I think I'll play some." Cassie started down the hall, then turned. "You guys comin'?"

"In a minute," Sarah replied. Cassie went down the stairs and Sarah turned a knowing gaze on her brother, her hazel eyes dancing. "I'd say that was received well."

"Yep. It was a good idea."

"Thanks *so* much for letting me know you were going to give it to her. I wouldn't have wanted to miss that, especially considering it's somewhat of a joint present." The sarcasm in her voice was obvious.

David rolled his eyes. "You seemed busy."

"Nah, I think you wanted the pleasure of giving her something by yourself. *You* like her."

David felt some heat come into his cheeks. "Of course I like her. Why else would I be friends with her?"

"That's not what I meant, and you know it." Now Sarah sounded amused.

David decided to end the conversation quickly. "That's nonsense, Sarah. But speaking of that subject, what's with you and William?" Now that Cassie had raised the idea, he was curious.

Now Sarah rolled *her* eyes. "Nothing, brother dear. I am merely trying to find out if he's genuine or not, and the best way to do that is to talk to him. If he's fake, he'll trip up on himself eventually. You should try it."

David grunted and went to follow Cassie down the stairs. "Coming?" he asked his sister. He didn't turn around, and so he didn't see the big grin on her face. He'd just confirmed her suspicions. She'd seen him blush. But she wouldn't let him know that. Not in a million years.

"And that brings me to the topic I'm preaching on today – grace." Pastor Peter Shelby looked over his congregation as he opened the sermon, his brown eyes evaluating the mood of the people seated before him. All looked attentive, which was good. The sanctuary chairs were about half full, reflecting the summer schedules of church attendees. Despite the sizeable area of the sanctuary, the pastor's voice was still easily audible in the balcony area near the steepled roof, thanks to the small microphone clipped to Pete's shirt and the small, nondescript speakers located throughout the room just below the wood trim at the top of the walls. "Before I start, I want to say that I was going to preach on a different topic today. But a few days ago God spoke to me and said I should speak on His saving grace today. I think He did this because there is someone out there today who needs to hear it. And I think even those of us who have been followers of Christ for a long time need a reminder of how we are saved, and just how amazing it is that we are.

"So, please open your Bibles to Acts 15:11." He waited for the rustling of pages to subside before reading the verse. "'We believe it is through the grace of our Lord Jesus Christ that we are saved.' This verse reminds us that we are saved not by good works, but by grace. Grace is God's forgiveness, which He gives us freely because He loves us. A common misconception of salvation is that it is because a person does good deeds that they get into heaven. That is not true. A person can live as a saint and still go to hell if they never accept God's free gift of grace – if they depend on their good works instead of believing in their hearts and confessing with their mouths that they are saved through Jesus' death on the cross. But good works alone do *not* get you to heaven, even if people expect them of us as Christians.

"You might wonder why someone wouldn't accept a free gift. It's because we, as humans, like to do things for ourselves. We don't like accepting help. We like to do things our own way, even if it's the hard way. God knows this. He's the one who gave us the free will to choose to take the hard way. He also knows that, no matter how hard we try, we can never get to heaven by ourselves because our sin and imperfection get in the way. So He sent Jesus, the only human without sin ever to walk this planet. He sent Him to die so that the barrier of sin, which separates us from God, could be removed. Jesus' death allowed God's grace to come to earth and be given to those who believed.

"Grace is God's forgiveness, but it is also His influence on us. Grace is a gift we don't deserve, the gift of salvation, but God gives it anyway, withholding what we do deserve because He is merciful. When we accept Jesus as Savior, grace washes away our sins – but it also begins working to change us from the inside." Pastor Shelby paused. He saw many people taking notes. Before he started talking again, he noticed the Thompson family sitting in the back. He also saw Cassie Pennington sitting beside Sarah, her eyes fixated on the pulpit. He quickly scanned the room for Ty and Leah, but didn't see them. He recalled his daughter Olivia saying that the Penningtons had been called away urgently for an undetermined length of time, but why would Cassie be here if her parents weren't? Making a note to himself to talk to her after the service, he pushed the matter to the back of his mind and proceeded with his message, but not before noticing a black-haired boy he didn't recognize sitting by David.

"Grace is also the strength God gives us to withstand hard times and keep going. Hebrews 4:16 says, 'Let us then approach the throne of grace with confidence, so that we may receive mercy and find grace to help us in our time of need.' This verse speaks of God's availability to His followers, telling us to approach the throne of grace, or God's throne in heaven, confidently – and He will help. This is a promise that I, myself, have often relied on. As many of you know, my father died several years ago from bone cancer. I went to the throne of grace daily during his final days and after his death to ask God for help in getting through each day as it came. God gave me the strength to be strong for the rest of my family, and also for my father as he slipped away. Receiving God's grace didn't keep me from sadness and grief, far from it. But I found comfort and peace in the midst of that storm, and that's what I needed the most.

"The throne of grace is open to all. All you need to do is ask in faith. When God promises something, He will fulfill it, and He promises in Matthew 7:7, 'Ask and it shall be given to you.' He is always right there with you in the midst of any storm, even if you think He isn't. And He has a plan and a purpose for each storm you find yourself in, as He says in Jeremiah 29:11, 'For I know the plans I have for you, declares the Lord, plans to prosper you and not to harm you, plans to give you a hope and a future.' He has a special plan for you and your life, a very unique plan for each of us, and He will see you through to the fulfillment of that plan.

"Now, God's gift of grace to us through Jesus, while free, does come with responsibility: the responsibility of extending grace to others. We, as Christians, are obligated to treat people as Jesus would and be lights in this world. He says this clearly in the Sermon on the Mount, where He instructs us to love our enemies. I know how hard that can be. As humans, we treat our friends well and *don't* treat people very well whom we don't like, or who are seen as being at the bottom of society. This tendency is what makes this order so hard to follow, and is why we need so much grace, which God is happy to give. He expects us also to treat others courteously and forgive freely, even if someone has hurt us badly.

"I struggle with this, because it's not human nature to easily forgive those who hurt us. But if we hold a grudge against someone and allow it to fester, we let a barrier grow between us and God, and must seek forgiveness ourselves before we can be capable of forgiving the person who hurt us. Because it's so hard to be forgiving and to extend grace toward those who hurt us, those who hate us, and those we just don't like, it makes those acts all the more powerful. It's what sets Christians apart from the world, what makes us different. And who knows? Maybe through that act of forgiveness you can draw a person to Jesus who otherwise would have been lost." Pastor Shelby spoke passionately, wanting his points to really hit home with those sitting in the sanctuary.

"Jesus' death made grace readily available. Not just for Jews, not just for those in the right society, not just for those who go to church, but for everyone, from the richest man in the world down to the poorest, from a newborn babe to a mass murderer sitting in prison. Many people reject God's gift of grace because they think, 'My sin is too great, too big for anyone to forgive, even God.' Well, if there are any people of that mindset in this congregation today, let me tell you: That's not true! That's the devil and your pride talking to you, saying there's no way you can be saved. If you listen to that, you'll wind up in hell for eternity. And believe me, that's the last thing God wants. John 3:16 says, 'For God so loved the world that He gave His one and only Son, that whoever believes in Him shall not perish but have eternal life.' Note the use of the word 'whoever.' Whoever literally means anyone! Therefore, everyone can be saved, and no one has 'sinned too much.' If Jesus hadn't come and shed His blood so we could receive grace and forgiveness, we would all be doomed to hell. But instead, God loved us enough to send His Son to save us, and no one, *no one*, is beyond His reach.

"This week, try to act with grace and forgiveness toward everyone you come into contact with. Try to see the world through God's eyes. God makes no distinction between people as being more or less likely to be saved. Everyone is the same, a wayward child who needs to find his or her way back to the Father who is waiting for them with open arms. For those of you going through hard times, go to the throne of grace and ask for help. You will receive it. There is as much grace as you need and more at the mercy seat. And remember, with Jesus as your example, why accept anything less? God bless you all." After closing in prayer, Pastor Shelby walked down from the pulpit and the congregation began to socialize and discuss the sermon.

Cassie felt stunned. It was as if the pastor knew exactly what she'd been going through over the past week. And hadn't he said that God had specifically told him to preach on grace because someone needed it? Pastor Pete had even mentioned Jeremiah 29:11. God always managed to astonish her. She smiled at that observation. That was why she followed Him, of course. She glanced to her right, where William was sitting. She was curious as to what he thought of the sermon. For once, she felt she could actually read the expression on his face, and it told her he was feeling shocked, too. Was it the part about grace being available for everyone? She decided she'd ask him later, when he'd had time to think about it, and when they were alone. Hannah's voice broke in on her thoughts. "I need to talk with some people before we go home, Ben. It shouldn't take too long. It's about vacation Bible school."

Ben nodded acknowledgment. "Alright. I'd like to talk with Pete. That word," he said, looking down at the kids, "was something we all needed to hear, I think." Cassie nodded, while the twins verbalized their assent. The adults moved off and left the teens to their own devices while they went about their self-appointed tasks.

"So William, what did you think?" Sarah asked curiously.

He started slightly at the question and answered with his face still facing forward. "It was... interesting. I've never really heard anything like that before." He sounded a little like someone had yanked the foundation out from under him. David caught it and Cassie saw him draw a breath to ask a question. She caught his eye and shook her head slightly. He raised an eyebrow inquiringly and she mouthed, *Later*. He nodded.

Just then, a familiar voice spoke up from behind them. "Well, if it isn't Cassie Pennington. I thought you were on a trip with your parents." Cassie turned toward the speaker with a smile. It was the pastor's daughter, Olivia – or Livvie, as she preferred to be called. She was a good friend of Cassie and Sarah's, and it was often lamented that she didn't live closer to them. As usual, her silky auburn hair was escaping its ponytail, and her brown eyes reflected her cheerful and lively personality.

"Hey, Livvie. Well, I was on a trip," Cassie replied, thinking of the adventure in the mountains, "but now I'm back."

"I can see that. Otherwise, you wouldn't be here, would you?" Livvie said whimsically. "But where are your parents? I don't see them."

"They're, um, still on the trip. It was getting to be more grown-up stuff, so I came home." Cassie winced inwardly at how weak that sounded. *Everyone* knew she accompanied her parents on trips even if it wasn't exactly for kids, because she generally found all things historical to be interesting. "I wanted to make better use of my summer vacation."

"She's staying with us," Sarah said, trying to help Cassie. Livvie shifted her attention to Sarah.

"So, I heard you and David went, too?" she asked, sounding slightly jealous. She often wished she could go with Cassie on trips. They always sounded so exciting.

Sarah caught Livvie's tone and laughed to dispel any tension. "Yeah, but it wasn't too exciting, so don't be jealous. That's why we came home, actually. It's more fun to be here with friends." Cassie and David both concealed snorts of amusement at Sarah's description.

Livvie grinned brightly, her brown eyes twinkling. "Well, of course. And since you're here..." She gave Cassie a hug. "Happy belated birthday! I went to your house on your birthday, but Mr. Thompson told me about the trip. Weren't you going to go on an overnight trail ride, though?"

"Thanks, Liv. And yeah, we were, but then the, ah, conference thing came up quick and so we went to that instead."

Livvie nodded. "But who's your friend here?" she asked, inclining her head toward William, who'd been listening to the conversation with interest.

"Oh, this is William. He's staying with us for the time being," Sarah said. "William, this is Olivia, but everyone calls her Livvie. Her dad's the pastor."

"Pleased to meet you," William said, smiling, as he extended a hand to her. He glanced at Cassie.

Livvie shook it, raising her eyebrows at his accent. "You're from England?" she asked. At William's nod, she went on, "What brought you across the pond?"

"Well, my, um, guardians went to the same conference Cassie's parents went to. They've known the Penningtons for a while and so when Cassie, David, and Sarah decided to go back home, they asked if it would be okay for me to tag along. The Thompsons didn't mind."

"Oh. So is this conference in England?"

"No," Cassie said. "It's in D.C." She really felt terrible about lying to her friend and asked God to forgive her as she uttered the words, but no way could she say what really happened. She'd sound nuts, and even though Livvie was a good friend, Cassie didn't want to put the weight of her secret on her. Besides, this was no place to discuss something like that, with all these people around. An awkward silence fell for a few minutes.

"Um, could someone tell me where the loo – er, where the restroom is?" William asked.

David took the opportunity to escape the conversation immediately. He liked Livvie well enough, but knew she was more of a girly-girl than Cassie or Sarah, and he had a feeling about what direction the conversation might take in the next few minutes. Besides, he had friends of his own he wanted to catch up with. "Sure. It's just over here." The boys walked off.

Livvie looked after them for a few seconds before turning back to Sarah and Cassie. "So how long have you known William?" she asked.

"A few days," Cassie said. "That is, I'd never met him before. Dad's told me about his, um, family, though."

"What's he like?"

"He's nice."

"That all?" Livvie continued to probe.

Cassie looked at her, puzzled. "Well, what do you expect me to say? I just said that I haven't known him long."

Livvie laughed. "You? Well, I suppose that would be the extent of what I'd expect *you* to say. Is he staying long?"

"I don't know. Why so curious?"

"He's cute."

Cassie groaned. She should have seen that coming. "Oh, for heaven's sake, Livvie, is that all you think about?" Her voice held a teasing note.

"Of course not. It's just kind of hard not to notice."

"Oh?"

"Well, *I* think so. What do you think, Sarah?"

"Yeah, I'd agree with that," Sarah said, suppressing bubbles of laughter.

Cassie rolled her eyes and shook her head. "Hey, I'm not blind, you know. I *have* noticed. I *can* make such judgments. I just prefer speaking of other things." She sounded somewhat plaintive. Livvie and Sarah grinned at each other.

"Well that's something I haven't heard too often from Cassie Pennington," Sarah said, "but I do think we can find other topics to talk about that don't cause such obvious pain." Cassie glared at them as they giggled, but smiled after a few seconds. It felt nice to have a regular, light-hearted conversation with her friends.

"So what did y'all think of the service?" Livvie asked, heeding Cassie's request.

"It was great," Cassie said. "Just what I needed, actually."

"Well, I'm glad to hear that, Cassie." All three girls jumped. They hadn't noticed Pastor Pete approaching. He stood behind his daughter. "I hope your trip was fun."

"It was okay," Cassie said, glancing at Sarah out of the corner of her eye. Sarah understood her warning immediately.

"I don't see your parents. Are they here?" the pastor inquired.

"No."

"That's too bad. I enjoy talking with them. How are you, Cassie?"

Pastor Shelby searched Cassie's face. He saw a deep sadness in her eyes, and wondered why.

"Oh, I'm doing alright. Thanks for asking."

The pastor nodded thoughtfully. "Good. Who's the young man I saw with David, Sarah? I didn't recognize him."

His daughter answered him. "That was William, Dad. He's staying with the Thompsons until the conference that Cassie's parents and his, um, guardians, I think he said, are at is finished. He's British."

"Really? Have you two known him long?" Pastor Shelby asked.

"Not too long, but he's very nice." Sarah answered. Just then, someone called Pastor Pete's name. He smiled apologetically at the girls.

"I've got to go. See you girls later." He walked off.

Livvie looked hopefully at Cassie and Sarah. "Would you guys like to come over to my house today? We'll be working on VBS stuff, and extra hands are always welcome. William can come too, if he wants." Cassie and Sarah exchanged glances. Under normal circumstances, they would have accepted at once, but given all that was going on...

"I think that's a great idea," Ben said, having been close enough to hear Livvie's offer.

"What's a great idea?" David asked, walking up behind his father with William following.

"Livvie wants us to come over to her house and work on VBS stuff," Sarah answered.

"What kind of stuff, Livvie?" David asked her.

"Oh, the usual. Making song sets, organizing pamphlets, preparing crafts for the kids, that sort of thing." David looked at his sister and Cassie.

William guessed at their hesitation. "Don't refuse on my account. I can find other things to do with myself."

"You're welcome to come, William. There'll be some other local teens, and an extra pair of hands is always welcome," Livvie said, smiling at him. She turned back to Cassie, who was thinking this could be a very interesting afternoon. "Please say you'll come. Marge'll be there, and so will Eric, James, and Jacquelyn. Kristina and John as well, and some others..."

"Oh, go on," Ben encouraged. "You all need something fun to do. There's plenty of time for other things. It's Sunday, the day of rest. Enjoy yourselves." Sarah and David looked to Cassie. She realized they were waiting for her decision. She looked at Livvie's hopeful face.

"Oh, why not?"

Decisions, Decisions

William looked around carefully to make sure he was completely alone. He was late in reporting to his father and didn't dare wait any longer. The others were caring for the horses, and he knew he had about half an hour before anyone would come looking for him. He was fairly sure they believed him enough that his absence wouldn't raise too much alarm, but knew they still doubted him enough to want to keep close tabs on him. He also wanted to be alone to process all the thoughts roiling around in his head. The day had presented him with two very different possible truths, and he had no idea which one to believe.

First, the sermon. Never in his life had he heard such things. He had been taught that God only saved those who helped themselves, not that salvation was free, as Pastor Shelby claimed, or that you had to pray to receive it. The best way to salvation that William knew was to rid the world of Satan's workers: the Brenwyds. But he'd looked up the Bible verses the pastor had read, and found them to be quoted accurately. If the pastor was right, William was headed for hell. He didn't like that thought. The sermon had emphasized that grace was available to everyone, but surely that was because the pastor just didn't understand William's situation. The Brotherhood couldn't be wrong. That would destroy everything he believed.

His thoughts turned from the sermon to the hours they'd spent at the pastor's house helping out. He had watched Cassie carefully and admitted that her actions lined up with what he had learned of her already. He had made some casual inquiries about her, and learned that her friends were quick to defend her. He discovered that Cassie had, in fact, been the object of some bullying, and her friends had assured him that she did absolutely nothing to deserve such treatment other than being herself. The way Cassie interacted so freely with her friends, and how they genuinely appeared to enjoy her company and have their wits about them, seemed to dispel his idea that Cassie had somehow enchanted them into liking her. But if he admitted that, it thrust everything he believed into doubt. Was it possible that the Brotherhood had Brenwyds all wrong? If so, why had they hunted them for so long? Wouldn't someone before him have realized that Brenwyds were not evil? And if they weren't evil, then how had they come into existence? William decided to get that story from Cassie as soon as possible. The Commander had taught him to gather as much information as possible before making decisions. True, at the time he'd been talking about planning raids and such, but William was sure that the instructions applied to this situation as well.

He realized that his questions all boiled down to two possible scenarios: either the Brotherhood was right and everyone else was wrong, or the Brotherhood was wrong and everyone else was right. He didn't know which one was correct. Furthermore, he wasn't sure which one he wanted to be correct. His training told him the Brotherhood was right, but his experiences over the past few days seemed to say the opposite.

He felt very disturbed about this inner turmoil. Every hour he spent with Cassie increased it. He wanted to blame it all on her – that it was Brenwyd witchcraft – but something told him it wasn't. At first he had easily been able to push his feelings aside, but now it was impossible. He had no idea what to make of it, and could not talk to anyone about it.

Distant shrieks and laughter diverted his attention. He looked up and saw that David, who had been using a hose to fill the water trough, was now aiming the water stream at the girls. Within several minutes a full-fledged water fight was in progress. The dogs also got in on the fun by knocking over the humans into the puddles they'd created. William smiled at their antics and felt some pricks of longing and envy. He'd never really had any friends. The Brotherhood consisted mostly of grown men with some young initiates, and it had been made clear to him at an early age that childish antics would not be tolerated. His play had consisted of learning to use the weapons of the Brotherhood with a deadly precision. As he'd gotten older and reached the traditional initiate age, he had hung out and practiced with the others his age, but he wouldn't consider them friends, not if he went off what he'd observed of friends this afternoon.

He shook his head, trying to shake the thoughts out. *Stop thinking like that, William,* he told himself, *envying a Brenwyd for goodness' sake! You certainly won't be envying her once the Brotherhood gets a hold of her.* He turned his back on the scene and took his cell phone out of his pocket, dialing and bringing it to his ear in one motion. On the second ring a gruff voice said, "Yes?" William took a breath, mentally preparing himself for the rebuke he was sure to get.

"Hello, Father." A pause.

"Why haven't you reported sooner? The Master has been most anxious." William winced slightly at the anger and disapproval underlying the words.

"I couldn't. They've been watching me too carefully. I had to wait until they trusted me more."

"What do you mean? Aren't you with Raymond?"

"No. Raymond and the others are dead. After you left in the airplane, the girl and two of her friends came down into the camp. Raymond attacked them, and he and his men all ended up dead. She and her friends are very skilled, and they have... animal guardians. I stayed hidden in a tent when they first came into the camp, then pretended to be a prisoner myself. They took me back to their house. We found out that her father is working on finding something to do with King Arthur, and we found a binder with all his work in it, but it's in Latin, so Cassie – the girl – has been working on translating it. Depending on what it says, there's a good chance that they may come to England on their own. If they do that, we can capture them there." As William waited for his father's response, he felt, to his surprise, that a slight sense of horror at what he'd just said welled up in him. He found that the idea of actually turning Cassie over sickened him. *Get a grip, William,* he told himself, *she may be a nice person, but she's still a Brenwyd! They're devil spawn!* His thoughts were interrupted by his father's voice.

"Excellent work, William." He sounded pleased. "Now we can get not just the girl, but Pennington's work as well. Get that witch over here as soon as possible. Report again when you learn more."

William knew he was about to hang up. "Father, wait! What is it Cassie's father is looking for that the Master wants?" William held his breath as he waited for his father to reply. William had learned a long time ago not to ask his father unnecessary questions, but his curiosity got the better of him with this one.

"You'll find out when the girl finishes translating. You must show the same surprise as the others so they do not suspect you." He hung up. William slowly put the phone back in his pocket, unable to believe his feelings. *I'm not supposed to feel sorry for them!* he told himself. But some part of him kept whispering that it was wrong, he was wrong, the Brotherhood was wrong. He tried again to mentally shove the feelings aside, recalling his father's words about emotions, but he'd never had such strong feelings before. He strode quickly from the woods, head down, not really paying attention to where he was going until he suddenly felt something cold and wet hurled against him, completely drenching the front of his clothes.

He looked up sharply, startled, into Sarah's apologetic face. "Oh, man, I'm sorry. I was aiming for David." She glared over his shoulder and William saw that David had taken refuge behind the tree that he himself had just stepped in front of. She had a bucket in her hand, which William guessed was the source of the water that had soaked him. For several seconds he felt completely at a loss as to how to respond.

A peal of laughter directed his attention to Cassie. She had a hose in hand and was soaking wet, with mud all over her clothes from being pushed down by the dogs. She looked quite comical. "You should see the look on your face!" she gasped out. William took in his wet front. He also noticed a bucket of water within reach. He hesitated a moment, unsure if he should really do it or not, but firmly decided to throw his hesitancy to the wind.

"I suppose there's only one thing to do in these situations," he said in a high-handed tone.

"Oh?" David inquired. He had a pretty good idea of what William was about to do.

William grinned at him mischievously, the first time David had seen such an expression on his face. He grabbed the bucket. "This!" he said as he threw the contents over Sarah.

She stared at him in shock for a few seconds, then grinned and laughed. "Oh, it's on now!" As the water fight resumed with even more intensity, William reflected that having fun like this was... well... fun. Nothing like it ever happened in the Brotherhood. It continued until Hannah came out and told them to dry off and clean up if they wanted any chance of dinner.

William strode quickly, not really paying attention until he suddenly felt something cold and wet hurled against him. He looked up sharply, startled.

Cassie leaned back in her chair, rubbing her eyes and stretching. Kai raised his head from his position at her feet. *Have you finished?* he asked, sensing her excitement.

"Yes," she said, feeling slightly awed by what she'd just read. Ever since they had discovered her father's notes, she had been working almost nonstop on translating them. She had also made an additional discovery in the secret compartment: the old diary she'd asked her father about. She'd gone back to more fully examine the drawer, wondering if it could be in there, and had found it at the bottom. She had looked inside and had discovered it was written in some ancient Celtic language and, unfortunately, she couldn't translate anything beyond the odd word or two of Latin mixed in. There were sketches inside, however – pretty good ones – of weapons, plants, maps, and even animals and people.

Several depictions of Seren and Excalibur captured her attention, and she studied them in detail. She noticed that in most of the Seren sketches, flames were drawn around the blade. She recalled her father telling her that, according to legend, Seren had been forged from a meteorite that had landed on earth in flames, igniting a forest and attracting the attention of a Brenwyd blacksmith. He had been commissioned to forge a weapon for the wife of the leader at the time. He used the metal because he found it to be very hard and durable. The knife was said to ignite with the fire of the meteorite when used by female members of the leader's family, the ones for whom it had been made, because the skill of the blacksmith was so great that he had tamed the flames to obey human will. Cassie hadn't thought the legend was true, but the sketches seemed to say otherwise. And given who she suspected had owned the diary, the book was a reliable source.

While scrutinizing the drawings, she made an additional discovery: the ones labeled *Caliburnus*, the Latinized word for Excalibur, were actually showing two different swords. They were very similar, both having a design engraved on the blade near the hilt, but the engravings were different. One showed a pair of dragons with their necks entwined and wings outstretched, while their bodies formed an intricate Celtic knot. The other was nearly identical, but had only a single dragon with a Celtic knot for a body. It was such a slight difference that Cassie doubted anyone else would notice. Under several sketches of the sword with the two dragons, she saw the words *gladius regum*, or "sword of kings." Cassie thought over everything she had learned of different King Arthur legends and of that time in history, but couldn't guess what the significance of the words might be. If the translation had simply been "sword of the king," she would have assumed it meant Arthur's sword. But *regum* was the possessive plural form of "king" in Latin, indicating the sword had belonged to many kings. Cassie didn't see how it was possible Excalibur had belonged to more than one king. Her dad had never mentioned anything of the kind, and he knew more about King Arthur than just about anyone. She knew Arthur had had two swords, but it was only the second that was called Excalibur. As her translation of her father's work progressed, the discovery was pushed from her mind, and by the time she finished it was completely forgotten.

Kai got to his feet. *What did you find?*

"You were right. Dad was on to something big. Very big."

What?

"I'll tell you when I tell everyone else, and that won't be until they're all here. Probably after dinner." She paused for several minutes, thinking. "But I think there must be something else," she mused to herself. Mr. Thompson was out at work, and David and Sarah had gone riding with William. They'd invited Cassie, but she'd declined. She had been glad to see that William was feeling more at ease with them. It lessened her suspicions, and made her hope all the more that he was telling the truth about breaking from the Brotherhood.

She went downstairs to where Hannah was working on bills in the kitchen. She looked up from the papers as Cassie walked in. "Did you finish?" she asked. Smokey looked over in Cassie's direction from where he'd been dozing in the sun.

"Yep. And it's a real eye-opener."

"I'd imagine. What was your dad working on?"

"I'd rather not say until everyone's here. I don't want to repeat it several times."

Hannah glanced at the clock. "Ben should be back soon, but no telling when the twins and William will be." Cassie nodded acknowledgment. She sat gazing out the window, lost in thought. Hannah thought she looked a little forlorn, a growing sadness evident on her face. It hurt Hannah's heart to see it. Cassie had always been cheerful and vivacious, but now she was more subdued, more likely to lose herself in her thoughts. "How are you, Cassie? Really?" The girl shrugged noncommittally.

"I'm okay, Mrs. Thompson." She paused, then went on. "I mean, I'm not great, but I could be worse. Sometimes, I even forget what happened for a brief moment, then I turn to find Mom or Dad but..." her voice choked a little, "... they're never there."

Hannah put her arms around her. "You don't have to hold everything in, you know. You can let your feelings out."

Cassie relished the comfort of the hug and took a shuddering breath. "I know. It's just... difficult."

"I can imagine." Hannah went back to her work after giving Cassie one last squeeze. "Why don't you go pay some attention to that mare of yours? I can't talk to animals, but she looked fairly irritated that she was left in the field."

"Mmm, yeah, she was," Cassie said with feeling, recalling the angry lecture she had received. "I'll go make amends now."

Time passed quickly for Cassie. William and the twins got back, inquiring about her project, but she deflected them with an "I'll tell you later." Then Mr. Thompson returned and everyone headed into the living room. Now Cassie was looking around at expectant faces, animal as well as human. She was conscious of the horses listening in from outside. The fact that Calico had deigned to come in the house, and that the horses were so interested, gave Cassie the idea that the information she was about to share was important to the animals at a deeper, more crucial level than the humans knew. She decided to ask Kai about it later. She took a deep breath as she opened the binder to the relevant section. She had checked her work several times and knew it was correct, but was still having trouble believing it. Feeling slightly unsure as to how to begin, she felt relieved when Sarah, unable to wait any longer, blurted out, "Well, come on, Cassie. We're not saving any time here. Tell us what you found."

Cassie cleared her throat and began. "I found out that Dad was working on the project of a lifetime. And if his assumptions are correct – and they usually are – it could be the find of the century." She had their full attention now, she could tell. "He was working on the assumption that every great kingdom, no matter how long or short it lasted, had to have had some kind of massed wealth from taxes or conquered lands or whatever. And also that the massed wealth could be found, like the 'Staffordshire hoard' found in that farmer's field in England. You know, that huge cache of Anglo-Saxon gold from the seventh to eighth centuries. Dad was looking for another treasure trove, also located in England, but from a hundred years earlier and consisting of more than artifacts of war." She paused for effect. "He was on the trail of King Arthur's treasure hoard." Everyone's faces took on a stunned expression, and silence reigned for several minutes.

"Are you serious?" David asked finally.

"Completely. I checked the translation several times. It's completely legitimate. And it makes sense as to why the Brotherhood would want to capture him and not kill him. They don't want him to find it and release it to the public. I think they want to find it for themselves and don't know where to start. But Dad has pretty much everything figured out."

"If there really is such a thing, why hasn't anything been found before now? There's certainly been enough interest in King Arthur to warrant a search for his treasure," Sarah said.

"Because no one else had what my dad had." Cassie held up the diary. "I found this in the secret shelf and I saw him using it one day last week when he was working. Based on how he refers to it in his notes, I think it talks about what Dad guesses is a probable location for the treasure. And if the person who wrote it is who I think it is, then it's a very reliable source."

"So who wrote it and what's the location?" David inquired.

"I'm getting to that. To answer your first question, Dad always refers to it as 'C's diary,' so the person's name starts with a C. He also indicated it was written by a woman, so I think... I think it's Caelwyn's diary." Cassie mentally asked Kai for a confirmation of the fact. He gave it. It didn't surprise Cassie that he knew. He picked up a lot of information around the house.

"The Brenwyd woman from your dad's stories?" David asked. Cassie nodded. From the corner of her eye, she noticed William straighten slightly as if with surprise at the information.

"Have you ever heard of Caelwyn?" she queried of him.

William nodded. "I've heard the name mentioned a few times. The Brotherhood doesn't like her. She was close to King Arthur, wasn't she?"

"Yep. Which makes this diary an invaluable historical source." Cassie frowned slightly. "But based on what I read in Dad's notes, he's been working on this project for years, so I don't think Caelwyn wrote the exact location down in the diary, unfortunately. Dad's had to do some guessing."

"If the location was such a secret, that doesn't surprise me," Ben said thoughtfully. "As I'm sure you know, your father has always wanted to prove Arthur's existence to the world. Finding a treasure trove dating to that period could help him do that. But it would have to be somewhere near a place associated with King Arthur, or else somehow state clearly that the treasure was Arthur's. It couldn't be just anywhere in the English countryside."

"Which is why he was investigating the possibility of tunnels running under Cadbury Castle as a location of the treasure," Cassie said.

"Not more tunnels!" Sarah groaned.

Cassie grinned at her. "Yep, more tunnels. They seem to be Dad's specialty. Tunnels running underneath the hill to a chamber where the treasure could be hidden. It would help explain why no one's ever found anything, because archaeologists haven't considered investigating the heart of the hill."

"So your father thinks that Cadbury Castle *is* the site of Camelot?" William asked.

"Yes. He figured it out based on stuff he read in the diary, I think. And the tunnels are definitely talked about in the diary, but not, I don't think, where their entrance is."

"So what do we do now that we know what your dad was working on?" Sarah asked after a few moments of silence. "I mean, it's interesting and all, but how is it going to help us free your parents?"

"Well," Cassie said slowly, "maybe not at all, but now that I know this, I want to go to England more than ever. Getting my parents out is the most important thing, but I wouldn't mind also taking a peep around Cadbury on the way to Carlisle. I may be wrong, but I think there's something more to this treasure trove than just the fact that it belonged to King Arthur."

"Something more? Like what?" David asked.

"I don't know. I just feel like there's something I'm missing that my dad realized about this treasure, and the Brotherhood knows it as well. Even if it belonged to King Arthur, I don't think that fact alone is a good enough reason to kidnap my parents." Cassie looked at William. "Any ideas?"

He shook his head. "Not a clue. Sorry."

Cassie turned her gaze to Mr. Thompson. "Well, Mr. Thompson? What do you say about a trip now?"

He was frowning. "It's still dangerous. And the fact that you think there's something more to it troubles me. You don't have any idea what it could be?"

"No, but in his notes Dad mentioned a Sadie Stone that he'd started working with. I looked her up. She works at the British Museum in London. She might know." Cassie paused for a moment, sneaking a quick glance at William as she debated whether or not to verbalize her next thought. "And there's another reason I'd like to meet her: to see whether she might have talked to other people about the project. If she did, that might be how the Brotherhood learned about it."

"A good idea," Mr. Thompson conceded.

David looked at him. "Dad, what other choice do we have except to go to England? We can't just let Cassie's parents stay in Brotherhood hands."

"We don't know anything about how the Brotherhood operates over there," Hannah put in. "They could be hoping we go and lead them to the treasure, if it exists. Or they could be watching to grab Cassie the minute she walks off a plane in England. It's very, very dangerous."

"You think I don't know that?" Cassie said. "That's why it's driving me crazy just sitting around here. It's really not any safer. Sooner or later, the Brotherhood will be back to get me. Even if I followed Dad's plan, they could probably still find me, and then that would put Aunt Janelle in danger. Traveling may actually be my best protection right now, especially to England. The Brotherhood would likely look in their own backyard last. It's not exactly a logical place to run to if you want to avoid them. But not everyone has to go."

"That's ridiculous, Cassie. Of course we'd go with you," David said.

"Hannah, why don't we go discuss this in the kitchen?" Ben said, rising from the couch. "We can talk without argument there." They exited, leaving the four teens waiting anxiously.

Cassie turned to William. "I assume your offer to guide us to the Brotherhood headquarters still stands?"

"Yes, of course. But what would you try to do first? Find the treasure trove or free your parents? That is, provided we go," he said.

We will, Kai said confidently. *The time is approaching and the prophecy is being set into motion.* The other animals affirmed his words, sounding eager.

Cassie looked at him quizzically. "Time for what? What prophecy?"

The time for the Brotherhood to reap what they have sown.

"What's that supposed to mean?" Sarah asked.

Exactly what I said, Kai replied, looking steadily at Cassie. She, David, and Sarah looked at each other, thoroughly puzzled. William observed this and became puzzled himself. Didn't Cassie know of the prophecy? Had her parents never told her? Did they even know? His question was answered by Cassie's next comment.

"What is this prophecy, Kai? Is this going back to why the Brotherhood Master wants me specifically?" She was looking at him with narrowed eyes.

She does not know? Gracie asked, sounding surprised.

Her parents thought it would be better if she was older before she learned of it, Dassah answered.

I think they were going to tell her on her birthday, Smokey added. *But then they were captured. We thought about telling her, but she was so distraught that we decided it was best to wait until she was calm and thinking straight.*

"Well, since now I'm not distraught and am thinking straight, could you tell me what it is I don't know about myself but everyone else seems to?" Cassie asked, trying to keep her frustration from creeping into her voice. If the animals knew something important she didn't, she wanted to know without more subterfuge. The others looked at her questioningly. She ignored them. After staring at the animals for a few more moments without response, she answered William's question. "Like I said, my parents are my top priority. They come first. It would actually probably be better to get them out first and then go after the treasure trove, since my dad is the one who knows everything." At that moment Ben and Hannah entered the room.

David asked his parents the question. "Are we going?"

Sarah was looking at them hopefully. Cassie switched her gaze from the animals to the Thompsons. William narrowed his eyes and waited for the reply.

Ben looked at each young face before he answered. "We have talked, and we both feel that it is hard to ignore the danger in the trip. However," he continued as their faces fell, "we have also agreed it may be more dangerous to sit here doing nothing, particularly for Ty and Leah. Therefore, I hope you all know where your suitcases are, because we'll be leaving as soon as I can get a few work things finished up." David and Sarah grinned at each other, excited by the prospect despite the danger. Cassie found her gaze drawn to William, wondering how he really felt about returning to Brotherhood territory. His face was set in hard-to-read lines, but she thought she detected that he seemed very conflicted over something and a little uncertain. Someone else would likely have assumed it was the thought of going back to where he'd run away from and the danger involved, but Cassie sensed there was a deeper, darker level to his uncertainty. He'd been looking at the floor, but raised his gaze suddenly, as if feeling hers. They stared at each other for a moment, trying to find one another's secrets. Cassie dropped her eyes first, wondering at the feeling that had just come over her, one that she had also felt when she'd first seen him in the tent – the sense that she'd seen him somewhere before, while knowing she had never laid eyes on him. It was an unsettling feeling.

Her thoughts were interrupted by a query from Sarah addressed to her father. "So when do you think we'll leave, Dad?"

"Tomorrow night, most likely. That'll give me time to tell my boss and get airplane tickets, and it will give us time to pack and dig out our passports."

"How long will we be able to stay?" Cassie asked.

Ben grimaced slightly. "That's the thing. I'm not sure. About a week, I think. But that's not enough time to conduct a thorough archaeological search, so that's probably out of the picture. We're lucky that I'm due for vacation time anyway."

"That's okay. Mom and Dad are way more important. A week should be plenty of time to rescue them, right, William?"

"Oh, yes," he answered.

His distracted way of answering caught Cassie's interest, but Hannah spoke before she could ask him about it. "Well, now that that's settled, I'm going to get ready for work. I have the night shift tonight at the hospital." She left the room, followed by Ben, who said he had work to do before the trip. The four teens were left to themselves. Cassie picked up a book and started to read it while David scanned through the newspaper.

Sarah thought that William seemed distracted and ill at ease. He was looking out the window, but the faraway look in his eyes told her his thoughts were miles away. He seemed so troubled that she couldn't bear staying silent any longer. "What is it?" she asked, drawing everyone's attention.

William looked surprised. "What's what?"

"What's on your mind?"

"Oh." William looked at Sarah's gentle, concerned hazel eyes and fought with himself over whether or not to ask his question. The answer wouldn't matter anyway, since the girl would be in Brotherhood hands long before a week was up, but he still couldn't help asking. He shifted his gaze to look deeply into Cassie's twain-colored eyes, trying to figure out just what this Brenwyd girl was all about. "What do you plan to do once we rescue your parents? You can't just come back here. They'd track you down again in a heartbeat. Even if you moved, they'd stop at nothing to find you again. No one's ever escaped the Brotherhood and stayed free for very long. Actually, no one's ever even had a successful escape as far as I know. As long as the Brotherhood exists, you'll never really be safe. How do you plan to avoid them?" He scolded himself as soon as he asked it. What did he care about her long-term plans, if indeed she had any? Why did he feel so interested in her safety? He saw that his speech had startled her, saw pain flare in her eyes, and also saw them fill with sadness. He realized she had thought of these things herself, when no one else was around, and had so far found no answer. She looked at him, almost pleadingly, as if asking him for help. Not being able to bear it, he turned abruptly toward the window.

Cassie gazed at William's back, trying to find the answer. Everyone in the room was completely silent, each trying to find their own solution to the problem, the issue that had been at the back of each of their minds since last week's events, but about which no one had had the nerve to ask. Sarah saw the expression on her friend's face and moved to put an arm around her. Cassie leaned into her gratefully. She started praying.

God, what am I to do? Danger lies on my every side, and I can't escape it. I need you. Oh, how I need Your help. William's right – they'll never stop hunting me, and I can't survive down here on my own. Help me face my enemies, remembering that You've already overcome the world and I don't need to fear it – because God, I am really, truly scared. Please, show me what to do, because I am seriously lost. I feel like the foundation of my life has been yanked out from under me, but I know, I know, that You have a firm grip on me and will never let me go.

She continued praying, and felt her fear become soothed. Jeremiah 29:11 came to her mind. She remembered what she'd told God that dreadful night, that she would trust Him no matter what. She reaffirmed the promise in her mind, and felt more confident. "Well, William, I'm just gonna let God handle that and do what I've got right in front of me. Who knows, maybe He'll commission someone to destroy the Brotherhood so it won't exist and I won't have to worry about it anymore." She said it in a joking kind of way, even though she knew God was entirely capable of doing such a thing, and so didn't understand why William whirled around with such force and looked at her with such a wide-eyed expression, or why the animals all started so violently. "What?"

Do you have any idea what you just said? Kai asked.

She looked at him, puzzled. "What do you mean? Don't you think it'd be nice if the Brotherhood didn't exist anymore?" She certainly thought it would be nice. Then maybe her life could get back to normal. Kai just looked at her disconcertingly, and she got the feeling she'd shocked him – *not* an easy thing to do. Cassie, Sarah, and David all looked at each other, trying to figure out if one knew something the others didn't, but only learned that they were all equally baffled.

Suddenly David thought of something. "Wait, does this have to do with that prophecy thing you mentioned earlier?" he asked Kai.

It has everything to do with it, Kai said. Cassie sighed and slammed her book closed in frustration. She was getting tired of all this subterfuge.

"Then for heaven's sake would you *please* just *tell* us what this prophecy is without all the mysterious talk?" she asked, exasperated. Instead of giving a reply, Dassah got up, went to the coffee table, gently picked up Caelwyn's diary in her mouth, and plopped it down in Cassie's lap.

Look in the back, on the last page, she said, sounding excited.

Cassie picked the book up and started leafing through the pages. "I can't read this, you know."

"What language is it?" William asked.

"I don't know. Whatever language was spoken in Britain in the 500s, probably something Celtic in origin." She reached the page Kai had indicated. "Now what?" she asked the dog.

Pry the page open, Kai answered, as if it were the most reasonable thing in the world. All the other animals in the room had risen from their positions and were making motions of excitement. All the humans stared at the dog, not quite sure if they'd heard him right.

"Pry the page open? Are you nuts?" Cassie asked, bemused.

Not at all, girl. Just do it.

Suddenly Sarah piped up. "He may be right, Cass. I saw something just like that in a movie."

"Just because it worked in a movie doesn't mean it'll work in real life, Sarah," her brother said.

"But it doesn't mean it won't," Sarah countered.

Cassie handed her the book. "Why don't you do the honors, then?" she said. Sarah accepted it with so grave an air and began to lift the page so solemnly, as if the information it contained could set off a bomb, that Cassie and David couldn't help laughing a little, though they tried to hide it.

Sarah looked at them with an expression of injured dignity and sighed dramatically. "The things I put up with," Sarah said to Gracie, who was sitting near her. "It makes me wonder why I decide to do anything for these people." The dog wagged her tail in understanding, though Cassie sensed she was just as amused as the humans. Sarah continued to follow Kai's instructions, turning the book upside down and shaking it slightly as she pulled gently on the page's edge. To Cassie's astonishment, a scrap of paper did, indeed, fall from a hiding place within the page, and she realized that two pages must have been glued together to hide the paper. Sarah looked at her brother triumphantly as she picked the paper up off the floor and handed it to Cassie. "See? Movies aren't all fake."

"My apologies. I shall give more credence to them in the future," he said dryly. He guessed from Cassie's expression of annoyance that the paper was in the same language as that of the diary.

It was confirmed by her next statement. "Fiddlesticks. I can't read it. *Now* will one of you mysterios tell me what this says?" she said, waving the paper in front of Kai's nose. "Unless any of the rest of you can read this ancient Celtic language." They seemed slightly disappointed.

Very well, Kai said. *I cannot tell you the exact wording, but–*

"I can read it," William interrupted. The others looked at him in surprise.

"You know this language?" Cassie asked.

He nodded. "Yeah. It's what was used during King Arthur's reign. It's called Brythonic, and it was the original language of the Brotherhood, so every member learns it. It comes in handy if you don't want anyone from outside to read something you've written."

"That makes sense," David mused. "I'd like that. Then I could write things without my sister being able to read them. Hey!" This last ejaculation came as a result of a pillow hitting his head, thrown by said sister.

"Say things like that when I'm not in the room, brother dear," she said sweetly.

Cassie grinned at their behavior. She handed William the paper. "All yours."

He scanned the paper and saw it was as he'd suspected. It was the prophecy that had led him to this room. He wondered if he should mistranslate it, as none of them would be able to catch the mistake, but then remembered that the animals would catch it since they knew what was written. He figured there couldn't be too much harm in translating it correctly. He cleared his throat and started to speak. "Here is a record of the last words of Caelwyn, advisor to High King Arthur Pendragon and leader of the blessed race of Brenwyds, as reported by her faithful companion, Dragon." He heard the others gasp, but didn't pause. "As she lay dying of wounds given by the black traitor, she issued a prophecy that foretold his doom: That one day a female of her line, working with the heir of Arthur, would bring down the traitor and his followers, and so start to heal the rift between humans and Brenwyds."

Total silence reigned. Cassie felt as if she'd been hit by a stone wall. No way could that prophecy be talking about her, could it? She thought back over all the weapons lessons her father had given her. He'd said it was so she would be able to protect herself, but had there been another motive behind it? It was obvious that her father had known of the prophecy. Did he really think that she was the one it talked about? And if so, why? She remembered that her father had said once that they were descended from Caelwyn, but she wasn't sure if he had been serious or not. She recalled the words Smokey had overheard that night: She was the one the Master of the Brotherhood had wanted. A chill came over her. Whether she was the one in the prophecy or not, the Brotherhood obviously thought she was, which meant that she must be descended from Caelwyn. And if that was the case, who was their "Master"? She thought she had a pretty good idea of who the traitor mentioned in the prophecy was, but that had been over a thousand years ago. It must be one of his descendants who ran the Brotherhood, she decided. More questions came crowding into her mind, more than she could think about at one time. She abruptly realized that everyone in the room was looking at her, William with narrowed eyes, David and Sarah with amazed expressions.

"Cass, could... could you be the fulfillment?" David asked softly.

His dark brown eyes gazed at her steadily, with an expression she couldn't read.

She swallowed, hard, before she replied. "I… I don't know. I've never heard of this before now."

"But are you a descendant of Caelwyn? That's the real question," William said.

Kai answered for her. *She is. And you are the one the prophecy speaks of, girl. The time is right. And this is why we did not want to tell you the night your parents were abducted.*

"Yeah… I'm sorry I went off on you guys. I should have known you knew best," Cassie murmured, still very much in shock.

It is alright.

"How do you know I'm the one it talks about? Dad did say once that Caelwyn is my ancestor, but just because she is, doesn't mean I'm the specific girl talked about," she said. "How do you even know this is a real prophecy and not just somebody combining poetic thinking with a hopeful idea or something?"

Kai looked at her with his liquid animal eyes – eyes that seemed to have seen centuries and gathered much wisdom – for several long seconds before he answered her. *Because I do. The stories say that one of her gifts was prophecy. It is true.* Cassie still wasn't completely convinced, but that seemed to be all he would say about the matter, as further queries failed to receive any satisfactory answer. The conversation was cut short by Hannah's announcement of dinner, but Cassie begged the others not to mention the prophecy to either adult, fearing it would cause them to change their minds about the trip. They agreed.

They all walked to dinner, but Cassie lingered a few moments. She felt a little upset with her father. He'd never told her about this prophecy. Why? Did he think he was somehow protecting her? That would be like Dad. So many things had happened in the last few days that she'd thought she would cease to be shocked by new developments, but man, was she wrong. As she stood gazing out the window at the landscape she knew so well, she wondered if she would ever see home again once she got to England. Immediately, she remembered how she'd thought the same thing when she first set out to rescue her parents, alone. *Of course I'll see it again*, she told herself again, and tried to dismiss such thoughts as she hurried to dinner. But the doubts remained, and questions plagued her throughout the night.

When she finally did sleep, her dreams were strange, following a beautiful woman with pointed ears and several men as they fought their way through various enemies to get… something. There were some conversations, but Cassie couldn't understand the language. In the final battle, one of the men fell, mortally wounded, but the woman took a wooden goblet from a bag, filled it with water, and put it to his lips, her lips moving in desperate prayer. Or was it song? Since the woman was clearly a Brenwyd, Cassie's dream-self suspected the latter. The man drank the water from the cup as the woman sang, and his wound healed. The last image Cassie saw before she woke was of the woman and men presenting the cup to another man, clearly a king as he wore a golden circlet on his brow. He looked startlingly familiar, but Cassie couldn't place him. The king looked at the cup, speaking to the others, and the woman put the cup back in her satchel. Cassie woke abruptly. It was still dark outside, and the clock read four o'clock in the morning. She lay in bed pondering the dream. The image of the cup in the king's hands kept coming back to her. She sat straight up as an idea came to her. She got out of bed and grabbed the diary, looking for a particular sketch. She found it quickly. It was the king she had seen. She stared at it as she realized the implications. "Could that be what the Brotherhood is after?" she murmured to herself. "If so, that would be the first time a dream has actually been helpful." She wondered whether or not to tell the others what she now believed was hidden in Arthur's treasure trove, and decided against it. It was a long shot, and she didn't want William to know of her suspicion. She still didn't trust him completely. Studying the drawing, she frowned. Something about the man seemed so familiar, yet she couldn't quite put a finger on it. Deciding to dismiss it, she climbed back into bed, and this time fell asleep quickly, sleeping peacefully for what remained of the night.

A Talk over Tea

Sarah looked out the airplane window down onto the sprawling buildings of London-Heathrow International Airport. She felt thrills of excitement course through her as the plane slowly began descending. She looked to her right, where her traveling companions sat. Cassie, who had been doodling in a sketchbook, was putting it away into the backpack that she'd brought in addition to her ever-present emergency bag. They all often joked that just about everything but the kitchen sink was in that bag, but they'd been grateful for it on more than one occasion. Cassie's face seemed devoid of expression, but Sarah knew her well enough to catch the wary and worried look in her eyes, as well as a spark of excitement. Beyond her, Sarah's dad was sitting in the aisle seat. The anxious look on his face was much easier to see. Sarah's mother had been unable to come because of her work, and Sarah suspected that her dad was relieved that at least one member of the family had stayed at home. Across the aisle, David and William sat together.

Sarah was happy to see her brother being more accepting of William. They'd discovered they shared several of the same interests and opinions, and had seemed to keep up a steady conversation throughout the flight. Well, when they'd been awake, anyway.

It was also good for David, in Sarah's opinion, to have some guy time. Because they lived in a fairly isolated valley some miles from town and both their parents worked, David didn't get to hang out with his guy friends as much as Sarah knew he would like to, and his closest guy friend had moved several months earlier. David didn't mind hanging out with her and Cassie, but Sarah suspected he had a girl overdose from time to time. It was too bad no boys their age lived in the valley.

Sarah still wasn't entirely sure what she thought of William. He seemed genuinely nice, and had showed on several occasions that he did have a good sense of humor. And he was good-looking, yes, but there was some sense of mystery about him that attracted her more than his looks. William definitely had a secret, but Sarah hoped more with each passing day that his secret wouldn't hurt them. There just seemed to be something slightly different about him, and she wanted to know what. In addition, when she'd first seen him she'd had a feeling that she'd seen him somewhere before, but had no idea where or when. She'd been racking her brain ever since trying to figure it out, but it remained an enigma. She hadn't mentioned it to Cassie or David.

She had also noticed that in the last few days, William seemed different from when they'd first met him. He appeared less sure of himself, more quiet, and Sarah thought she saw hints of an internal battle raging inside when she looked at him. She hadn't discussed any of her observations with David or Cassie, not wanting to burden the latter with more suspicions and worries, and knowing the former would accuse her of liking him enough to make a habit of studying his every move. Sometimes Sarah wished she were an only child, although more often than not she was grateful for her brother. Yeah, she admitted to herself that she did like William – but as a friend, nothing more. She was pulled from her thoughts as the plane landed, and dismissed them to ponder later.

Sarah wanted all her wits about her. She'd gotten lost in Heathrow several years earlier and had no wish to repeat the experience. She'd been able to find her group only after being paged over the public address system. It had been one of the scariest events of her life (until last week), and was hands-down the most embarrassing. On this trip, before they'd even left the airport in Virginia, David had already teased her about getting lost and told William the whole story. William had looked amused, but he hadn't laughed, which Sarah appreciated. In her opinion, Heathrow was easy to get lost in with all the different terminals, shops, and people. She expected some more teasing from her brother before they reached the rental car area, and he lived up to her expectations. But he stopped teasing when Cassie took her hand and declared that if Sarah got lost, she'd be lost with her and David would be responsible for finding them, as the brother and best friend. Despite Cassie's words, however, Sarah sensed that her friend was nervous herself and wanted some moral support.

Fortunately, no one got lost. Soon enough they collected their luggage, plus dogs (who had insisted on coming despite Cassie's attempts to dissuade them), and headed to the rental car area.

"So where are we meeting this lady again?" Sarah asked her dad. Before leaving the States, her dad and Cassie had arranged to meet with Dr. Sadie Stone, someone none of them had heard of before, but whom Cassie's dad apparently trusted. Sarah knew Cassie's main goal in meeting the woman was to figure out if Dr. Stone had been the means by which the Brotherhood had discovered Mr. Pennington's project. Cassie didn't think that the woman was directly responsible, but thought that she may have unknowingly mentioned it to the wrong person.

"At the British Museum, but then she said we'd go to a restaurant to get something to eat, and also to talk," he answered. Sarah checked her watch. It was 11:30 in the morning, local time.

David rubbed his stomach. "I hope they have more than tea and crumpets. What they gave us on the airplane wasn't very filling."

"They will," William reassured him. "Shepherd pies are pretty filling. I'm hungry enough myself to eat a horse."

"Excuse me?" Cassie asked. She'd been lost in thought, but William's comment had caught her attention and now she was glaring at him. She knew it was just an expression, but she disliked it.

"Uh, I meant a cow. I'm hungry enough to eat a cow," William amended hastily.

"I thought so," Cassie said, before quickening her pace to catch up with Mr. Thompson. Sarah chuckled, wishing she could get inside Cassie's head and figure out what she was really thinking. Cassie hadn't tried as hard as she could have to keep the dogs at home, which told Sarah she was feeling insecure about this expedition. She also suspected that the prophecy William had translated was weighing heavily on Cassie's mind. It had been on Sarah's too. It seemed incredible to her that a prophecy from over a thousand years ago would be about Cassie, assuming it was accurate, but Cassie said all the animals were dead certain. *But why Cassie?* Sarah wondered. It obviously hadn't happened yet, because the Brotherhood was still around. *Unless,* the thought occurred to her, *it happened but the Brotherhood re-formed.* That would be just great... but somehow it just didn't seem to fit. *So if the prophecy is true, who's to say it isn't going to happen in the future?* Sarah recalled Kai had said something about events or timing being right. She thought back over all the crazy stuff that had happened over the last week, taking into account that they were walking knowingly into the Brotherhood's lair, and admitted it would kinda make sense for Cassie to be the one talked about.

But then what about the stuff in it about Arthur's heir? she wondered. *How does that come into play?* She thought Arthur had died (or disappeared, or whatever) childless, so how could he have an heir? Well, there was that story about Mordred being Arthur's illegitimate son, but Cassie's dad had said it wasn't true – and if he said it wasn't true, it wasn't true. Sarah used to wonder how he could know so much about Arthur and be so sure of himself, until one day recently when Cassie said the knowledge had been passed down in their family since the time of Arthur's reign. But if Arthur did somehow have descendants, why say *the* heir instead of *an* heir? And how exactly would they go about finding the heir of a legendary king from fifteen hundred years ago? And assuming they could find the heir, how would they persuade him or her that they weren't completely nuts? Her thoughts wandered to Cassie's cryptic remarks about suspecting there was more to the treasure trove than it appeared. She hadn't put forth a theory as to what, which was unusual for her, but that didn't mean she hadn't thought of one.

"Sarah, watch where you're going!" David's voice cut into her thoughts. He'd stopped directly in front of her and she'd bumped into him. Sarah decided to save her deep thoughts for a time when she didn't have to pay attention to what she was doing.

"Hello, hello! Welcome to London," the woman said with a friendly smile. Cassie studied her. She wasn't particularly tall, standing a couple of inches below Cassie's five-foot-four-inch frame. Her hair was a soft shade of blonde and her eyes were a welcoming brown. She wore a clean-cut business suit, and had an air of efficiency and professionalism about her. Cassie guessed that this must be Dr. Sadie Stone. The woman walked up to Ben and shook hands, confirming Cassie's guess by introducing herself. She added, "I was glad to hear from you. I was beginning to wonder why Professor Pennington hasn't responded to any of my messages."

Ben returned the handshake. "I'm Ben Thompson. I'm glad you were able to meet with us."

"My pleasure. Now, please introduce me to these young people." Dr. Stone turned slightly to the teens. Cassie thought she saw a flicker of surprise in the woman's eyes when her gaze rested on William, but it was gone too quickly for her to be sure.

"Of course. This is my son, David; my daughter, Sarah; a friend of ours, William Douglas; and that's Cassie over there." He gestured to each as he named them and Dr. Stone greeted them all pleasantly, but it was obvious that Cassie was the one who caught her attention.

"I'm so glad to meet you in person, Cassandra. Your father has told me much about you."

"Really?" Cassie asked, a little wary.

"Oh, yes," Dr. Stone said, smiling at her. Cassie wondered just how much her dad had told this woman. Not that she minded her knowing the basics, but there was a limit to how much Cassie liked people knowing about her at first meetings. "And what are your dogs' names?" Dr. Stone queried.

"Kai and Dassah."

"Really? Those are unusual. I don't think I've ever heard those names before."

"They're nicknames actually. Kai is short for Kaiser and Dassah is short for Hadassah.

"Ah, I see. The German name for emperor, and a brave Jewish queen of Persia."

"Yes." Cassie leaned in toward the doctor slightly, lowering her voice. "How long have you worked with my father?"

Dr. Stone regarded Cassie for a minute, eyebrows slightly raised. "You don't know?"

"No, ma'am."

"Hmm." Her brown eyes darkened as if in thought. "Well," she said brightly after a moment, "let's go to lunch. I'll answer your questions there, where we can talk in peace. I'm sure you're all hungry after that trip."

The small restaurant where Dr. Stone took them, overlooking the Thames River, had only a few people in it. They took an outdoor table so the dogs could stay with them. David was relieved to find that William had been right about the menu. While they waited on the food, Cassie once again brought up the project.

This time, Dr. Stone was more than willing to talk. "Your father contacted me about a month ago, Cassandra," she began. "He said he thought he was onto something that could rewrite early British history. I actually hear variations of that line quite often in the archaeological field, so it was the source that intrigued me more than the declaration. I had heard of Professor Tyler Pennington, and of the discovery of those tunnels north of here a couple of years ago." Cassie, David, and Sarah all exchanged knowing glances. If only people knew how those tunnels had really been discovered. "But I wasn't sure why he'd want to contact me. I study the Roman occupation of Britain, and he focuses more on the Dark Ages. I asked him for more information and he obliged. He said he thinks that there is more to Cadbury than meets the eye." She paused. "He then told me of the tunnel network he believes lies deep under the hill and surrounding fields. I admit I was skeptical. Why would ancient Britons build a series of tunnels under a hill, even if it had once been a city? He said he didn't think it was the Britons at all. He thought it was–"

"A group of people who lived alongside the Britons but are unmentioned in historical records," Cassie cut in, anxious to get to what she considered the relevant part of the conversation.

Dr. Stone looked at her in surprise. "Yes, but he wouldn't tell me who he thought these people were, or why there should be no mention of them in history." *I'll bet he didn't,* Cassie thought. Her father was of the opinion that Brenwyds had constructed the tunnels, and no way would he go around telling people that. Dr. Stone continued speaking. "If you already knew, Cassandra, why are you asking me? And where is your father, anyway? I haven't heard from him in over a week."

"Oh, well, he, um..." Cassie stumbled.

Mr. Thompson saved her. "He was called away unexpectedly on some urgent business for an unknown length of time. It was very sudden and pretty mysterious. We don't know much about it, but we think it may have something to do with this project, so we decided to come see you and find out if you could shed any more light on the subject."

Dr. Stone studied him, as if trying to gauge the truth of his words. Her eyes narrowed, and for a second David thought he saw a glint appear in them. It passed quickly, but it made David feel slightly uneasy, though he couldn't say for sure if he'd really seen it or not, and if so, what it had represented. From the corner of his eye, he saw Cassie straighten a little, as if she'd also seen it. "Well, that's certainly strange. Especially as I think that you had a birthday recently, Cassandra?" Cassie started, surprised, but Dr. Stone just smiled. "Oh, don't be alarmed, dear. Your father mentioned it the last time we talked, that's all. How old are you?"

"Fourteen." Cassie wondered why the doctor kept calling her Cassandra. It made her feel like Dr. Stone was reproaching her. She was starting to get a very strange feeling. She couldn't say why, but she had a strong urge to get up and run from the restaurant. Cassie glanced around quickly, but didn't see anyone who could constitute a threat. "When was the last time you talked to my father?"

"The 14th of June, at about 10:00 p.m. London time." David, Sarah, and Cassie all exchanged looks. June 14 had been the date they'd set out on their camping trip.

"Why were you talking so late?" This query came from William, which surprised the others. He hadn't said much up to this point.

Dr. Stone hesitated for a minute before answering. "I had just gotten back from a trip to Cadbury, which he'd asked me to take to find some possible sites to start investigating. I also found out that no digs have been scheduled yet there for this summer. Your father was nearing the end of his research. Besides, it was only five o'clock his time."

There was silence for a few minutes as they concentrated on eating. Cassie turned over all the information in her head. Based on what Dr. Stone had said, it made perfect sense that the Brotherhood would take her parents now, just before her father was ready to start dig work, which Cassie had suspected already. Now she needed to know if Dr. Stone had mentioned the project to anyone else. "Dr. Stone," Cassie said, "did you talk to anyone else about the project? I know my dad would have kept it as secret as possible."

Dr. Stone narrowed her eyes at her. "Yes, your father did tell me he wished the project to be kept secret. I assumed he had his own reasons for secrecy, so I didn't pry. I never spoke of it with anyone other than your father until today, with you. Is there... a specific reason why you ask?"

"Just wondering. My dad is a private person even at home, but I wondered if he was a little more public with other historians. So, no one knew what you were working on with him?"

"No," Dr. Stone said. "I spoke of it to no one." She paused. "Although, sometimes I would be working and some co-workers would come and talk to me, so they may have glimpsed something."

Cassie kept her facial expression neutral, but she felt extremely puzzled. If Dr. Stone hadn't told anyone, then how had the news leaked out? Had a Brotherhood operative managed to put the puzzle pieces together about what Dr. Stone was working on based on some glimpses? Or had they broken into her office and left no trace? Cassie also started feeling more and more uncomfortable, like warning signals were going off inside her brain, and it was making her feel wary. She looked up and down the street, wondering if the Brotherhood was about to pull off an attack. An urgent plea from Dassah was a welcome excuse to get up. She looked at Mr. Thompson. "I need to take the dogs on a walk, to let them take care of business. Is that okay?"

Ben nodded. "I think so."

"There's a nice park just up the block and across the street where many people take their dogs," Dr. Stone put in. "It's a lovely place to walk as well." They quickly paid the bill and made their way to the park Dr. Stone had indicated. It was fenced and Cassie saw other dogs running around, so she let Dassah and Kai off their leashes. She watched them take care of business, then start playing to get all their excess energy out. She felt herself relaxing. It was easy, standing there, to forget the reason why she'd come to England at all. Dr. Stone was conversing amiably with David and Sarah's dad, so the young people were left to themselves.

"So what do you think of her?" Sarah asked.

Cassie took a minute to collect her thoughts, playing with the locket at her neck. "Honestly, I'm not sure. But something around here is making me feel... jumpy. It could be her, or could be something else, but I don't like it."

"What about her would be making you feel jumpy?" David asked. "She's been very nice." He had decided to try Cassie's method of looking for the good in people, and he was being honest. Dr. Stone certainly hadn't shown any reason to mistrust her.

"I know." Cassie was frowning. "It's just... I don't know... I've got this odd feeling, and the more I think on it, the more I feel like it's about her."

"An odd feeling?" William asked, sounding a little skeptical. "You doubt her just because of a feeling?"

"Dad always tells me to pay attention to my instincts. It's kept me out of trouble several times. And you left the Brotherhood because of a feeling," she reminded him.

"The situation was very different," William covered quickly. "I had a moral issue with wantonly killing a fourteen-year-old girl. You're saying that you mistrust a person you just met who has been nothing but polite, someone your dad trusted, just because of a feeling."

Cassie frowned at him. "Not everything has to be backed up by hard scientific proof. You said you trusted your instincts. Is there something wrong with me trusting mine?" She looked at him carefully. "Are you doubting me because I'm part Brenwyd?"

"Of course not. I was just saying that it doesn't make sense. In the same vein, you gave me a chance. Won't you give her one?"

"I never said I wouldn't. I was just saying that I have an odd feeling that may or may not be about her. There is freedom of speech in Britain, isn't there?" Cassie said tartly, starting to feel irritated. Why was he so fixated on that comment? David and Sarah exchanged glances as the conversation heated up, wondering how to diffuse the tension.

Fortunately, Kai interrupted before the argument went any further. *She has a bad smell*, he declared as he and Dassah walked up.

William swiveled his head to scowl at the dog. He'd been hoping that if the discussion continued he could finally determine whether Cassie told the truth or not, and he wasn't appreciative that Kai had interrupted. "What do you mean she has a bad smell? She smells fine to me," he said, not fully thinking about the comment before it was out of his mouth.

"You took note?" Sarah asked with a humorous twinkle in her eyes, jumping at the chance to lighten the mood. William rolled his eyes. He'd gotten used to the gentle teasing and wordplay that accompanied conversations with Cassie and the twins, so now he decided to play along with Sarah. *After all*, he reflected, *I did ask for it with that comment.*

"Oh, yes, of course. Didn't you notice? She's wearing a very pleasant fragrance," he said with such a straight face and serious tone that Sarah actually thought he might be serious. William chuckled at her confused expression, forgetting his annoyance. "Joking, Sarah. Joking."

"Oh," she said, feeling her face go red in embarrassment for taking him seriously. David and Cassie burst out laughing, and William joined in. Then Sarah did, too, albeit sheepishly, and even the dogs thought it was amusing.

"Oh, dear," Cassie said between laughs, having gotten over her irritation. "You've been hanging around us too much, William. You're losing your proper attitude."

William sighed dramatically. "I'm afraid you're right, Cassie. Even the most proper Englishman would have trouble staying that way after spending a week with you backwards Americans. But I imagine I will regain it after being here for a few days," he replied with mock seriousness.

"Oh, we're backward, are we?" David asked.

"Well, the colonies broke from England, didn't they? Definitely backward thinkers," he retorted. Everyone was laughing hard, probably more than was necessary, but it was a relief to laugh after having such depressing thoughts and worries on their minds for days. William once again reflected that, in moments like these, it was fun to just go along and not pay much attention to the fact that Cassie was Brenwyd and he'd have to turn her in... That thought led him back to Kai's original statement. "So what did you mean, Kai?" The others stopped laughing.

Something about her smells wrong. I would not trust her.

"Dad did trust her," Cassie put in thoughtfully, knowing that part of William's argument was valid. "And he's good at judging people's character."

Appearances can be deceiving, girl. I agree with Kai. There is definitely something wrong with that woman, Dassah said. *Your father never spoke with her face-to-face. He could have been deceived.*

"Maybe we're just being paranoid," Sarah suggested. "After last week, we're all on edge and suspicious. We're probably just reading into her too much."

The conversation was cut short by the arrival of Dr. Stone and the twins' dad.

"What have you been laughing about?" Ben asked.

"We'll tell you later," David said.

"It must have been very amusing," Dr. Stone said.

"It was," Sarah said. "But you had to be there."

Dr. Stone smiled. "I see." She turned her gaze to the river. Ben took advantage of the pause to say he was going to use the restroom and get the car. He left, and an awkward silence rose. Dr. Stone broke it by turning to William with a smile, but something about the smile struck Cassie as odd. She couldn't say what, but this lady was really starting to bother her. Again she felt the need to run, but stronger this time. *Sarah's right,* she told herself. *I'm being way too suspicious.* "Mr. Thompson tells me that you're from the Carlisle area," Dr. Stone said to William.

"Uh, yeah. I am." William wondered why Mr. Thompson had told the woman that.

"I know many people in that area. I wonder if you know any of them," she said over her shoulder as she started to walk down a path. She stopped when she realized no one was following. "I apologize. I rarely get the chance to get out of the museum on such a gorgeous day, and I want to take full advantage of it. This is a lovely walk. Why don't you come with me, William, and we can see if we know the same people?" She walked off before waiting for an answer. William looked at his companions. They looked as puzzled as he felt (and probably looked).

"Should I go?" he asked. Normally he wouldn't think of asking permission from a Brenwyd to do something, but this lady was starting to make him uncomfortable. Maybe Cassie's words were getting to him.

Cassie shrugged. "Well, I don't really see any reason not to," she said, sounding uncertain. "You might have the best chance outta all of us to figure her out, being the same nationality and all. Especially if it turns out you know the same people."

William accepted this logic. *She may be a Brenwyd,* he thought, *but she does have sense.* He hurried after the doctor. "Maybe if you told me their names..." At this point the two walked out of even Cassie's hearing. She and the twins looked at each other, each knowing what was on the others' minds: there was something strange about this.

At the moment, William was feeling even more puzzled than the other three. Dr. Stone had deliberately singled him out to talk, but so far she hadn't said a word, hadn't even answered his question. They stopped along the park fence at a point that gave a good view of the river through the trees. The Thames was chugging along as it always did, with the currents and eddies carrying everything along with them. Looking back, William could see they also had a clear view of Cassie, David, Sarah, and the dogs, still where they'd been left. Dassah had found a stick, and Cassie was throwing it for her and Kai.

William returned his attention to Dr. Stone and was shocked by the look on her face. Her friendly smile had become a look of absolute hate and loathing, her brown eyes dark and ominous. Following her line of vision, William realized that the recipient of this look was Cassie. That made no sense. Why would Dr. Stone feel such hate for her project partner's daughter, whom she had never met before? She shifted her gaze to him, and her expression became a stern frown. "What do you think you're doing, boy?" Her light, easygoing tone was gone, replaced by one of harsh rebuke.

William had no idea what she was talking about. "Ma'am?"

"Don't pretend you don't know what I'm talking about. Traveling with a Brenwyd! Yes, I know who you are, William Douglas. I know your father. Where is he? And how'd he miss the girl? I led them right to her doorstep!" She sounded angry.

"You... you're a Brotherhood member?"

Dr. Stone rolled her eyes. "Of course, boy. How do you think the Brotherhood found out the Penningtons' secret? They found it themselves? Please! Without my help, they would still be trying to figure out if they were even Brenwyd. I was the one who alerted them to the professor's theories and thoroughly researched his family tree. They were close as it was, but not quite close enough. But I suppose they didn't tell you that?"

"Um, no ma'am."

"Hm. Typical. Well, you still haven't answered my questions. Where is your father and why are you traveling with *her*?" William's brain was scrambling. Who was this woman? There were no women members of the Brotherhood, not that he'd heard of. She must be just an informant. He decided to answer her questions for the time being.

"My father's back at headquarters. I... I'm bringing the girl to him." Dr. Stone stared at him. William felt a sense of shock at what he'd said, and was surprised by it, as he'd been surprised by the feeling of horror he felt when telling his father their movements. He realized, with crystal clarity, that he didn't *want* to turn Cassie over. She didn't deserve it. He tore his eyes from Dr. Stone's gaze and tried to focus on something else, anything else. *Don't think like that, William!* he told himself. *That's traitor talk!* His eyes found Cassie and he studied her. She was scratching Dassah and saying something to David, probably something funny, because she had a smile on her face. From here he couldn't tell what color in her eyes was dominant, but it was probably blue. Her titian hair was in its usual braids, but they weren't very tight and several strands framed her face, held back by her headband. She looked like a normal teen enjoying some time at the park. She certainly didn't look evil, much less like she was descended from fallen angels.

"I see. Using deception to get her right where you want her. Very clever." Dr. Stone's voice brought him back to the conversation. He looked at her again, and her eyes searched his. They apparently found something they didn't like, because they darkened even further. "But you seem to be having second thoughts?" Her voice was soft now. It reminded William of a serpent's hiss.

"No, of course not. I just–"

"Oh, don't try fooling me, boy. The father fooled me as well in the beginning. So seemingly kind, so seemingly genuine. But don't be tricked by appearances. The evil in Brenwyds comes with the ability to project an aura of seeming virtue, but inside they're plotting to bring us down. Don't fall into her trap. You're an intelligent boy. You can overcome her charms." William felt like the woman was reading his mind.

"I know my duty."

"Yes, but can you perform it?"

"Of course I can," he snapped. "Father is counting on me."

"Then how were you planning to go about getting the girl to him?"

William hesitated. "We... we're going on to Cadbury today. I was going to contact my father to tell him to bring some men and intercept her there. If I call him soon, he can be there by evening."

"Why not just take them to headquarters and have her captured there?"

"Because... she's smart. She doesn't completely trust me, and I know David doesn't. It would be better to nab her before she thinks better of this excursion and decides to head home."

"Hmm. You make a good point. Brenwyds are cowards by nature." William thought that obviously this woman had not met Cassie. "And it would be embarrassing for you, to say the least, to have gotten her so close only to have her escape. I could contact your father for you, if you want."

"Sure, that's probably a good idea. I may not have an opportunity to do it."

"How many men should he bring? One for each?" That surprised William.

"One for each? Is that necessary? It's just Cassie who's Brenwyd."

"Think, boy. I know the Commander's taught you how to use your brain. The others know too much for us to let them go. They know about the project and the general location of our headquarters. And they are closely acquainted with *her* and her family. It's too dangerous for them to go free."

"Oh, right." William wasn't sure he liked that. Then again, he wasn't sure he liked the idea of betraying Cassie into Brotherhood hands. Sure, he'd been trained from birth to hate Brenwyds. He'd dreamed about being the one to completely extinguish their race from the earth. But the Brenwyds he'd imagined destroying had been faceless, nameless, not people he'd come to know and appreciate. *Oh, get over yourself, William!* he yelled at himself. *She's a Brenwyd, a child of the devil! You're not supposed to appreciate her. She must be a powerful witch for you to feel like this. And the others are just as bad, having aided and abetted her and her family.* "Of course. But I think there should be more than four. They're fierce fighters and won't let themselves be captured easily. And then, there are the dogs to think about."

"Fierce fighters, you say? Who trained them?"

"The girl's father, and he did it very well. They killed the men Father left behind to catch the girl, and likely would have killed me if I hadn't pretended to be a prisoner myself." It was much easier to speak of Cassie as "the girl." "The girl" made it sound like it could be anyone, made it less personal.

"And they believed you?" He nodded. She sounded impressed. "Well, that's a job well done. How long have you been in her company?"

"About a week."

"Ah, no wonder you feel a little reluctant. She's had plenty of time to cast her enchantment."

"No one's cast any enchantment over me."

"Not anymore, now that you've been talking to someone who knows the truth." Her tone softened. "You've done well, William. If you tell me your phone number, I'll send you a text letting you know the time and place your father says."

"Alright." William gave her his number.

"I'll call headquarters as soon as you leave. We'd better go back now. We can't let them get too suspicious." They headed back.

Sarah looked at William curiously. "What did you talk about?"

William gave her what he hoped looked like a genuine, reassuring smile. "Oh, not much. Turns out, we do know some of the same people around Carlisle."

"Really?" she said. "Small world." *If only you knew,* William thought.

Dr. Stone smiled her friendly smile. "I need to get back to the museum now. It's been lovely meeting all of you. Good luck on the rest of your trip."

"Thank you for your time, Dr. Stone," Cassie said. "I really appreciate it."

"Don't mention it, dear. It's a treat for me to spend time with you young people. Goodbye. Do let me know if you find anything." She turned and started walking in the direction of the museum, just as Ben was coming back.

"Do you want a ride?" he called after her.

She looked over her shoulder without stopping. "Oh, no. I'll enjoy the walk back. I don't get out enough." And with that, she disappeared among the people on the sidewalk.

Ben looked at the teens. "Ready to go?"

"Yep," David said. Cassie and Sarah nodded. William made no response, simply staring blankly at the river.

"Are you ready, William?" Ben asked.

"What? Oh, yes. Quite." His tone made the others look at him.

"Are you feeling alright, William?" Sarah asked with concern.

"Yes, I'm fine. Just a little tired."

"You can sleep in the car," Ben said. They headed toward the vehicle. Cassie watched William closely. Something was wrong with him, and she was pretty sure it had nothing to do with being tired and everything to do with the conversation he'd just had with Dr. Stone. She almost thought she saw a guilty look in his eyes as he looked at them.

"Are you sure you're alright?" she asked him quietly. They were a little behind the others. "You seem shaken up. Was she really that bad?" He looked at her, and she thought he looked miserable.

"Oh, no, not at all. She's quite nice, really. I think your feelings are off. And I'm just tired. Been switching time zones too much." With that, he quickened his pace and pulled ahead of her and the dogs.

Something is wrong with him, Dassah said.

Yes, Cassie agreed. *I wish I knew what.*

Kai bared his teeth a little. *He is up to something. Watch him.*

Maybe he just feels a little overwhelmed, returning home and all, but marked as an enemy by his former friends. She hoped it was the case. Kai wasn't so sure.

I will be keeping a close eye on him. I suggest you do the same.

I have since the day we met, Kai, Cassie said. *I think he really needs God more than anything else.*

Everyone needs the One, Dassah said. *We must show him the way to Him.*

We will, Cassie said. *We will.* And the threesome quickened their pace to catch up with the others.

Betrayed

David studied William in the rear view mirror. He was acting more normal now, debating some of the finer points of the King Arthur legend with Cassie (a dangerous pastime, in David's opinion), but David could see a slight uneasiness in his eyes. He knew Cassie probably saw it as well. After they'd gotten into the car, William had slept for about half an hour, proving that he was tired, but David also had a feeling that the conversation with Dr. Stone had really upset him. Each of the teens had tried in their own way to pry out of the British boy what had gone on, but each time he'd stymied them.

He may not be the most trustworthy person, David thought, *but he's not dumb.* Cassie's animated tone caught his attention, and he tuned in to her and William's conversation. They were debating whether Arthur had drawn Excalibur from the stone or gotten it from the Lady of the Lake, as legend claimed.

"A mysterious lady rising from a lake to give Arthur a sword? That does not make sense," William was saying. "Not that being the only person able to pull it out of a stone makes sense either, but I have an easier time seeing where that might have originated."

"But the legend had to come from somewhere," Cassie argued. "All legends and myths, no matter how far-fetched, must be based on grains of truth, or else people wouldn't keep telling them. Take elves, for example." William looked confused. David didn't blame him. The way Cassie's mind moved and made connections was beyond him a lot of the time.

"What do elves have to do with Arthur?" William asked.

"Nothing. Well, not really, anyway. I was just using them as an example that all legends, or most anyway, have at least one small grain of truth in them. Of course, elves have lots of truth to them; it's mainly the name that's fiction, but anyway–"

"Whoa!" Sarah interjected. "Are you saying elves were real?"

Cassie gave her a look as if to say, *Really?* "Sarah, you have seen my ears, right?" she asked, sounding amused.

Sarah went red. "Oh. Right. I guess I should have thought of that. Looks like you weren't too far off after all, David."

"Huh?" David said, startled by his sudden inclusion in the conversation.

"You know, what we were talking about coming back from the campsite the first time," Sarah reminded him.

"Oh, right. Well, you suggested it," David said.

"Suggested what?" Cassie and William said at the same time.

David turned to face the back seat as he answered. "Well, it was right after you'd galloped off, Cassie, and we were trying to figure out your weird behavior – hey, what did set the animals off, anyway?"

"They sensed what Kai now thinks was a Brotherhood member. They weren't exactly sure at the time, but, well..." Cassie's voice trailed off. "You were saying?"

"Well, I made a comment that maybe your behavior had something to do with what was under your headband, and Sarah said, 'What, you think she has pointed ears and is part elf?' Or something like that," David finished.

"Hmm. Not too far off. I actually thought that myself on the day they became pointed. And now you know where that legend came from," Cassie said.

William raised an eyebrow. "Became pointed? You weren't born with pointed ears?" he asked curiously, sounding surprised.

"Heavens, no. They became pointed a few weeks after my tenth birthday. Really shocked myself when I looked in the mirror that morning."

"Then it did happen while we were away," David said.

"The morning after you got back, actually, before you came over."

"Really?" Sarah asked. "No wonder you seemed a little upset."

"Yeah, well, now you know." There was a short silence.

Sarah looked at her friend curiously as a thought struck her. "Cassie?" she asked.

"Yeah?"

"Can Brenwyds do magic?" Cassie looked at her carefully, not sure of where the question was going.

"Why do you ask?" she asked cautiously.

"Well, in lots of stories, elves are magical and can do magic. And you were saying how legends generally have grains of truth, and Calico mentioned something about increased mental talent, and healing, and how people got scared of Brenwyds. Not to mention how Chance was slashed by a sword yet the wound looked months old when we got to your house. And then there's the whole Brotherhood notion that Brenwyds are witches, and what you said at the camp about Brenwyds and magic. I've been meaning to ask you about that, but I kept forgetting," Sarah said.

"I see. The answer to that is... complicated. No, not really," Cassie corrected herself, "just a little hard to explain."

"Why?"

"Well, it's *not* magic, not at all. It's... ugh, how do I say this?... listening and fixing what sounds wrong." There was silence in the car for several minutes.

"Could you clarify that?" David finally asked.

Cassie sighed. "Well, magic like you're probably thinking of, with spells and enchantment and whatnot, Brenwyds *cannot* do and *do not* do. Those things go against the laws of God. Remember that story in the Bible about Saul going to a medium? That magic was not of God, because the power did not come from Him, though it was real. Brenwyds are completely opposed to that." She paused for a moment, thinking. "Okay, so Brenwyds have enhanced senses, right? And not just keen vision or hearing. They can sense things, hear things, that normal humans can't. Like... the songs living things have in them that usually only God hears."

William started to look more interested. "Songs? What do you mean?" he asked, almost eagerly.

"Well, so God made everything on the planet, right?" Cassie said.

"Right," three voices said.

"So all living things have a song, like, programmed into them, kinda like DNA, and it's like a continuous praise rising to God. That's what He intended it to be, anyway. Now, with all the evil in the world, lots of people's songs are twisted and not at all like they're meant to be. Brenwyds can hear those songs if they want to. They tell a lot about a person. Animals have them too, but theirs generally aren't messed up, unless they're hurt or sick. When that happens, a Brenwyd can listen for their song, recognize how it's supposed to sound versus how it actually sounds, and sing the right melody that then heals the wound or illness. It works that way for people, too. It's actually a natural process. People back a thousand years ago didn't really understand it; they just knew it was strange and different and looked like magic, so that's what they called it and why they came to fear Brenwyds so much. It's just a talent. God gave it to the original Brenwyds and it's been passed down ever since." There was another silence. Cassie felt herself blushing. She'd refrained from telling them about her unique ability until now because she hadn't wanted to freak them out.

"And you can do that?" Sarah asked. Cassie nodded. "That's so cool! So that's why Chance's wound was healed. You fixed it... with his song. No wonder you have such a good voice."

Cassie nodded. "Yep."

"Do you have any other abilities like that?" William asked.

"Not that I know of. Frankly, I've got enough weird abilities. I really don't want any more," Cassie said with some feeling.

"Weird? I don't think it's weird. It's useful," David said. He personally thought those sorts of abilities would be pretty cool. But then, they did come with the risk of being killed by a diabolical organization. That wasn't so cool. He could see why Cassie was perfectly content with the abilities she already had.

"And you can't use it for anything other than healing?" William asked. He had heard that Brenwyds worked their magic through songs, but the way Cassie explained it made it not seem like magic. This might be his only chance before she was captured to have her speak freely about her abilities.

Cassie looked at him. "Well, yes, to put it in brief terms. I don't fully understand it, but Dad told me a few weeks ago that Brenwyds could use songs and counter-melodies to battle evil."

"How?" William pursued the point.

Cassie shrugged. "I don't know, exactly. Dad told me that he thought it had something to do with finding and singing a melody that somehow ran counter to an evil song, which would be an actual spell or something like that, and the singing of the countersong would destroy the evil one, but he said that the exact practice of it was lost during the Middle Ages when Brenwyds were being persecuted. A lot of things were lost."

"That's too bad," Sarah said.

Cassie nodded. "It is." There was a thoughtful silence. "Now, where were we, William?" Cassie said, shaking herself out of her thoughts.

"Huh?"

"You know, our debate. Where were we before we went off on this tangent?"

"Oh. Um, you were saying how most legends have a least one small grain of truth in them." He paused. "Wow, we really went off topic. From Excalibur to elves to Brenwyd abilities."

"Ah, it's not so far off. There's a story Dad told me that Excalibur and Seren were forged from the same meteorite by a Brenwyd smith. One time, I had this conversation with a friend when we started by reviewing the government systems of Rome for a test, but by the end of it we were discussing the pros and cons of various horse breeds. *That's* way off topic."

Ben broke into the conversation. "I hate to interrupt, but we're nearly there. The hill should appear through the passenger side window in about two minutes." The young people all looked out the window, and sure enough, the hill came into view. Despite the fact that it was called "Cadbury Castle," the hilltop was bare, any man-made structure having crumbled long ago. Much of the hillside was covered by trees, but there were some clear, grassy areas where four ridge lines were visible, evidence of ancient earthworks used for defense. The hilltop was also bare of trees, covered only by a carpet of grass.

"Well, it looks the same as ever," Cassie stated. A gleam of excitement came into her eye as she made her next statement. "But I can't wait to see what may be lying underneath."

William stared at his phone screen, slowly absorbing the meaning of the characters displayed. Dr. Stone had kept her end of the bargain, and they were coming. *9:30 @ castle*, the message read. *Get them there.* William glanced at his watch. It was 3:15. *Father must be just starting,* he mused, thinking of the long drive from Carlisle to Cadbury, which could be up to six hours. The real trick would be persuading the group to go out that late. How to convince them? Leave something important on purpose, discover it was missing, and convince them he needed to come back? No, that wouldn't work; it was likely only Mr. Thompson would come with him, and he needed all four. Unless… unless he could get Cassie out by herself, without the dogs, knock her out, call his father and have him pick them up. Then maybe, just maybe, the others could stay free. William shook his head. His father would simply make him go get the others. He kicked the ground in frustration. Why was he even doing this? It turned his stomach, when it shouldn't. He hadn't felt this way when witnessing the deaths of other people of Brenwyd blood, so why was this one so different? Was it because she really was a powerful witch?

No, it is because you know her, that contrary part of him whispered. *You know she does not deserve this. Why not tell her now, give her a warning? She has been nothing but kind to you. If she really were evil, she would have killed you when she found you. And what of the others? What have they done to merit being captured, besides being loyal to their friend? Do you really want their blood on your hands? You know what will happen to them, to them all, eventually. Why turn them in? Has your own father ever treated you with the kindness they have?*

Shut up, William told the voice. *I'm my own person. Dr. Stone was right, Cassie must be powerful, whatever claims she may have made in the car about only being able to heal.* He remembered that Cassie had mentioned that Brenwyds could tell a lot about people based on their "songs." If that were true, why hadn't she exposed William already, or Dr. Stone for that matter? Perhaps she hadn't thought of it, content to trust them at their word. That thought made him feel strangely ashamed.

"Goodness, William, that's quite an expression. What's up?" Sarah's voice startled him and he looked up abruptly.

"Nothing. Just thinking."

"About what?"

"Nothing important."

She looked unconvinced. "Then why are you torturing the grass?"

William looked down and saw that the grass was all twisted and broken in his vicinity. "Oh. I, uh, was just thinking pretty hard."

"Must be important to be thinking about it so hard."

"It's not." He started walking, trying to get away. It did no good, as she just followed him.

"Are you sure?"

"Yes, Sarah, I'm sure. Please stop asking." She was silent. He stopped and turned. Her mouth was set in a frown, and the usual humor was gone from her hazel eyes. "Where are the others?" he asked.

"They're checking out the sites Dr. Stone thought might have ways to get to the tunnels. We were wondering where you were, so I volunteered to come find you. But I see you're busy thinking, so I'll leave you alone now." She turned as if to walk away.

"Sarah, wait!" He put a hand on her arm, and she swiveled her head to look at him, surprised. "I really don't mind. My thoughts weren't any good anyway. I'm sorry."

She gazed at him thoughtfully. "Alright, I forgive you." An awkward silence rose.

William realized she was looking at his hand, which was still clutching her arm. He released it quickly. "Sorry."

A smile broke through her expression and she chuckled. "Well, I'm not quite sure why you feel so apologetic, but I accept. Mind if I take a guess at your thoughts?" He shrugged. "You probably feel a little lost. You were taught that Brenwyds are evil, were trained to hate them, but your feelings got in the way of what you were told was your duty, and then you were abandoned. Now you're finding out that Brenwyds aren't really all that different from regular people, and it's making you confused. And we're back in your home country, headed to Brotherhood HQ, where you're now seen as an enemy. That's enough to make anyone nervous." He stared at her. It wasn't exactly what he'd been thinking just then, but close enough. "Am I right?"

"Close enough. How'd you know?"

"I didn't. I just guessed. I've made it a habit to study people. It's interesting to me. I've found out a lot that way. You've seemed really conflicted, especially over the last few days, ever since you translated that prophecy."

"Planning to go into psychology, are you?"

"Maybe. But that's off topic. The point I want to make, William, is that we do care about you, and so does God. He knows your thoughts even better than I do, because He knows thoughts before people even think them. He knew you even before you were born, knows what you'll become. You're at a crossroads right now as you're seeing that the doctrine you've learned is all wrong, and that's a lot for anyone to take. But you're keeping it all locked in, and talking to someone about it would probably really help." She wasn't looking at him directly, and was rushing through her words as if she wanted to say them but was embarrassed. Her cheeks had gone slightly pink.

He just stared at her, amazed by her insight and her words. "Are you... offering?" The question made her cheeks turn a darker shade of pink and he realized she was blushing.

"N-no, I mean, if you want to, I wouldn't mind. I was just saying..." She seemed to be at a loss.

William was touched by how concerned she seemed for him. He desperately wanted nothing more than to pour his inner turmoil out to her, but he restrained himself. She would hate him, and tell Cassie, and he would get into a huge amount of trouble with his father and the whole Brotherhood organization if he botched this assignment. Still... "It – it's not the sort of thing I can talk about with someone, Sarah. It's complicated."

She raised her eyes to his, and nodded slowly. "Well, if you can't talk with any of us about it, you could always talk to God about it. He's great at problem solving." William hadn't thought of that. Where he came from, God was acknowledged, but never really prayed to by anyone on his level. That was done by the higher-ups, like his father. At least, that was what he had always been taught. After spending a week with Cassie and the Thompsons, he wasn't so sure.

"I don't know how," he found himself saying.

Sarah grinned, her dimples showing. "That's okay. There's no real right or wrong way. Like I said, God already knows your thoughts. He knows what you mean even if you can't articulate it just right. I generally talk to him like I do to other people, and Cassie talks to him like that even with other people around." William had noticed that about the Brenwyd girl. It was one of the many things about her character that was at odds with Brotherhood teaching.

A shout from up the hill diverted their attention. "Hey! What are you two doing?" David was looking down at them. "Sarah, I thought you were going to find William and bring him back."

"I'm in the process of doing that, David. We're having a conversation."

"Then have one while you're walking. Dad doesn't want any of us out of sight from the others for too long."

"We're coming, we're coming," Sarah answered. She and William trudged up the hill, William thinking hard on her words. They made him feel even more strongly that the Brotherhood was in the wrong, but it was too late to turn back now. He had to go through with the mission.

Cassie pored over her translation of her father's notes. Somewhere there had to be his thoughts on where the entrance to the tunnels could be located. She was curled up in a chair in the hotel room she and Sarah were sharing, with Dassah and Kai on the floor beside her. Sarah was reading and listening to her iPod on one of the beds. Mr. Thompson, David, and William were in the room next to them, with a connecting door, closed at present, linking the two rooms. The hotel where they were staying on the way to the Brotherhood headquarters happened to be only about five minutes from Cadbury Castle. That afternoon, they hadn't had much luck in finding possible entrances. They'd found the locations given them by Dr. Stone but, without the proper equipment, they couldn't tell if they led to a tunnel system or not, and no way could they get the right equipment to the hill without going through the proper channels and raising a fuss.

She must have let out a big sigh, because Sarah looked up from her reading. "What is it?" she asked.

"Sarah, why am I doing this?"

"Doing what?"

"Looking for tunnels under the site of an ancient hill fort. This is my dad's work, not mine. If all this hadn't happened, we would be back in Virginia, riding the trails and hanging out with our friends like we're supposed to do over the summer, not here with the threat of the Brotherhood looming over our heads." Dassah licked Cassie's hand comfortingly.

Kai raised his head from the floor. *What* you *think you should be doing, girl, is not necessarily what the* One *needs* you *doing. He knows how all this will turn out, and will guide you. Do not be afraid.*

"I'm not scared. Well, no, I am. I just don't want to be doing this. I want to be home, have my parents home, and be *normal.* Is that so much to ask?" Cassie said plaintively.

No, but the One wants you here, so here you are and here we are. Do not be like Jonah and run from your calling. Just accept that He would not give you a task you are not ready for, Kai answered.

Cassie held back a sigh. Sometimes Kai was just too philosophical. "Just keep reminding me."

"Kai's right, Cassie," Sarah piped up. "And you're not alone, you know. You've got the dogs, me, my dad, David, and William. We stand with ya."

"But what about that prophecy?" Cassie asked. "*If* it's true and *if* it's about me" – Kai and Dassah both looked at her irritably at the insinuation that it might not be true – "then I'm supposed to fight and kill the head of the Brotherhood and knock the whole organization out of existence! I'm only fourteen, and barely that! Why is all this happening now and not later, when I'm older?"

Because the One loves to use those who think they are too weak, too young, or otherwise unable to do the things to which He has called them, Dassah said. *Why not right now? You have mastered your knife work, and have learned to hear the songs. The One thinks you are ready, therefore you are ready. Do not doubt yourself, girl.* Cassie thought about that. It did kinda make sense, but it didn't really make her feel much better about things.

"I don't know the answers to all your questions, Cass," Sarah said, unaware of Dassah's response. "But I do know this: You'll be able to handle anything that happens, because God has to check out anything the world throws at you before he lets it hit ya. And," she smiled a little, "who says you have to know what you're doing? Just do what you know's right, and God may just use those actions to throw the Brotherhood down."

Cassie looked at Sarah, smiling slightly. "You make it sound easy. Maybe you should do it."

Sarah laughed. "Thanks, but it's your job. I wouldn't want to mess it up for you." Cassie grunted.

"Are you in the middle of something?" William said from the doorway. The girls started.

"No," Cassie said.

"How long have you been standing there?" Sarah demanded.

"Just long enough to hear that last comment." He stepped into the room. David and Mr. Thompson followed him.

"What is it?" Cassie asked.

"William has this idea on where the tunnel entrance may be,"

David said. His dark eyes glinted with an even mixture of suspicion and excitement.

"Oh? Where?" she asked William.

He cleared his throat. "I think on the northwestern side of the hill that faces toward the Tor at Glastonbury. I was running through all the Arthurian folklore in my head, and considering the aura of mystery surrounding both places, I think it's fairly plausible. Cadbury's not so far from Glastonbury, after all. And I think I remember seeing some odd rocks on that side of the hill this afternoon," he answered.

Cassie thought about it for a minute. "That's as good a guess as any. I remember seeing those rocks. We can check it out tomorrow."

"And that's where the rest of this idea comes in," David interjected.

"Oh?" both girls asked.

William looked away from them, out the window, and hoped they'd buy his reason, though that hope was battled with by another, stronger hope that they wouldn't. "I think we should check it out tonight. If we do find the tunnel entrance, we don't want it to be in the middle of the day, when there could be people around. It could become a media frenzy, which is the last thing we need. The Brotherhood would be onto us in a heartbeat. But if we find it at night, no one'll be around to see. Also, we could use shovels to dig, which we can't in daylight."

Cassie frowned. "We can't use shovels and stuff like that on the site without permission. It's illegal. And I'm not so sure about going out at night."

"We don't have to dig up anything. And besides, we really can't spend too much time here before going on to Carlisle. If we stay in one place too long, the Brotherhood will find out we're here. They have excellent intelligence forces. We need to keep moving. And nighttime is the best time for doing things you don't want other people to see." Cassie probed him with her eyes, trying to figure out what he wasn't saying. He did have a point about needing to move quickly. The Brotherhood was sure to be watching her movements, trying to figure out when best to capture her – and she had no doubt they would keep trying until they succeeded. And if she did manage to free her parents, they wouldn't really have time to stop and figure out the treasure's exact location afterwards. The Brotherhood would be on their heels, and they'd have to be really creative in how to get back to the States without being recaptured. Cassie hadn't thought much about it, because her brain was on overload with all the things she was already worrying about.

She looked at Mr. Thompson. "What do you think?" she asked him.

"William's idea does have merit, and so do his points. We weren't planning on stopping here long, anyway. I don't see anything obvious standing in the way, unless we're all just too exhausted. But you're the one with all the knowledge, Cassie. It's your decision," he said. "My main concern is that it's completely dark outside." *Well that's just great,* Cassie thought. She asked the dogs for their opinion. Dassah said she wouldn't mind going back, but she wouldn't mind waiting. Her main opposition was that the sun had gone down. Kai said that if they did go, they should go prepared and wary.

"Does anyone really feel tired?" Cassie asked.

Sarah shook her head. "Our bodies are thinking it's five hours earlier. I think it'd be kinda fun to go poking around after dark. I brought a flashlight." David agreed with his sister. Cassie realized she was the only real opposition. Part of her thought, *Why not? It's not like anyone else will be out there at this time of night, and I would rather be out there doing something than sitting here doing nothing.* But part of her warned of danger.

William saw her hesitation. "We don't have to go; I just thought we might as well, seeing as I don't think any of us feel like falling asleep."

Cassie shrugged, making up her mind. "Just so long as there aren't any artifact thieves lurking around, I don't see why not." The Thompsons laughed, and the group got ready to go. David noted that William looked tense and seemed a little nervous. He wondered why, as it had been William's idea to go out at night. He wanted to take William aside and ask him about it, but didn't find an opportunity. Before leaving the room, Cassie made sure that everything that might come in handy was in her emergency bag, and that her knife was in a position for her to grab if the occasion called for it. She had a strange feeling she would need it.

The trip to Cadbury Castle was quick, but the hill looked different in the dark, more ominous, the shadows of the trees more forbidding. They made their way over to where William thought the entrance might be. Kai and Dassah sniffed around. The trees were clumped together tightly here, as they were all around the hill.

"So, William, did you have any definite ideas on where to look and what to look for?" David asked.

William started slightly, as if he'd forgotten David was there. "Um, not... not really. I was thinking, maybe there would be a marker of some kind, maybe hidden under the grass. It's grown up since Arthur's time, and there could be anything beneath the ground. Also, we should look around the trees carefully, since I doubt they would have been here when this place was still a functioning hill fort, and they could easily be hiding something."

"True," Cassie agreed, kneeling on the ground near an especially big tree, putting her hand on the trunk as she studied the earth. There was a large rock nearby. David wondered if maybe she was sensing something the rest of them couldn't with her special song-listening ability. She took her bag from her back and started rummaging around for something, but stopped abruptly and tensed. The dogs circled back, teeth bared at the darkness. David started to ask what was wrong, but stopped when he saw William's face. The moon was full and stars bright, providing light to supplement their flashlights, so David could make out his expression, and it spooked him. A look of complete anguish had fallen over him, as if he was about to do something he already regretted.

"Cassie, what's wrong?" Ben asked softly.

She stood, keeping a hand on her bag. "Something's out there. The dogs say it's not friendly." The whispered words had barely left her lips before David glimpsed several dark figures descending upon them from the trees. Cassie whipped a knife from her bag – since when had she started keeping a knife in her bag? – and charged one of them. David saw glints of metal in their hands. Strangely, the metal seemed to reflect dull flames in the dim light. The dogs each rushed a figure, but before anyone made contact, a shriek from Sarah made everyone stop short. Her hazel eyes were wide in fear, and her breathing was shallow. A sword was at her throat, and a dark figure was behind her with an arm around her chest.

David started to run toward her, noticing his father doing the same, but the figure holding her snarled, "Stop! Don't anyone move, or the girl dies." He turned the blade and scratched her neck to prove his point. Ben halted abruptly as a man stepped in front of him and leveled a sword point at his stomach. David stopped, his mind whirling. He knew who the men must be, but how had they known where the group would be? It had been less than an hour ago that they'd made plans to come out here at night, but the Brotherhood had known and set a trap, somehow anticipating their movements... David's thoughts stopped spinning with such force. He realized what had happened. They had been duped. He turned to William, glaring at him angrily. The look on William's face told David everything he needed to know. Oh yes, he understood all too well.

The man holding Sarah spoke again, this time addressing Cassie exclusively. "You've led us on a chase, witch. More than we expected. But you have lost, so put down your weapon and tell your dogs not to attack. If they do, they die. If they kill any of my men,

David turned to William, glaring at him angrily. The look on William's face told David everything he needed to know.

your friend dies." Cassie glared at him, but slowly bent and placed her knife on the ground. Her eyes turned a little in the direction of the growling dogs, and they left the men to stand by her. "That's better. William, did they bring any other weapons?" David saw William remake his expression into the unreadable one he used most of the time.

"No," he answered the man. From the corner of his eye, David saw Sarah looking at William in horror. He saw sparks of anger in Cassie's eyes, but also sadness, as if she were disappointed. Looking at his dad, David saw that his eyes were dark with anger. Another man was standing several feet away from David, and two more moved toward Cassie. She looked around, taking in the whole situation. David could see her mind working. She took a step toward the man holding Sarah, hands out in a gesture of surrender. David had a pretty good guess of what she would say next, and he was right.

"Alright, take me. But please, leave my dogs and friends alone. They haven't done anything to deserve this." Cassie was sure he would completely disregard her suggestion, but she had to try anyway. The man smiled at her, not at all a nice smile.

"Sorry, witch, but we can't let them go. They know too much. And according to my information, your dogs and friends helped kill some of my men." Glancing at one of the men, he continued, "Get the rope, Edward, and muzzle those dogs. Can't risk them getting uppity." Cassie stiffened and the dogs bristled in outrage at the suggestion of muzzles. She started to protest, but one of the men near her smacked her hard across the face. The force, combined with the surprise of the blow, caused her to stumble back a few paces.

"Hey!" David said angrily, turning toward the man.

William stopped him before he went a foot. "Leave it," he muttered under his breath. "It'll go easier on you."

"Oh, will it? Why should I listen to you, *traitor*?" David growled. William turned his face away so David couldn't see his expression.

The man holding Sarah laughed. "You shouldn't have trusted him, boy. But you did. Brenwyds and their friends are always so easy to trick." He looked at William with approval. "Well done, William."

"Thank you, Father," William said. Cassie looked at him in surprise. *Father*? The two looked nothing alike. William caught her gaze and nodded slightly. His face was completely unreadable. Rage boiled inside her. How could she have trusted him? And how could he do this to her after learning she wasn't a witch? *No, wait*, she told herself, *the prophecy*.According to that, she was supposed to bring down the whole organization. Her heart sank right down to her toes. Of course he would turn her in. She remembered seeing him struggling, and now guessed what it had been about. His training had won out over his conscience.

The man came back with the rope and proceeded to tie all their hands behind their backs. They had a hard time muzzling the dogs, and it was only because Cassie intervened that the scene didn't become ugly. As it was, several of the men got bitten. Instead of angering their commander, it seemed to please him. He looked at Cassie's dogs in a way she didn't like. It reminded her of the way men eyed things when they hoped to make a profit. The men also gagged her. She couldn't imagine why, unless it was to stop her from "enchanting them." The thought gave her some amusement, although it's hard to feel amused when you're being captured at sword point. Once the captives were secure, the Brotherhood escorted them to two waiting vans. Cassie wondered if they'd drive all the way to Carlisle that night. It was nearly ten o'clock, and Carlisle was about six hours away. They were shoved rudely into the back of one van and the doors were locked. The dogs were taken to the other van. Cassie, David, Sarah, and Ben all looked at each other, each reading the despair in the others' eyes.

Sarah leaned her head over onto Cassie's shoulder and tears started streaming down her cheeks. "Why? Why did he do it?" she asked softly of no one in particular. They all knew who she was talking about, but no one had an answer. David figured Sarah wouldn't appreciate hearing what he was feeling about William right now, but if he ever got near that boy with a sword... he'd better watch it. Cassie looked up at the ceiling and started to pray, knowing it would take a true miracle of God to free both themselves and her parents now.

William stared up at the stars as the last man passed into the trees, his arms wrapped around himself as if to ward off a chill. He couldn't believe how he felt right now. The expression of horror in Sarah's eyes haunted him and stabbed his heart, as did David's accusatory glare. Cassie had looked at him with disappointment, like she had expected this all along. That also hurt. He tried to shake those thoughts aside. He should be feeling triumphant right now, having lured the most powerful Brenwyd in centuries into the Brotherhood's grasp. His father approved of him. This was sure to confirm him as a full Brotherhood member. It was all he had ever wanted, yet he felt like he was going to throw up. He collapsed to his knees. Why on earth had he decided to go through with this, even with Dr. Stone's urging? He wasn't sure how much of a difference it would have made if he had confessed to the others what he was really about – perhaps the Brotherhood would have tracked them down anyway. But at the very least, he wouldn't be feeling so bad.

He located the North Star, the one that had always guided sailors without fail, and wished he had someone to guide him as faithfully. He heard someone behind him and got up hastily, turning toward the person. It would definitely not be good if one of the Brotherhood men saw him showing remorse. It was a man named Edward, one of the few men toward whom William was partial. "Time to go," he said. "We can't stay long."

"Are we driving the whole way back tonight?"

"No, we'll drive for a couple of hours, then stop at a safe house where we'll stay for the night, then continue in the morning." They walked to the vans together. William would be riding in the van with the dogs, for which he was grateful. He didn't think he could deal with riding in the other van right now. As he buckled himself in, a realization hit him: it wasn't just Cassie he had betrayed. He had also betrayed himself.

Finding Truth

Twi grazed methodically, tearing, chewing, swallowing, and then starting the whole process over again. Fire and Penny stood near her, Dreamer and Chance a little farther away. The afternoon was growing old, and Twi knew that the woman would be out soon with dinner. The day was muggy and hot, but the flies weren't bad. All in all, it should have been a perfect afternoon, but Twi felt no pleasure, only worry for her girl. She had no idea what the girl could be up to, but knew that she had a penchant for getting into trouble. The other horses worried about the group as well, frustrated that they were stuck here when their people were over there. Twi wasn't sure where this "England" was exactly, but her girl had explained that it was across a very big, very salty body of water called an ocean, and the fastest way to get there was to fly through the air in one of those mechanized birds that flew overhead sometimes. Twi didn't trust those metal things; they looked dangerous. She accepted that it was not possible for her to go with her girl on this trip. But that didn't mean she had to like it. She shook her mane. There was always the Ability, but she'd never used it before the capture, and that had been a short distance to somewhere she knew very well. She'd never even told the girl about it. She was surprised the girl hadn't asked, but guessed she had forgotten about it with everything else going on.

Fire sensed the black mare's distress. He nickered comfortingly. Horses didn't really use words when communicating among themselves. The gelding was also feeling anxiety, and not just about his own boy. He had picked up on David's suspicious attitude toward William, and all the animals sensed something amiss with the boy.

Hannah walked out of the house to prepare the evening grain, wishing that her family were here. It was odd to be the only human around. Gracie trotted on ahead of her, sniffing various objects. Hannah had noticed that all the animals seemed to be hypersensitive lately, and guessed it was because of the past week's events. The horses saw her coming and hurried to their buckets, whickering eagerly. She didn't need Cassie's talent to know what they were thinking. She prepared the grain quickly and, after dumping it, she watched the horses chow down on the food before she headed back up to the house.

Twi finished her grain, thanking the One, as she always did, that her girl had found her and persisted in taming her even after others had said she should quit. Otherwise she, Twi, would not be enjoying this fine dinner. She was about to go back to grazing when something stopped her, a sense that all was not right. She paused, wondering if the sensation would repeat itself. A sudden wave of emotion hit the horse, and Twi shook her head to try to clear her thoughts. She sensed despair, horror, anger. Something was very wrong. The mare probed the feelings cautiously. Suddenly she understood and whinnied angrily, lifting her forelegs to paw the air in a rear. She became aware that Fire and Dreamer sensed what she did, while the other horses looked on in surprise. Smokey and Calico, who had been lounging in the sun, came running. *The girl*, Twi said, *she is in trouble. I must go.*

But how? Smokey asked. *She is too far away. You should not even be able to hear her.*

Twi snorted. *A regular horse would not be able to, but I can,* she said.

Ah, Calico said, *the Ability. Can you use it?*

What Ability? Smokey asked. Calico looked at her littermate as if he'd just questioned that water was wet.

The *Ability. The one the people's horses received as part of the Blessing.*

Oh, I see. You have this Ability, Twi?

Yes, as do Fire and I, Dreamer said. *We were all born from the same dam, you know.*

Then what are you hanging around here for? Penny asked. *Go! Humans, even Brenwyds, need help often.* By this point, Hannah had come running out of the house to investigate the source of all the hullabaloo.

Gracie raced into the paddock ahead of her. *What is wrong?* the dog asked.

They are in trouble. We must go, Fire said.

Gracie cocked her head questioningly, then nodded in understanding. *Then go. I only wish I could go with you. Tell Dassah and Kai they had better get my people home safe.* Gracie went to the gate and stood on her hind legs, manipulating the latch.

"Gracie, stop!" came Hannah's voice, but it was too late. The dog pushed the gate open and Twi, Fire, and Dreamer ran out in a flash. Hannah watched in bewilderment as the horses sped past her, picking up speed until their legs were blurs beneath their bodies. Then their bodies also blurred, the air around them seemed to bend and – they vanished. Hannah stared at the spot where her children's and Cassie's horses had just been, but there was no sign of them. Turning to look in the paddock, she saw Gracie trying to re-latch the gate, but all the other creatures were looking at the spot where the horses had disappeared, as if waiting for them to reappear. Hannah shook her head slowly. She had never seen anything like it. It seemed like magic.

Suddenly feeling weak, she sagged against the fence, and pulled her cell phone out to call Ben. Checking her watch, she saw it would be nearly ten where he was, but she figured he wouldn't mind. She needed to find out if Cassie knew any explanation for this. She heard his phone ringing, but no one picked up. She frowned slightly, thinking it was a little odd, but shrugged aside her concern and left a message, guessing that he was asleep. She went back to the house slowly, wondering what on earth she had just witnessed. She had never heard of horses doing anything like she had just seen. She hoped they would be back soon. As she sat down in the living room, a sudden urge to pray for the group in England struck her. Hannah knew when urges came from God and wasted no time obeying.

"God, please keep my family safe. Obviously, something is going on over there, so please help them overcome whatever obstacle they've encountered. Give them wisdom and clear judgment." As she continued praying, she realized that it was William whose name passed her lips most often. "Okay, God. William has been having a tough time ever since we met him, but I'm guessing that he's having an especially difficult time right now. Please fill him with knowledge of You and draw him to Yourself. He is caught between two radically different places mentally right now, and he needs You to help him out, whether he realizes it or not." She continued praying for the better part of half an hour, beseeching God to do whatever it was He was asking her to pray about. Eventually, she rose from her knees, feeling a little unsteady. She tried calling Ben again, but again got only voicemail. Worry started to take hold. Once more, she went down on her knees to ask God to keep watch over the group and bring her family back to her safely. Little did Hannah know it, but the safe return of her family and dearest friends depended on one boy, and he was in desperate need of guidance.

William stared out the window at the English countryside speeding by. They'd been on the road for a little less than two hours, but the driver said they would be stopping soon. William felt some relief that his father was riding in the other van. He didn't feel up to dealing with him right now. He felt absolutely miserable. His conscience nagged him, yelled at him, and told him what a terrible person he was. He tried to shush it, but it did no good. His attempts were too feeble. He felt numb, incapable of doing anything. *Buck up, William,* he told himself. *She would have been caught eventually, anyway. You just hurried the process a little.* The thought didn't comfort him. The dogs staring at him didn't help either. He wasn't well versed in animal behavior, but he could tell they were angry. And it didn't take a genius to figure out who was the source of their anger. At least Kai had refrained from speaking to him. If the dog had started lecturing him, William was sure he would have broken down, which would have earned him a severe reprimand from his father and snide comments from the other men.

He should be tougher than this. His father was one of the most feared men in the whole organization, coming second only to the Master. He'd been doing this since he was William's age, when he'd joined the Brotherhood as an initiate. William had certainly never seen his father show remorse for any of the awful things he'd done. Instead, he reveled in them, always eager for his next chance to cause anyone of Brenwyd blood harm, so great was his hatred of them. He had trained William to follow in his footsteps, starting him much younger than the usual Brotherhood initiate. As a result, William was much more skilled in weapons use than the other initiates his age in the organization. He was even more skilled than most of the men, and as a result had been surprised by Cassie's skill level when he'd sparred with her for practice back in the States. He had won the bout, but she'd made him really work for it. Some of her skill he attributed to the super-human fast reflexes he'd heard Brenwyds possessed, but most of it was because she had been taught extremely well. William had been curious as to how well her father fought, and wondered where he could have learned such skills.

The van slowing to a stop brought William out of his thoughts. He'd been so preoccupied that he hadn't noticed when the van had turned onto a dirt road, indicating that they would be stopping soon. He quickly hopped out, surveying the surroundings. A small house was in front of him, built with small windows as though the inhabitants didn't want anyone to see in. There was a large dirt area in front of the house where the vans were parked. William guessed that the house could accommodate large numbers of people if necessary, something all Brotherhood safe houses could do in emergencies. He caught a glimpse of another building in the backyard, and figured it was a stable. The opening of the van doors attracted his attention. His father and several others stood around the van into which Cassie and the Thompsons had been thrown, with weapons drawn just to show how futile it would be to try to escape. Other men were taking the dogs out. William heard a lot of growling and snapping, but on the whole, Kai and Dassah seemed to be cooperating, likely as a result of Cassie's influence. William backed up until he was in the shadow of the van he'd ridden in, hoping he wouldn't be spotted by the captives. His father hauled them roughly out of the van.

Sarah and David came out first. Sarah looked understandably scared, but there was also a steely look in her eyes that told William she could handle herself just fine if an opportunity arose to escape – not that it would. William found himself deeply upset that Sarah had been captured as well. He didn't at all approve of the rough treatment she and David were receiving. He knew it was completely unnecessary. He also knew that if they had been captured before last week, he wouldn't have seen anything wrong with it. Mr. Thompson came out next, and just to be sure he wouldn't try anything, one of the men put a sword to Sarah's throat. She looked incredibly annoyed. "Is that really necessary?" she asked. "It's not like we have anywhere to escape to." She spoke bravely, but

William detected a quiver of fear in her voice. He retreated farther into the shadow of the van.

The man next to her hit her hard across the mouth, causing her to release a startled cry. William felt like throttling him. He could tell David felt the same way, as he tried to wrestle out of the grip of the man holding him, but in vain. "Prisoners do not have the right to speak, girl. Be quiet," the man ordered Sarah.

Mr. Thompson tried to pull away from the man holding him. "Don't touch my daughter," he said with a hard edge to his voice.

William's father intervened before things could go any farther. "No talking. And do not harm them. The Master wants them brought to him uninjured." He dragged Cassie out of the van as he was saying this. William noted in surprise that she was gagged. Why would they have done that? Her eyes were downcast, but she held herself erect. Her gaze flicked to her dogs, avoiding the men. William saw the anger in her face as she looked at the muzzles. He assumed some kind of silent conversation occurred between them.

"Alright, let's get them in the house. Separate the man from the kids, and make sure the witch is secured so she won't try to escape. They're tricky, these Brenwyds." The Commander looked Cassie over. She raised her gaze to stare at him coolly, with obvious disdain and no sign of fear, her eyes like ice. No other person would have noticed, but William saw a flicker of hesitation in his father's eyes as he met her gaze. William didn't really blame him. Cassie's stare was hard to meet. In some ways, it reminded him of the Master's, but *his* stare could be ten times more intimidating. His father moved his hand toward her head and ripped the headband from it, revealing her pointed ears. Murmurs rippled through the men and they looked at her more closely. "Well, gentlemen," William's father said. "Any doubts as to her identity?" All shook their heads, and he looked pleased. "Very well. Let's get these prisoners secured."

As Cassie turned toward the house, her eyes met William's. She stared at him, but it wasn't the accusatory glare he'd been expecting, nor was it the look of disdain she'd given his father. Instead, it was full of sadness... and pity. He stared after her, bewildered. Was it possible she felt pity for him? How could she? He had betrayed her, lied to her, and gotten her and her friends captured. Now she was facing certain death sooner or later – but, William knew, not before the Master had her begging for it. William winced at that thought, but he knew it was true. He'd seen it before and he could never forget it. How could she feel anything but anger toward him?

"William?" William jumped. He hadn't realized his father hadn't gone in with the rest of the men.

"Yes, Father?"

"Aren't you coming?"

"Oh... yeah. I was just... um..." His voice trailed off. He felt his father studying him.

"You feel guilty," he said. William started.

"No, sir, it's just..."

"Don't try to fool me, boy. You've just been exposed to them too long. Sadie told me how confused you seemed in London." It took William a minute to remember that Dr. Stone's first name was Sadie. "Brenwyds can cast powerful spells, son, and this girl is strong. I don't blame you for your confusion, but..." – he stepped closer, and William saw a gleam in his eye. Was it pride? – "you overcame it! You proved yourself stronger. What you're feeling right now is just the aftereffect of her spell. You already beat her when you delivered her to us. You can shake off this residual enchantment." His voice became more affectionate than usual. "You did very well. You were able to get her to trust you, and none of my men would have been able to do that. The Master wants to commend you personally." He stretched out an arm and clumsily enfolded William in a stiff hug, patting him on the back. William felt his throat tighten, and started feeling a bit better. It wasn't often he got praise from his father, and never like this. "As a reward, he wants me to tell you that you will oversee the group... and set the time and manner of their deaths."

William's stomach roiled and his spirits plummeted to new depths. He was in charge of *that*? It was considered an honor in the Brotherhood, but he felt horrified to the point that he felt sick in his stomach. "Then the others are to die as well?" he asked.

"Of course. We can't let them live. You know that." His father examined William's face more closely. "Is it that dark-haired girl?"

"What... what do you mean?"

"I mean, have you taken a fancy to her, boy?"

"Sarah? No, it's just–"

"There's no 'just' about those things, boy. If you want my advice, forget about her. She consorts with Brenwyds and is no better, and you said she helped kill the men I left with you. Women... women only end up hurting you."

William frowned. He wondered at the slight choking sound in his father's voice. He'd never heard a thing like it from him before. "I'll remember that, Father."

His father nodded, his face turned so William couldn't see his expression. "Good. Come, let's go in." He started toward the house, pausing to wait for William.

The last thing William wanted to do was to go into that house and be the subject of all their accusing glares. "Um, if it's okay, I'd rather stay out here for a bit. I'm not tired, and it's a nice night."

His father looked at him carefully. "Alright." He went into the house. William looked after him for a moment, and then meandered around to the back of the house. He needed to calm his thoughts. His father had said he felt like this because of a spell, but William didn't think so. He remembered Cassie's description of Brenwyd abilities earlier, and he knew she told the truth. It just wasn't in her nature to be deceitful. He knew that from having been around her for eight days. Had it really been only eight days?

He stopped short. If Cassie was genuine, then the Brotherhood must be a fake! But if it was, how could it have survived through the centuries? Was Cassie an exception? He thought back on all his training, all his learning, and knew the main thing the Brotherhood preached was that Brenwyds were evil. He paced as he thought.

But Cassie wasn't evil. She and her friends were the best people William knew. They cared for each other, were loyal to each other, and trusted each other. They'd welcomed him, and while they hadn't trusted him entirely, they had accepted him and made him feel... what? What had they made him feel? It was something he hadn't experienced before. He stopped pacing as he searched his mind, trying to come up with a word, and when he did, it shocked him. Cassie, David, and Sarah, along with Ben and Hannah, had made him feel *loved*, and special, just by being himself. He wasn't sure what to make of it. He couldn't remember his father, or anyone else, ever making him feel that way. In the Brotherhood, everyone was treated mostly the same and no one made time to talk about hard issues. It was all focused on ending the "Brenwyd Threat," as they called it. Except now William knew there was no threat. Brenwyds were just regular people trying to live their lives as normally as possible. He started pacing again.

He thought of the strange mixture of sadness and pity in the gaze Cassie had given him. She knew more than he did about his situation. He realized now that he was trapped, trapped in an organization that hunted humans out of fear. He marveled at her ability to feel sympathy for those she should hate, those who hated her. Suddenly, he remembered something the pastor had mentioned the previous Sunday, something that might explain her behavior:*Because it's so hard to be forgiving and to extend grace toward those who hurt us, those who hate us, and those we just don't like, it makes those acts all the more powerful. It's what sets Christians apart from the world, what makes us different.*

That's what makes Cassie different, William realized. *She believes in a God who loves everybody, even though many don't acknowledge Him, and she tries to be like Him in any and every way she can.* He remembered reading in the Thompsons' extra Bible, while flipping through it trying to find the Bible verses from the Sunday sermon, that after Judas Iscariot betrayed Jesus, his conscience smote him so hard that he hanged himself. While William had no desire to hang himself, he realized just how like Judas he was. He, too, had betrayed someone he knew was good and innocent, and he was also feeling extreme regret. But what did he do now? He sure didn't want to follow Judas' example. What did he want? He wasn't sure. He thought back over the past week, thinking of the things he'd experienced, and realized what he wanted. He wanted what the others had, the peace that seemed to comfort and surround them. He wanted God. But would God take someone like him, someone who'd betrayed his only real friends to an evil organization? More of Pastor Shelby's sermon filtered through his mind, about how Jesus died to make grace available to everyone, not just a certain select group. The pastor had even made the comparison between a newborn baby and a mass murderer, how they were both offered the same grace. Was it really true?

He stopped in mid-step and looked up at the sky, at all the billions of stars in the heavens. The world had changed much since Creation, but the stars had remained the same. Always constant, always shining, always able to guide people home. He knew he needed God. But would God have him? He thought back to the pastor's sermon, trying to recall exactly what he'd said. He'd said that lots of people reject God's grace because they decide they've sinned too much. But then he'd said that anyone who thinks that is mistaken. He'd quoted some Bible verse, what was it? Oh, yes: *For God so loved the world that He gave His one and only Son, that whoever believes in Him shall not perish but have eternal life.* The pastor had particularly stressed the word "whoever." William recalled Cassie's expression, and knew she had somehow found it in herself to forgive him. He could no longer deny the truth that was staring him right in the face.

He knelt on the ground, hoping no one was looking out the house's windows. He tried to think of what to say. He'd never prayed before. He had a vague idea it should have a lot of*thees* and *thous* and such and sound very reverent, but he wasn't quite sure how to word it. Sarah's voice came to mind, saying, *There's no real right or wrong way. Like I said, God already knows your thoughts. He knows what you mean even if you can't articulate it just right.* He remembered his conversation with her at the Castle. He figured he may as well give it a try.

"God, I haven't really talked to You before. Sarah says You don't really care about doing it a certain way, so I'm just going to try my best. I... I need You. This organization, what I've been taught, it's all wrong. I see that now. I'm sorry, really sorry, that... that I betrayed Cassie and Sarah and David and Mr. Thompson. I was trying to do things on my own, but that doesn't work. God, I really, really, truly feel awful right now. I can't describe it well enough, and I don't really want to. I don't know what to do. I'm stuck. I need You to be with me. I believe now that You're good, and You sent Jesus to die so He could save us. I know that Brenwyds aren't evil; it's people who are, people who are scared of anything different. Please, don't let my mistake cost them their lives. I couldn't live with myself. And... I'm sorry I ignored You for so long. Even with examples right in front of me, I really messed up. Please forgive me. I can't keep living like this."

William continued to kneel on the ground, but he sensed that he wasn't alone. He felt a peace wind through him, and he knew that his prayer had not been in vain. God had accepted him, welcomed him, and William got the feeling God had been waiting for him. A smile broke through. "Thank you." He continued reveling in the presence of God. It wasn't dramatic; there were no angels singing or bells ringing or anything. It was just the knowledge that he had found the truth, and that he was saved. He stood, no longer feeling the guilt he had earlier. He still felt some, yes, but he knew now that he had acted out of fear and ignorance, and God would not count it against him. He also knew that he had to fix his mistake.

He turned to go into the house, his mind settled and calm, but a slight movement from the trees caught his eye. Curious, he turned and walked toward the trees. "Is anyone there?" he called. There was no answer, but William thought he heard a soft nicker, as if a horse was standing there. He knew it was ridiculous, but finding a horse out here wouldn't be the strangest thing to have happened to him this week. He saw the movement again and focused on it. A large shadow moved away from him, paused, turned a little as if beckoning to him, and then continued on. William followed, curious. The shadow moved into a shaft of moonlight, and he saw it *was* a horse – a very familiar-looking horse. But it couldn't possibly be the one he was thinking of. The horse kept going, and William followed. After traveling out of sight of the house, the horse (William now saw it was a mare) stopped and whickered, as if calling. Two more horses emerged from the trees, a bay gelding and blue roan mare. The black mare he'd been following turned, and William saw a white star in the center of her forehead. He stared. "No way," he muttered, looking at all of them. But there was no denying the horses' identities. They were Cassie's, David's, and Sarah's horses. But how on earth had they gotten from Virginia to England? No way could they have hidden in the luggage.

The horses looked at him as if he were a problem. "Um… what are you guys doing here? And how did you even get here?" he asked, even though he knew they couldn't answer him. Cassie's mare, Twi, stepped up to him, looking him in the eye. He saw a reflection of himself in her brown eye, looking confused, but calm.

She snorted. William felt a little wary, as he'd heard from David and Sarah how wild the mare had been when Cassie had acquired her. Even Cassie had had difficulty training her, finally succeeding the morning her father had been going to call the vet to put her down. Cassie was still the only one who could ride Twi with the assurance that the horse wouldn't act up, and even she kept a close watch on her.

William wasn't quite sure what the mare was up to, but he jerked in surprise when he heard a female voice in his head, clear as day, asking, *Can you hear me?* He stared at the mare. She huffed. *Do not just stand there looking like an idiot. Can you hear me or not? I guess that you can, based on your expression.*

"Uh, if you're the one asking if I hear you, the answer is yes."

The horse looked pleased with herself. *Good.* Then she did something that surprised him even more. She rammed her head into his chest with such force he was knocked flat on the ground.

"Ouch!" He sat up, rubbing his chest. "What was that for?"

For betraying my girl. It is a good thing you just came to your senses about the One, or I would kick you so hard you would never get up. She glared at him so angrily, ears pinned, that William knew it was no idle statement.

"Oh, yeah. I guess I deserved that."

You did. She backed away, ears slowly rotating to their usual position, and William got up, albeit a little cautiously.

He looked at the other two horses. "Do you guys want to knock me down, too?"

The question appeared to amuse them. *No, we let Twi take care of such things*, a male voice said. It was David's gelding, Fire. *We must move on to more pressing business.*

"Okay." Suddenly the reality of the whole scene really hit William. "Hang on, how am I able to hear you guys? I'm not Brenwyd." The horses looked at him with... curiosity? Puzzlement? Surprise? It was hard to tell.

No, you are not, a female voice said, but it wasn't Twi's. It was gentler than the black mare's and must belong to the roan, Sarah's mare, Dreamer. It even sounded a little like Sarah. William realized that each horse sounded a bit like their rider. *But it was given to all animals of Brenwyds the ability to communicate with any humans we choose to.*

William frowned. "Brenwyd animals? You're like Kai? And you still haven't told me how you managed to cross an ocean."

Yes, we are like Kai, though the girl does not know it. As for how we got here, we ran, Fire finished, like that explained everything.

William wasn't sure if the horse was joking or not. Did horses joke? He would have to ask Cassie at some point. "You ran," he said dubiously.

Yes. Brenwyds were not the only ones blessed by the One. He also blessed their animals, which is why we have special talents. To horses, He gave the ability to travel very quickly to reach destinations when the need is great, allowing us to bypass the distance between places. I am not sure what you humans would call it. We sensed our people's distress and came to help them. That is why I led you here, Twi said.

William still wasn't clear on how they'd gotten here, but decided to think about it later. "You want me to help you free Cassie."

And my boy, Fire said.

My girl, too, Dreamer added.

Twi bobbed her head up and down. *You are correct. I saw you petition the One, and the One always forgives. Therefore, you can now be trusted*, she said.

"The One... you mean, God?"

That is what humans call Him, yes.

Okay, William thought. *They want me to help them free their people. That makes sense. What doesn't make sense is the fact that I'm conspiring with horses.* "So, what do you want me to do?" he asked.

The horses all looked at each other, like, can-you-believe-he-just-asked-that? *You are a human. You were part of this organization. You can get them out and to us, and we will take them to safety,* Fire said slowly, as if it was the obvious thing to do but William was a little slow.

"Oh, right. Of course. I should have thought of that," William said, a little sarcastically. He was getting the feeling that horses didn't think in complicated ways. There was no doubt that they were intelligent, but to them everything had a simple solution. *And,* he admitted to himself, *it's a pretty good idea. It just needs a little more detail. Okay, make that a lot more detail.* "So, any idea on how to get them out?"

That is your job. Humans are better at thinking through all the details, Dreamer said, confirming William's idea. Twi snorted agreement, ears pricked forward alertly as she gazed at William with intelligent eyes.

"Let me think for a few minutes." He closed his eyes so he wouldn't have to see the three pairs of eyes looking at him. It was a little intimidating having three horses stare at you so expectantly, and horses didn't blink as often as humans did. There was no way he could free them tonight. His father would have them too well guarded. The thought gave him pause. If he did this, his father would hunt him down with the same determination he did Brenwyds, if not more. The whole organization would want his blood. He remembered years earlier, when he was eight, how a Brotherhood member had turned traitor but had been caught. The man's screams as he died still made their way into William's nightmares occasionally, and the event had seriously traumatized him. In fact, he now realized that the memory of that event had, subconsciously, been one of the forces driving him to go through with his mission. If he was caught, he would face the same fate.

To his surprise, he found he didn't care anymore. He had no real ties to the Brotherhood now, and his father... he would deal with that later. He had asked God to not let his mistake cost Cassie her life, and now he knew God was calling him to be the rescuer. He thought for a little longer, then hit on a plan. "Alright, here's what we'll do." He shared it with the horses, who approved it, then he hurried back to the house, hoping to get a chance to talk to Kai and Dassah with no one else in the room. He couldn't risk raising suspicion. He felt stronger now than he ever had before, more sure of himself, and he knew it was because he would never have to face another battle alone. He was no longer fighting for darkness and lies, but for light and truth. He made a mental note to find Cassie's bag. She would need it. Besides, he knew she kept a Bible in there, and he had some serious reading to do.

Change of Plans

Cassie looked out the window, hoping they'd reach their destination soon. By her calculations, they'd been traveling for almost four hours, so they should be getting close. Her muscles were cramping, and her hands were completely numb. She closed her eyes, thinking over events. William's betrayal hurt to think about, but it was impossible not to think of it. She still had a hard time believing it. He had seemed so genuine. And yet, it all made sense now. She recognized now that the internal struggle he'd been fighting had been over whether to turn her in or not. She had thought that he was merely having difficulty changing his mindset about Brenwyds. When she thought of the act, she felt intense anger, but when she thought of the person, she could only feel pity – and disappointment that he'd given in to the Brotherhood. She had seen the look on his face after they'd been jumped at Cadbury. There had been a pained look in his eyes. She'd seen it again that night at the safe house, even more clearly. He truly regretted what he'd done, but there was no going back now.

On the way to the safe house, Cassie had recalled Pastor Pete's challenge to treat everyone with grace. She had decided to apply it in William's case because, as the pastor had said, if Jesus was to be her example and he had been able to forgive his crucifiers as he hung dying on the cross, how could she do anything but forgive William? She could do no less, but that didn't mean it wasn't a struggle. She still felt that she would very much like to smack him, given the chance. But she had a feeling his father had driven him to it. Perhaps, if he'd been with them even one day more, he wouldn't have done it. But it was no use thinking about what might have been. She had to focus on what had happened, and the result, and try to think of a way to get herself, her friends, and her parents out of Brotherhood hands. So far she hadn't been able to think of anything, despite hours of prayer and thought.

The van jerked to a stop, and the others struggled to sitting positions. They hadn't gotten much sleep the night before, and so had caught up that morning. The van started again, and Cassie assumed they'd passed some sort of checkpoint. The van stopped again several minutes later, and Cassie heard doors opening and closing. They had arrived at their destination... wherever it was.

Ben looked at the kids, trying to encourage them. "Everyone just stay quiet, okay? We'll get out of this. God's still with us."

Sarah nodded, a scratch on her throat. "Just as long as they don't hold a sword up to my throat again," she grumbled. She strongly disapproved of the Brotherhood using her to keep the others in line. Despite her somewhat flippant comment, however, Cassie could see the fear in her eyes. She was scared, and it made Cassie feel guilty. She should have insisted that only the minimum number of people necessary come on the trip. She knew the danger. What kind of person knowingly led their friends into danger? Then again, she reflected, the twins had made the choice. But knowing that didn't do much to ease her guilt.

Before anyone could respond, the back door opened, and William's father – Cassie wondered what his name was – looked in. "Behave yourselves and it'll go easier on you," he warned gruffly before jerking David, who was closest to the door, out of the van. Cassie came out last. The bright sunlight momentarily blinded her, and when she blinked the glare out of her eyes, she saw a whole lot of men – and, surprisingly, some teenage boys – looking at her curiously. She felt sudden sympathy for zoo animals, who had to endure such looks every day. She moved her gaze from the men to the building behind them, her eyes widened, and she gasped – or would have, if she hadn't been gagged.

It was a castle, something straight out of the Middle Ages, made of stone. It was three stories tall, with one square tower that looked Roman-designed, and three others that looked more classically medieval. The upper-story windows had bars on them. It even had a stream like a moat around it, though there wasn't a drawbridge. Cassie guessed that she was looking at the main part of the castle, and knew that the wall extended around a courtyard that would have been used by peasants as a shelter during times of war in centuries past. There would also be areas for a smithy, a kitchen, a tanner's shop, and anything else the inhabitants might need to survive. Medieval castles had been made so the people living in them could be self-sufficient during a siege. Judging by the condition of the road and thick forest around them, she guessed they were pretty far removed from any town. Further examining the castle, she realized that the front part was much older than the rest, and she guessed that the rest had been added after castle-building took hold in Britain, and had been grafted into the original design. The original building must have been built in Roman times, judging by the architecture, and hadn't even been a castle but merely a large, stone building that took characteristics from both Roman luxury villas and military outposts.

The castle was black, and looking at it made Cassie's blood run cold. She felt like the hairs were standing up on the back of her neck, and she had goosebumps on her arms. This place seriously gave her the creeps. The atmosphere seemed like the stuff of nightmares, and it gave her the feeling that something terrible and deadly lurked just behind her. She couldn't help but glance back over her shoulder, just to make sure nothing was creeping up on her. Despite the fact it was a beautiful, sunny day with a slight breeze and comfortable temperature, the sky appeared dim to her, the air stifling, and something inside her screamed at her to leave, that this was a place of danger. The only word that she thought truly described the sensation was *evil*.

Cassie felt a rough shove from behind, and almost toppled over. She added numb legs to her list of body parts that either hurt or didn't work correctly. She looked around for her companions and saw that each was being held firmly by a Brotherhood member. Sarah looked relieved that this time no one was holding a sword to her throat. Cassie's ears caught the sound of growling, and Kai and Dassah came into view, the former being led by William. He looked at her, and she noticed that he seemed more comfortable than he had the night before, more confident, and looked like he was trying to communicate something to her silently. She glared at him, and a faint smile came to his lips. Was he *enjoying* this? Maybe she should rethink her character evaluation. Perhaps his regret had merely been a passing feeling.

William's father's voice boomed from behind her, and she winced at the loud sound near her sensitive ears. "Well, men, today is a great day for the Brotherhood," he declared. "The witch has been caught and outwitted – and at last, the great witch's bloodline will come to an end." A chorus of cheers met this statement. Cassie had a feeling she would not like learning what the latter half of it meant. She wondered who the "great witch" was. "And the one who enabled us to capture her is one of our youngest members, my son William." William nodded acknowledgment, but as Kai chose that moment to act up, Cassie couldn't see his expression.

Kai, settle down. We can't escape right now, she said, knowing that escape at any time was highly unlikely, and yet refusing to believe it was completely impossible.

I know, girl. We will escape later. It is all part of the plan.

What? What plan?

You will see. Be patient. I will tell you later, when there are no distractions. Cassie felt perplexed. Had the dogs come up with an escape plan? It wasn't impossible, but fairly improbable. Animals in general, she knew, were not given to thinking up escape plans for situations such as the one they found themselves in at the moment. William caught her eye and winked, as if he knew something she didn't. It was almost like he was trying to reassure her about something. But what?

"Now, we must secure this witch and her friends properly. It would not do to have them escape," William's father said. Laughter met this statement, and Cassie remembered William had said that no one had ever escaped the Brotherhood. Yet. "The man will be secured away from the children." Ben's head snapped to attention and he looked like he was about to protest.

Be quiet, Cassie heard Kai tell him. *It will be alright.*

"And I think we'd better put the witch in our, ah, special quarters, away from the others." *Oh dear,* Cassie thought. *I don't like the sound of that.*

William's voice surprised her. "Actually, Father, I think it may be better to put the... witch and her two young friends in the same cell, but chained securely so they can't reach each other. She isn't really so powerful after all." His voice had become scornful, but Cassie thought she saw the faintest traces of worry and tension in his eyes. She wondered at it. "I mean, *I* was able to trick her. What could the harm be in putting them in the same cell? It's not like they could escape. And it would take fewer men to guard them in one cell than in two separate cells." The yard had gone quiet. It was rare that anyone suggested changing the Commander's orders, but William was one of the few people who could get away with it. Very occasionally, that is.

His father looked at him critically, and William prayed he

would agree. Otherwise, the plan would not work so well. "Hmm, good point. Not to mention they may find some meager comfort in company." His tone said that he obviously didn't expect them to find much comfort. "I guess it couldn't hurt. You," he said, turning to a man, "take the adult to our... other guests. I'll take the kids to the first level myself." From the corner of her eye, Cassie thought she saw William frown ever so slightly, but he didn't raise any objection.

"And the dogs, Father?"

"Take them to the stables. Make sure they can't get out."

"Of course." William and the other man pulled the dogs around a side of the castle, and Cassie got the feeling the dogs were just making a show of resistance.

Do not worry, girl, Dassah said before she rounded the corner. *All will be well. The One is watching over us.* The dogs disappeared around the corner, and Cassie raised her eyes, blinking back tears. *I will not cry,* she told herself firmly. Movement at one of the barred windows caught her attention. She focused on it. It looked like... Mom? Cassie felt more tears threaten to break through. It *was* Mom, and she saw Dad behind her. Their eyes met, and she saw tears on their faces. She had never felt so useless as she did at that moment. Her parents were there, but she was powerless to reach them.

She looked away, unable to bear the sensation of being so close, yet not close enough. She hated feeling this helpless. Her eye caught the figure of a man standing at another window, watching what was happening in the driveway. He was clothed in dark pants and a black polo shirt, with a sword at his side and light brown hair. She locked eyes with him. They were gray, and somehow familiar, like a half-formed face seen in nightmares made flesh, though his expression looked pleasant enough. She shivered. She could tell that the malevolent atmosphere of the castle generated from this man. He started to smile, but suddenly his expression changed to one of confusion, and he turned abruptly and was lost to her view.

Movement at one of the barred windows caught Cassie's attention. Her parents were there, but she was powerless to reach them.

William waited until the other man was out of sight before speaking to the dogs. “Great acting, guys. You may as well make yourselves comfortable, because nothing will happen until after nightfall. I’d remove the muzzles, but...” He shrugged. “It would look suspicious.”

Kai looked at him with a gentle light in his eyes. *It is alright, boy. You have proven yourself to have good instincts. We will be patient.*

“Good. I’d better get in before they start wondering where I am.”

Wait, Kai said as William started to turn. *That man. Is he truly your father?* The question surprised William.

“Yeah. Why do you ask?”

What of your mother?

“My mother died giving birth to me. I never knew her.” There was a long silence.

I see, Kai said finally. He didn’t sound convinced.

“Why did you want to know?”

Curious. You are nothing like him. Generally pups reflect their parents. William studied the dog curiously. Kai turned and lay down, an obvious end to the conversation. William headed up to castle, wondering at the dog’s questions. Of course his father was his father. It was an odd question, but he’d noticed Kai was a bit of an odd dog. It meant nothing. He pushed the thoughts aside and concentrated on finalizing the details of what would happen that night, wondering if it was possible to get in to see Cassie’s parents.

Leah stared down at the scene before the castle, not wanting to believe her eyes, but knowing it was true. She choked down a sob, catching Ty’s attention, and he came to stand by his wife’s side. “What...” he started to ask, but then he caught the full magnitude of what was happening outside. Leah felt him tense. He muttered something under his breath, but Leah didn't catch it. They gazed down at their daughter, bound and gagged, standing in the middle of a mob, with Ben, David, and Sarah nearby. Cassie looked up, and she spotted them. Her eyes went wide, and Ty could tell she was on the verge of tears. How had she been captured? He recalled the Commander saying something about his son planning to bring her in. Apparently, he had succeeded. Ty felt anger burn in his chest, and also a sense of failure. He was supposed to protect his family, but he'd only caused their capture. They watched as Cassie and the others were roughly shoved into the castle. They stayed at the window.

"Oh, Ty, what happens now?" Leah asked. "What happens to the prophecy?"

Ty put an arm around her waist. "The prophecy still stands. It will happen. We just need to have faith." He hoped he hid the doubt in his voice from Leah. He was also trying to convince himself.

"Do you... do you think they'll bring her up here?"

Ty wished they would, but he knew better. "I doubt it. She'll be lucky if they leave anyone with her. They're all convinced she's a powerful witch. They'll watch her very closely." Leah leaned against his chest. "Leah, we can't lose hope. God hasn't forgotten where we are. Cassie will try any means at her disposal to get out, and so will I. And don't forget the dogs. I saw them being led off somewhere."

They stayed a little longer at the window, then Ty returned to his task. Leah sat on the bed. Being a captive was really very boring, she thought idly. They don't give you anything to do. The sound of footsteps in the hallway didn't surprise them. What did surprise them was Ben Thompson being shoved into the room. He stumbled and braced himself against the wall. "The Commander thought you might like some company," one of their guards said. "The work should go faster now. Your daughter's here, too, so you'd better not try anything funny."

The door closed, and Leah heard the lock click. She rushed over to Ben. "Are you alright?" she asked.

He grimaced, rubbing his arms. "I will be. Riding on the floor of a van for four hours with your hands tied behind your back is not the best way to travel." He turned sad eyes on Ty. "Ty, I'm sorry. I should have seen the threat."

"No, Ben, this isn't your fault. The Brotherhood's just trickier than we thought," Ty tried to console him.

Ben shook his head. "No, I was the adult on the expedition. I should have been more concerned about going out at night." Ty and Leah looked at each other, puzzled.

"What expedition?" Leah asked.

"The one that was supposed to eventually rescue you. But, now..." Ben raised his hands helplessly.

"Rescue us?" Ty asked. He sighed. "I should have guessed Cassie would come after us. But she convinced you all to come?"

"Let me put it this way: she would have found a way to come even if she hadn't gotten permission. She went after you that night, you know, and just missed you leaving in the plane."

"What?" Leah exclaimed. Ben nodded.

Ty shook his head. "I thought I raised that girl with a modicum of sense."

"You would have done the same thing, Tyler Pennington," Leah scolded, "So don't you go criticizing our daughter. You can't be surprised."

"Well, no, but I would like to think she picked up some ability to accurately assess risk in emergency situations and act accordingly," Ty said.

"She picked up the first part of that well enough," Ben said. "She knew the danger. She left before any of us knew what was going on and even tried to leave David and Sarah behind."

"Tried?" Ty asked. "They followed her? Good grief, do any of our children have sense?"

"I wonder," Ben said, smiling a little. "I wasn't pleased, but neither was I surprised. I would have tried to go after her myself, if only to convince her to turn around, but you know I have no riding skills whatsoever."

Ty chuckled. "That's true enough. She told them, then?"

"Not exactly. She was about to when Penny appeared at their campsite with the news, so Cassie rushed back out on Twi to see to Chance–"

"I saw he was hurt," Leah interjected. "Is he alright?"

"He's fine, but it would have been a different story if Cassie hadn't gotten there in time." And with that, Ben told how Cassie had wakened him and his wife with a strange phone call, then went on to describe the discovery at the Penningtons' house and the subsequent journey that the three teens had taken through the mountains. He told how they'd met William, discovered Ty's project journal, and decided to go to England. He ended with meeting Dr. Stone and the capture at Cadbury. Ty and Leah were silent for a while after he finished, processing all the information.

"So the Commander is William's father?" Ty asked. Ben frowned. "The man you described leading the expedition."

"Oh. Yes, he is."

"Humph. I wonder what his wife's like," Leah said. "I never saw any wedding band on his finger."

Ben shrugged. "He may just not wear one. And after seeing his father, William must favor his mother in looks. They look nothing alike."

"Hmm," Ty mused. "How old is he?"

"Fifteen. That's one piece of information he told us that is true." Ben scowled. "I should have been more suspicious of him."

"Perhaps he feels bad," Leah said.

Ben harrumphed. "I doubt it." They were interrupted by the door opening. The guard looked in.

"You've got a visitor." He stepped aside and a boy about fifteen stepped into the room. Leah guessed that this must be William. Ben straightened and scowled at the boy, leaving no doubt about his identity.

The boy gestured toward the door. "You can go, Kirk. I'll be safe enough. I wish to question them in private." His voice was quiet, but commanding. The guard didn't look happy about it, but he obeyed.

No sooner had the guard left and shut the door than Ben leaped to his feet. "What do want with us, boy? Come to gloat?" he asked harshly.

Leah saw pain flare in the boy's eyes, but his tone of voice remained calm. "No, not at all." He turned his gaze to Ty and Leah. "You must be Cassie's parents. She looks like you." He smiled at them, but it was a hesitant, nervous smile.

Leah saw her husband studying him, and she wondered what he was thinking. She herself was finding it hard to feel anger toward the nervous teenager standing in front of her. "Yes, we are," she answered. She could see how Cassie had been taken in. He had a very trustworthy face.

"I'm William, but Mr. Thompson probably already told you all about me." He paused, searching her face uncertainly. "You're not... are you going to yell at me?"

"I should tan your hide," Ben said angrily. "But that guard outside the door would come to your rescue. If you just came to stare, you should leave." His voice was cold. Leah couldn't recall having ever heard him speak like that before. "I hope you're pleased with yourself."

William's face contorted into an expression of deep regret. "I'm not." He went to the window. "I haven't got much time. Basically, I feel really terrible about all of this. I have no excuses. Yell at me all you want, but please, hear me out."

Leah's motherly instincts were aroused. He looked very forlorn standing there. She went over to him and placed an arm around his shoulders. He looked at her, surprised. "Of course we will," she said, giving him an encouraging smile.

He took a breath. "I want to help you escape," he said in a rush, looking at them anxiously for their reactions.

Leah blinked. "What?"

"I want to help you escape, and I will," William said, sounding steadier with the confidence that they would hear him out completely. "I've already got a plan. Well, actually, the horses thought of the framework. I just provided the details, but anyway–"

"Hold it," Ty said. He looked sternly at William. "Why are you becoming so helpful all of a sudden? It's because of you that my daughter is a prisoner. What's in it for you if you help us escape? And what horses?" William met his gaze squarely.

"A clear conscience before God," he said quietly. Ty raised his eyebrows at the answer.

"What would you care?" Ben asked. "This organization exists to prevent people from believing in God."

"I care because... because I met God last night. I know now I was wrong... really wrong. I'm really sorry. Please, forgive me. I know I don't deserve your forgiveness, but I really need it." He said the words quietly, with dignity.

Ben could tell from his eyes that he spoke the truth, and could also see how much the current situation pained him. He softened his gaze on the boy. "Alright, William. I'll give you another chance," he said.

William's face lit up. "Really?"

He sounded so surprised, Ben had to smile. "Really. It may take some time for any of us to fully trust you, but I'll try."

"That's all I'm asking." His tone became more businesslike. "Now, I need to make some modifications to the plan, because I didn't think they would put so much space between you all, but it should still work if we can coordinate everything right."

"You still haven't answered my last question," Ty put in. William looked at him quizzically. "What horses were you talking about?"

"Oh, Twi, Fire, and Dreamer." The adults all looked at him incredulously.

"Excuse me?" Ben said. "Last I checked, they were all in Virginia. Don't tell me they caught a ride on the plane and we never noticed."

William chuckled and shook his head. "I don't really understand it, but apparently they all had the same dam, and that dam could trace her lineage back to the Brenwyd horses, and when God blessed the Brenwyds, he gave their horses the ability to travel very speedily over long distances, whatever that means. I couldn't get a clearer explanation than that."

Ty's face showed sudden comprehension. "Brenwyd horses you say? Interesting. Yes, legend says that Brenwyd horses were able to move miraculously quickly. It added to the mystery surrounding the Brenwyd people. Apparently, Brenwyd horses can reach speeds regular horses can't, and when they reach those speeds they can sort of... slip, I guess, or transfer from one place to another instantly."

"So, like, teleporting horses?" William wasn't sure he'd heard correctly.

"Basically," Ty said with a grin. "But, getting back to the escape plan?"

"Right. So, there are tunnels running under the whole castle, but as far as I know, no one has explored down there except for me. Everyone knows about the tunnels because they've been there since medieval times, but few people ever enter, and I'm pretty sure the Master is the only one besides me who knows how to navigate them. If we can get down there, I know a tunnel that leads into the forest, where the horses will be waiting. They can take you to safety."

"How many horses are there?" Leah asked.

"Just the three at the moment, but Kai is going to talk to some of the horses in the stable to see which ones would be willing to help. Once you've gotten far enough away on horseback..." William shrugged. "It's really up to you. Or if, as you say, they really teleport or whatever, you could use them to get home."

"And what will you do?" Leah asked. "You can't stay here."

"I'll escape on my own. I know how to get around undetected, and it's unlikely I'll be first on the list of possible suspects."

"It sounds risky," Ty said.

"It's the best I could come up with. Believe me, it's your best bet."

"How do you plan on getting us down to the tunnels?"

William sighed. "That's the part I'm not completely sure of now. I'd counted on everyone being kept in the same area. Then I would have gotten you all out on some pretense, and I'm planning–" Ty held out a hand to stop him.

"No, don't tell us any more," he said.

"What?" William asked, confused. "Why? If you don't know what to do, it won't work."

"But we also won't be able to tell anyone exactly how you escaped if we're questioned."

"What do you mean?"

The three adults locked glances, each reading what was on the others' minds and agreeing. "What I mean, William, is that you should concentrate on getting Cassie and the twins out," Ty said. "Don't worry about us. We'll get out eventually. But it's more important that you all get away from here safely."

William looked at Cassie's dad in shock. How could he be suggesting such a thing? He couldn't escape on his own, not without William's help. He gazed into Ty's green eyes, trying to figure out his reasoning. Suddenly he realized what prompted the self-sacrifice. "It's the prophecy, isn't it?" he asked.

"You know of it?" Ty asked, surprised.

"Why do you think the Brotherhood was so keen to get their hands on Cassie?" William asked him. "Killing off all of Caelwyn's descendants has been a longtime goal of this organization because of that prophecy – and they've succeeded for the most part, except for your family."

Leah's eyes widened. "Then it's true?" she asked.

William shrugged. "The Brotherhood thinks so. And frankly, now you had better hope so. Especially if you're going to stay."

"Would this be the prophecy you mentioned finding in a journal several years ago, Ty?" Ben asked.

"Yes. Everything seems to be coming together. There's one thing I'm still not sure about, but I'm sure that it will be made clear in time." Ty focused back on William. "Does Cassie know of it? I had planned to tell her on her birthday, but as you know, some outside forces intervened."

William nodded. "Yeah. She found the journal it was in, and the animals all kept mentioning it, so she asked what they were talking about."

"The animals know about it?" Leah asked.

"Yeah. Based on what Cassie said they said, I think they've been waiting for it to happen for a long time." William looked at his watch. "I'd better go now. Can't risk raising suspicions. I just thought... that you'd like to know what was going on, and how sorry I am. And... I'm glad to have met you."

Leah smiled at him. Her smile made William feel content inside. "It's been a pleasure meeting you. Tell Cassie," she sighed, and her smile was replaced by a wistful look. "Tell Cassie we love her, and we *will* be together again, no matter what."

William nodded. "I will." He headed out the door.

"Did you get the information you needed?" they heard the guard ask him.

"I did," William responded, and the door closed.

Leah looked at her husband. "I think we just got a miracle," she said.

Ty pulled her to him and kissed her. "I do believe we did," he agreed.

Ben stared at the door, shaking his head slowly in wonder. "Well, this day is full of surprises," he said. "The one who betrayed us is now our only hope of rescue. God does have a sense of humor, I do believe."

Leah laughed. It had been a long time since she'd laughed. "That He does, Ben. That He does."

Escape

Cassie drooped, feeling completely drained. Her hands were chained in cuffs to the wall in what she guessed was the castle's dungeon. The walls were cold stone, and the lone window was high, small, and barred with iron. The door was dark wood and also had a small, barred window. It was better than her imagination had anticipated, but still not at all pleasant to be in. David and Sarah were with her, but they were merely tied to rings on the wall with rope and so they didn't feel the pain and lethargy she did. Wherever the manacles touched her body, it felt like her skin was on fire. The metal even looked like it was surrounded by flames, though Cassie was sure it was just her imagination. The sensation had lessened somewhat after several hours, but the constant pain wore down her energy like nothing she had ever experienced. She had no idea what the metal was, and she wasn't sure she wanted to know. She tried to shift into a more comfortable position, but a new wave of burning pain swept through her, and she gasped.

"Cass? What is it?" came David's voice. The cell was dim, as their only sources of light were a dying lamp hanging by the door and what little light managed to come through the window. Both sources had been steadily growing dimmer since the three had been thrown into the room. Cassie could normally see well even in dim light, but for some reason her vision now seemed to weaken as the light dimmed.

"It's this metal. It burns." They had taken her gag off, thankfully, but it wasn't like anyone helpful could hear them even if they yelled.

"Burns?" Sarah asked, sounding concerned.

"Yeah, it feels like my wrists are on fire. It was worse before, but..."

"That's weird," Sarah said. "Is it really that bad?"

"Let's put it this way: I think I'd rather break my leg again like I did when I was eight than stand this for much longer."

David frowned in concern. "That's not good. Do you have any idea what the metal is?" he asked, eyeing it. Cassie shook her head. "It actually kinda looks like it's on fire," he commented.

Cassie glanced at him, surprised. "You see it, too? I thought it was just my imagination. It's definitely not actual fire, but it doesn't feel far from it," Cassie said. She looked at the floor, sighing. "Guys, I'm really, really sorry. You shouldn't be here." The guilt she was feeling for getting them into this predicament was enormous.

David shook his head. "Cassie, you can't blame yourself for what William did." His voice grew angry at the thought of William. "We're the ones who chose to follow you. If it's anyone's fault, it's ours, but none of this would have happened if William had had the sense to see that the Brotherhood is wrong."

"I think he did," Sarah said. "Remember how unsettled he seemed as we got close to Cadbury? And on the hill, when I was talking to him, it was really obvious he was torn about something. It had to have been about turning us in. I don't think he wanted to do it at all."

David scowled. "But he still did it. Don't make excuses, Sarah," he said harshly.

Cassie sighed. "I think David's right, Sarah. However torn he was, he still did it, even if he does feel regret."

"Feels regret? What gives you that idea?" David asked, sounding dubious.

"His expression afterwards."

"He seemed to be in a pretty good mood this morning."

"Yes, but Kai kept saying something about a plan, and William did make it possible for us all to be together. I'm grateful for that."

David narrowed his eyes at Cassie, getting a sense of the direction in which her thoughts were turning. "You think he may try to help us escape? Cassie, I know you like thinking the best of people, but the guy betrayed us and now we're locked up in a medieval dungeon. How can you still see him in a good light?"

"The struggle Kai put up with William on the way to the stables was an act. I got the sense that William is involved in the plan Kai kept mentioning. Both he and Dassah seemed in hopeful moods. Something has happened since last night that's put them in a better mood. Remember what I told you about Bob Mallory?"

"Cassie, this is more serious than someone continually cheating or even continually bullying someone."

"I know that, but he had outside circumstances that drove him to it. I think William did, too. Did you see his father?"

"Yes, but William was out of touch with him the whole time he was with us."

"Do you know that for sure?"

"I'm reasonably sure." David gave her a look, and shook his head. "Jeepers, Cassie, I think you might try to see a good side to the devil himself."

Cassie chuckled and shook her head. "No, I draw the line there. I'm also not inclined to think kindly of the Brotherhood Master. But anyone else? Sure."

"What are you two talking about?" Sarah asked.

"Don't worry about it," David said. "But going back to this escape plan idea. Have you talked to Kai since we saw him last?"

"No, I think he's out of range. So if there *is* an escape plan and William's involved, he's going to have to tell us himself," Cassie said.

"He was supposed to be 'helping us' before, and he betrayed us," David said. Cassie and Sarah looked at each other. Each saw in the other's eyes that they had chosen to forgive William, for whatever reason, and knew that David needed to as well.

"David, you've got to stop feeling so bitter. It's not Christian," his sister chided.

"William betrayed us, and now we'll be killed. I'm not supposed to be mad at him?"

"Well, you've been mad at him. Now you need to try seeing things from his perspective. Or actually, try seeing things from Cassie's perspective. He could have been forced into it. But even if he wasn't, Jesus would forgive him, so you need to as well." David was silent. He knew the truth of their logic, but he didn't think he was ready for that just yet.

Suddenly Cassie cocked her head slightly, listening to footsteps in the hallway outside. She heard muted conversation, then a key turning in the lock. The three friends looked at each other, wondering what would happen now.

Standing outside the cell, William felt huge butterflies in his stomach. Talking to the parents, he'd had no idea how he would be received. But their ability to forgive him so easily amazed him and gave him heart. He hoped their children would be as open. Technically, according to the plan, Kai was supposed to tell Cassie what was going to happen so she could tell the others. But inexplicably, Kai had been unable to make contact with Cassie, so now William had to risk a visit to the cell to let them know the plan. He would come to the cell after dark to take them somewhere for some official-sounding reason, but in reality he would lead them to the escape tunnel. He still wasn't sure about leaving the parents, and decided once he got Cassie, David, and Sarah into the tunnels safely, he'd come back for them, or at least try. He'd spent a large part of the afternoon down in the tunnels, and had drawn a map, which he'd stashed in Cassie's bag so they wouldn't get lost. He'd put her bag and a couple other bundles with some spare clothes and food in a crevice just inside the entrance they would be using. He'd gotten the horses to the tunnel exit, a camouflaged hut in the forest a few miles from the castle. He'd never been able to figure out why there was an exit in the middle of the woods, or why there were tunnels at all, but had never asked, not wanting anyone to find his secret place for privacy.

William needed to explain the plan to the three captives, but he also had to convince them he had no ill intentions toward them. *Like* that *will be easy,* he thought. *Well, I suppose it's better to convince them now than have them doubt me during the escape.* He wondered why Kai hadn't been able to contact Cassie. "Just be quick," the guard said. "Are you sure you don't want company?"

"Yes. My questioning will be more effective if I am alone."

"Be careful. Never know what Brenwyds will do."

William smiled condescendingly at him. "I have been in this one's company for over a week. I think I can handle her." With that, he pushed the door open and stepped inside, closing the door behind him. Cassie, David, and Sarah were staring at him, the girls with more incredulity, David with more anger and suspicion. William noted how pale Cassie was, and looked at the manacles on her hands. His eyebrows came together angrily when he saw they were devil's iron. The incorporeal fire around the metal gave it away. With an angry exclamation, he crossed the cell, dropped down next to her, and tried to take one of her hands, rummaging around in his pocket.

She jerked away from him. "What do you want?" she asked, voice tight, though with what emotion William couldn't tell.

"Right now, to remove those manacles. You're going to need your strength."

"Oh? For what? An escape?" she asked sarcastically, but William made a note never to underestimate her ability to interpret comments.

"Actually, yes. Now will you let me get those things off?" She stared at him, wondering if she'd heard him right. She'd put the question to him to see his reaction, but hadn't expected such an offhand answer.

"Escape?" David asked, eyes narrowed at William. "Why would you help us escape?" Before answering, William took Cassie's right hand, brought his pocketknife out of his pocket, put it in the lock, and started to fiddle with it. His father had shown him how to pick locks, but it had been awhile ago and not with this kind of lock.

"Because I don't want my mistake to cost you your lives. And, if I *don't* get you out, your horses will trample me.

"What?" they all asked.

"No joke. They really said that. Well, only Twi actually said it, but the others–"

"Whoa-ho, there boy. Are you telling us that our horses are here? Like, *in England?* And you are somehow communicating with them?" Cassie sounded astonished. The mention of the horses seemed to make all three back down from their defensive position, for which William was grateful.

"Yeah." He twisted the knife in the lock and heard it click. "Got it," he said as he opened it, taking it from Cassie's wrist. "Oh my gosh." Her skin was burned and blistered, and William feared it would scar.

Cassie examined her wrist, frowning. "What is that metal?"

"You don't know?"

"No. Should I?"

"I should think so. It's called devil's iron. I don't know why, but it's appropriate. Lots of Brotherhood weapons are made from it because, well, it continually burns anyone with Brenwyd blood. If a full-blooded Brenwyd was left with devil's iron touching them too long, they'd die. It's slow and extremely painful, so the Brotherhood really likes using it. No wonder Kai wasn't able to reach you." He moved to work on her other wrist. As he worked, he was aware of David's suspicious gaze on him. "Can you heal yourself?"

Cassie blinked. "Maybe. Let me try." She concentrated on her wrists, closing her eyes. She tried to listen for her song, but wasn't able to hear it. For that matter, she wasn't sensing anyone else's song either. She opened her eyes, feeling a sense of panic start to build. "I can't sense the song. That's not normal."

William shook his head. "It is after you've been chained for several hours with devil's iron. I've heard it disables Brenwyd abilities, but I wasn't sure. You should be able to do it after a while." Cassie looked relieved at that explanation.

"So how did our horses get from Virginia to England and how are you communicating with them?" Sarah asked, repeating Cassie's question. "Did you discover you have a minute amount of Brenwyd blood or something?"

William chuckled but didn't look at her. "No. They said they have this ability to travel speedily over long distances in an emergency, and Mr. Pennington said–"

"You've seen my dad?" Cassie asked breathlessly.

"Yeah. He's okay, and so's your mom. Mr. Thompson's in with them. They're a lot better off than you guys. But anyway, he said they do something like teleportation."

"Teleporting horses?" David sounded skeptical, unknowingly parroting William's reaction a few hours earlier.

William smiled. "Why not? Apparently, when God blessed the

Brenwyds, he gave their horses the ability to traverse long distances almost instantly when the need was great. Pretty handy ability for battles and such."

"They're descended from Brenwyd horses?" Cassie asked.

"You didn't know?"

"No, they never told me," she answered, frowning. She would have to have a serious talk with the animals about hiding things from her. It seemed like it was becoming a habit. "So they're like Kai in their ability to talk to people?"

"Yep."

The second manacle fell from Cassie's hand and she breathed a sigh of relief. "Thanks."

"Don't mention it. I just wish I had some first-aid supplies. Now, getting to the escape plan. I'll come back here after dark with some pretext for taking you to my father. We'll get to a certain hallway, and the power will go out. I can pre-program it, but that means we have to stick to a strict time schedule so as to be in the right place at the right time."

"You can do that?" Sarah asked.

"Yeah. I've got a knack with technology."

"I wasn't even sure they *had* anything technological here."

"Oh, yeah, that's a definite affirmative. You should see the information center. So anyway, the power will go out, and in that moment, you guys will twist out of the grip of whoever's holding you. Then you'll all run down a small side hallway that'll be on your left. I'll follow you after taking care of the others with us. Actually, Cassie, I'll make sure I'm the one holding you so I can let you know when the lights are about to turn off. Escape my grip right then, and make it look convincing – then the men will think your Brenwyd abilities caused the power outage."

"I *really* can't do those sorts of things, William," Cassie said. "It's like I said in the car. I can only hear animals, and heal using songs."

"I know that, but the others don't. It could create an extra fear factor that would make them hesitant to go rushing off after you. Brotherhood members are actually pretty superstitious. There's a secret entrance to underground tunnels that you'll use to escape. I'll show you where it is. It's across the hall from a big tapestry. Once we get down into the tunnels, I'll go get the dogs. There's another entrance in the stables, and I'll send them to you. I've put a map in your bag, Cassie, which is near the entrance with a few other things. I highlighted the way out. Follow the map, and your horses will be waiting at the tunnel's exit in the middle of the woods. At that point, it's up to you. Carlisle is east of here, but I wouldn't go that way. If you want my advice, use the horses' ability and get back to Virginia. You'll have some breathing space, but not much. Then you'll need to go into hiding."

"But what about you?" Sarah asked. "You can't stay here. It's too dangerous."

Before he could answer, David cut in. "Why should we trust you, anyway? You're the one responsible for this predicament. Why are you being so helpful now?"

William sighed. "Well, you shouldn't trust me, but you don't really have a choice. No one has ever escaped from here since one time near the beginning of the Brotherhood, back in 516 A.D. or something like that, when a whole group of Brenwyds managed to escape."

"Really?" Cassie asked. "I thought you said no one had ever escaped the Brotherhood."

"I wasn't counting that. Most people here don't, as it was in the Brotherhood's early days. I'm not sure how it was done." He paused. "I'm turning against the whole organization by doing this, and my father will be the first to hunt me down. But I'm doing it because I want a clear conscience, and, well, God told me to." He looked at the floor. "I need you to trust me. Otherwise this won't work. If you don't trust me now... I don't know when there'd be another chance. I've seen what can happen to prisoners, and I don't want it to happen to you. Helping you escape is the only thing I can do to prove I mean it this time, and I know it's a big thing, but you just have to trust me." He kept looking at the floor and so didn't see the look passing among the three, which said that they'd trust him.

David took in a breath. He could tell William was serious. Besides, if Cassie was feeling sure about him this time, that probably meant he was trustworthy. Cassie had very good instincts about people. Sometimes it was almost uncanny, but it had gotten the trio out of dicey situations before. "Alright, William. I'll trust you."

William looked up and met David's eyes. He saw that David was still wary and suspicious, but also saw a willingness to follow the plan he had presented. David nodded slightly in acknowledgment of what he saw, and William nodded slightly in return. He understood that David would reserve his complete trust until he was convinced on his own that William was now a friend. William glanced at the girls. "What about you two?"

"William, we were on your side before you came in," Sarah said. "You should have heard our conversation. Cassie has this penchant for constantly looking for the good in people even when they're mean to her." William looked at Cassie.

She nodded. "That is true. I prefer having an optimistic outlook of the world, compared to Mr. Pessimism over there."

"Hey, I had reasonable concerns," David protested, then glanced at William. "No offense."

"None taken," William said. "I'd have your attitude if our roles were reversed."

"But what about the parents? Can you get them out?" Sarah asked.

William hesitated a moment. "That was the original plan, but they're pretty far from here and that's what I didn't count on, though I'm really kicking myself that I didn't. I talked to them about it, and Cassie's dad told me to forget about them and get you guys away. But I'm still going to try to get them out after helping you guys." He looked into Cassie's eyes. "Your mom said to tell you that they love you, and that you'll all be together again... somehow." He saw tears forming in Cassie's eyes, but she kept them from spilling.

"Thank you. But William..." She took a breath. The next words were hard to say, but she knew she had to. She had to trust God that everything would come out alright. "I think... I think my dad's right. You can't risk getting them. You'll be caught. You need to come with us."

Sarah looked at Cassie in surprise. "Why shouldn't he try?" she asked. She certainly didn't like the thought of her dad in Brotherhood hands if she was able to get out.

"Because the Brotherhood won't harm them. Not yet. They need my dad to lead them to Arthur's treasure, and they're likely using my mom to get him to cooperate. Your dad provides more incentive. They wouldn't risk harming him and my mom, mainly just threatening them, at this point anyway. Am I right?" she challenged William.

"Probably. But this could be their only chance," he warned her.

"It won't be. Remember the prophecy."

"So you *do* think it is about you," David said.

"At this point, it's our best hope."

"Good point."

"So you really want me to go with you?" William asked. "I'd probably be more useful to you still on the Brotherhood inside."

Cassie looked at him levelly. "And how would you explain it was on your watch we escaped?"

"I can be pretty convincing. And if I did come, I'd just slow you down."

Cassie smiled slightly. "Granted, but you're still coming with us. No argument."

William held her gaze and nodded slowly. "Alright, if you really want me to." He stood. "I'll be back later, but for now..." He searched the cell until he found what he was looking for. He picked up a rope. "I need to reattach you to the wall, Cassie, but this won't burn, though it may hurt your blisters."

"I understand. And I'll be okay, just as long as these won't burn me. But won't the guards notice you switched it out?"

William chuckled. "Are you kidding? They wouldn't dare come in here. They might act tough, but you scare them. The ropes are a precaution in case someone happens to look in, but if they ask about them, I'll just say my father said you'd been in the chains long enough." He quickly reattached her to the wall, though not too tightly so as not to irritate her skin more than necessary.

"That's true enough," Cassie agreed. She paused. "Are they really that scared of me?"

"Yeah. The rumor is that you are an extremely powerful witch and quite dangerous to be around."

She looked at him, disbelieving. "You're kidding, right?"

"No. As I mentioned earlier, a lot of the Brotherhood members are pretty superstitious. So on the one hand, while everyone's happy that you're a captive, they're also very wary of what you might do to get back at them."

Cassie blinked. It sounded completely ridiculous. A bunch of grown men terrified of a captive fourteen-year-old? She eyed William suspiciously. "You didn't have anything to do with that, did you?"

He looked at her innocently. "Me? Now why would I do a thing like that? But you have to admit, it works to our advantage." Cassie set her mouth in a thin line and didn't answer. William turned to leave.

Sarah's voice made him pause. "William?" He turned toward her. Her hazel eyes were sparkling and alive with hope. His heart lightened. "Thank you."

He smiled at her. "Well, you guys are the best people I've ever known. I'm not my father. I couldn't live with myself if I turned my back on you." With that, he opened the door and disappeared through it. The three left behind all grinned at each other, marveling at the way God worked and feeling much better, now that they knew they wouldn't be staying in the cell much longer.

William saddled his horse, feeling exhilarated. They forgave him! They really forgave him! He breathed a prayer of thanks. His horse, a bright chestnut gelding named Phoenix, turned his head and shoved him playfully, happy his boy was back and sensing his good mood. William rubbed the white blaze on his head affectionately. He wondered if there was any possible way he could get all of them out, not just Cassie and the twins. Perhaps he could get the parents out during the confusion of the blackout if he acted quickly... Footsteps warned him of someone approaching and he turned to see his father striding toward him. *Uh-oh,* William thought. *I hope nothing's been discovered.* "Hello, Father."

"I understand you have been asking questions of the prisoners," his father said, cutting right to the chase.

William prayed his father did not suspect anything. "Yes. I had some questions about the project I needed answered."

"I see. What were these questions? Did you get the answers?" He sounded suspicious.

"I was wondering if they had any clearer idea about the location we're looking for at Cadbury, and I wanted to know where the notebook is. I didn't get direct answers, but I think I can puzzle them out."

His father nodded, but gave him a long look. "Alright. But before you do something like that again, please tell me first."

"I will."

The Commander turned to go, but turned back, apparently remembering something. "Oh, one more thing. The Master wants to see the witch first thing tomorrow morning. I would like you to take her to him. He wants to hear your account firsthand, in front of her."

"Me?"

"Yes, you. You brought her in." His gaze turned harder. "You object?"

"Oh, no," William said hastily. "I just didn't think I'd be presenting her to him myself the first time he saw her."

"Why not? You're the one who let us capture her. Such deeds come with rewards." He turned to go. "Enjoy your ride," he called back over his shoulder.

William stood frozen. He looked at the stall Kai and Dassah were in. "Did you hear that?" he asked in a low voice. He saw both dogs nod. Phoenix looked at his boy curiously, wondering at the change in him, but very happy to see it. William hurriedly finished tacking up. Getting Cassie out had just gotten even more important. Once the Master saw her, there was no way William would be able to set her free.

Cassie felt excited, and every sound from the hallway made her look eagerly toward the door. They were going to escape! William had turned out to be a friend after all. It had been dark for about an hour now, so William should be coming soon. "Cassie, settle down a little. We don't want anyone thinking something odd is going to happen," David said. She smiled at him.

"I know, I just feel so excited. The Brotherhood will *not* like it when their most valuable captive escapes from right under their noses." Suddenly she heard several people walking down the corridor, and heard them stop outside the door. The friends all looked at each other. This was it. The cell opened, and William entered with the guards and two others behind him. He looked at them coldly, no emotion apparent in his blue eyes. Cassie felt a pang of doubt. Was this a set-up after all? Never mind the fact that she could think of no reason why William would go to such lengths to arrange such a set-up.

"My father has summoned you to him for questioning because you would not answer me satisfactorily this afternoon." He knelt by Cassie and gave her a quick wink, reassuring her. He quickly untied her bonds to prevent questions about why she was merely tied to the wall and not chained. "Now don't try any enchantments, witch, or I *will* ask my father to remove your friends from your cell." Cassie gave him her best glare as he tied her hands behind her back, but loosely so she would be able to escape the rope easily. He also gagged her, which she had been expecting. He pulled her to her feet, but her legs had fallen asleep and she fell back against him. He shoved her forward, but not so roughly that she fell over. "Walk on your own, witch." Two other members of the Brotherhood had tied David's and Sarah's hands behind their backs. William scowled at the soldiers. "Only the witch is to be restrained with rope. The others won't try anything with my dagger to her back. Just keep a sharp eye and a firm grip on them," he said, drawing a dagger from where it had been strapped to his side and pressing it against Cassie's back.

One of the men grunted. "Are you sure?"

William laughed scornfully. *He's a really good actor,* Cassie thought. "Trust me. I know how they think. And my father ordered it. You will behave, won't you?" he asked David, as if daring him to say no.

David glared at him, but William detected some excitement and amusement in his eyes. "Yes. But if I ever get my hands on a weapon without them around..." David let the rest of the sentence hang.

"Goodness, David, no need to be so upset. It was your mistake to trust me, after all. But enough talk. My father is not a patient man," William said contemptuously. He was finding this whole dialogue strangely amusing, probably because all the people participating in it knew it was just an act. He decided to get going so he wouldn't start laughing, either from nervous tension or from how well they were fooling the Brotherhood men around them. He waited until David's and Sarah's hands were freed, then prodded Cassie gently with the dagger to get her to walk forward, knowing they had to get to the right spot in the hallway in time. One man went ahead of them, while two others kept firm grips on David and Sarah. The last man brought up the rear. As they reached the side hallway entrance, William whispered into Cassie's ear: "*Now.*"

She spun out of his grip and kneed him hard in the groin. He dropped to his knees, gasping. It really hurt. Then she brought her hand across his face in a hard slap, knocking him over. She'd taken him seriously, and he saw a satisfied look in her eyes, as well as some amusement. He supposed he did deserve to be hit that hard. "Get her!" he shouted to the other men. The two men not holding anyone lunged toward her, but at that moment, the lights went out and the group was plunged into blinding darkness. David and Sarah, having expected the power outage when they saw Cassie break free of William's hold, used the sudden shock of it to immediately fight free of the men holding them. They had paid careful attention to where each guard was, so they were able to go off memory to free themselves from the men's grips. Sarah followed Cassie's example, while David threw a hard punch and socked the man in the jaw.

Cassie quickly freed her hands from the loose binding and pulled her gag down. She decided to do a little acting herself. "Do not try to follow me, or I shall kill you. This is only a token of the powers I possess," she said, deepening her voice a little for effect. She saw the men falter, and grabbed the hands of David and Sarah, who were standing uncertainly, being unable to see. She could see, but barely. Her friends started, but followed her when she hissed, "Relax, it's me. Come on." She figured the men's fear from her threat wouldn't last long. She saw William gesture down the hallway and the threesome wasted no time in running down it, Cassie guiding the other two. She halted them when they reached the end, as she made out the tapestry William had talked about. It was too dark to see the picture on it. Cassie whirled as she heard footsteps run up behind them, then relaxed as she discerned William's profile.

"I knocked them out," he said, a little breathlessly. "But we need to start moving before the alarm gets out. Someone's probably already wakened my father with the news about the power outage." He pulled the tapestry aside and pressed a hand on a spot on the wall. Behind them, Cassie heard the faint sound of hinges and turned to see a door opening in the wall.

"Does anyone else know of these passages?" she asked.

"All the Brotherhood members know *of* them," William said. "But the only one besides me who knows how to navigate them is the Master, and we should pray we don't run into him. My father might also know how to navigate them, but if so, he's never mentioned it to me. Don't worry. If everything goes according to plan, we'll be well away before they realize what has happened. No one knows that I know my way around the tunnels. I never told anyone because I use them when I want to be alone. They won't think we used them to get away, not immediately, anyway." He held them back as he brought a flashlight from his pocket and flicked it on, revealing a steep stairway that led down into darkness. Cassie noticed a red mark on his face where she'd slapped him.

"I didn't hit you too hard, did I?" she asked.

He chuckled. "No less than I deserved. I'm fine." They quickly entered the passage, William leading the way. "Come on," he said. "We need to get the dogs." He shot Cassie a quick glance. "And if we can move fast enough, I may be able to get your parents out." They quickly descended the stairs, David closing the door behind them securely. William paused for a minute at the bottom, and brought some bundles out of a crevice. Cassie felt relieved to see her emergency bag was one of the bundles.

"You saved it?" she asked.

"Yeah. I figured you'd want it."

"Thanks." She investigated the bag and found, to her surprise, that her knives were inside. "I thought the Brotherhood confiscated my knives."

"They did," William said. "I confiscated them back."

"Thanks, again."

"No problem." He reached into the crevice again and brought out three swords. He handed two of them to the twins and buckled the third around his own waist. "We may need to defend ourselves, though hopefully we can get out of here without too much of a fuss." He looked apologetically at Sarah. "I'm sorry there's no bow, but we don't have many and if I took one it would have been missed."

"It's okay. I don't mind." She fastened the sword around her waist. "You boys and Cassie can handle the fighting. I'll be the reserve force, if needed."

"Which way do we go?" Cassie asked.

"This way. Hurry." William led them through the labyrinth of tunnels. After about ten minutes, he halted at a crossroads. "You guys stay here. The way to the horses is to the left, but the dogs are straight ahead. I'll go get–"

Cassie abruptly clapped a hand over his mouth. He started. "I hear footsteps," she whispered. "Someone's coming from the right." She removed her hand from William's mouth. "Sorry."

William felt a chill run down his spine. It could only be one man. "That's not good," he said. He looked around. "There's a niche to the left we can hide in." They went down a side passageway and crouched down, pressing closely against each other. The footsteps became audible to the other three, and red torchlight lit the tunnels in the direction of the footsteps. Cassie realized that there were two men coming in their direction. The teens pressed even closer to the wall. Cassie was able to hear the men's conversation.

"He did well, Commander. You raised the boy well." The voice was unfamiliar, but Cassie knew who he was talking about.

"Thank you. I admit, I wasn't sure why I decided to act as I did, but it seems to have paid off." That was definitely the Commander. And he was talking to the Master? Cassie felt her skin grow cold, and her heartbeat seemed impossibly loud in her ears.

"It has, indeed. Once the girl is dead, we shall be that much closer to stamping out the Nazarene's religion once and for all, and Caelwyn's words shall no longer hold any power."

"And then we can finally claim our rightful place in the world," the Commander said, sounding greedy. Cassie wondered what on earth they were talking about. She could tell the others could hear them now, too. The men were coming ever closer. The thought occurred to Cassie that if they got much closer the prophecy might come true that very night. She hoped not. Frankly, the idea of killing so many people that the organization would cease to exist both sickened and terrified her.

"Yes," the other man said, sounding very satisfied. "With the Brenwyds out of the way, nothing stands in our way. Those calling themselves Christians cannot defeat us. They're too weak." The teens jumped as a loud ringing tone permeated the tunnel and echoed back. Cassie clapped her hands over her ears. "What's that?" the Master asked, sounding alarmed.

"My pager," the Commander said, switching the sound off. "Something is wrong. We must go back." The light and footsteps retreated rapidly down the tunnel from which they had come. Cassie waited until she could no longer hear the footsteps before giving the all-clear.

"What on earth was that about?" Sarah asked, looking at William.

He shrugged. "I have no clue. But that pager alarm that went off, it's only used in emergencies. Someone must have found the men I knocked unconscious. A power outage wouldn't merit an emergency alarm." He looked at them. "I'll go get the dogs, but now I don't think we can risk trying to get your parents. Stay here. If I'm not back in fifteen minutes, follow the map to the tunnel

"I hear footsteps," Cassie whispered. They went down a side passageway and crouched down, pressing closely against each other.

exit. The horses will be there." With that, he sprinted down the tunnel, not waiting for any objections to be made. Cassie had taken her own flashlight out of her bag, so they still had a light. They all looked at each other worriedly. Cassie looked at her watch and marked the time. Ten minutes slowly passed in silence, and then fifteen, with no sign of William.

As the minute hand marked seventeen minutes, Cassie looked at her companions. "I'm going after him."

"Not alone, you're not," David said. "We're going with you." There was no time to argue the point. They hurried down the tunnel William had disappeared into.

As they got farther along, Cassie felt Kai and Dassah. They were excited, but not in a good way. *I'm coming*, she told them.

Hurry, Dassah said. *He needs help, and we are still muzzled.* Cassie accelerated into a sprint and sped ahead of her friends, who had trouble keeping up. They reached the exit, but Cassie held up a hand, signaling them to stop. She heard voices, loud voices. They crept cautiously up the stairway. The door at the top was slightly open, but not enough that anyone would notice the presence of a secret door.

"Taking the dogs, William?" a voice was saying. It sounded young.

"I told you," came William's voice. "My father wants to make sure the girl won't try to grab them. I'm taking them to a safe place." He sounded on edge.

"I don't know. You're acting weird. Why don't I come with you? Those dogs are fierce."

"What, you don't trust me?" William shot back. "I've been with this organization much longer than you have. Why would I turn traitor?" He was gradually sounding more agitated.

"That girl could be enchanting you into doing it."

Cassie had heard enough. She drew her knives and slipped through the door, David and Sarah on her heels. Their sudden appearance from the tunnels startled William, but it startled his adversary even more. He was a boy about William's age, maybe a little older, with brown hair and brown eyes. He backed away in shock, dropping his hand to his hip where Cassie saw he had a sword. He recovered himself quickly and drew it. "Get back, witch!" he said.

Cassie hoped there wasn't anyone else in the vicinity. "William, get the muzzles off the dogs and get back in the tunnels," she said. William glared at her, but knew that now was no time to protest. He started to do as she asked.

The boy looked a little wild-eyed. "Release him, witch! William, resist the enchantment!" he lunged at Cassie, and she blocked. She sidestepped and tried to get a blow in on his head to knock him out, but he parried the strike. She concentrated on defending herself, trying to get a feel for the boy's style. But as soon as William removed his muzzle, Kai lunged at the boy, knocking him to the ground, and Cassie snatched up his sword. He looked into the dog's face fearfully. Cassie didn't blame him.

"Don't kill him, Kai, there's no need," she said aloud for the boy's benefit. She knew Kai had no intention of harming him.

The boy started to struggle, but a snarl from Kai and a growl from Dassah checked him. "Please don't enchant me," he begged. Cassie found it both amusing and alarming that he was so scared of her.

She knelt down next to him and took the gag from around her neck. "I'm not going to enchant you," she said. "I'm not a witch. I can't do enchantments." His eyes narrowed suspiciously, but Cassie gagged him before he could make a response. She looked at William. "Is there any rope around here?" she asked.

"Not any we could reach fast enough. We need to move. I *told* you to stay put and go to the horses if I didn't get back in time." He sounded reproachful.

She gave him a look. "Yeah, knowing us, did you really expect us to do that?" she asked.

William smiled ruefully and shook his head. "I hoped," he said. Cassie looked back at the boy, who was now glaring daggers at William. He couldn't talk, but his look said, *Traitor*. William knelt next to him. "You know, Pete, I discovered something most interesting on my latest assignment. Brenwyds are really more human than the Brotherhood is. I suggest you think on it." With that, he swung the hilt of his sword onto the boy's head, causing him to go limp. Cassie checked his pulse and found it still strong. She hugged her dogs, and they wagged their tails and licked her.

"Guys?" Sarah said, looking out the window. "We should go. I don't like the look of that." The others looked out the window and saw a buzz of activity going on around the castle, and a group of men heading toward the stable.

William saw his father, and he did *not* look pleased. "Yeah, going would be a good idea," he decided. He looked at Sarah and gestured to the door. "Ladies first." She grinned at him and headed back into the darkness of the tunnels. Cassie went next with Kai and Dassah, then David, and William went last, shutting the door quietly a few minutes before the men reached the stable.

A New Start

The Commander was *not* happy. He and the Master had been disturbed during a discussion in the tunnels by his emergency pager going off. Upon arriving back in the castle, they'd found the power out and three men knocked out cold in a hallway – two of whom had been assigned to guard the girl – with a rock on the floor indicating what weapon had been used. Worst of all, she and her friends had gone missing – along with his son. One of the men who hadn't been knocked out as hard came around quickly, and what he said astonished the Commander and the Master. He said that William had come to the cell with another man, telling the guards his father wished to interrogate the prisoners because he'd been unable to receive the answers he'd wanted that afternoon. The report raised a suspicion in the Commander's mind, but he dismissed it as ludicrous. He talked to several others as they came around, and all verified the first man's account. Their consensus was that the girl had kidnapped William to force him to show her the way out, and was using enchantment to keep him from raising any alarm. The Commander knew William was still in a state that was susceptible to her enchantments, so it made sense, especially given his visit to her earlier. A quick search of the castle had turned up nothing, so they were expanding the search onto the castle grounds. The Master had gone to his rooms to try and find her using his own means.

The Commander knew he had to find her, or his life could be in very serious danger. The Master was by no means pleased by this turn of events, and the Commander knew someone would pay. He entered the stable with some other men and went to his horse, but was distracted by a commotion raised near the tack room. "Here now, what's all the fuss?" he growled. He shoved into the room and saw one of the initiates – Pete, he thought his name was – lying unconscious on the floor. The Commander cursed. "Check the dogs," he ordered. A man left and returned quickly.

"They're gone, Commander," he said. The Commander balled his hands in frustration. What had gone wrong? They'd had her in their grasp, locked in a cell, with devil's iron, no less, but she had managed to escape. Not for long, though. Not if he could help it. He noticed the man looked like he wanted to say something else.

"What is it?" he barked.

The man jumped nervously. "Your son's horse, sir," he said.

"What about him?"

"He's gone."

"Gone?"

"Yes, sir, gone. None of the other horses are missing."

The Commander looked at him incredulously. "William went for a ride just this after–" he stopped as his idea resurfaced. *Impossible,* he thought. *The boy wouldn't.* He gazed around him. "Did anyone see William return *on* the horse?" he demanded. A round of negative gestures met his query. He looked down at the boy. "Wake him up," he ordered. A man went and grabbed a pail of water and flung it over the boy. He jerked to a sitting position, spluttering. "Who knocked you out?" the Commander demanded.

The boy blinked, then realized who was addressing him. He scrambled to his feet, staggering as if drunk. "Commander!" he said, saluting shakily.

"Answer the question, boy," the Commander said in a softer voice. The boy was clearly afraid of him. That was good.

"Well, Commander, you see, I was here, and then... and then he was here and I was feeling suspicious and–"

"Stop this chatter and get to the point! Who knocked you out? The witch?"

"N-no, Commander. It was... it was your son." Everything went quiet, and the Commander grew very, very still. Pete swallowed nervously.

When the Commander spoke again, his voice was ominously quiet. "Are you sure?"

"Y-yes sir. He was helping *her* escape. He was trying to take the dogs to her, but I was questioning him and suddenly *she* came out of the wall with her friends."

"Out of the wall."

"Y-yes sir. Out of nowhere, it seemed. She had knives drawn. I tried to disarm her, because I thought she was enchanting William, but that big dog knocked me down, and she gagged me. Then William knelt by me, and he said..." he stopped and shuddered.

"What did he say?" The Commander shouted, his black eyes dangerous.

Pete was shaking like a wet leaf caught in a gale, stunned by the force of the question. "He said... he said that he'd learned... that Brenwyds are more human than we are." Shocked silence met this remark at first, then the men all started whispering.

The Commander whirled on them, his eyes filled with anger. "Silence!" he bellowed, and all went quiet. The Commander took a breath to steady himself. His voice shook with restrained fury. "It appears we have a traitor on our hands." He glared at all of them. The men avoided his gaze nervously. Never had they seen their Commander so enraged. "And we all know how we deal with traitors." It was a statement, not a question. "You will all look for this traitor with the witch. Show him no mercy."

"B-but, Commander," Pete said nervously.

The Commander turned on him. "What?"

"I-isn't it p-possible t-that sh-she enchanted him into h-helping her? William wouldn't–"

"You will not say his name!" the Commander shouted. Pete went white. "No, I should have known. He knew exactly what he was doing. He always knows exactly what he's doing, and he knows the consequences." He stared out the window. "Where did they emerge from the wall?"

"Th-there, s-sir." Pete stammered, pointing. The Commander examined the wall and pressed on a section, revealing the entrance to the tunnels.

"Do we follow them, Commander?" one of the men asked.

The Commander stared into the passageway, hating what he was about to say. "No."

"No?" the man repeated, surprised.

"No." The Commander confirmed. "I don't know how to navigate down there by myself. No one but the Master does. Or so I thought." His voice was ragged, but full of hate. "We will have to wait. Go back to the castle." The men quickly filed out of the stable, leaving the Commander staring at the open door long after the last man had left. "Why, William?" he said softly. "Why?" And there in the stable, with only the horses watching, tears began to leak from the Commander's eyes, tears of sorrow and anger. The boy for whom he'd had such high hopes and expectations had disappointed him so bitterly. But in disappointing his earthly father, William had pleased his eternal one.

Cassie buried her head in Twi's mane, breathing deeply of the mare's scent. Twi nuzzled her hair, as happy as Cassie about the successful escape from the Brotherhood's headquarters. *I am glad you are alright, girl*, the mare said.

Me too. I wasn't so sure I would be.

The One works for our good.

That he does. But Cassie still felt a sense of failure inside. She had escaped, but her parents were still prisoners. Her only glimpse of them had been from several stories below, as she had entered the Brotherhood headquarters. She missed them so much. Twi knew her rider's thoughts.

We will get them, girl. Do not worry and be sad. Instead, be happy in what you have done tonight. You have already taken a step toward freeing them by escaping yourself. The One is not done yet.

Cassie smiled. "How did you get so wise?" she murmured.

It must be having you as my girl for the past two years. One of us had to become wise. Cassie chuckled. Sarah and David were also going through reunions, though they were still getting over the fact that their horses were able to talk to them without having to use Cassie as an interpreter.

"So after all this time, *now* you decide to start talking to me?" David asked Fire, sounding peeved.

Fire tossed his head and mussed David's hair with his muzzle. *If I had, I would have had to explain Brenwyds, and Cassie was not ready to tell you yet,* he said unapologetically.

"Humph. Still not a good enough excuse." The others all chortled. Cassie noticed that William seemed a little downcast. His horse, Phoenix, stood beside him quietly. Cassie had exchanged words with him, and he seemed very polite. Cassie sensed pride from the horse about his rider's actions, and she got the feeling William's aid in helping them escape resonated with him on a very deep level. She wondered at it, but knew it wasn't polite to ask such queries when she'd just met the horse.

"Are you alright?" she asked William.

He nodded slowly. "Yeah. It's just... well, you know. I betrayed the Brotherhood, and they'll be out to get me now."

"William, you did the right thing. I don't know how I can thank you enough."

He smiled at her, a little tentatively, but it was a real smile. "Just consider it making up for my blunder. I really don't mind. You guys are way nicer than any of *them*." He swung up on his horse, and the others followed his example. William had managed to smuggle three extra sets of tack out through the tunnels during the course of the day, so Cassie and the twins didn't have to ride bareback. Cassie had her emergency bag slung on her back, knives belted around her waist. David and Sarah each carried one of the bags of provisions William had stored in the tunnel. William had some other things in his saddlebags. Cassie wasn't sure exactly what, but probably anything he thought might come in handy. William turned and started rifling through one of his saddlebags. "Before I forget, Cassie, I have something for you."

"What?" she asked, then gasped as he produced a notebook from his bag. "The translation! You saved it?"

"Yeah. I figured we'd need it, if we're going to get to the treasure first. I hope you don't mind, but I looked through it, and I have an idea of where to look – if you want to go to Cadbury, that is."

"I don't mind," she said, taking the notebook and putting it in her bag. "Where should we look?"

"Just so long as it's legitimate this time," David put in.

"David!" his sister scolded. "Don't tease him like that."

William chuckled. "I think I deserved that, Sarah. And it is real, I promise. But first, are we going to Cadbury? You could go home. It'd be safer." The foursome started walking away from the exit.

"We're going to Cadbury," Cassie said. "There's no sense in staying around here with the Brotherhood out looking for us. For that prophecy to come true, we're gonna have to cross with the Brotherhood again, and we know they'll be going to Cadbury eventually, maybe even with my parents. Also, since we couldn't get my parents out this time, I want to know what exactly is in that treasure chamber that caused Dad to be so secretive."

"Do you have any ideas?" David asked.

Cassie hesitated. She did have an idea, but it seemed a little far-fetched to her, especially since it had, for lack of a better term, come to her in a dream. "Maybe, but... I'd prefer to get there first. If it really is so important, I don't want the Brotherhood getting their hands on it. Let's go to Cadbury." It made the most sense, but the statement brought her up short, for some reason. Was it really the best path to take? In her mind's eye, she saw a tall, iconic hill rise with a single, solitary tower at its top, dominating the landscape around it. She knew what it was. She had never actually been to the place, but she had seen it from the top of Cadbury Castle. "Actually, what about Glastonbury?" she asked, mildly surprised to hear the words come out of her mouth, but she knew the instant she uttered them that they were the right course to take.

"Glastonbury?" Sarah asked. "You mean that place near Cadbury with the big hill and the tower on it... what's it called, Glastonbury Tor? Why? Is it important?"

"I just think we should go there, that's all."

"You just think we should go there," William said dubiously.

"One of the first things to know when traveling with Cassie," Sarah said, "is that generally it's a good idea to go where she thinks we should go, because she's right most of the time. Actually, more like all of the time."

"Really," William said, clearly skeptical. "Is this back to the... oh, never mind. Glastonbury sounds fine."

Cassie eyed him. "That was a rather sudden change of mind."

"I just remembered what you said about Dr. Stone, and that was right, so I figured you might be right about this, too.

Cassie blinked. "What do you mean I was right about Dr. Stone?"

"Oh... right, I didn't mention it earlier. She's actually a Brotherhood informant. She's the one who told on your family, and she really pushed me to... you know."

"Are you serious?" Cassie asked.

William nodded. "I'm not trying to shift blame or anything, but she's one of the main reasons I went through with it."

David chuckled and looked upward. "Cassie, I give you permission to say, 'I told you so.' I promise I will not doubt your instincts again."

"I thought you might have learned that by now," Sarah said.

"What?" William asked.

"Cassie said that there were probably outside forces that pushed you. I didn't really believe her," David explained.

William looked at Cassie. "How do you know these things? Get these feelings? Is it some sort of Brenwyd trait?"

Cassie shrugged. "I don't know. Dad's never mentioned anything that it might be. I just get hunches and feelings, and they turn out to be right. I really don't know why."

I believe it does have something to do with your Brenwyd blood, Kai said. *But I do not know what it is called.* Cassie sighed. Another unidentified Brenwyd trait – she seemed bursting with them.

"Cassie," Sarah said, seeing her expression. "It's okay to be different. We don't mind. If you have some trait that makes you have always-right hunches, that's a good thing."

"And useful," William added. Cassie glanced at him. There seemed to be something else on his mind.

"What?" Cassie asked.

He looked at her. "What?"

"That's what I'm asking you. What?"

"Why are you asking me that?"

"Because it looks like you want to say something else."

"Oh." He paused. "Well, I would like to ask you a question."

"What?"

"Why did you trust me? Before, I mean? Especially with this... always-right hunch thing you have."

She frowned. "I had no way of knowing whether you were genuine or not. I had to judge by your actions. The hunch thing… I only get them once in a while. Honestly, I just wasn't sure about you, but as I've said, I like giving people the benefit of the doubt."

He looked puzzled. "But didn't you say in the car on the way to Cadbury that you tell a lot about people by what their… song sounds like? I don't know anything about what all that is supposed to sound like, but mine was probably pretty messed up. From that, you could have known that it wouldn't be a good idea to trust me."

Cassie blinked. She was amazed by his candidness about his fault. "Oh. Well, you know, I never thought of using my ability like that. That's actually a very good point. Why didn't I think of that?"

"Maybe God didn't want you to," Sarah suggested.

"Maybe," Cassie said. "But I think I'll make a note to check people's songs from now on. Thank you, William."

"Um, no problem."

"Anybody know how far it is to Glastonbury?" David asked.

"I think it's somewhere a little over 550 kilometers," William said.

"550 kilometers is about 340 miles," Cassie mused. "That's gonna take at least a week, guaranteeing we can stay on track and keep up the pace."

"I have a compass," William offered. "I can keep us on track."

"But can we afford to take that long?" Sarah asked. "There's no telling what might happen in a week." There was silence as they considered that.

"Could we use whatever this transfer ability thing is?" David suggested.

"You all could," William said. "But Phoenix isn't a Brenwyd horse."

Not to mention Kai and I cannot transfer, Dassah commented to the horses and Cassie.

We have to know where we are transferring to, Twi said. *Or our rider does. The reason we were able to come to you was because we used your presence as an anchor. Has anyone been to this Glastonbury?*

There was an all-around negative response. "We have the time," Cassie said confidently. "If we keep pressing onward, we have the time."

"Is that another hunch?" William asked.

"Sort of. I know where Dad is on his research. He still needs to work out a couple of things and if I know him, he'll slow down as much as possible, especially since he doesn't have all his notes. It'll take him over a week, maybe two to get everything finalized enough to actually start a dig. I doubt anything will happen to any of them during that time."

William nodded. "That's right. The Master needs the other two for incentive. He'll only harm them if your dad refuses to share his finished research about the treasure."

Are we going to move faster? Dreamer asked. *We must get some miles between us and this place.*

"She's right," David said. "We need to speed up. A straight week of riding across English countryside. *That* should be fun." He didn't sound entirely convinced.

You will survive, Fire said. *Remember, I am the one who has to carry you for that week.*

Well, it won't hurt you, Dassah said. *It is just what you need, in fact. It will take off your chubbiness.*

I am not chubby! Fire protested.

Cassie laughed. "We'll be taking some breaks, don't worry. We'll make it through. Remember Philippians 4:13: 'I can do all things through Him who gives me strength.'"

"Right. Just keep saying that every hour or so," David said.

"What if we run into people or have an accident or something? We don't even have helmets," Sarah said concernedly.

"You know what, Sarah?" Cassie said. "I'm not going to worry about all the things that could possibly go wrong at the moment.

God will watch over us. He's helped us survive this far, so I think He'll help us survive a week of riding with no helmets." Cassie sensed approval from all the animals at her statement. "Besides," she added with a hint of a grin, "our horses know better than to throw their riders, don't they?" All four snorted at the implication that they didn't know how to take care of their riders, and didn't deign to answer otherwise.

Of course they do, Kai said, sounding amused. *Can we get going now?*

"We had better," William said. "Even though the Master's the only other one who knows how to navigate the tunnels, you can bet he'll be leading a search party through soon."

Cassie let out a deep sigh, looking up at all the stars. Despite the danger, a peace settled over her. She knew God was watching over them. She lowered her gaze from the sky and squeezed Twi into a gallop, and the mare obliged eagerly. She thought she heard David say something, but paid no heed. She just rode on, letting her worries leave her, and reveling in her freedom. She always felt freest when galloping on Twi's back. The mare loved to run and she almost flew over the ground. Cassie made sure she didn't go too fast, but the feeling of complete freedom was all the stronger when she considered she might never have ridden Twi again. She looked back at her companions – gentle Sarah, protective David, mysterious William – and decided there were no other people she would rather go adventuring with. They all had strengths and weaknesses, and all supported each other. Even if William was a new addition to their group, she knew that now she could trust him like she did David and Sarah. She wondered what he would do if the prophecy was about her and if she cast down the Brotherhood. He had no other family. A thought started forming in her mind. She kept it to herself, not even asking Kai what he thought. She would mention it when everything had been set right. For now, she knew she had a job to do, and she planned to do it well.

Glossary of Horse Terms

Bay: One of the most common horse colors, a bay horse has a brown body with a black mane and tail. The lower legs are also black, unless there is a white leg marking.

Blaze: White facial marking on a horse, resembling a wide stripe running up and down the horse's face between the eyes.

Blue roan: A very rare horse color, with many white hairs mixed into a black coat, making it lighter.

Bridle: Piece of equipment placed on a horse's head for riding, containing the bit and reins that a rider uses to direct the horse.

Canter: A horse's second fastest gait. Each stride is three beats.

Chestnut: Another very common horse color. Brown all over, generally with some reddish tones.

Dam: A horse's mother.

Gallop: A horse's fastest gait. Each stride is four beats.

Gelding: Male horse who cannot make foals.

Girth: Long strap that is fastened around a horse's belly to keep the saddle on.

Halter: Resembling a bridle in basic structure, but with no bit or reins. Used to lead horses when they are not being ridden.

Mare: Mature, female horse.

Star: Diamond-shaped facial feature between a horse's eyes.

Tack: The equipment used on horses when ridden, including the saddle, girth, and bridle.

Trot: A two-beat gait. Faster and more bouncy than a walk.

Whicker: A soft sound made by a horse, used when calling another horse or a person in close quarters, or used in anticipation of something (generally a treat).

Coming Soon: Book 2

Finding Secrets

Brenwyd Legacy continues as Cassie and her friends journey to Glastonbury, where they meet a mysterious woman who holds the key to their past – and their future.

Suddenly thrust through a musical "time slip," the teens find themselves in a kingdom ruled by none other than the legendary King Arthur.

Before they can return and finish the rescue mission they began in their own era, the four friends discover that they have a vital role to play in this one. To preserve the legacy of a kingdom that has fascinated imaginations for centuries, they must first uncover several secrets.

Caught in a race against time and a battle against the original Brotherhood, will Cassie and her friends be able to find the answers to their questions in time to save the kingdom... and themselves?